PRAISE FOR

The Hindenburg Crashes Nightly

"A coming-of-age story through a very dark glass. Stylistically dazzling and strong in narrative flow, [with] passages of great poetic beauty."

—*San Francisco Chronicle*

"With sensuous prose and vital characters, this first novel by James Jones Award–winner Hrbek fearlessly explores the wracking entanglements of two lovers in flux. . . . Hrbek's meditation on love and suffering twists along exquisitely. . . . He builds scenes with a tight economy of timing and detail, so that a tension resonates well beyond their conclusion. . . . Hrbek's portrait of the heart is magnetic, difficult, strange . . . well worth the read."

—*Publishers Weekly*

"A poignant novel of love and loss . . . *Hindenburg* compels, illuminating as it does the sometimes murderous rites of passage young men must traverse to reach healthy and sane adulthood."

—*Baltimore Sun*

"Lovely and engrossing. . . . Hrbek's characters are viscerally real. . . . Their reality makes their traumas that much more believable, more meaningful."   —*Ft. Lauderdale Sun-Sentinel*

"Hrbek writes with appealing lyricism; and he knows how to deliver a bravura sex scene."

—*The New York Times Book Review*

"A story of the heart—original, passionate, and brave."
—Peter Landesman, author of *The Raven* and *Blood Acre*

"A compelling story of obsessed passion . . . written in the intense first-person narrative tradition of Scott Spencer's *Endless Love*. . . .

THE HINDENBURG
CRASHES NIGHTLY

Greg Hrbek

Perennial

An Imprint of HarperCollins*Publishers*

Excerpts from Georges Bataille's "Story of the Eye" copyright © 1977 by City Lights Books. Reprinted by permission of City Lights Books.

A hardcover edition of this book was published in 1999 by Avon Books, Inc.

HarperCollins books may be purchased for educational, business, or sales promotional use. For information please write: Special Markets Department, HarperCollins Publishers Inc., 10 East 53rd Street, New York, New York 10022.

First Perennial edition published 2000.

Library of Congress Cataloging-in-Publication Data is available.

ISBN 0-380-80543-X

00 01 02 03 04 RRD 10 9 8 7 6 5 4 3 2 1

Acknowledgments

I am grateful to James A. Michener and the Copernicus Society of America and the James Jones Literary Society for financial assistance; to Maria Massie at Witherspoon Associates; and to Jennifer Hershey and Hamilton Cain at Avon Books.

Sincerest thanks to Ann Imbrie and Frank Conroy for invaluable guidance and support; to David and Diana for their faith and sacrifices; and to Dede for years of inspiration and love.

THE HINDENBURG
CRASHES NIGHTLY

PART ONE

1 / Will you believe me when I tell you they were one and the same? The girl whose tears I tasted, whose scent I washed from the tips of my fingers (the smell of verdant moss, of a humid day broken by rain)—and the woman whom academics in worn tweed jackets would introduce as a journalist with the lyrical voice of a poet. The girl I'd met in, of all places, a church—and the woman I loved while her husband was scaling the Antarctic slopes of Deception Island, recording for posterity the spectacle of eighty thousand pairs of breeding chin-strap penguins . . . It has been many years since my last confession. I find it difficult to proceed. I have been an adulterer (though until that last dinner party on Russian Hill, I was a monogamous one). I have been a murderer (though here one runs into issues of semantics, the question of whether silence equals complicity). Hard to believe that, once upon a time, I myself had been called to the holy life. Then I shook the hand of Lindsey Paris. It was Easter Sunday. The morning of my First Communion. The service over, the hall empty, and the two of us in full view of the perpetual flame, the fire of God burning inside red-tinted glass. Her feet were bare and I had to pee. She was fifteen, I was seven. That morning, the character of my faith was irreversibly changed—and I began to dream a long, elusive dream.

My parents named me after St. Thomas Aquinas. But that dim monastic figure meant little to me, so I considered my patron the disciple, the doubter, infamous for his refusal to believe without visual proof. As a boy, I made a vague connection between the legacy of my name and my father's career as an optometrist; but I knew the choice had been my mother's. My mother, who had lived two years as an aspiring Carmelite in the South Bronx, who I felt should have known better. When I sensed myself falling from grace, she was the one I blamed. "Why didn't you call me Judas?" I said. "Why didn't you just name me Judas?" She was pregnant at the time, breathing oxygen from a portable tank—and I was full of an angry fear because I knew, with some pale and errorless instinct, that time was growing scarce. That minutes and days were being depleted at an alarming rate. Months could be counted on the fingers of one hand. And years were already extinct. The morning after her funeral, those words I'd spoken grew more important, far more brutal than they had been in actuality. I had to apologize. Since that day, my heart has burned the way hearts do when their longings are locked away forever.

She had given me literature on the subject.

At six weeks, the fetus could fit into a walnut shell, yet a tiny heart was beating a hundred times a minute. At eight, budding arms and legs had grown clusters of fingers and toes. By twelve, at the weight of one ounce, it had all its important organs, and was moving freely in its bath of amniotic fluid. At fourteen, knees tucked up and arms folded, it lay in the position I still automatically assumed on cold nights. Living silently on her oxygen, on the pumping of her heart. Claiming, bit by bit, more and more of her life. Taking by instinct. When I was with her, I felt I was keeping watch, guarding against some sudden internal trespass. Sometimes, like an animal marking territory, I believed I could intimidate that fetus into going back to its point of origin—some collective void of nonexistence. I didn't want to kill it. Just halt its progress, return it to nothingness.

Then Lindsey came back.

How strange it was to see her again. After nearly a year. After everything that had happened the summer before. I was ten now; she was eighteen. June 1975. The first day of my summer vacation. My mother well into her second trimester. Dad and I were on the porch, hanging the bronze eagle I'd won at Prize Day, when she walked up the lake road and turned into our driveway. What could I do but hold that eagle, its wings spreading far out on either side of my bare chest? I'd never given a second thought to walking around shirtless in the summer; suddenly, I felt skinny and undressed.

"Hey," I heard. From up on the ladder, my father requested the bird, the relinquishment of which would result in virtual nakedness.

"I don't think this is the right spot," I said.

"Kid, I'm acrophobic. Hand me the damn bird."

I gave it to him and my heart started pounding in earnest. I considered flight, but how long had I been waiting for this moment? How many times had I told myself it would never come? I watched my father awkwardly trying to hang the eagle on an old nail. Meanwhile, Lindsey moved into my peripheral vision. Still far enough away that I could glance surreptitiously. She'd cut her hair. She wore a striped tank top, cutoff jeans, sandals. My father cursed softly in the realm of the wasps. I looked up at her face, and our eyes met. Then she started toward me.

"What's going on?" she said.

"We're hanging the eagle."

"I can see that. But what's the problem?"

I shielded my eyes and hazarded another glance. "He's scared of heights."

"Who are you talking to?" Dad said.

"Nobody."

"Lindsey Paris," she said. "If you don't mind my saying, Mr. Markham, I think you're going to have to get onto the next step."

My father gripped the top of the ladder, allowed the eagle to dangle from one hand, like something dead, like something he'd lately shot from the sky. Slowly, he backed down—and I saw on his face that expression of surrender he'd come to wear more than any other. My spirit sank, and at the same time filled with new life to see him hand the eagle to Lindsey. To watch him give up. To watch her climb those steps without fear, and hang a prize I didn't even want over our front door.

       ⌐

I spent that summer in her father's Duster. Driving through the countryside, over farmland and into small villages, collecting signatures and donations in support of nuclear disarmament. *Our technology is developing faster than our knowledge of ourselves,* Lindsey would say. *We have to slow down, before it's too late.* I'd display topographical proof of downwind radiation. *Ma'am,* I would say, *do you know that the American government has been waging nuclear war against its own citizens for the last thirty years?* We stood outside grocery stores in Cornwall and Kent, asking old people, ladies with kids, local businessmen for a minute of their time. We posted flyers in restaurants and town halls. On long, shaded porches, above buzz-cut lawns, we talked to people through their screen doors, and informed them of the perils of the arms race. The first week, we collected twenty signatures and a little over two hundred dollars. Most days, we had to be back in Bethlehem by two o'clock. Lindsey had the afternoon shift at Stosh's Cone-U-Copia. Sometimes I'd sit at a corner table, nursing a cone, watching her scoop ice cream and make sundaes. The high school boys hung around too. They knew her hours and stopped by to talk to her, ask her out on dates in their used Trans Ams. Lindsey handed them their waffle cones, along with her regrets. "They've got fuzzy dice hanging from their rearview mirrors," she'd explain to me later. "I wouldn't get in a car with them if you paid me." That summer, I was the only boy she drove with—and the only one she let into her room.

    Lying on her shag rug, I'd read books or fold newsletters while, on the bed, she read bigger books or typed envelopes, legs crossed on a psychedelic-paisley blanket, an electric Smith-Corona humming and clicking beneath her fingers. Kool-Aid in tall, sweating glasses. Joni Mitchell on the stereo. Lindsey told me about Latin American revolutions, boat people in Vietnam, draft evaders in Canada. My eyes wandered the room. A piece of underwear, not much larger than my own, lying beside the rattan hamper. The shadowy visage of Che Guevara above the words HASTA LA VICTORIA SIEMPRE. Her bureau mirror, which from a certain spot on the floor reflected the bed. Reflected her lying down, typing, leaning over; the downy curve of her neck, the dark line between her breasts; or her eyes, already focused on me, the image of me on that glassy plane. It got so I would just show up, walk in the house, walk up to her room. Sometimes I ate dinner there, watched television. *The Streets of San Francisco, The Partridge Family, The Mod Squad.* On those nights, I didn't want to leave. The phone would ring at eight-thirty or nine; and on the way home I'd cry beside the lake, staring at the illuminated square of her window. What had happened last summer? Had it all just been an illusion? But it must have been real. Because in church, Father Coine was still remembered in the list of the faithful departed, and in the cemetery there was a headstone bearing his name. Yes. He was dead, and there was no bringing him back. No way to change the things that had happened. No way, it seemed, to break the promise I'd made her . . .

One afternoon, I brought her to the foot of our rock wall, to my father's aluminum toolshed. I pushed open the bent door, shaking the entire structure. The light of the yard crept in and the darkness was colored with gray, dull green, brown. Inside, spiders crawled on long, thread-thin legs across the floor, the walls, over bags of peat moss and tools caked with dried dirt. Lindsey lay down on her stomach with me, our eyes almost level with the cool concrete floor. I looked at her out of the corner of my eye. So close, she was barely in focus.

"They're Daddy Long Legs," I said.

She stretched an arm into the shed and made a ramp, touching her fingertips to the concrete. A spider climbed on and she lifted it out, rising to her knees, then easing her legs crossed.

Out in the sun, its round body was a vivid mahogany, its legs so delicate. It walked a spiral up her bare arm and crested her shoulder, disappearing onto her back.

"They don't spin webs," I told her. "Did you know that?"

She shook her head as the spider hiked back over her left shoulder, walking the blue-and-orange trail of her tank-top strap. It crossed onto her tanned skin and descended along the line of her throat. Impulsively, I reached out a hand, placed my fingers in the spider's path, on her breastbone. It sidestepped me. Then, through a thin film of perspiration, I slid my fingers across Lindsey's skin to intercept it. She drew her body away and I was suddenly filled with fear. I withdrew my hand. The moistened tips of my fingers grew cold in the air. The wind filled the silence, a gentle rush from far off, like tambourines; and in a moment, the leaves and smaller branches of the maples were sounding and moving above us. The tree's brittle seeds, tiny helicopter rotors, spiraled down out of the branches. When I finally looked at Lindsey, she was crying.

"I'm sorry," I said.

She shook her head. "It's not your fault."

But I knew it was. I turned to the lake, to the land beyond where there had once been a meadow of tall grass, full of life and sound. It was all gone now. The earth out there was brown, as barren as a moonscape; and as if for the first time, I understood what we'd been telling people all summer. I understood the text of those newsletters. I knew that my mother didn't have long to live. And what else was left to know? There were some things in life—actions and events, mistakes you make—that can't be changed or reversed. The consequences last forever.

⌐━━┐

Ten years old. A new, navy blue suit. The arms a bit too long, the shoulders a bit too broad; and so I would always remember feeling especially small that day, dwarfed by everything that surrounded me. From the backseat of a dark sedan, I looked out at my mother's old neighborhood. Tiny brick houses crammed onto city blocks. The choppy waters of Long Island Sound. The Throgs Neck Expressway, which, in her youth, had been undeveloped land: a place to play in the daytime, and to wander with your beau at night. Ahead of us, the taillights of the hearse glowed red, and I felt us slow down. They blinked a steady yellow, and I felt us change direction. Sitting beside me, my father held my hand. He'd stopped doing this under normal circumstances some time ago, and now I wished he'd let go, as it seemed hypocritical and backward to me. An action which belonged to another life—one we'd never live again, no matter how many of its tendernesses we tried to resurrect. From the opposite seat, my grandparents' eyes would occasionally wash over us. My grandfather's pupils swam behind his thick lenses, like little dark goldfish warped by the curvature of their bowl. My grandmother's, ringed with mascara, still held the memory of the stained tears she had shed back at the funeral parlor.

There, we had viewed the body for the last time.

I'd knelt before the coffin with my father, understanding that I was to say a prayer, or some kind of farewell to her. My mind was a void, and my eyes strayed from her face to the electric candles that stood at either end of the coffin. Flame-shaped bulbs whose filaments silently flickered—on, off, on—in random syncopation. Flowers banked along the walls. A giant heart-shaped wreath stood in one corner, with a shiny banner which read, "Our Sympathy." It was all tasteless and painfully insulting. Who were the people in this room? Relatives I'd never met or even heard of. Men with slicked-back hair, in leisure suits and tinted glasses. Women, reeking of perfume, who embraced me with alien arms and muttered consolations in a cheap accent. In the back, by the thick metal curtain which divided us from another party of mourners (the place was like a motel, I thought to myself, a disgusting rented room), my aunt Sophia held my brother. Almost a week old, he would occasionally gurgle. From time to time he burst out crying. And when this happened, the room went misty and my body shivered strangely. I felt my father's hand touch down on my shoulder. Felt myself standing up, moving away. Turning away. Looking up, I found Lindsey standing just inside the door, wearing a dark sleeveless dress. Her hand reached out and drew me toward her, into her warmth. I found she was a little shorter than my mother. When I hugged her, my face rested against the hard bone of her chest; I could feel her rib cage against my arms. She took my face in her two hands and kissed my forehead. Lovingly.

"You came," I said.

She nodded, her eyes sweeping over the room, and guided me into the lobby. At the far end, the other family loitered about in greater numbers; a couple of young children were playing with action figures on the tile floor. The deceased, I imagined, was some distant family patriarch, a man who'd lived a long and detailed life. No one would be ruined by his departure. He would float, with a kind of natural buoyancy, down a tributary stream of memory. Lindsey and I found a couple of chairs in our less populous region of the hall, beneath a dim painting of a schooner cresting an ocean wave at sunset. A ceramic ashtray, filled with cigarette butts, gave off an old and nauseating smell.

"You look really nice," Lindsey said.

"It's too big." I displayed my hands, the knuckles just peeking out from under the cuffs.

She shrugged, leaned closer, and straightened my tie. We'd spent the entire summer together, but only now did I notice that the light shading of her freckles flawlessly matched, in color, the hazel strokes in her irises. How many hours this summer had I spent out of the house? Away from my mother? Now, as Lindsey let go of my necktie, as her face withdrew and her lips maintained a gentle smile, I felt a new kind of disbelief, a different kind of fear. Today was an ending, but not my end. I'd wake up tomorrow. Still alive. And lonelier than I'd ever believed possible. My body was filling with an unbearable pressure. I shut my eyes, tried to swallow, but found my throat was blocked. In the other room, my brother began to cry again, and biblical words seared themselves into my mind: *I'm not his keeper. I never will be.* I wanted to climb onto my chair and scream this at the top of my voice. I took a deep breath and my lungs filled with the smell of dead fire, smoke, and charred grass—it was only the cigarettes in the ashtray.

"I hate him," I said.

"What?"

Both of us became aware of footsteps clacking over the floor, growing distinct from the background noise. It was Marco standing over us. His feet traced shapes over the olive-green tiles.

"Leave us alone," Lindsey said.

Her face was angled away from him, her dark hair a curtain obscuring half of her face. My cousin cleared his throat.

"I just . . . wanted to say hello . . ."

"Get the fuck away from me," she said, her voice trembling violently.

Yes, that was it, I thought to myself. I wanted to curse. Stand up on this chair and curse at everyone. Family, friends, and total strangers.

"I have to go," she told me, and in the cool breeze from her departing body, I looked up at Marco. He ran a hand through his hair, gave me a brief, sympathetic smile—and the hurt beneath it, his own private wound, was strikingly apparent. As he started to turn away, I heard myself pronounce his name. A name I'd tried to avoid saying for over a year now. He looked back at me. Completely open. Vulnerable and compassionate.

"I hate you," I told him. "I fucking hate you."

———

As we drove away from the Bronx that August evening, I questioned whether we'd ever go back. My uncle Vincent and aunt

Carmela returned to Connecticut with us, following our station wagon along the dark country roads. They would stay with us for a few days, until we got resettled. But I was certain this was merely the epilogue of my experience with them. The tenuous connection between me and my mother's family had been permanently severed. How could they ever forgive us? How could they ever forget that she had died in our care? By the time we got home, it was nearly ten o'clock. My brother was put to bed. The rest of us sat out on the deck under the stars, the moon up above us, its blue-gray light draped over everything; and I waited for a falling star, for some sign in the heavens that never came. Finally, my aunt and uncle kissed me passionately good-night— and my father, sitting on the edge of a redwood chair, held his arms dramatically open, as if he were about to begin a sermon filled with comforting parables. But he said nothing. Only hugged me, leaving the warm impression of his lips on my cheek. Upstairs, in what had been my mother's sewing room and study, Matthew slept quietly in my old crib. On one white side, Humpty Dumpty sat grinning and oblivious atop his wall; on the other, a little girl whose name escaped me ran from a spider dangling from a thread which had vanished over time. I watched him for a while. His tiny fingers were curled into a half fist. I wondered what his dreams looked like, if he had any.

It was nearly midnight when I crept downstairs. Outside, the moon, almost full, hung over the east end of the lake. Dangerously bright and heavy. Shards of it floating like jetsam on the surface of the water. I had never been in the canoe at night; and in the darkness, as I glided away from the little sand beach, the sound of the paddle against the water was loud and crisp. It seemed it could carry for miles. Without my mother to steer, I alternated my strokes—a few starboard, a few port—moving away from the moon, toward the far shore, where the white bark of the birches gleamed. One light was on inside the circle of trees. The lantern above the front porch. I felt the canoe run aground, and carefully I disembarked. Pulled it up to the grass. Walked, through the endless chirping of the crickets, to the side door. On the concrete step, I removed my damp sneakers and socks, then stepped inside.

Upstairs, the door of Lindsey's room was open a crack. I stood there, listening for her breathing, hearing only the distant throb of a grandfather clock. Hours might have passed. Mystery swirling in the black silence on the other side of her door. Finally, I pushed it open. On the bed across the room, Lindsey lay beneath a light sheet, one bare arm exposed to the air. To touch her arm, I thought. To run my finger along its softness. I whispered her name and waited. And as my vision adjusted to the dark, I could see that her eyes were open. Lifting an arm, she reached out to me, in a way that seemed at once imploring and hesitant. As if she'd been waiting for me to arrive, and hoping I wouldn't. I crossed the carpet. I knelt beside the bed and felt my hand slide into hers.

"The moon's beautiful tonight, isn't it?"

The window's curtains were thrown wide open. In the light, her skin had the undying quality of marble; a dull shine slipped over her hair. For a long time she kneaded my palm with her fingers—and then she whispered that I could stay there. I could stay. The top sheet warm, the pillow suffused with the smell of her; and though I gripped her hand as if it were the one I'd just lost, I understood that this was not the love I'd felt for my mother. This was something else. Something desperate and unnamable and premature.

"We're going to be all right," she said.

She smoothed the hair back from my face, and kissed my forehead.

⌐_⌐

For the rest of the summer, I will wake up repeatedly in a bed which is not my own. The sunlight falling in bright yellow trapezoids on Lindsey's shag rug. Her pillow smelling faintly of perfume, that rustic scent like pine needles or bark. I wake up facing either the wall (the Peace poster; the laundry hamper; on the carpet, a bra or tank top which has missed its mark) or the windows, and the streaming leaves of a willow. Always: her teenage arms mooring me from behind. Her breath warm on the back of my neck. While at my house across the lake, my little brother, only days old, lies oblivious. Does he know yet that something is missing? Her hand slides along my forearm, into my fingers half curled at my chest. Sometimes I fall back into sleep. Sometimes we just lie there, each knowing the other is awake, unwilling to dismantle an embrace that is as fragile as a spider's web. We love only at night, in the dark, and it seems to me that all of those nights are the same. My heart beating wildly. My body shivering, as if the air is cold.

"It's okay," she whispers.

But her voice sounds uncertain, heavy with realizations that wait in the future, just out of our reach, just beyond our vision. She draws me close, into the soft warmth of her body. Holds me from behind. The stereo playing low. The crickets' nocturnal orchestration. How long do I lie there, trying to force myself into sleep? Wanting to lose consciousness . . . and not wanting to. Am I the one who turns toward her? To smell her breath, lush and narcotic. A finger touches my cheek. She holds my face with both hands, wills me to look into her eyes. When I do, I think I can see myself there, full of the future—and behind me, all the things I've ever done. All of life, it seems, compressed into a single convex image. Outside, the trees take a great collective breath. Then, gently, her lips close over mine. A trembling, almost impalpable pressure.

For a moment, panic. But only for a moment.

Then I am on the other side of a wall. Where sound is beautifully dampened. Where a serene exhaustion begins to settle over me. I feel myself grow weaker, and slowly surrender, as if to the irresistible embrace of water. The next few hours are like that. Like sinking through fathoms and leagues, past coral reefs and sunken galleons, monsters of superstition, to the blackness of the ocean, where the fish glow like stars, shooting through a watery night.

2 / We never talked about those nights, or the days which had inspired them. Not even obliquely. Not until she had been married for two years. Not until we were lovers in an official adulterous sense, and I'd come in view of my own inner landscape. Primitive. Sordid. Populated by unforgivable things. It was the summer my brother ran away from home. He was sixteen. By way of explanation, he left a 3-D postcard in the bathroom, hidden in a box of feminine napkins. On the front, the Virgin Mary appearing to a little girl at Lourdes. On the back, in chicken scratch: "I beseech you not to send the police after me for I am carrying a gun, and the first bullet will be for the policeman, the second for myself." On a Greyhound bus, he fled New England, journeyed across Pennsylvania, through Iowan corn, over the Great Plains and the raped land of Nevada—

But I am getting ahead of myself.

Before any of that, I lived the days of my truest and most honest happiness. Back, then, to the Middle West. Twenty years old and Chicago has been created for me alone. A theater to stage the epic production of my young adulthood. The Art Institute is putting all kinds of wacky ideas into my head. I am more than an "experimental animator." More than a budding genius. A postmodern article about the theocratic divinity of the hand of the animator has had a particularly intoxicating effect; and when I look at my little puppets of wire and clay and rubber, when I see them move across the screen, I half believe that I have filled them with breath. When in fact their movement is just an illusion, created by the rapid progression of a series of still images and the limitations of the human eye. But I want nothing of truth. There I am at nearly midnight in the old editing room, at the old Moviola with the foot pedals. And here comes Carolyn Kuxhausen in her pleated skirt, bearing takeout food. She smells like lo mein and L'Oréal. In that Minnesota accent which makes my eardrum purr: "I'm wearing my diaphragm."

———

I'd met her at a candlelight vigil—held in remembrance of a kid who'd been killed below my window in a drive-by shooting. She and I spent a lot of time at the Shedd Aquarium (she was a lover of the cold-blooded); in cafes talking about Kate Chopin and Virginia Woolf (she was also an English major at the U. of C.); and one pre-dawn, after a lengthy acid trip along the shore of Lake Michigan, in the emergency ward of Mercy Hospital, where a little squeaking voice inside Carolyn's head was removed with the aid of a common turkey baster, and found to be an earwig (an incident which, as any entomologist will tell you, occurs only in the realm of myth). At twenty, I considered myself a virgin, and in the beginning it took me some time to achieve the minimum stiffness required for coitus. Carolyn had been extremely sweet, if somewhat oblique about this, advising me to look upon the act not as a performance as much as a rehearsal. By the spring of '87, two years into things, we were in love. I'd started calling her Moonshot, as according to family legend she'd spoken her first complete sentence during the televised landing of Apollo 11. Then one night the phone rang, roused me from sleep. Lindsey's voice was like the touch of an unseen assailant. I didn't move. I didn't speak.

"Are you there?" she asked.

I cleared my throat. "I'm here, yes. I'm right here." Carolyn was there too, sleeping as she did through ringing phones, tempests, shots fired by the guns of teenagers—everything except insects in the ear canal.

"Where are you?" I asked.

"I'm in Lima."

"Peru?"

"Yes . . ."

Trailing the phone cord, I walked into the bathroom, shut the door, sat on the lid of the toilet. Carolyn's pink diaphragm case, a tube of contraceptive jelly, rested on the edge of the sink. I was naked, I smelled of sex; and this condition of mine, though surely unknowable to her, nonetheless filled me with fear. I hadn't seen her in several years. I was expecting, I suppose, to never see her again.

"I thought you were in Nicaragua," I said.

"I came down here with a friend of mine, a photographer, to do a story . . ." Her voice trailed off. What I'd thought to be some kind of echo resulting from the international connection proved to be the sound of her breathing; there were hairline cracks running through her voice.

"Are you all right?"

"This place is fucked up," she said. "There's no hope. There's no morality here."

I realized I was completely out of my depth. It wasn't just ignorance of Peruvian politics. I considered hanging up. Disconnecting the phone. Instead, I surrendered to pent-up emotion. I allowed a tear to track uninterrupted down my cheek.

There was a long silence.

"I have your letter," she finally said. "I carry it with me."

I stared down at the tile floor of the bathroom. Noticed the slow drip of the shower head. That letter, that mundane document written at the age of eighteen and sent to the Managua office of the *San Francisco Chronicle*. Its contents: my transfer from Brown, the move to Chicago. The thrill of being here. Eating food from Thailand and Africa. Riding the El at night. The feel of a Bolex camera in my hands, of my first dailies lighting up a dark screening room. A detailed description of my neighborhood, poor and dangerous (this detail to impress, to prove my fraternity with a woman who lived in a region where people were disappeared daily). In the last paragraph, I hazarded sentiment. A hope that we'd know each other always—that I understood, as she'd once told me, that people drift apart and come back together again. That I loved her, no matter what.

"Can I ask you something?" she said, her words burning like a fuse across continents.

"Yes . . ."

"If I came to Chicago . . . would you see me?"

I closed my eyes, heard my girlfriend in the other room, turning in her sleep.

"Of course," I said.

"Because I'm leaving," she said. "I need you."

⌐_____⌐

Oh, Carolyn.

Did I really wait for her on the steps of the Art Institute? An autumn chill cutting through my jacket, and guilt like some wounded animal, trembling in my chest. Twenty-two, with sideburns and my hair pulled back in a loose ponytail. Sitting at the foot of all that beauty and history, waiting for an old lover.

"Hi, Thomas."

My heart slid into a hot groove at the sound of her voice. I rose up. I opened my arms. What do I mean to say? That the form, the mass of her body filled all the empty space I'd nearly forgotten about? Or that the emptiness was her, displacing the form and substance of me? Holding her on those steps, I felt at once old and childlike. I looked at the premature gray winding through her dark hair (as if she'd been caught in a gentle silver rain), at the lines on her face which had once appeared only when she smiled. She was thirty years old. Still, it seemed I was looking at the girl she had once been. Desperate and confused and filled with impossible guilt. Was she seeing me in the same way? A boy whose mother lay buried in a distant hole? The boy who had come to her of his own volition?

"Don't cry," I said.

"Look at your hair," she whispered.

"Look at yours."

"I know. Can you believe it?"

I reached out and touched it; her eyelids fluttered and closed, like the wings of a bird coming to rest. "It's beautiful," I said.

———

About a week later, I returned to those steps—with Carolyn. She wanted to see the Roy Lichtenstein retrospective. Lindsey had been gone for days, but the taste of her sex was still on my tongue, her profession of love surging through my veins like an illegal drug. Suddenly, Carolyn's hand was just the hand of a girl. Just some girl from St. Paul whom I'd happened to have spent countless hours with. Whom I'd started calling pet names, and had joked with more than once about the specifics of our wedding day. But that was before. Before my mind began to flood again with fear and guilt, a boy's wild dream of an ancient future. I sat my girlfriend down in the midst of Lichtenstein's Haystacks, and heard the truth pour out of me in a relentless whisper. *My cousin who was here last week . . . the journalist . . . she's not my cousin . . . I knew her . . . growing up . . .* I told her almost everything, and Carolyn's face strained in a peculiar manner, as if she were trying to translate the words of a language she understood only marginally. When I was through, she took a deep breath and said, "I want that photograph. The one of us camping on the Apostle Islands." She ran a hand over my hair, and exited the way we had entered . . . For some time I walked through the immaculate rooms in a daze, hardly seeing the work on exhibit, until I reached the image of a blond-haired woman singing plaintively into a microphone, her skin, irises, lips shaded with the artist's trademark dots. I could almost hear her crooning the words which hovered over her head, enclosed in a speech bubble and bracketed by musical notes. THE MELODY HAUNTS MY REVERIE. Outside, on those steps, all of Chicago seemed to be humming along. Those stenciled dots invaded my vision, swirled over Michigan Avenue. I leaned into one of the Doric colums. "Are you all right?" someone asked. An anonymous motherly voice. "I'm fine," I said—and by the time I opened my eyes, she was gone.

___

About a year later, she married one of the hottest cinematographers in nature documentary. A bit of a madman, but a madman with a heart. The kind of guy who, on the shores of Patagonia, would fight off tears as he filmed from the beach (killer whales charging the sea-lioned shallows . . . plucking tender pups from their parents . . . tossing the mutilated bodies around like wet rags), then, outfitted with scuba gear and amphibious camera, against the advice of local divers, would not only lie in the surf to get low-angle shots from the point of view of a hapless seal, but, farther out—motorboat anchored to a forest of kelp, the dorsal fin of an orca slicing through the water—would submerge himself in the whale's attack channel—underwater visibility, five to ten feet—and roll film until the black-and-white mass appeared in the murk like a Reaper of the deep. The obsessed derangement of an Ahab, and the bleeding heart of a New Deal Democrat.

I should have hated him.

The mere thought of him should have turned my stomach, the way it did at first, when he was just some nebulous phantom stealing Lindsey away from me on another coast. The sound of his voice should have made me sick, the way it did that day on the rocks above Cliff House—when the two of them, silhouetted against the panorama of an indigo ocean, bound by a pink cloth, circled the sacred fire in a vaguely Hindu wedding ceremony. The fact is that even on that day—the day I met Philip Davenport, the day I was certain I'd lost her to him—I couldn't deny an affinitive phenomenon, like a current produced by opposing electrical charges.

"You know," I told Lindsey at the reception, "you're not really married. You only circled the fire six times."

She raised an eyebrow. "Seven."

"Six," I repeated. "Believe me, I was counting."

In the background, the band was playing "Up, Up and Away" with a string-bean Indian doing an Eddie Van Halen solo on a sitar. Lindsey was gorgeous, wrapped in a misty-thin sari, nibbling on fluorescent tandoori chicken. Her long hair braided, tassels tied onto the ends; a peacock, painted with henna, unfurled its plumage up the inside of her arm. Six months before, Philip had proposed to her in the snowy folds of the Himalayas, where he'd been shooting bharals for a segment of *National Geographic Explorer*. After a consciousness-lifting episode with a yogi sage, and much meditation under the fir trees, they decided to be married Hindu-style. If not for the restrictions of the San Francisco transit authorities, Philip would have steered himself to her house on the back of a white stallion.

"You're going to like him," she said. "You have to like him."

"*Like* him? What are you talking about?"

"You two have a lot in common—"

A round of applause cut her off, and the band drifted into a trippy interlude. The sitar player was sitting down now, turned inward, communing with the instrument. A piercing, soothing sound, like mental acupuncture. Philip emerged from the dispersing crowd, head swathed in an orange turban which appeared to be concealing the overgrown hemispheres of a giant alien brain.

"Here comes the Maharaja now," I said.

The skirts of a long imperial dress, colored violet red,

swept across the dance floor as he wandered over, pointed at me to indicate he knew exactly who I was. He had a light beard, the inexplicably authoritative look of a guy who'd seen it all before forty. Regarding Lindsey and me, he knew only that we'd grown up in the same town in Connecticut; that we'd known each other (despite a few lengthy estrangements) for fourteen years. There wasn't much else to tell, much else that would have made sense. She presented me now with a manual flourish, as if I were a prize worthy of canned cooing on a morning game show.

"This is the kid. *The* kid," he said.

I smiled weakly as he extended a hand. To shake it, I had to ease mine into the dark cave of his elongated cuff.

"Great," he said vigorously. "I'm really pleased you're here. Pleased to make the acquaintance of a stop-motion animator."

I shrugged.

"O'Brien, Harryhausen," Philip said. "I imagine you've studied their stuff pretty extensively."

My ears pricked up at the sound of these names. My personal idols. The masters of my trade. The fathers of King Kong and a brood of giant monsters transfigured by the magical power of the A-bomb.

"Don't take those names in vain," I said.

Phil looked at me seriously. "Wouldn't dream of it. Stop motion's a marginalized art."

Across a spread of mangoes, papayas, and loquats, Lindsey was resting her head in her hands, gazing at her husband. I felt a violent revolt in the region of my heart. What the hell was I doing here? And then I remembered: I was laying my dreams to rest. I was twenty-four, still a boy. I had my whole life ahead of me, et cetera, et cetera.

"Why don't you take Tom to the den," Lindsey said, "while I save my mother from that pornographer. Did you invite that guy?"

Philip kissed her chastely on the cheek, then led me to a

small room off the dance floor, dimly lit and thick with the lush odor of hashish. A couple of guys wearing fezzes squeezed past us, shaking Phil's hand on their way out. A hookah sat in the center of the floor—a porcelain Buddha trailing a long, snaky tube.

"I know this is going to sound crazy," he said, loading the Buddha with fresh crumbs of hash. "I mean, I shoot nature flicks. The name of the game is capturing reality. But *King Kong* was my inspiration. You ever use one of these?"

"Not exactly."

He demonstrated. In turn, I drew a cloud of epicurean smoke into my lungs, then expelled it. Like fog, it hovered between us.

"I was nine or ten," he said. "And all I wanted to do was get to the South Seas with an old hand crank. Just like Carl Denham. I wanted to meet those natives, get on the other side of those giant gates, and film. The girl I wasn't so sure about, but the camera . . ."

I nodded, remembering the meadow behind my old house in Connecticut. I knew the impulse. I knew exactly what Philip was talking about.

"What do you think about *Kong?*" he asked. "From an artist's standpoint. Archaic? Just a museum piece?"

I shook my head. "It's beautiful. More than beautiful. Everything . . . down to the way his hair bristles."

Philip snapped his fingers to confirm the value of this minute detail.

"Its antiquity is an asset," I concluded. "It looks like newsreel footage."

"So for you too . . . an inspiration."

"Well, yes and no," I said, feeling a light-headed, intellectual abandon. "For me, it was Harryhausen. Chaos as opposed to action. Destruction as opposed to death. Watching his movies, it was like being high at the age of eight. Familiar things built in miniature. The Capitol Building. The Golden Gate

Bridge. Then some other force—some unfamiliar force demolishing them. Of course, I knew the real things were still intact. But their images had been destroyed. The paradox bent my mind."

"The art of iconoclasm," Philip said.

"Exactly," I said, nodding. "Exactly."

Again, we inhaled from deep in the Buddha. The drug tightened its hold. My mind darkened—and then was illuminated by memories of a night in Chicago, about one year distant. After coming inside her, I'd rested my face against her belly. Beyond the soft field of her pubic hair: the faint odor of the two of us.

"What was it like?" I heard.

Like? Beautiful. In the morning, the evidence of her shuddering orgasm on my shoulder. A hickey. A gunshot wound. Stigmata—

Suddenly, I remembered where I was, and found Philip two feet away, his image wavering like a genie in a veil of lamp smoke. Had he just asked me what I thought he'd asked me? That turban and the extraterrestrial brain within—was it continually engaged in the art of mental telepathy? I was completely baked.

"What did you say?"

"When she was a kid," Philip asked, "what was she like?"

I took a deep, measured breath. "She was a teenager when I met her. Sixteen, seventeen."

He nodded, as if I'd just begun a promising oral history.

"What I mean is," I said, "she wasn't really a kid anymore."

"Let's not get hung up on semantics," Phil said.

I shrugged. "She was upset politically. Smart but angry. She put a lot of ideas in my head."

"About what?"

"Vietnam, mostly. The truth, you know, and I wasn't really sure what to do with it. After Saigon fell, I'd see the refugees on the news, boat people. Orphaned kids. I asked my parents to adopt one, I had this extra bunk bed in my room. I said we owed it to them, and my dad looked at me like he'd just found my membership card to SDS."

"A Nixonite, your dad?"

"Like riding first-class on the *Titanic*."

He smiled, thin lips parting in an impish fashion, the peppery hairs of his beard seeming to shift, like iron shavings moved by the power of a magnet. I could see it, ridiculously enough—the attraction. A modest male beauty, unknown to (or absently dismissed by) its possessor. His life, his catalog of experience. Isn't it what I'd always wanted for myself? First-hand knowledge of the world, of exotic lands, endangered species. I'd yet to set foot on another continent.

"Have you seen a condor?" I asked. "In the wild, I mean."

"Andean," he said. "Not California."

"Andean condors," I whispered.

"Fucking huge, Tom. This wingspan. So big. They're enough to make you believe in God."

"How'd you get started?" I asked. "In cinematography?"

"Well, like I said, there was *Kong*. And we had this Super 8 Bell & Howell. I started shooting outside. Ant hills, butterflies, whatever. My dad helped me cut stuff together. But it was the shooting. Containing some creature in the viewfinder, not knowing what it was going to do. The unpredictability of nature."

We sat for a few moments in a weighty silence; then Philip spoke again.

"The seed sown in childhood blossoms into the tree of life. Like you and Lindsey. To be honest, I can't help but feel a little jealous."

I stared at him. The groom. Decked out, pulsating like neon, in impossible regalia.

"Fourteen years," he went on. "She loves you, you know. In a way she'll never love me. Like a brother."

My mind chafed at this classification. Then Philip forced that smile, his beard shifting under the influence of some emotional magnetic field.

"More than a brother," he said. "Like someone she can't live without."

I took my final hit. The hookah gurgled like a mountain stream, the hash glowing like hot coals. The memory of child-hood, of Lindsey and me, was frighteningly intact. A miracle of paleontology hidden in rock, and excavated by the cooled smoke of a magic narcotic. I looked again at her husband. She was right, I did like him. And now I saw the primary reason why. Because he posed no threat. He was here not because of who he was, but who he would never be. She didn't love him. All of this—the ceremony, the party, the costumes—it had all been motivated by fear. Of something desperate and irrevocable. Something that had grabbed us one distant summer when we lost ourselves to each other. Grabbed both of us when we were weak, and would never let go.

⌐⌐

It pains me to recall that Philip was, in part, responsible for all this. It was he who put me in touch with Lane, and Lane who offered me a job at Kinetoscope, a stop-motion studio in San Francisco which at that time was producing episodes of *The New Davey and Goliath*—a revival of the sixties children's show about a mischief-prone Christian youth and his dog of uncanny intelli-gence. I fairly gagged on the scripts: corn-syrupy-sweet tales about how to navigate the treacherous waters of the modern world with a simple faith in the Lord. But I tried not to take my frustrations out on Davey, little Christian of clay and rubber, passive soul that he was. I faithfully reminded myself of why I took the job. A steady income, and after-hours use of the studio to mount a full production of my graduate-school thesis film. The story of a little boy who works the graveyard shift in the belly of the *Hindenburg*.

First and foremost, this was a career move.

But what else was I thinking as I dismantled my life in Chicago? Packed my things into the trunk, the backseat of my ancient Mustang, and started west. I entered California from the north. I drove down the coast, and saw the ocean surging green around the offshore rocks, fairy-tale groves of giant redwoods, the sweeping arms of the Golden Gate Bridge reaching out to embrace me . . .

We had rules.

The Articles of Our Adulterous Constitution.

No intimate contact when Philip was in town. No intimate contact—period—in the house she shared with Philip. No references to our intimate contact when Philip was within a hundred-yard radius.

In the beginning, our affair was conducted within the confines of my one-bedroom apartment on Dolores Street. Meetings were rare and followed the pretext of dinner or coffee, a movie, or an aimless walk through some used-book store. Slowly, quiet shame was displaced by familiarity. We began speaking each other's names at the apex of passion. Traveling on weekends to anonymous places along the coast or deep inside national forests. We started sleeping in her house, which was soon filled with objects (beds, chairs, bathtubs, Oriental rugs) that, it seemed, rightly belonged to me, as works of art and wonders of archaeology belong to those invaders who manage to plunder them. How, in that case, was I going to take possession of the second-floor porch, and keep intact the view of the bay, the headlands, the bridge? Out there—late at night, when surrounding windows fell dark—her face, her body, washed in the city's ambient light, put me in mind of sculpture, of inanimate things come to life. When I was not working, I was thinking of her. When I wasn't with her, I was waiting. Like one of my puppets, frozen on a tabletop set. Waiting for a hand to reach down and move me another few millimeters. Waiting for my own hand to wave, for a smile to break over my lips, a tear to fall from my eye. Waiting to fuck a married woman. And when I did, I felt I had been set into infinitesimal motion. A camera shutter opened and closed, exposing a single frame of life . . .

A Saturday morning in my apartment.

Sunny and fogless. Down on Dolores Avenue, the leaves of the palm trees quivering like the vibrating strings of huge musical instruments. In my kitchen, Lindsey stands naked fom the waist down, cooking omelettes filled with salmon and Brie. Greeting me, as I return bearing the newspaper and fresh croissants, with an expression which tells me she is feeling more than the opiate calm of orgasm.

"It's gorgeous out there," I say. "At the risk of sounding superlative, it's the most gorgeous day I've ever personally witnessed."

"I'm hiking the Dipsea Trail with Terry this afternoon. Want to come?"

I stare at her while she layers fish and cheese into a bed of eggs. Until she turns, her lips parting in a smile which promises all sorts of impossible things. "Come here," she says; and I step up behind her, rest my hands on her stomach, my lips on her neck, and I am saturated with a love that hangs thick in the air, like pollen. The city's flowers are laden with it, and the bees carry it in their bellies . . .

Shall I go on?

About afternoons spent in museums; under the giant chandelier of the Castro Theatre; on the rocks of Twin Peaks after dark, the city below us swelled with light, and a terrifying void over the Pacific; or in her car, driving south on Route 1. The ragged end of California an arm's length away. Hundreds of feet of vertiginous cliff. Then the ocean, the blue edge of the world bending. The day is clear and hot. Lindsey drives in her bare feet, wearing shorts and a halter top. Siamese-cat sunglasses with white frames and green-tinted lenses. Hair pulled back, bound at the neck by a silver barrette, save for one curling strand that flutters about her cheek. Her upper body bathed in sun, and a delicate shadow between her breasts.

"How's the writing going?"

"Don't ask," she says. "You're a distraction."

"Me?"

"Yes, you. I put your flowers in my study."

"And?"

"I smell them and I think of you. My mind wanders."

She slows for a hairpin turn, maneuvers us around an outcropping of rock.

"My hand wanders," she adds.

Biting down with girlish embarrassment on her lower lip, she grasps one of my hands and guides it to her chest. Her breasts are warm with sunlight, still swollen from her period. A few miles on, we park in a turnout. A zigzag path provides access to the shore below, and we hike down with a blanket and Lindsey's diaphragm. The beach is completely deserted. We are hidden from the road by the steepness of the cliff. I prepare the contraception, watch her insert it between her legs. Then I dip my hand in the ocean, wipe her labia clean of spermicide, and lick her until the salty taste of the ocean is gone, until the salty taste of her has replaced it. I push inside her, in mind (as always) of the conjugal prescriptions of the ancient Chinese masters. I time my fiercest thrusts to the arrival of the breakers, and Lindsey's cries are lost in that sound. There is no one in sight, surely no one within earshot. Still, when she climaxes I press a hand over her mouth, and I come seconds later with her fingers touching my face, lazily and blindly . . . The sun pours over us like molten wax. The vultures circle above. I doze off and when I awaken, my head is in the hollow between her shoulder and chest. Beyond the gentle slope of her breast, I can see in the offshore distance the monumental rocks, the water splintering against their mass. Solid. Real. My fingers tighten around her hand as an icy cold stings my toes. She stirs, turns toward me. Her eyes don't open, but her hands reach clairvoyantly for my face. I feel the warmth of her breath. The gentle somnolent pressure of her lips. And the magnetic pull of the past. "The tide's coming in," she says; and as she moves away, rising to her knees, gravity seems to go with her. Between her legs, her dark hair is wet with semen. The coastline falls silent and the ocean gathers strength. Breathes itself in . . . then exhales on the sand.

3 / Before brothers and stepparents. Before the pregnancy that will take her life. Before terms like "pulmonary edema" and "rheumatic heart disease," there were summer mornings. Waking up to the feeling of her fingers smoothing my hair. As we walk to our little sand beach, the world is still in darkness. A thin transient fog lies along the surface of the lake. The trees are black silhouettes against a slate-gray sky; and in that sky a handful of stars are still holding onto life. We ease the canoe into the water, alongside the dock. We climb in and push off, my mother steering in the rear. No sound but the liquid plunk of my paddle. The crickets deep in sleep, the birds only beginning to stir. Up ahead, a few feet from the far shore, there is a meadow, a field of tall grass. It is perhaps a half mile square, but it seems to stretch on forever. Growing and growing. Fading into the foothills of the Appalachians. To me, it is a living presence. In the rain, it asks for a strange sympathy; in the wind, the brown stalks brush against each other and whisper enigmatic things, messages you sense to be important, but cannot understand.

"Look, Tom."

As an orange sun bleeds across the sky, the field loses its icy grayness. The grass ignites with a gentle embryonic fire, and I imagine that somehow she is responsible for this. For hue and tint, for a sudden leap into life and color. The field changing from red to yellow, the pine green of the distant hills. At this moment, we might be on the Colorado or the Missouri, floating at the edge of a new frontier, like Lewis and Clark. The sun touches my back, the world grows bright, and I feel an anticipation which seems to open my life to endless possibility. Staring at the field, I see my own private wilderness, as wondrous to me as any foreign place on the map. Soon the air is warm. The dragonflies come out by the dozens to feed and perform their invisible skywriting. One of them sits down on the bow beside me, to model the shiny blue-green tint of its body, its incredible wingspan. The transparent, netted wings quiver, as if communicating in code, then lift the insect away. I follow its flight to my mother, her face tilted to the sun, her eyes closed. A soft wind blows over the field, and with a slow rolling movement, the grass seems to awaken.

⌐———⌐

I prayed in those days. In my head at night and out loud in the living room. I called my mother and father to worship, and they knelt before me through complete repetitions of the Catholic Mass. My sermons were lengthy extractions from the biography of Abraham Lincoln; my vestments Mom's silk scarves, draped around my neck, cool and caressing when I moved my head. I stood behind the coffee table, hands folded. The plastic chalice I'd bought at the religious-articles shop rested at my fingertips, brimming with wafers of compressed Wonder Bread. On the turntable, the Monks of the Abbey of St. Pierre de Solesmes moaned a Requiem for the Dead. Their chanting was gorgeous, like the sound track to a dream. All this started in the Bronx, my mother's homeland, where my cousin, Marco, had guided me to a rendezvous with the miraculous.

Fall, 1971. I was nearly seven.

My parents had flown to Florida, leaving me at my grandparents' house, one block equidistant from Long Island Sound and the Throgs Neck Expressway. It was a Tuesday, Grandma's day off from the factory where they made the cloth calendars. She had bingo plans for the evening, but in the meantime wandered the house in a pink nightgown. Her hair, still as dark as my mother's, rose above her head in daring, extravagant curls. In the living room, Grandpa sat in the La-Z-Boy recliner, reading the *Daily News* and coughing. I'd been there a day, and was beginning to experience the madness of the shipwrecked, when Marco arrived.

"This place is a drag," he said, peering down the hallway.

His mother was an exotic-looking woman from Ecuador; and Marco, fifteen at the time, had inherited her olive complexion and an accent which put me in mind of coconut trees and fishing boats floating in turquoise water.

"Anyone alive in here?" he shouted.

A series of hacking coughs from the adjoining room. Grandma appeared at the top of the stairs.

"What do you two think you're doing?"

"Hitting the road," Marco said.

She gave him her worn-out look, the precise meaning of which was always difficult to ascertain. She wore this expression more than any other and used it to communicate a wide array of mental states: fatigue, confusion, skepticism, impatience, hurt feelings. I imagined it had first crossed her face during childhood, on the boat ride from Italy. She'd worn it in the shadow of the Statue of Liberty, in the processing center on Ellis Island. Gradually, all other expressions had been submerged beneath this surface of ambiguity.

"That's a great idea," Grandpa said from the next room. "Take a trip down to City Hall. Give my regards to these bastards." We heard him slap the newspaper.

"This is no day for politics," Marco said. "But a day for nature."

"What are you talking about?" my grandmother said weakly. If my cousin uttered another vaguely poetic line, it looked as if she might slip into a coma.

He bounded up the stairs and whispered in her ear. I could see the veins that ran up his forearms, the biceps hardened by the free weights in his basement.

"Take the bus," she said. "Not the train."

He borrowed some money and we headed out, walked over the Expressway and past the open doors of a bus on Tremont Avenue. In a few more blocks, we reached the elevated tracks. Subway cars racing. The roller-coaster sound of wheels grinding against metal. Soon we were rattling over the rooftops of the Bronx, sharing a car with a wide variety of people. Some were black, some white. A family across from us conversed in Spanish. A guy at the end of the car slept on a stretch of seat.

"I've been doing some very interesting reading . . ." Marco said, showing me his latest issue of *Psychology Today*, ". . . about women's sexual arousal."

He had a subscription and sometimes shared the results of particularly compelling studies. Once, over the phone, he had tested whether I would turn out to be a dove or a hawk, and determined I could go either way. In the course of casual conversation, he referred to things like Pavlovian conditioning and the Oedipus complex. His mom was always saying he'd be the next Sigmund Freud. In my mind, he was already a genius.

"It turns out," he said, "that women get as turned on by erotic stimuli as men. That means they're not just interested in romance. They like to get down to business and do it."

Marco opened to the article and handed me the magazine. I flipped through. The columns of words had emboldened headlines like "Sexually Sophisticated Students" and "Knowing When You Throb or Tickle." There was a graph with jagged lines that looked like primitive cave drawings and a photo of two objects: one resembled a lasso; the other, a test tube.

"What are these things?"

My cousin smiled and ran a hand through his thick black hair. "That's how they test how turned on you are."

The first, he explained, fits around the penis; the second, inside the vagina. The subjects listened to sexy tapes and somehow the researchers wound up with this prehistoric graph. I turned the page to find a full-page ad for a book called *How to*

Pick Up Girls! The mail-in coupon at the bottom had been clipped. Marco told me this was the handbook for the sexual revolution. As soon as he got it, he was going to ride down to Fordham and start putting the principles into practice in the student union. He said he was going to cause some immediate fluctuations in arousal.

━━━

We got off at 180th Street and walked down blocks littered with garbage and filled with sound. In front of a paint-sprayed apartment building, a couple of guys with huge Afros leaned into a headwind of music blaring from a nearby window; one wore a suit jacket with no shirt or tie. Soon we were in a caravan of families, some carrying cameras and lunch coolers, in sight of the entrance to the Bronx Zoo.

"Ever been here?" Marco asked.

I shook my head. "My parents don't like the city. I think they're scared of it."

"There's nothing to fear but fear itself," he said, paying the cashier. "And the occasional mugger or rapist. The occasional giant ape falling off the Empire State Building. You know the scene."

We walked up to a nearby map, enclosed in glass.

"Take your pick. Africa. Antarctica. Australia."

He put his hands on his hips, like a superhero, as he studied the map. His shirt had a half-length zipper, pulled all the way down. The metal loop dangled at his sternum, and a few chest hairs were visible between the shiny metal teeth.

"How about World of Birds?" I said.

We followed the signs to a giant concrete building, sitting on the top of a hill, like a castle. Lila Acheson Wallace World of Birds. Inside, the inhabitants cavorted in re-creations of their natural habitats—*Arid Scrubland, Forest Floor, In the Treetops.* Most of them lived without a glass shield; by the magic of an optical illusion, they were guaranteed to never dart into the darkened hallway. The larger, nobler types—the Birds of Paradise—were another story. If they could talk, who knew what else they might figure out? On the other side of a window, they perched on knotty branches, gigantic and colorful.

"I'd like to see them flying," I said. "I'd like to be in the jungle with them flying over my head."

"In that case," Marco said, "come with me."

He led me upstairs to a doorway labelled THE JUNGLE. Opening the door like a valet, he invited me with a flourish of his arm onto a catwalk two stories high. Here, sunlight poured from a high glass ceiling and feathers flickered like prism spectrums in the air. Trees stretched toward the light. Cords of vines flowered purple and violet. A wall of rock rose at our side, spotted with moss and gleaming with a trickle of water. The room was completely open, no barriers, real or imagined. We shared the air space of the birds. Below, some strutted on the jungle floor, under the fan-like leaves of giant ferns; others sat in the trees, level with our eyes, calling out; a few floated above, in the dizzy space between branches. This was Madagascar, damp and moist and exotic. I looked up to where Marco had been standing, but he was gone. How long had I been staring? I squinted up into the white light and watched a beautiful parrot descend from the heights, its wings long and elegant. Deep majestic colors spilled toward me. Dark blue. Bright red. A flash of yellow. Fixed in place, I shut my eyes and felt it land on my shoulder, fasten its toes lightly through the material of my shirt. My eyes opened to a spotty haze, the prelude to a faint, which slowly dissipated. Then I shifted my eyes to the right, straining the muscles. The bird was a blur of downy color, like something seen through a kaleidoscope.

"Whoa, cuz," I could hear. "Jesus H."

The bird shifted, its claws tickling my shoulders. I smiled, suffused by an honest and buoyant feeling. I was completely calm, starting to relax my motionless body, afraid only that the bird would leave me, when I heard the approach of footsteps. A few feet away, a man dressed in a caretaker's uniform came to a stop. He stretched an arm toward me, and the parrot lifted itself from my shoulder. I could see all of it now, wings unfolding rich colors, carefully layered feathers. It settled on the man's arm, where it nodded approval.

"I didn't mean to," I said. "It just came down."

He smiled through a thick beard. "No problem," he said. "Just extremely unusual."

He wore a gray shirt with patches above the pockets: "Ornithology" on one side, "The Wildlife Conservation Society" on the other. I looked at his face, his long hair, his unruly beard. I'd seen him before. In a movie. Standing in a river. One of Mom's favorite movies. He lifted his arm and the bird took off, its brilliant colors leaping to new life in the sunlight.

    ⌐⎯⎯

A while later, we were eating hot dogs at the edge of The Veldt. A twenty-foot gorge ending in a murky stream protected us from various man-eating species, supposedly lurking nearby. I was starved and arriving at wild conclusions.

"That guy looked just like John the Baptist. He had the beard, the hair, everything."

It had been a long time since Marco had last analyzed me. I could tell by the look in his eyes, the forked gaze of the psychiatrist, that he was working up some ideas, some explanations, even as he offered his full attention.

"Let me tell you what happened," he said.

I scooted to the edge of my bench. Leaning forward, he told me facetiously that my parents had messed around with acid before I was born. I was having hand-me-down hallucinations.

"It perched on my shoulder," I said. "You saw it."

He nodded and recaptured his air of professionalism, drew

deeply on his soda. "It's like out of all those people, you were chosen."

Chosen. Like Noah or one of the Twelve. I glanced around the little court, filled with men, women, children, babies. If I stood up on my bench, shouted for their attention, and told them my story, none of them would believe me. They'd shake their heads, laugh, return to their lunches. They were all of them heedless, on a simple visit to the zoo. Not us. Not me. For the chosen, everything had a meaning beyond the visible.

"I never thought I'd say this," my cousin said. "But in this situation, we may have to put the workings of the mind aside. This could be something else."

I looked down at my paper plate, and discovered half a hot dog where I was certain there'd been nothing moments before.

"I finished this hot dog," I said gravely.

He held up his hand so I wouldn't disturb the assembly of his thoughts, then pushed his tray aside, leaned his elbows on the table.

"I'm going to tell you something, cuz. Now, there's a lot about our parents we don't know. When you're a kid, you don't realize your mom and dad lived a whole life before you were even born. But they did. For instance, what do you know about your dad?"

"He was in the Air Force. He was a good artist."

"Anything else?"

"Once, he ate two Thanksgiving dinners."

"You've proved my point," he said. "You don't know much about him, do you?"

I thought it over. "I guess not," I said.

"What about your mom? What do you know about her?"

I opened my mouth and nothing came out. Incredibly, my mind was a blank. Did I really know nothing of her past?

"She went to Egypt," I remembered. "She saw the pyramids."

Marco nodded slowly, looked out at the yellowish grass of a counterfeit Africa.

"Thomas," he said, "your mother was a nun."

I felt a brief flare of heat in my chest. According to my cousin, it was Julie Andrews all the way. Two years in the Carmelite Convent in the Bronx, before she met my dad in that bar in Flushing. Later, the propensity for holy drama had been transferred to me in the womb, through chromosomes.

"It's hereditary," he said. "Like the Partridge Family is in touch with music. You're in touch with God."

        ⌞   ⌟

For all the magic it held, World of Birds did not house the most impressive members of the species. The predators, the possessors of epic wingspans, lived in outdoor shelters, cages of chicken wire at the center of the zoo. On the way to this place, where I would see for the first time a living eagle, autumn leaves littered the paths. Some had left their imprints, like shadows, on the concrete; others parted only now from their branches to drift down on us. The air was cool, satisfyingly bracing, and my body felt weightless, pulled forward by some gentle guiding force. The bird (a violet touraco, the caretaker had called it) seemed to fly with me, just out of my sight.

Perhaps I'd been lucky, favored by Fate, in the right place at the right time. Or maybe the bird's action had been a personal compliment, allowed by something in me, some intrinsic communion I had with nature. Or, most fantastically, maybe my wildest suspicions, backed up by the know-how of my cousin, were actually correct. Today I'd been called to the holy life. From a certain perspective, it made perfect sense. It was in my blood, in my love of the stained-glass windows of our church, my superhuman ability to stay awake until the end credits of *The Ten Commandments*.

"I have to warn you," Marco said. "This eagle's only got one wing. It's an amputee eagle."

"One wing?"

"They found it wounded someplace. They had to cut the wing off."

We walked past the gorillas, who watched us with spooky intensity. It seemed they were seeing into my mind.

"The last time I was here," Marco said, "a guy handcuffed himself to the eagle's cage. It was a war protest. Pandemonium. The vultures were screeching. This guy was yelling about Indochina. The eagle was flapping her wing."

He shook his head.

"Crazy shit, man. You're lucky to be seven. By the time you're eighteen, the draft just might be over."

I had no idea what he was talking about. No idea he was two years away from eligibility, and didn't believe for a minute we were really pulling out. Suddenly, he stopped dead in his tracks.

"Son of a bitch," he said.

He was staring up the path, at two people feeding each other French fries. A boy and a girl, both teenagers.

"I want you to sit down," he told me, indicating a nearby bench. "And don't move. Just wait for me. I have some business to attend to."

The couple seemed surprised to see him. The boy's face— olive-skinned and Spanish-looking—went blank. The girl, lost in an oversized jacket, smiled weakly. Out of my hearing, they started talking, pointing at each other, as if there were something wrong. The girl offered Marco a French fry, and he slapped the little cardboard boat out of her hand. Ketchup stained her face and the front of the jacket. I found this vaguely amusing.

"That's my jacket," the other guy said.

The girl's hand flew up and grazed my cousin's cheek. Then my body went rigid, something gripped my insides as Marco, without hesitation, slapped her sharply in the face. The owner of the jacket made a clumsy lunge. My cousin grabbed him by his clothing, pushed him across the path, and slammed his back into a waiting tree trunk. "The next time I catch you two sharing fast food," he said, "I'm going to feed your ass to the fucking gorillas." The girl felt her nose, then inspected her fingers as if for blood; the guy, who had the wind knocked out of him, struggled for breath; and my cousin, waving to assure me that everything was now under control, rejoined me at the bench. He stood over me, raking his fingers through his hair. I wasn't afraid of him, though I thought perhaps I should be.

"Girl trouble," he said. "You're lucky you're seven."

The tone of his voice, the look on his face, served as a kind of apology, an assurance that this unexpected volatility would never be turned upon me. He was still Marco. The kind of guy who took you to the zoo on a Saturday.

A brother.

———

I will meet her, several months later, at the most important cere-mony of my life since my baptism. It is Easter Sunday. Christ has risen. Look at me on that morning. In a white Oxford shirt, turquoise trousers, and a maroon clip-on tie. Full of the Holy Spirit, the certainty that I've been brought into this world for a saintly purpose as deep and mysterious as the ocean. The service over, my class is filing out into the young spring warmth. A recording of bells rings out from the top of the church, a gentle rain of sound, as we assemble for photographs on the lawn, beneath the statue of the Virgin. Our religious instructor, an old man in a lemon-yellow blazer, smiling and winking. Father Coine in glowing white robes, as if dressed in light. His reddish-blond hair almost crew-cut; small eyeglasses resting on the bridge of his nose, lenses fashioned by my father; a faint Irish accent. Cameras click and several flash bulbs go off, impotent in the light of day; a couple of movie cameras purr like mechanical cats. In my mouth I can still taste the pasty blandness of the host as we disband into a giddy chaos. Father Coine walking among us, calling each of us by name. We are giving him skin, our hands slapping against his thick palm and fingers. I emerge from this crowd and sight my mother. Red dress the color of poinsettias. White gloves. A lace mantilla resting on her long black hair. She bends down to kiss my cheek.

"Congratulations. You looked great."

"It didn't taste like anything," I say.

"It's not supposed to."

"Where's Dad?"

She points behind me, and I see him approaching with Father Coine, whose voice you can hear from miles away. He speaks loudly and rapidly, conditioned by his work at the prison in Danbury. He lives not far from us, in the parish rectory, which sits at the end of the tall grass. Only in winter, after heavy snow, can I see it from my room, its chimney sending soft gray smoke to the sky. The rest of the time, the grass is thick and healthy. Hiding things, making me forget. He and my father are talking about the revolution in modern eyewear. The miracle of the soft contact lens. It is my father's radical opinion that eyeglasses will one day be the dinosaurs of optometry, and that even contacts will eventually be made obsolete by the healing power of laser beams. In this way, he is forward-thinking.

"I'll stick to the old spectacles," Father Coine says.

We pose for two photographs, his hand resting on my shoulder, the folds of his vestment touching my bare arm. I have told him about the violet touraco. He knows of my aspirations to the priesthood, and has offered me a position, when I come of age, beside him on the altar. I will light the candles. I will present to him the flasks of water and wine, and ring a small bell to signal the magic of transubstantiation. For now, he claps me on the back and moves off to be captured on other strips of film, his robes shimmering in the sunlight.

___

On the back lawn, a long table covered with white cloth features arrangements of cookies from the Little Cake Box, and giant glass bowls filled with red liquid. I ladle out a cup and attempt to mingle. I strike up a conversation about baseball, but it spends itself quickly, and I end up back at the refreshment table, studying cookies. Most of my fellow communicants are public-school kids with whom I have a tentative bond; my friends from Mount Carmel are mostly Episcopalian and live across the border in New York State. My best friend, Roland, lives in Bethlehem, but he is an atheist. At this moment, he is probably in Cornwall or Kent, eating crepes for brunch, trying sips of his mother's mimosa. While here at St. Edward's, I have tasted, for the first time, the Body of Christ. I cannot get over its weightlessness, its lack of flavor. I am still waiting for some quantifiable change, some shift in my perception, a leap in my intellectual prowess.

"Hello, Thomas."

This is Catherine Paris, who in her frilly white dress looks like something plucked from the top of a music box. For weeks, she has been talking about her pious cousin, Ruthie, who, upon receiving the Sacrament of Penance, saw a blinding light, fainted, and woke up to a world shining at its edges, the fingerprint of God impressed on her soul. Daintily, she picks a pink cookie from the tray and takes a minuscule bite. A moment later, her sidekick, a redhead with a case of freckles, arrives and copies the action, complete with pinkie extension.

"Catherine had a rapture," she says, pigtails aquiver.

"Sure," I say.

"She did, whoever-you-are."

"That's Thomas, Kelly. Don't you remember? Doubting Thomas?"

"Oh, yeah . . . No wonder you don't believe us."

"I thought your cousin fainted," I say. "I didn't exactly see you faint."

Catherine sips demurely, dismissively, from a Dixie cup. "There's such a thing," she says, "as a polite rapture."

Moments later, I'm heading for the church. I am not sure where exactly I am going. Just that I want to put some space between me and this girl, between me and her strawberry-blond hair, her missing front tooth, and her bee-stung lips. I know her from preschool. From the days when she had a sweet smile, a wet mouth suggesting the cloying stickiness of honey or tree sap; it was this detail, and the vague questions it raised, which motivated me to kiss her in the coat closet one morning, initiating an affair that our young teacher labeled cute and liberated. We saw *Pinocchio* together, and at appropriate moments, she grabbed my arm in the buttery dark; we went to the Great Danbury Fair, where we posed for pictures at the ankles of the giant Uncle Sam . . . But that is all in the past—she has turned out to be an unbearable priss.

I use the side entrance, feeling a sudden need to pee. The church is empty now, the main lights off, and the faint echo of my shoes on the tile floor is ghostly. I pass in front of the altar and genuflect. The bathrooms, hidden in a small foyer, have old-fashioned silhouettes painted on their doors: a man wearing a top hat, holding a cane; a woman with a parasol, skirt bowing out like a parachute. The men's room is locked, so I walk out to the hall and wait under one of the stained-glass windows. I stare at the tabernacle, the home of Christ's body, seemingly built of pure gold and ivory. Beside it, the perpetual flame burns inside red-tinted glass.

A few seconds later, the door to the women's room opens. The featureless image of the lady disappears, and a girl emerges. Teenage. Black hair, long and parted in the middle. Sunglasses with round lenses. Flung over one shoulder, a brown suede jacket fringed with shredded leather. Blue jeans with elegantly curved cuffs. Sandals on her feet. She is seemingly oblivious to me as she wanders slowly past the flag of the Vatican, trailing her hand over the wood of the front pew. Finally, she slides out of her sandals, lets her jacket drop to the floor, and then steps up onto the altar. I watch her run her bare feet over the velvety carpet. I watch her make her way, languidly, to the tabernacle. And something sparks in my chest as she reaches for the doors, and finds them locked.

"Does this thing open?" she says.

I think she is speaking to herself. But then she turns and looks at me. She repeats the question.

"There's a key," I say.

"Huh?"

"There's a key."

"That figures."

I glance at the bathroom, listen for a flush. None forthcoming. The church is unbelievably quiet, and the words we've spoken seem to still be resonating; they seem to float in the air somehow, they seem to have bodies and shadows. She disembarks from the altar, walks toward me in her bare feet. She is wearing a daisy in her hair, just above her left ear.

"Were you in the Communion group?"

I nod as she leans her forearms on the end of the first pew.

"Congratulations," she says flatly.

"Thanks."

"So I guess you know my sister. Catherine Paris."

"Your what?"

"Did she tell you that story? About our cousin and the rapture?"

"Yeah, but—"

"I don't believe in lies. I believe in getting the truth out in the open. So let me tell you something. My little half sister's full of it. Cousin Ruthie didn't have any raptures. She happens to have epilepsy."

I look at her, still trying to work out questions of familial connection.

"Epilepsy," she says. "It's a disease where your brain sort of short-circuits, then you fall over and have a fit. When it happened to Ruthie, they had to stuff a shirt in her mouth so she wouldn't bite off her tongue."

She gives a wry smile, the implication of which is unclear to me. There is a long pause, during which she stares at me from behind the darkness of her sunglasses. I can see, beyond her, the open doorway to the lawn. The trees and grass bloom with color as the sun emerges from behind a cloud. A moment later, the stained-glass windows on the far wall light up like giant lanterns.

"Nice tie," she finally says.

"It's a clip-on."

She nods, as if in contemplation of a significant fact. "What's your name?"

"Tom."

"Tom. Hi, Tom. Where are you from?"

I point in the direction of the sacristy. "Just up the road."

"Up the road. That's a great place to be from. Where, exactly, up the road?"

"On the lake."

"Really. The maroon house?"

I nod.

"I live in the white one . . . or I used to."

Something in her voice sets me at ease, a melancholy, a nostalgia which is completely unexpected. She straightens up, walks back to her belongings, slides into the sandals. Still, all is silent in the bathroom, and I am growing less and less concerned with this. The longer I stare at her, the more familiar she looks. Did I meet her in the days when she still lived here—or is it just that I've seen others of her kind on television? Heard my father, more than once, berate them with that special bitterness he reserves for the foreign and the unique. I can feel curiosity winding its way through my insides. As with most things my parents disapprove of, I am feeling attracted to the mere idea of her.

"How old are you?" I ask.

"Fifteen."

"Do you always dress like that?"

"This old stuff? I just wear this on holy days of obligation."

"But you're a hippie, right?"

Very slowly, jacket over her shoulder, she walks back to me. Leans against the wall. Leans down. I can see my reflection in the black lenses of her glasses. Then she removes them. Her eyes look strangely naked, her face young. A rose-colored pimple dots her left cheek. Some hair has fallen into her face, and she smells faintly of pine needles, of autumn leaves. I feel heat blossom in my chest. Not fear or anxiety or excitement. But something new and different. Something larger and more powerful, around which these other feelings merely orbit, as planets orbit a sun.

"Do you know," she asks, "what a left-wing radical is?"

"Yes . . ."

"What . . ."

I give this a moment of serious thought. Finally, from the interior of the men's room comes the sound I am no longer waiting for.

"A kind of bird," I say.

⎣⎯⎯⎯⎦

A few minutes later, I was back outside, pulling off my tie, unbuttoning the top of my shirt. I saw my mother by the refreshment table and ran to her. Somehow the world looked different. Bright and colorful, the edges of things sharply defined. Had the Body of Christ opened the aperture of my eyes? Or was it something else? My mother crouched down, asked me, smiling, where the fire was. What did I want to tell her? "Monica!" someone called. She turned, and I saw her face in profile, angled upward and blessed by sunlight. Her skin smooth and white against the dark curls of her hair. A brown beauty mark spotting the curve of her cheek. Pearls shining in her earlobes. The mantilla, white and delicate as snow . . .

She was beautiful! Beautiful!

4 / Twenty-six years old and dialing their number. Because my eyes were throbbing. Because I didn't think I could handle it that night. The concentration it took to look at her and not gaze. To chat amiably, to limit physical contact to a kiss on the cheek at arrival and departure, when all I could think about was steering her upstairs . . . Three rings and then the answering machine. A couple of seconds of music. The keyboard solo from "Riders on the Storm." Then Philip's voice, deep and lush, laced with some ancestral residue of the untamed West. *"This is Phil and Lindsey's answering machine. Speak to us."* A crash of thunder from the record album (a collector of vinyl, Philip, an activist in the lost battle against digitization), then Lindsey's voice, a playful improvisation in the background. *"We can't come to the phone right now, at this very moment."* Suddenly, the machine clicked off. The man of the house picked up. His "Hello," after the oceanic rhythm of the Doors, sounded post-orgasmic to me.

"It's Tom," I said.

"What's up, pal?"

"Am I . . . interrupting something?"

"I'm doing a model kit with Zach."

I felt a slackening of tension in my chest. "I can't make it tonight."

"Bullshit," he said.

I gave a weak laugh. "I'm serious. I've been shooting all day—"

"Listen, kid. Listen when I tell you that your attendance here tonight is not voluntary. This is nonnegotiable. You have to be here."

I balked again and he handed the phone over to his son, fruit of a previous marriage, whose seven-year-old logic I found difficult to resist.

"We're expecting you," Zach said. "It's nonnegotiable."

"Do you know what nonnegotiable means?" I asked.

"Yeah, it means my dad had a brainstorm today."

Phil took the phone back.

"What," I said, "is that supposed to mean?"

"I don't know what he's talking about. The kid's a wise-butt."

"Ha!" I heard in the background.

"So six-thirty, seven," Phil said. "And, Tom . . ."

"Uh-huh."

"Dress up a little."

⌊___⌋

Two weeks earlier, they had celebrated their second wedding anniversary with a bonfire on Ocean Beach. About thirty guests. Merlot flowing as if from the biblical jugs at Cana; four hibachis smoking (two out of four exclusively vegetarian); Philip holding court as always, lecturing about Jack London's round-the-world voyage in a doomed boat of his own design; and in the center of it all, a pyre worthy of any operatic heroine. The sun had set, the Pacific rushed at the beach. In the hollow of a sand dune, a hundred-odd yards from the proceedings, I knelt, and Lindsey straddled me, her skirt concealing everything below our waists. She climaxed almost immediately, twice in rapid succession. I couldn't come inside her, there was nothing to halt and kill my sperm, but she hadn't stopped moaning before her lips and fingers were embracing me.

"We'd better go," I said.

She told me to keep quiet. Her breath heavy, an angry energy in the act she was committing. When I told her it hurt, she whispered something filthy and clichéd; and though the sentiment only bruised my heart, I nonetheless felt a surge of blood, and then the silent approach of orgasm. She often denied me something in these final moments. Tonight, for some reason, it seemed I couldn't allow that. So I closed my hands around her neck and head, and as I felt the vibration of that familiar tone, that absolute pitch, as if a tuning fork had been struck in some deep and unchartable part of me, I held her there. When she tried to pull away, I held her down on me . . . afterward, the ocean took deep trembling breaths, the reeds whispered in the offshore breeze. Lindsey produced a pack of cigarettes and angled her face away from me as she smoked. In the distance, the bonfire licked at an ebony sky. I reached out, touched her cheek, and something warm and wet fell onto my fingertip.

"Why did you do that?"

I didn't answer. I stroked her hair, her forehead. I managed to extricate the cigarette from her fingers. I kissed her. In her mouth, beneath the thicker coating of ash, I could taste my come; and its presence there filled me with remorse, and a fear I couldn't identify.

"I'm sorry," I said.

"That's not good enough. I want to know why."

"I didn't ask you . . ." The sentence evaporated; I took a breath. "I wanted to go back."

"I was trying to move and you held me down."

"I'm sorry, Lindsey. I'm sorry we did this. I didn't come here intending to."

She stared at me in the grainy, colorless light. Below us, the breaking waves were white lines bleeding over a terrifying darkness, like wounds ripping open and healing again and again.

"I don't believe you," she said. "I think this is exactly what you intended."

A moment later, without another word, she was on her feet and walking down the dune. Her body going dark, becoming an inky silhouette. I watched her walk slowly toward the bonfire, which was casting into the air evanescent tongues of flame, and my mind felt dazed by a force more potent than alcohol. By the giddy rate, growing ever faster, at which passion was refined, like some raw mineral, into anger—into a fuel that powered us, burned out, and left an emptiness that felt exactly like love.

We'd had rules.

By that night on the beach, they'd all been broken. Our affair was six months old, and there were moments now, growing ever more frequent, when it seemed I'd do anything to own a little more of her, when the trespass against Philip meant nothing to me. At these moments, I stepped up to a kind of gateway, beyond which common sense and morality were nonexistent, where established physical laws were irrelevant. A place where one need never experience beauty from a meaningless distance . . . I had realized, sometime earlier, that I had hopes for the future. Specific and concrete. One night, at a northern inn overlooking the ocean, I had told her for the first time that I loved her. And after that night, things began to change. Her eyes avoided me in the daylight. A nameless tension charged the air between us, like a summer heat which leads inevitably to a darkening sky. At night, when we came together, the sound of pleasure and release was like the breaking of a windowpane, or the forcing of a lock. Something which demands investigation. We chose to close our eyes and feign sleep . . . How much longer could this continue? How much longer before Philip saw us, the light catching the two of us at a new and revelatory angle? How many more mornings would we wake up together, stumble forward blindly, and ignore the fact that we were, in truth, sliding backward? As if our universe had expanded as far as it could, and was now beginning the process of contraction. Racing back to the point of its birth.

Their house was in Russian Hill, a posh neighborhood balanced on some of the steepest streets in the city. There, cars curb their tires and look as if, at any moment, they will lose their grip and surrender to gravity. When conditions conspired, you could hear from their doorstep the bell of a cable car ringing softly in the distance, as I did on the evening of that last dinner party. I'd pressed the doorbell and was looking down Jones Street, into the chasm of the Marina District. Then, softly in the distance: *cling clang, cling clang.* The bay was colored a rich sky blue, the sun slanting in from the west.

"What's the password?"

I stepped back, found Zach's head peering down from the second floor. "Cephalothorax," I said.

He ducked back inside, and my heart started pounding in its traditional rhythm. The front door opened. Philip, a glass of champagne in hand, regarded me for several seconds in the light of the foyer, which approximated the glow of an old oil-powered streetlamp.

"What?" I said.

"You're early," he said, smiling. "You're chronically early."

As he led me up the stairs, I detected the smell of fresh flowers, and heard a strange sound emanating from above. "What is that?"

"Hmm?"

"It sounds like a moose is dying in your living room."

"Oh, that. It's a *shakuhachi*. I was at Tower Records this afternoon. This guy plays flowerpots tuned with water."

The stairs led directly into the living room, which had a high ceiling and enough square footage to easily house the Steinway baby grand that no one knew how to play. Zach was on the hardwood floor, confronting the *Oxford English Dictionary*.

"I can't find it," he said.

"You remember the word?"

"Cephalo-throw-ax."

"Thorax," I corrected. "It starts with C. Not S."

"C?"

"A soft C," I said. "Like 'cereal.' "

Zach backtracked to the beginning of the alphabet, the pages making thick flapping noises. It was at this point that I noticed, in the corner of the room, on the top of a faux-marble pillar, what I assumed to be a stuffed animal. A giant white bird. Epic wings unfurled as if in flight, it stared at me with glassy eyes.

"Where'd that come from?" I asked. "Is that from F•A•O Schwarz?"

"Antarctica," Zach said. "It's a wandering albatross."

"It's real?"

I stepped up to the bird, tentatively stroked its downy chest. The wingspan must have been six feet.

"Champagne?" Philip asked me.

"Sure. Thanks."

Footsteps descending from the third floor. Lindsey. Whom I hadn't seen or talked to since the bonfire. A glass of red wine in hand. Burgundy dress of crushed velvet, shirred waist with a half-length skirt and black fishnets. No shoes, as she always entertained in her stockinged feet. My body charged with a familiar friction. A headlong rush of tenderness and desire, and something darker riding underneath it. She didn't look at me, just wandered soundlessly around the room in those stockings. Below me, the pages of the dictionary were snapping sharply while Zach whispered to himself, "Cephalothorax, cephalothorax." Lindsey sipped her wine, her eyes avoiding me needlessly.

"The bird," I said to her. "It's real."

"It's dead," she said flatly.

I relieved Philip of my champagne. Once his right hand was free, he reeled Lindsey in, his lips contacting her forehead. My eyes shifted to Zach, whose hands pressed at the edges of the dictionary, as if he were pinning a wrestling opponent. "I have to check the soup," I heard her say; she touched her stepson's shiny dark hair. "You going to break out that silver, Hi-Ho?"

"Uh-huh . . ."

She headed for the kitchen; I realized I was halfway through my drink, and I hadn't had it for more than half a minute.

"So what do you think?" Phil said, pointing to the bird. "We were shooting penguins off the Peninsula. I found this poor son of a bitch with his right wing broken. He looked up at me like he'd been there for weeks, waiting for some sentient being to happen by and put him out of his misery."

"I thought you weren't supposed to interfere with the cycles of nature."

"Yeah, whatever. Some . . . Spaniard on a black-market seal-hunting expedition probably nailed him with a slingshot."

"They still do that?"

"What, carry slingshots?"

"No," I said. "Hunt seals."

"South Americans don't recognize any law except the one coursing through their bloodstream. The law of the conquistador. But he's beautiful, isn't he?"

"He's gigantic."

"Lindsey hates it," he informed me.

By this time, Zach had found the word and proceeded to spell it for us. Then he defined it. *The head and thorax regarded as a single part in certain crustaceans and arachnids.* His lips—long and full, almost femininely elegant—parted in a smile which was a perfect echo of his father's.

"Hey," Phil whispered, "could you go set that table?"

Zach left the dictionary on the floor, where it looked likely that someone would trip over it, then passed through the French doors, into the dining room.

"What was that business on the phone before?" I asked.

"Nothing. You look interesting." He fingered my shirt. "Was this made in the last decade?"

"Give me a break."

"So," he said, "what did you think of Jacqueline?"

"Who?"

"Jacqueline. The graphic artist . . . I introduced you right over there."

I shook my head; I couldn't remember what the woman looked like.

"You didn't call her," he said. "What about the Kurosawa flick, the sushi? It was perfect, she was wild about you."

"I appreciate your effort. But I don't date people who think that art can be produced with software."

"I sympathize, kid. But you don't have to go down in history with her. Just have some fun. She goes to mosh pits."

We sipped our drinks in the context of a xylophonic plunking. Funeral rite for a dying moose.

"Can I ask you something?" he said. "No judgment attached. Just man to man."

I looked at him.

"Are you gay?"

"No," I said calmly. "I'm not."

He nodded. "Then what? You're a celibate? Or you're too good for every woman you cross paths with. You have to fuck Georgia O'Keeffe?"

"I'm just not dating."

"How many times can you repeat that sentence?"

"Chicago," I said; this was my perennial one-word excuse.

"Kid, that was three years ago."

"We were practically engaged," I said.

"Not even officially. You act like you lost your wife of two decades in a tragic accident. How can you be so hung up over an academic?"

"I just can't deal with starting the process over from scratch."

"What process? Why is every woman a prospective wife? What do you want to get married for? You're twenty-six."

"I want some permanence. I want some certainty."

"Do yourself a favor, Tom, and take this advice. Don't spend your life chasing that stuff. It doesn't exist."

"If marriage is such a diseased institution," I said, "then why are you married again?"

"Because I've learned my lessons. I've parted with my illusions. I met an independent woman."

"And what was Claire?"

"Claire was a permanence seeker. It's not marriage that's diseased, it's the existent culture. You know what our culture has become? A culture of panic. Of panic-stricken permanence seekers."

"I'm not in a panic," I said.

"Yes, you are. You're paralyzed with panic. You've become subservient to loss. You're suffering the loss of things you haven't even obtained yet."

The doorbell rang. Phil gave me a long, fatherly look before he left me alone with that bird of legend. I bent over the coffee table, spread some cheese on a cracker. Through the French doors I could see Zach and Lindsey setting the table. She flicked a finger playfully against his earlobe, whereupon he requested she bend down as if to receive a secret; then, deftly, he wet his pinkie with saliva, and inserted it in her ear canal. It had been only two weeks, but it seemed she'd been sequestered for the better part of eternity. I'd passed the time with friends I didn't feel close to, coming home to a dark, silent apartment or just working through the night at the studio. I masturbated daily, thinking only of her; and in the sober moments afterward, I tried to articulate what I meant to her. I couldn't anymore. I couldn't see . . .

"Tomás," Zach said. "What are you staring at?"

A moment later, Phil crested the stairs with a guy I'd met at a previous party. A grade school friend from Montana, now a screenwriter in L.A. If I remembered correctly, he'd sold a script which was floating in the realm of the dead and unbaptized at Miramax, and maintained an arsenal of vague, imprecise language.

"Jackson, you remember Tom," Phil said. "He's an animator."

The screenwriter shook my hand. "I've got a lot of respect for anyone left in the animation industry." Without further ado, he turned to Lindsey, who made a soundless approach in those stockings. "Christ," he said to her, "you should come with a Surgeon General's warning."

"What the hell is that supposed to mean? That I'm cancer-causing?"

He ignored this vulgarity and took her hand. "Let me kiss this hand," he said. "Let me kiss this acerbic hand."

Two more people arrived—a guy Lindsey knew from when she wrote for the *Chronicle* and a woman opening an organic restaurant tentatively named The Call of Nature. This latter guest was a friend of Lindsey's from the old days in the Haight. Known in that past life as Saffron, she now went by the name on her birth certificate, which, having been told, I immediately forgot. The reporter's name was Schroeder, like the pianist in the "Peanuts" strip, and he talked obsessively about strange stirrings along the border of Kuwait, the exact location of which was contested by the restaurateur, who had once worked at a falafel stand with the purported son of an Arab sheik. What promised to be a fine fracas was diffused when Philip pulled out his first printing of some priceless world atlas—left to him in the last will and testament of Columbus or Admiral Byrd—and opened to the map which would soon become a household geographical image.

"To the south of Iraq, bordered on the *east* by the Persian Gulf—"

Again, the doorbell.

"You want to get that, Hi-Ho?"

Zach was already on his way to the stairs. "Tomás, c'mon."

"You can't open the door?" I said.

"It might be a stranger."

I nodded slowly, descended beside him, champagne glass in

hand. Stepped into the foyer. Zach pulled the door open, an effort which put me in mind of an archaeologist opening the vault of some pyramidal tomb.

"Hi, Miss Nile," he said.

"Hey, Zach." The woman looked up at me, smiled the nervous smile of someone arriving at a job interview. "Nile Treadway," she said.

"This is Tom," Zach said. "What's your last name again?"

"Aquinas."

Zach screwed up his face. "Tom Aquinas. He's an animator. He's the guy I went to Chinatown with. Remember, the story from show-and-tell, when I barfed the pot stickers?"

Nile smiled again, this time with a kind of nostalgic sarcasm. "We used to have a student-teacher relationship."

"Really," I said, trying to work up a stunned tone. Trying to conceal the fact that I knew exactly who she was. The same Nile who, several years before, had often answered the phone at Lindsey's apartment, and never failed to give the impression of being anchored in the balmy waters of hedonism. The same Nile whom Lindsey claimed not to have seen in over a year. The physical image was throwing me for a loop. Of African lineage, no older than I, and possessing a flagrantly displayed beauty which conformed to none of my preconceived notions of lesbianism. She removed her jacket, and Zach led her upstairs by the hand. Her thick heels clacked against the steps. She wore black bell-bottom pants and a tight matching top. In defiance of all rational thought, I felt lust overtake me, like a wave I'd mistimed.

"What's that noise?" she asked.

"What noise?" Zach said.

"Sounds like an elk is dying up there."

As we entered the living room, under the gaze of the albatross, Lindsey tried without success to conceal her alarm—the look of someone confronting an emergency as unlikely as it is inevitable.

"Wow," she managed. "Isn't this a surprise?"

"Yeah." Nile clasped her hands behind her back.

"Sort of like *This Is Your Life*," I kicked in.

"I ran into Nile at the Modern today," Phil said. "I have no explanation, but this knockout had no plans for the evening. Other than grading finger paintings." He turned to me. "You guys know each other, right?"

"Actually, no."

"You've never met?" he said. "I can't believe it. You've lived in town for, what, a year now?"

I nodded, and found Nile studying me as if I were inanimate, a sculpture composed of found objects.

"Actually," she said. "I feel like we have met."

"I don't think so," I said.

"Do you shop in that sex boutique on Filbert? The classy one, I mean, with the lingerie and the expensive toys."

Phil gave a snort through his nose, which put me in mind of bullfighting and Hemingway.

"I love that place," Nile said. "I thought I'd seen you in there."

"You said you teach kindergarten?" I asked.

"Once upon a time."

"It was a very progressive curriculum," Phil said.

Lindsey took a long sip of wine. Her lips were practically marinating in it. Her ex-lover smiled again—and a pair of dimples, which can be termed only as cute, were chiseled into the brown skin of her cheeks.

━━

Glasses of Cabernet Sauvignon. Bowls of squash soup and sourdough bread. Zach orbited the table with a giant pepper mill, and I reviewed the evening's delegates: The Screenwriter, The Host (at the patriarchal end of the table), The Flower Child Turned Restaurateur, The Reporter, The Hostess (Beloved of the Stop-Motion Animator), The Son from The Host's First

Marriage, and finally, seated at my immediate left, The Ex-Kindergarten Teacher—one to put all clichés of her professional breed to permanent rest. We talked about Los Angeles, the antique humidor of an Academy Award-winning director . . . entered, borne forward on Philip's nautical prose, the epic mist of the Polar Front, and gazed up at islands of ice, immaculate sculptures turning colors in the waning Antarctic light . . . debated with Saffron the possible drawbacks of defecatory double entendre in the name of a culinary establishment, vegetarian or otherwise . . . approached, then veered away from the sore subject of Lindsey's still-unfinished manuscript . . . and sat entranced while Zach—whose uncanny talent for the art of the monologue brought to mind Spalding Gray or Lenny Bruce (depending on the day's sugar intake)—told the tale of a previous dinner party, at which his uncle Simon, a usually mild-mannered longshoreman, had wound up under the table, removing the shoe, ripping open the stocking, and sucking the toe of a woman who was not his wife.

"What did she *do?*" Nile demanded.

"She said . . ." (and here the young prodigy managed to communicate a timeless tension between womanly outrage and the laws of Emily Post) " 'For your information, Mr. Davenport, that polish is known to cause cancer of the tongue.' "

The table, which by now was a wasteland of salmon carcasses and empty bottles of wine, exploded with laughter. The screenwriter's fist overturned his plate in a show of artistic fraternity. Philip grinned with fatherly disbelief. And Zach stole furtive glances at the only person whose reaction appeared to carry any weight for him: his spiritual guide from the land of afternoon naps, whose chair was jacked up against mine and whose perfume, a heady distillation of lilacs or roses, had been lulling me into a heightened state. She began to applaud and her elbow hit me solidly in the sternum.

"Jesus," she said. "I'm sorry. Are you all right?"

"I'm great."

"I didn't realize I was so close to you."

"You're pretty close," I said.

Her eyes were huge and dark, her lips full and on the verge of betraying inner hysteria. "Tom, I'm really sorry."

So this was Nile. Lindsey's ex-lover. Philip's latest idea. The reason my attendance tonight was not voluntary. I looked down the table at Lindsey, who hadn't directed a sentence at either one of us for the entire meal. Was it possible that *she* was in on this? That she was trying to phase me out by introducing me to someone else—someone utterly irresistible, not to mention my own age? Perhaps she had confessed everything to Philip, who, considering his fondness for me and his general predilection for philanthropy, saw only one thing to do: find me another woman.

"I'd like to propose a toast," the screenwriter said. Glass raised, he surveyed the table, and his eyes came to rest on Lindsey. "To a hostess whose culinary gifts are preceded only by her measurements."

There was a dead silence, save for the sound of Zach blowing his nose into his napkin.

"Is this guy for real?" Lindsey asked, without amusement.

"Jackson," Phil told him. "Sit down. Before my wife has to hurt you."

Nile turned to me in a clandestine fashion. "Who is that guy?"

"He's a friend of Phil's, from grade school."

"Do you know what he said to me before? He said I have childbearing hips. What kind of offense am I supposed to take to that? Is that an insult or a lecherous comment?"

"It could be either," I said. "He's an ambiguous kind of asshole."

"Are you sure you're all right? Anything broken?"

She touched my hand apologetically, and during the subsequent pheromonal commotion, I met Philip's eyes. He gave me a grin full of good-natured envy. A smile designed to make me feel important and somehow indebted to him. To make me see the beauty of being twenty-six and unmarried.

———

Migration back to the living room. Philip arranged some logs, kindling, and newspaper in the fireplace, and struck an oversized match. Zach and Nile played "Heart and Soul" on the piano. Lindsey sat on a large round ottoman, legs crossed in a demure but sexy fashion, and in the bright, early moments of the fire, she seemed young and vulnerable. I'd been right earlier in the day. It hurt to look at her. She was, without a doubt, trying to avoid any and all contact. I found myself doing the very same thing with Nile. But why? Tonight, for some reason, the question felt more solid and disturbing than usual. Why did I rarely date, and if I did, refuse to cross the threshold of a strange woman's apartment? At some point, Lindsey left the room, and I waited a discreet thirty seconds before following. I walked through the dining room, past the kitchen, into the dark hallway that led to the rear of the house. The light was on under the bathroom door. I knocked. A pause before she answered.

"Can I come in?"

"No, you can't."

I stood there, considering the fact that the door didn't lock. I placed my hand on the knob and turned it. A moment later, I was alone with her, the door closed insecurely behind me. She was staring at her reflection, touching up her lips.

"Interesting," I said.

"What?"

"Your ex. I didn't think that was your type."

She didn't look at me. "She used to be more earthy," she finally said.

"I thought you two were estranged."

"We are."

"So why'd you invite her?"

"I didn't," Lindsey said.

"You didn't know she was coming?"

She capped the lipstick, picked up her wineglass, and faced me. Her lips were burgundy. Like the wine, like her dress. I stepped up to her and she angled her face to the floor. She said no, but I touched her chin and forced her to look at me. We hadn't kissed since that night on the beach, and when our lips came together it felt as tireless, as necessary, as the act of breathing.

"Stop it," she said, more to herself, it seemed, than to me.

"You're beautiful," I told her.

She tried to push me back. "Can you leave? Right now?"

"Let me kiss you first, down here. Just once."

"Absolutely not. Stop it."

From somewhere in the distance, Zach shouted, "Tomás!"

"I want to smell you," I said. "I want to taste you."

Again we kissed, and this time I eased my tongue into her mouth, placed a hand on her breast. Her nipple grew hard. I held it, delicately, between two fingers.

"Let me lick you," I whispered.

Then, from the other side of the door: "Tomás!"

Lindsey pulled back, her wineglass shattered against the floor. The doorknob turned, the door opened a crack, and I pushed it shut, held it firm.

"It's just me," Lindsey said.

"What happened?"

"Nothing."

Red liquid beaded on the white-tiled floor, shards of glass glittered.

"Where the hell is Tomás?"

"Honey, don't use that word," Lindsey said, her voice shaking.

After a moment, we heard him walk away. His footsteps receded. He shouted my name in a new direction. Lindsey and

I stood there for a few seconds, not speaking, just staring down at what we'd broken.

"Okay," she finally said. "I want you to leave. Leave the house now. Tell everyone you're feeling sick." She opened the door, peered into the hallway, then moved outside. "I'm serious, Tom. Get out of my house. I don't want to see you. I don't want to see you again until Philip goes to New Zealand. I want you to keep your place, and if you don't, I'll end this, I swear to God."

Very slowly, I stepped around the glass. I walked toward her and leaned against the opposing wall.

"I'm not leaving, Lindsey. I'll clean up the glass if you want, but I'm not leaving."

"Fuck you," she whispered.

"You haven't called me in two weeks. You haven't looked at me all night. You're not going to kick me out."

"I don't owe you phone calls or conversation. I didn't ask you to come here. What are you doing here?"

There was a long silence. The question concerned far more than tonight, far more than my presence at this gathering. From the living room: a burst of collective laughter, and the gravelly baritone of Tom Waits, who was singing about gray skies and yesterday. Lindsey pulled some hair out of her face, tucked it behind her ear. Then she looked at me; the sight of me seemed to drain her of energy and color. Her eyes were wet, and when she spoke again, her voice was weak and broken. She said, "What do you want from me?"

⎣⎯⎯⎯⎯⎯⎦

In the living room, I poured myself a fresh glass of wine, and walked up to the second floor, looking for Zach. If I could be alone with him for a few minutes, a particular peace would soothe my insides. I saw him rarely, but when I did I felt this inexplicable warmth, an amazement at the bond which had sprung up between us without effort or complication. Soon after my arrival in San Francisco, with his father's permission, I'd asked him to be the model for the main character in my film. I did some sketches, built him in miniature from plasticine and foam rubber. Told him he would be the pilot of a zeppelin. Showed him my model of the new and improved *Hindenburg,* his place at the helm inside the glass-enclosed nose—and his hazel-brown irises expanded, as if to admit the burgeoning vision of his own fictional future.

He lived with his mother in Ashbury Heights, but he had a bedroom here too, with his father written all over it. Every time Phil returned from a shoot, he'd take Zach to F•A•O Schwarz and buy him a stuffed representative from Africa, India, New Zealand, wherever he'd been for the past two or three weeks. The place was like a haven for the escaped inmates of a zoo, the last stop on the Davenport Underground Railroad. Here, lions lived in harmony with gazelles and zebras; penguins discussed climatological difference with lizards; and a boa constrictor curled around the feet of a giant polar bear. Beneath the population of mammals, fish, and reptiles, there was a bed, a desk, a Macintosh computer, a bookcase full of Chris Van Allsburg and Eric Carle. The sketches I'd done at the studio were framed and hanging on the wall, my signature in the lower right corner. I was standing in the doorway when he marched up the stairs, with Nile in tow.

"There you are," he said. "Where the hell have you been?"

"Waiting here for you."

"I wanted to show you something."

He walked past me, into the room. Nile paused in the doorway with me, gave me a smile. "How's it going?"

"Fine."

"You've got some lipstick right there," she said quietly.

I felt a slow burn in my chest as she licked a finger and erased evidence from the corner of my mouth. Zach thrust a stuffed animal into my arms.

"What is it?"

"It's a sloth," he said. "A three-toed sloth. It lives in the Amazon. It sleeps sixteen hours a day. It comes down from its tree once a week. Do you know why?"

I shook my head.

"To take a shit."

"Hey," Nile said. "You need your mouth washed out with soap?"

His face went momentarily blank. He feared her; she had power over him.

"I'm just kidding, Hi-Ho." She touched his head. "Who did the drawings?"

Zach pointed at me as he fell onto the bed, and I half expected the birds on the mattress to scatter and take flight.

"That's amazing. The lips." She sat on the bed with him. "You have your dad's lips, you know?"

Cradling the stuffed sloth, I watched Zach gaze at Nile dreamily. Then I looked at her and found her looking at me.

"You and Miss Nile should check out the view," Zach said.

"What?"

"From the porch."

He pointed his thumb in a northerly direction.

"I'd like to stay up and talk," he said, eyes closing against the pink fluff of a flamingo, "but I've got a soccer game in the morning."

━━

Out on the porch. An impassioned lecture about the secrets of animation technique. Discussion of kindergarten as microcosm. She said she loved my eyeglasses. I was hooked by her creamy brown skin and the weird candor of the admission that she would soon turn yellow if she didn't get some sun. It was dark and pleasantly cool. In the distance, dewdrops of light shone along the steely web of the Golden Gate Bridge. The fog was massing out there. We could smell it.

"So how do you know Phil?" she asked.

"Phil? I know Phil through Lindsey."

Nile seemed vaguely puzzled.

"We grew up together," I explained.

"Back East?"

I nodded. "What about you?"

"Well, I know Phil through Zach. And Lindsey I met at a seance." She rolled her eyes. "It's a long story with a tragic ending."

Again I nodded, but deeply this time, as if my head were pumping oil from deep inside the Earth.

"We were together for a while," she explained. "Before she got married. The ending is really more ironic than tragic. Lindsey and Phil met each other in my kindergarten."

"You're kidding," I said, but I already knew the whole story. How Zach, not yet six at the time, had been given the lead role in Nile's magical-realist production of *Anansi and the Strange Moss-Covered Rock*. How Phil had passed up a dream shoot in Alaska to watch his son's debut, and Lindsey had come to see what her lover was billing as the best ensemble work since *Gilligan's Island*. At some point, at Zach's request, I watched the event on videotape, stunned by his flawless delivery of memorized lines, and an occasional glinting twitch of the eye which was undeniably evocative of Robert De Niro. In between scenes, the camera panned slowly over the capacity crowd—the prideful faces of family, teachers, and friends—and updated the budding attraction between two strangers, laughing and chatting away at the latter end of the alphabet line: the divorced father of the star and the lover of the director. As for Nile, the unwitting producer of this secondary drama, she had somehow managed to avoid the lazy objectivity of the camera. "Where's your other teacher?" I remember asking Zach, who was too engrossed in the record of his own talent to care.

"About that time," Nile said, "is when I developed my theory."

"What theory is that?"

"My theory that the world isn't composed of matter, but of irony. And each of us actually has an 'ironic structure,' as opposed to a genetic one."

"You're challenging some basic notions of science," I told her.

"I'm not talking about *science*," she said, turning the word over in her mouth like a bite of bad fruit. "I mean, I am talking about it, but only to the end of denying its validity. My real point is that the world operates on an entirely different set of principles, as different from science as science is from religion, and as objectively true, relative to science, as science is true, relative to religion."

"Wow," I said.

"Exactly."

"Exactly what?"

"Exactly wow," Nile said. She smiled, and as she bent over to lean against the railing, the material of her pants stretching tightly over her ass, an unsettling tension established itself in the region of my loins.

"I'm not saying there's no such thing as genes or DNA," she went on. "Just that those terms are misnomers. What we're coded with is irony. We're tagged, like animals in a study."

"It's scary," I said. "It's a truly frightening notion."

"No shit," she agreed. "I'm scared out of my goddamn wits."

"So you're saying that whatever particular type of irony we're coded for, there's no way to avoid it? To avoid becoming its victim?"

She took a long sip of her wine. "Are you a Catholic?"

"How'd you know?"

"You're persecuted, semantically. You're talking about avoidance, victimization. You're talking about predestination.

The will of some external force. I'm talking about something organic. Not something that's unavoidable, but something that's un*deni*able."

"Have you gone to the authorities with this? I mean, don't you think someone should know? Foucault, or at the very least Bill Cosby?"

"God," she said. "I'm drunk."

I watched her ease herself into a wrought-iron chair. She crossed her legs, slumped down, and, tilting her head to the sky, spoke to the stars.

"She looks amazing tonight, don't you think?"

"Who?" I said.

"Lindsey Paris."

In the semi-darkness, her neck and collarbone, exposed by the cut of her top, looked bronze, meticulously sculpted. I leaned on the railing, stared at her until I didn't dare anymore. My eyes swept over the bay, settled on the slow, rhythmic pulse of the Alcatraz lighthouse.

"I'm drunk," she repeated. "And you've got quite an erection."

I glanced back at her, found her head resting sideways on her hand, an expression of laboratory interest on her face—a zoologist studying the behavior of some newly discovered species. I tipped back my drink and reviewed a panicked host of possible responses.

"Sorry about that," I finally said.

Nile waved a hand at me. "Don't sweat it. I know that dicks work in mysterious ways. Just because a guy has a hard-on doesn't necessarily mean he's sexually excited. Just because you have one right now doesn't mean, necessarily, that you're turned on by me. I had this boyfriend who'd get hard during games of chess, but only if we played to a stalemate. If I asked him, he'd drop his drawers and show me, but it wasn't sexual. It was like the rigid dynamism of the pieces got transferred to his penis. It's a perfect example of irony theory: the oxymoron of a non-sexual erection. Do you see how this all fits together?"

"I do. I really do," I said, completely disoriented.

She downed her glass with a flourish, rose to her feet, and parked herself beside me. Leaning down on the railing, imitating my pose, she nestled an arm up against mine. In a ridiculous silence, we watched the lights of Sausalito, winking like gold deposits at the foot of the headlands. My heart raced. Strangely, there seemed to be tears pushing at the backs of my eyes.

"These are beautiful earrings," I said, embracing one with my finger, brushing the downy southernmost tip of her lobe.

"African fertility goddess," she said.

A moment later, we were tasting wine on each other's lips. A single kiss without the use of our hands. Something experimental. Nile pulled away and turned, smiling, back to the bay.

"Tell me more about Gumby," she said.

⎣＿＿⎦

Downstairs, the fire was cracking and hissing, a piney smell threading through the air. There was a kind of argument in progress. Nile and I kept an instinctual distance, and no one appeared to notice our return.

"Don't look at me," Philip was saying. "Lindsey's invited everywhere I go and she never comes. She's got a standing offer."

"She also has a career," Saffron pointed out.

"For a while, yes, she was quite busy with her book. It was a resounding success and then the tour ended. Then she started another book."

"She has a grant, Phil."

He screwed up his face, like someone playing Charades and trying to get across the idea of irrelevance. "I'm well aware of that. I'm proud as hell. I don't see how it precludes a couple of weeks of travel."

"Writers need to write," Saffron stated.

"A commonly held misconception," said the screenwriter.

"Listen. Just one example." Philip paced to the edge of the Oriental rug, farther away from his wife. "I just had a shoot in the Amazon. Army ants. Most brutal insects on Earth—the fuckers can devour a cow, an entire cow, in under an hour—but that's beside the point. We're staying with some Indians whose entire way of life is threatened, about to go down the shitter, thanks to Brazilian rubber interests, and Beaner here wants to stay home and write treatises on how armed violence is the way to Utopia."

"You're so fucking reductionist," Lindsey said.

"Phil," Saffron said, "if you're so concerned about the Indians, and I'm not saying you shouldn't be, why don't *you* write about them?"

"He'll be too busy saving the ants," Lindsey said, gazing into her wineglass.

"Did you just use the word 'reductionist'? Beaner?"

"Stop calling me that, goddammit."

"Hey," Nile said.

Attention shifted to the two of us. Lindsey regarded me confusedly, as if she'd been under the impression that I'd left the premises, as if she couldn't quite figure out how I could be standing next to her ex-lover.

"You guys shouldn't be so combative about this," Nile said. "It's clear that Phil just wants to spend some quality time with you, and he doesn't know how to express himself except through a show of hostility. I used to teach kindergarten. Believe me, this sort of conflict isn't uncommon."

Phil snorted through his nose for the second time in a single evening. "You're so fucking wry. In anyone else, the quality would be obnoxious. In you, it's like icing on the cake."

Nile had traversed the Oriental rug and was now seating herself beside Lindsey on the ottoman. She clasped her hand, and I felt an odd sensation, a disquieting mix of eroticism and jealousy. "Your husband just wants you at his side," she said. "A rifle in your hand, a charging rhino in your sights. He's turning the old hand crank and at the last possible second, you put a bullet in the poor brute's brain. Then one of your pygmy slaves snaps a picture for the den wall."

Stepping over to the stereo, Phil removed a spent album from the turntable. "You have a rather antiquated vision of nature photography. Completely defunct, in fact."

"Still," the reporter said. "It's true, isn't it, in terms of ethics, that many of the early pioneers of your field were . . . well . . . little better than big game hunters."

"And Raymond Carver beat his wife. So what? Just as many were motivated by the consequences of human behavior." Gingerly, Phil slipped the record into a paper sleeve. "They saw film as the only way to preserve disappearing species."

"Phil, of course, falls into the latter camp," Lindsey said. "So he's not opposed to the concept of taxidermy." With a leisurely motion, she indicated the stuffed albatross.

"You *shot* that bird?" Saffron said.

"Don't be ridiculous. It died of natural causes."

"That's right," Lindsey said. "He didn't kill it. He's preserving it."

"This does raise an interesting question," the reporter said, "about the entire notion of preservation. The preservation of images versus the conservation of living things. The very action of photography is basically one of capturing. Locking the image of an animal in a succession of frames. The space in between is even reminiscent of the bars of a cage."

Phil waved him off as he searched for another album.

"I mean, I respect your work. I'm even sympathetic to it. But animals preserved on film—whose benefit is that for?"

"This is amazing," Philip said. "With all the concrete, quantifiable offenses perpetrated against the natural order, you guys can sit here wasting time deconstructing cinematography?"

"There *is* the question of that albatross to resolve," Nile said.

"Fuck the albatross. We're talking about film. And film makes people think. There's no force more capable of changing values, and therefore society, than motion pictures. Tom, why the hell aren't you saying anything? Obviously you're the only one in the room who understands the power of it."

Everyone turned to me.

"I like your movies," I said. "I like the funny things the animals do."

A contagious snicker ran through the room. Nodding gravely, Philip cued up a new record, asked us all how we were fixed for drinks. From her place on the ottoman, Nile gestured to me with her glass. I walked over and took it, with a subtle chivalric flair, from her hand.

"Lindsey?" I said.

Her eyes rose from the rug with the metallic torpor of a pair of submarines. She looked at the glass in my hand, and then she looked at me.

"No," she said. "Thanks."

In the dining room, Philip was measuring out for himself and Jackson immoderate doses of very expensive scotch.

"Sorry about that," I said. "I wanted to make a joke. I agree with you, of course."

He waved me off. "Forget about that. I want to know what you think."

"About what?"

He glanced surreptitiously in the direction of the living room. "About Nile."

"What do I think? Of her?"

He waited.

"She's the most gorgeous thing this side of Jupiter."

His head nodded in a sage-like fashion. "Your convergence here tonight is not accidental."

"You don't say."

"I ran into her today at the Modern. In the surrealist exhibit. Saw her enveloped by this Dali, the one with the flaming giraffes.

And after I acknowledged my own sexual uprising and made peace with it, I thought of you."

"I thought she was gay," I said irrelevantly.

"She's confused," Philip clarified. "And confusion can be a highly erotic state of mind."

"That's what I need," I said. "Confused eroticism."

"You've got it exactly backward. It's erotic confusion."

"I'm moved by your charity, Phil. But didn't she spend a year in bed with your wife?"

He studied me with an expression of scholarly amusement, as if I'd just employed some archaic linguistic construction. He uncorked the wine, and I handed him Nile's glass.

"Is Lindsey in on this?" I asked.

"In on what?"

"You know what. On trying to set me up with her confused ex-lover."

"No. This is my baby."

"Well . . . don't you think the idea would upset her?"

He gave me back Nile's glass, refilled and sporting a faint impression of her lips along its rim. "Tom, you're a sensitive guy. It's an admirable trait, but you indulge it to a fault. Lindsey is over her. Frankly, the whole affair was lukewarm for both of them."

"Really . . ."

"Loosen up. You're always walking on eggshells around here. I bet Lindsey would love it if you two got together."

I took a contemplative sip of the drink in my hand, then realized it wasn't mine.

"You do find her attractive."

"Who?"

"Nile."

"I could write sonnets," I said.

Again, that fatherly bobbing of the head as he handed me my rightful glass. We walked back through the French doors, into the bachelor-pad saxophone of Stan Getz, and I felt his hand greet my spine.

"My boy," he whispered, "you have neither lived nor loved until you've had sex with a lapsed lesbian."

As though I were a miniature sailboat, he gave me a gentle push in Nile's direction. Fresh drinks in hand, I glided to her side.

5 / Summer, 1974.

School has ended. My best friend, Roland, has departed for the Far East. In Connecticut, the days are long and hot. The smell of freshly cut grass, the hum of stinging insects. At six o'clock every night, Walter Cronkite speaks to us of the arms race, the Arab oil embargo, and Patty Hearst. The Supreme Court and the Oval Office. Taped conversations and the withholding of evidence. With increasing frequency, Mr. Cronkite uses the word "impeachment," after which the camera lingers on his paternal visage, his shadowy mustache; then the screen is usurped by the rolling fog of Raid Jungle-Tested Yard Guard, the rich shag beauty of Ozite Carpet, or the giddy image of someone taking the Nestea Plunge. In those days, Bethlehem had one grocer, one pharmacist, one gas station. The nearest bank was twenty minutes away, the closest movie theater a good forty. We had a barber, a candy store, a luncheonette. We had a church, we had one man of God—and when he died, it seemed to be proof of a new and irreversible motion. That summer, our exhausted nation began to fall into its deep myopic sleep. I remember our leader, waving with incongruous triumph from the doorway of a helicopter, as years before, in the Land of Oz, in the unconscious mind of a little girl, a deposed wizard had waved from his hot-air balloon. I remember Father Coine's coffin being lowered into the ground, beads of holy water clinging to its surface. There were members of the Catholic Archdiocese in liturgical headdress. There were state officials with badges and guns. Investigating. Searching for answers. But the truth would always remain locked away. In my mind. In Lindsey's. Summer would end, and autumn would come in the colors of fire.

                      —

A lot had changed since I'd last seen her, since we'd spoken in the darkened nave of St. Edward's. I was two years older, and I now read books without illustrations, owned a Little League uniform, and experimented with the use of curse words. Most important, I had discovered in myself an artistic lucidity, and had abandoned dreams of the priesthood for a career as a political cartoonist. Working from photos in *Time* and *Newsweek,* I sketched Nixon and Brezhnev, capitalizing on the comic potential of noses and eyebrows. My parents bought me expensive pencils, gray gum erasers, and professional drawing pads. They told me I had a natural gift for caricature. I spent my days sketching, swimming in the lake, reading books at the waterfall. C. S. Lewis, Roald Dahl, Madeleine L'Engle. I walked into town, past the church and the statue of the Virgin; past the Civil War monument and the Mobil station with the old-fashioned pumps; past my father's optometry office and the Town Hall, until I reached the candy store.

It was there that I met her again.

In the pleasant smell of unsmoked cigars. Among the shelves filled with chocolate and bubble gum. In the presence of the old, unfriendly proprietor who looked remarkably like a bullfrog reading the *Daily News.* Afternoon. The sky dark, and that cellar-like room about as bright as the bottom of a murky pond. Thunder in the distance, an atmospheric purr. For the privilege of browsing the comic books, I bought a pack of baseball cards. He responded by punching the keys of the ancient cash register, which always read NO SALE. Then I disappeared into the second of the two aisles. Lined up along the wall: *Batman, Doctor Strange, The Fantastic Four.* I sat down on the painted concrete floor, picked up a Marvel title I'd never seen before. *Son of Satan.*

According to page one, the main character was Daimon Hell-strom—spawn of the devil, born of woman. I breathed in the smell of the cigars. The window half open, admitting a cool breeze, barely enough light to read by, and the gentle drum roll of the rain . . . The door creaked. Footsteps. A girl's voice.

"Rolling *what?*" the bullfrog croaked.

"Papers," she said.

A long silence.

"Forget it," she finally said.

The footsteps approached my aisle, turned into it, and stopped beside me. I looked over at two feet strapped into worn leather sandals. From above, the rustling of magazines and a few drops of water. I raised my eyes slowly. Cutoff jeans, a tank top soaked with rain, and a face I had not forgotten staring down at me.

"You trying to look up my skirt?" she said. " 'Cause I'm not wearing one."

"I beg your pardon," I said, and returned immediately to Daimon Hellstrom, who was blazing a trail of fire across the sky.

"You beg my pardon?"

I nodded, not taking my eyes off the page.

"Isn't that a little polite for a seven-year-old?"

"I'm nine," I said.

"Oh, nine," she said. "My sincerest apologies."

She crouched down and I glanced at her in the dim light. Yes, her. Long black hair dripping with rainwater. Eyebrows arched as if in contemplation of some unasked question. A dusting of freckles so light, it seemed with a gentle breath I might blow them from her face.

"You look familiar," she said. "You a friend of my sister's?"

"Not really."

"I've seen you somewhere."

Behind the counter, a transistor radio was receiving unintelligible transmissions. It crackled loudly as our host lowered the volume, and suddenly, the store was as silent as a mausoleum.

"I know," she said. "That time at the church. I didn't recognize you without a necktie."

"Time to move along," we heard: a voice which was deep and swampy.

"What's his problem?" she said.

"I don't know."

"You're just going to leave? You haven't finished your reading matter."

"It's okay."

A single punch rang out from the register; the cash drawer jangled as it sprang open.

"That means hurry up," I said, making to return the book to the shelf.

She rolled her eyes and stopped me, grasping my wrist. She slipped the book underneath her tank top, fastened one end inside the waist of her shorts, affording me a brief but opulent view of her stomach; then, placing a hand on my back, guided me toward the door.

"We beg your pardon," she said as we crossed the bullfrog's line of vision.

Outside, the rain was coming down hard and steady, and the world appeared content to be wet. We ran for the awning of the market two doors down, and there she removed the stolen item. She started to hand it to me when she noticed the title and the cover: the red-caped Daimon Hellstrom fighting a hairy goat monster above the caption, ONE BY ONE, THE TAROT CARDS ARE TURNED, AND THE FUTURE THEY FORETELL IS . . . DEATH. Amusement broke the cool criminal look on her face.

"By the way," she said, "I'm Lindsey Paris."

Her right hand was extended. The fingers long and feminine, a large opalescent ring on her middle finger. I shook her hand, and cleared my throat.

"I'm Thomas Markham."

Rain sounded against the sidewalk, the canvas of the awning above us, the top of a car parked nearby. It would be a long time before it let up, before the pregnant clouds would spend themselves and the sun would issue its forgiveness; so it didn't surprise me when Lindsey stepped into the grayness and the falling drops. "Let's do this again sometime," she said. A conspiratorial smile. Then she was gone, running up Main Street, in the direction of Massachusetts.

⌣

As dusk hardened into night, the lake, the field beyond, the hills in the distance were still as a photograph, old and fading and grainy. In a pair of cutoff jeans, I sat on the end of the dock, dangling my bare feet in the water, looking across the lake at Lindsey's house. I'd never stolen anything from someone who wasn't a blood relation, and the comic book was exerting an incisive pressure on my mind. It was filled with references to exorcism, demons, the occult, and something called the Legion of Nihilists. I really wasn't interested in this subject matter. If I had to be a partner in a theft, I wished the stolen item had been an issue of *The Fantasic Four* or *Batman*. Throw it away, I thought. Ditch it in the woods, or shove it to the bottom of the aluminum garbage can. Yet when I'd reached our driveway, the hot asphalt steaming after the rain, I headed for the garage. I hid it in an old chest of drawers, beneath a supply of sandpaper my father rarely used. It seemed to be pulsing out there, with the silent sinister throb of evidence. Why had I been unable to discard it?

I heard something fall and break.

The sound was so far away, so powerless against the silence of dusk, it might have been nothing but memory. Then it happened again. A crystalline smash that carried over the lawn and hung suspended. I rose to my feet, the dock swaying gently under my weight, and saw my mother's silhouette in the kitchen window. Strangely motionless. My father called out to her from another part of the house. Why didn't she answer? A few moments later, he spoke her name again, this time in a tone I'd never heard before, a tone which sparked in my mind the beginnings of impossible images—and all at once, night seemed to fall. The sky dark and filled with stars. Fireflies lighting up and fading out. The air suddenly cold, colder than was possible, against my bare chest and shoulders. I started running. My wet feet slipping on the grass. The back door whining as I flung it open. The television on in the basement and losing its vertical hold. At the top of the stairs, I found the kitchen floor glittering with shards of glass, my parents standing in an awkward embrace.

"You're not choking?" my father said. "You weren't eating?"

With her eyes shut hard, my mother was struggling to breathe.

"Lie down. Try lying down."

He eased her to her knees, then lowered her head into his lap. But panic entered her eyes. She lost her breath completely. Suddenly, she clamped a hand over her mouth and coughed from deep in her throat. Her palm came away red, stained with thick, bloody saliva. There was a rush inside my head, an unrecognizable sound. My father ran for the telephone; and as he dialed, the rotary wheel unwinding in slow-motion, I found myself walking forward. A pinprick on the tender arch of my bare foot. Then I was kneeling beside her, holding her hand, sick to my stomach and my eyes burning. Her beauty had been transformed into something grotesque and urgent. An elastic string of saliva, colored pink, dripped from the subtle cleft of her chin. I turned. On the countertop above, the radio murmured; and a small lamp, the one which featured on its base a statuette of St. Francis, shone its soft light down on us—while miles away, on the other side of a gleaming sea of glass, my father was speaking in clipped sentences. Speaking some other language. I couldn't listen. I couldn't look at my mother. I locked my eyes on St. Francis. On the dove resting placidly in his hands. From inside the radio, a man with a Southern accent spoke in a pained and hopeless tone. He was saying something about America. He said we'd lost our moral compass.

⎯

The situation was neither a mystery nor an emergency. As a girl, she'd had rheumatic fever. She remembered being home from school for a month, the aching in her joints. She remembered her family taking turns sitting with her, reading to her. Though no doctor had noticed then, and in fact twenty years had passed with hardly a single symptom, the infection had affected a small piece of her heart, which simply needed special care now. As long as she followed a new set of rules, everything would be fine. There were three kinds of medication. Naps every afternoon. A restricted diet. My father closed his office and spent his time steaming vegetables and cutting fruit. He didn't want Mom exerting herself in any way. But there was only so much my father could do. I got the feeling he just wanted to be present in the house, listening, hearing everything that transpired. Before long, Mom's gratitude for his attentiveness soured; she grew snappy and impatient. Even when there was space between us, we all got in each other's way, like three astronauts in a cramped capsule.

This went on for nearly two weeks before a rescue team arrived from the Bronx: Uncle Vincent, Aunt Carmela, and Marco. Vincent, on vacation from the Thirty-fifth Precinct, had decided to sacrifice a few days at Jones Beach in the name of brotherly love. A man who believed in a good, solid tan, my uncle spent as much time as possible in the sun, wearing a bathing suit that looked like a bikini. Tall and muscular, he had a commanding, handsome face, perfectly white teeth, and roving eyes which implied a mutual understanding I could never quite grasp. He showed up on Sunday in a cowboy hat and called me "partner." His Ecuadoran wife, my aunt Carmela, looked, as always, darkly, futuristically glamorous. Like a model in a fashion magazine, my aunt pushed the boundaries of everyday cosmetics, using experimental shades of makeup—gold lipstick, bruise-purple nail polish—which, combined with her olive skin, put me in mind of extraterrestrial Amazons. When she held my face in her hands and kissed my lips, I half expected to be brainwashed or turned into a statue made of the same alien ore which decorated her mouth. When she spoke, I wanted to lie in a tub of warm water, close my eyes, and just listen.

"This boy is going places," she said, a hand resting on Marco's knee.

We were sitting on the deck, in the shade of the wind-out umbrella table, sipping iced tea. My father had finally relented and gone to the office; Uncle Vincent was in the kitchen preparing lunch.

"Tell your aunt Monica what you're reading now."

My cousin rolled his eyes in protest.

"Civilization and Discontent," Carmela said. "Freud, at the age of eighteen. I don't know where he gets it."

"Now and then," Marco said, "the intelligence gene skips a generation."

Carmela eyed him suspiciously, tapping one of her large gold earrings with an eggplant-colored nail. When he cracked a smile, she slapped him on the knee.

"Half the time," she said, "you don't know whether you're being insulted or not. It's the curse of giving birth to a psychiatrist."

The screen door opened and my uncle stepped out with a tray of sandwiches and raw vegetables, naked except for his skimpy bathing suit and cowboy hat, his brown skin still shiny with tanning oil. "Lunch," he said, "is served."

"For God's sake," his wife said, "put some clothes on." Then, her voice growing exotic, she added, "Unless you're going to streak for us."

He gave her a wide-eyed, indignant look. "Madam, I am an officer of the law."

"Yeah, well, what about those cops in Boston?" Marco asked.

Vincent placed the tray on the table and selected one triangular quarter of a turkey sandwich. He used it for emphasis as he spoke. "Those men forgot their solemn oath . . . to keep it in their pants."

While we ate, my relatives recounted their favorite streaking stories. A thousand students at the University of Georgia. Naked people on Wall Street, at the Vatican, riding motorcycles, parachuting. Jail sentences in South Korea. A homosexual hairdresser who ran nude through the Hawaii state legislature and then explained, "I am the Streaker of the House." This individual was subsequently arrested and charged with open lewdness.

"My sister's not amused," Vincent said.

Mom, who had been gazing absently at the lake, turned back to us. "Oh, it's just sort of sad, you know. Our society's become so absurd. Democracy's in crisis and all anyone can do is take their clothes off in public."

"Well," Carmela said, crunching a carrot stick, "I, for one, enjoyed having something to laugh about for a change."

I offered my own personal theory, stolen from an episode of *Star Trek,* that it was all the fault of alien micro-organisms which had broken through the atmosphere carrying a rare strain of space madness. A moment later, my uncle began to twitch as if suddenly stricken with my fanciful disease. He stood up and feigned a loss of motor control. At any moment, it seemed he would tear off his bikini and complete our already extensive understanding of his anatomy.

"Do it!" I shouted, laughing wildly. "Do it!"

"Don't you dare," Carmela said.

My mother struggled to keep a straight face, and Marco observed him with a studious expression, as if through the two-way glass of a psychiatric ward. Finally, he stopped. Kissing Mom on the cheek, he moseyed off, returned to the blanket which waited down on the sand, the bathing suit covering about half of his rear end.

"You've got to admit," Marco said, "he's got a nice butt."

⎳

After lunch, my cousin and I walked along the lake road, then up the dirt path which led to the waterfall. We sat on a rock above the pool. A few feet away, water dropped along the mossy face of the cliff, as Marco lit up a small homemade cigarette. The smoke smelled like burning resin. Like the incense lit on feast days at church.

"How old are you?" he asked.

"Nine. Ten in January."

"Going on ten. That's the end of the single digits, man. You're going into fourth grade?"

"Fifth," I said. "I skipped first. Remember?"

"So you're a year younger . . . than the other kids in your class."

I nodded.

"How does that make you feel?" he asked.

"Weird, sometimes. But it's all right, mostly."

He drew on the cigarette, held the smoke in his lungs, then exhaled a pungent cloud. "You realize," he said, "you're entering a very volatile stage of life. Have your parents talked to you yet? About sex?"

I shook my head.

"I didn't think so. See, they wouldn't consider the fact that your friends are a year older than you. That imbalance has to be compensated for, or the pressure on your psyche is going to be a problem later. It's like tires. If you don't rotate them at the proper times, they wear unevenly. You get what I'm saying?"

I shrugged, and Marco explained to me that psychosexual disorders had their origins very early in life. He told me about a seventeen-year-old boy who, for as long as he could remember, had felt and acted like a girl, and in fact wanted be surgically transformed into one. This was known as a sex-change operation and the resulting individual a transsexual. Though this particular person had eventually been cured—through behavior modification and electroshock therapy—things would have been a lot easier if he'd just been properly educated in the first place. My cousin removed his sneakers and socks, and segued into a rambling lecture on the male and female sex organs, the act of intercourse. I listened, with a queasy fascination, to news of a milky fluid which would one day emerge from the hole in my penis. How many other changes did my body plan to implement without my permission?

"What's it like?" I asked him.

"What?"

"When it comes out, is it like peeing?"

He smiled and shook his head. Then he pointed to the top of the falls, maybe thirty feet above the pool. "Imagine you're standing up there," he said, "on the very edge. And you're going to jump because you know it's safe. The pool is deep enough and you won't hit any rocks, it's a guarantee. So you let yourself go. You're a little nervous, but you feel great while you fall. And when you hit the water, it's warm. It closes all around you. You're light, and you can breathe down there."

"You've done it?"

Pursing his lips, my cousin gazed pensively downstream. "Girls," he said. "They're funny. Some are still confused about their own liberation. Sometimes they don't like it at first. But once you get into it, the old attitudes fade away."

I watched the water falling and splashing into the pool below, a thing as relentless and unceasing as the crashing of ocean waves or the beating of a heart.

"How about a swim?" Marco said.

"We don't have any bathing suits."

He placed a finger on his temple, closed one eye. "We'll do it in the nude and air-dry."

I looked all around, down the path and over my shoulder.

"Come on, there's no one around. Anyway, what does it matter? This is the Age of Aquarius."

He slipped off his shirt, revealing a muscular chest and the shadow of a few black hairs. His arms were strong as well, and I remembered the free weights in his basement, which he and his father used. He took off his shorts and briefs. His penis bounced up and down; it was half erect. Soon, I too was naked and easing myself into the cold water, my own penis shriveling and my testicles retreating to somewhere deep inside. Still, it was thrilling to be naked outdoors, to exist in a completely natural state. To run the risk of being charged with open lewdness. Marco submerged himself, and a few moments later, so did I. Under the surface, the sound of the waterfall was like something real heard in the context of a dream. I imagined the water was warm. That I was light, and I could breathe.

—

The next afternoon. Front seat of my uncle's car. Cool air blowing through the open windows. The radio playing at excessive volume as Marco and I drove down Main Street. The otherworldly rhythm of the music—the music of black people, the music of *Soul Train*—seemed to undermine the credibility of our village center. There was something about the homogeneous white storefronts, a truth that kept slipping out of my grasp.

"Maybe we should turn this down," I said.

"I feel mean!" Marco sang along. "Like a sex machine!"

We clattered over the defunct tracks of the Housatonic Valley Railroad and into the parking lot of Cone-U-Copia. Inside, the air was cool, and a few people sat at the small round tables. Father Coine stood at the counter, surveying the tubs of ice cream, wearing his black shirt with the white clerical collar.

"Sweet Mother of Mercy," my cousin whispered. "Who's that?"

"Father Coine," I said.

"Not the holy man, dummy. The girl."

I stepped closer to Marco. Had she been there a moment ago? Cone in hand, Lindsey Paris was engaged in animated conversation with our local priest. It had been over two weeks since the incident at the candy store. Seeing her now, I felt myself charging with a familiar fear, as if we'd been made partners in some scholastic activity, a game or science experiment from which there was no escape.

"You know her?" Marco asked.

"Not really."

A moment later, Father Coine glanced in our direction. He announced my name at a volume that turned every head in the place. His hand shot out like a switchblade. There was an embarrassing hush, a universal pause in the consumption of sundaes and cones, while I crossed the room and slapped him five.

"How's it going, buddy?"

"Good."

He looked at Marco pleasantly.

"This is my cousin," I said. "From New York."

Marco extended his hand and pronounced his full name with that lyrical accent of his. He shook Father's hand, and then he shook Lindsey's. She wore a halter top, straps tied at the shoulders, three pointless buttons falling in a vertical line between her breasts. Her stomach was completely bare. I felt Father's hand touch down on my shoulder.

"Lindsey, have you met Tom?"

"Sure," she said. "You might say we have a history."

My cousin raised an eyebrow. I thought I could feel, for the first time, sweat forming under my armpits without the aid of exercise. The counter girl handed Father his order. Butter pecan on a sugar cone, chocolate sprinkles. Then he told us he had to be on his way, his green eyes glimmering like emeralds behind the lenses of his eyeglasses.

"That guy's cool," Lindsey said as he walked away. "Like

Berrigan." She leaned toward us, confidentially. "We're gonna start a little underground."

"Sign me up," Marco said.

"You into liberation theology?"

"Not exactly. But I was a draft evader."

She gave him a skeptical look.

"I'm serious," he said. "I lived in Canada for two years. In an igloo."

"And now you live in New York," she said.

"Park Avenue."

"Uh-huh."

"Okay, the Bronx. And I wasn't really a draft evader. I was a conscientious objector."

Lindsey tried, unsuccessfully, to fight off a smile. I, for one, didn't see what was so funny.

"Where are you from?" he asked.

"San Francisco," she said. "Upper Haight."

"Far out," Marco said.

"It is. Extremely far out."

Her eyes met mine, and I looked away immediately.

"So," Marco said, "you two know each other."

Lindsey nodded and licked her ice-cream cone. "It's a Bonnie-and-Clyde-type thing."

———

A few minutes later, we were all together in the front seat of the Chrysler. Marco to my left, navigating with one hand. Lindsey Paris to my right, talking about the next great threat to the national consciousness. The Bicentennial. Like Vietnam before it, this event was supported by a massive propaganda campaign designed to eclipse a host of governmental ills, chiefly Watergate and the failure of the war. She had recently joined a radical organization called the People's Bicentennial Commission, a Washington-based group seeking to build a mass revolutionary movement for a totally restructured America. Last December, in Massachusetts, they'd turned the first official event of the Bicentennial, a reenactment of the Boston Tea Party, into a giant impeachment rally.

"You were there?" Marco said.

"It was beautiful, man. We hung the bastard in effigy, then we burned him."

Her naked leg was easing into mine, like a ship drifting off course. My cousin went for the gear lever and his elbow hit my arm.

"Give me some room, cuz."

I inched to the right.

"Do you realize," Lindsey said, "that July Fourth, 1976, was going to be the crown jewel of the Nixon Administration? He was going to preside over it like some kind of living myth. He thought he was going to be the new George Washington. Is that sick?"

"Nixon," my cousin said, shaking his head as if at some tragic automobile accident.

"Now it's just another hopeless attempt to distract us. Like China and the POWs. Of course, he hasn't got a prayer now, it's just a matter of weeks now. But the danger is, once he's gone, they'll really crank up the machine, try to hypnotize us with that crap. Bicentennial, bicentennial. Tell us to pull together, heal the wounds, stand up for America, march in a parade. It's all so predictable. It's like a goddamn script. And the worst part is, everyone'll play their parts."

"Not me," Marco said. "I've got a lunch date. At the Kremlin."

"Don't you get it?" she said. "This is psychological warfare."

At the mention of his field of expertise, my cousin's face grew suddenly attentive, then reflective, as if he were reevaluating everything Lindsey had said in a new and more interesting light. Meanwhile, she searched through her shoulder bag, pulled out two pins, and handed one to each of us. Marco's read "Jail to the Chief," mine read "Don't Blame Me—I Voted for McGovern." I looked up at her and she gave me one of those smiles, the grin of a wolf in sheep's clothing. The radio playing. The wind blowing into her long dark hair. Dappled sunlight splashing over the three of us, like luminous rain.

⌐────⌐

In the days following, my cousin walked around like a paralytic who'd miraculously regained the use of his legs. He told me that love was a many-splendored thing. He told me about being with Lindsey Paris on the Appalachian Trail. Walking, looking at views, hearing the birds and the bees. He described more than once how her nipple had hardened between his fingers, a little pebble of flesh. Every day, he was either with her or lazing around reading books that she had lent him about revolution and social change. At night, he came home late, sometimes after I'd fallen asleep. If I was still awake, though, we'd walk down to the lake and he would smoke one of those homemade cigarettes, after which his mind was given to the formation of strange comparisons. He said the world of night was like a bowling ball. He said that girls were like fruit—when they played hard to get, you had to soften them up, like a nice mango. One night on the dock, he let me try a little. I waited for similes and metaphors to start sprouting in my mind. Nothing seemed to happen. But then I saw the stars up above us, some of them long dead, but their light still traveling through space; and as I thought about her, I had a strange and fearful sensation. Some kind of realization about time and change. I looked down the sand beach, at the canoe lying beached on its side, and imagined paddling silently across the lake, into the reeds below her house. Floating there. Staring into the windows. Waiting for her to fill a square of light, while fireflies whirled through the tall grass like the jets of some busy country, taking off and landing on hidden runways.

Saturday morning. Breakfast on the deck, under the shade of the wind-out umbrella. My parents and aunt and uncle were there; Marco was still asleep. While I ate bacon and fried eggs, I considered the imminent broadcast of *Sigmund and the Sea Monsters,* the adults' conversation only dimly registering until I heard mention of the sticker on the door of my father's optometry office.

"What sticker?" my mother said.

"The Bicentennial sticker. It came in the mail."

My father sorted through the bacon in search of a crispy piece, a process which my mother observed with a patient stare, one of those stares that presaged argument.

"You're saying you refused to sell her sunglasses—"

"That's right," Dad said.

"—because you had a political disagreement."

"She can buy her sunglasses at the drugstore."

Aunt Carmela's bracelets jangled against her juice glass. "Marco seems to think she's very sweet."

"Marco," Vincent said, "has got a hormone imbalance."

The doorbell rang. Two cheerful tones. While my aunt got up to see who it was, I busied myself mopping up egg yolk with a slice of toast. I'd missed the beginning of this conversation, but the outline was easy enough to piece together; and I had the creeping suspicion that I was in the process of getting myself into trouble. First the comic book, biding its time out there in the garage. Then the pin. "Don't Blame Me—I Voted for McGovern." It had been missing for two days now, and I'd begun to fear that my father had found it and was waiting for an opportune time to lecture me. Hadn't I once heard him loudly refer to that man as an apologist for the Communist world?

"Have you met her?" my mother asked me.

"Who?" I said.

"Lindsey Paris. From across the lake."

I shook my head automatically. Dip toast into egg. Chew carefully. About three seconds later, my aunt reappeared, escorting onto the deck our surprise visitor.

"Everyone," Carmela said. "May I present the girl in question."

"Morning," Lindsey said. "Hi, Tom."

There was a sudden flare of heat in my chest. Silence while my family waited for me to return the greeting. I said hello and then, totally against my will, glanced at my father. He was already looking at me, wearing on his face the dull, ruthless expression of a courtroom judge. Introductions were made. Vincent offered his seat. I wanted nothing more than to be elsewhere, safely entranced by Saturday-morning television, but it seemed a sudden departure would be more incriminating than staying put.

"Has anyone heard the latest?" Lindsey asked.

We all looked at her as she stirred sugar into her coffee.

"The Supreme Court voted unanimously. He's got to give up the tapes."

My father dropped his fork onto his plate, tossed his napkin onto the table, and exited. No sooner had the deck door swung shut than it opened up again. Marco stepped out in a bathrobe, a towel draped over his shoulders. He looked like a prize fighter about to enter the ring.

"Hiya," he said.

Lindsey gave him a lazy salute.

"How about we go on a hayride," he said, buffing his wet head. "You got any hay around here?"

Regretfully, Carmela informed him that they had to be in Danbury in an hour. My mother had a hair appointment, and my aunt didn't have a driver's license. Marco turned to his father, whose hand was already up, forefinger rocking back and forth like a metronome.

"I'm on vacation," Vincent said.

Marco took all this in stride. Sometime before, he'd told me the three general pointers for picking up girls. Number two was "Act your age." He made a date with Lindsey for noon.

"You'll have to forgive us," Mom said, standing up. "You caught us at a bad time."

"No problem." Lindsey crossed her legs and sipped her coffee. "Maybe to make up for it, Tom would be willing to walk me home."

"Perfect," Vincent said. "Everyone's happy."

He gave us all a white smile and went inside to strip.

⌐

A few minutes later, Lindsey and I were on our way around the lake. It was still morning, but the sun burned hot through a sky that hadn't offered rain in days. As we walked, she told me all about herself. Until she was nine, she'd lived right here on the lake. Then, in the spring of 1967, her parents divorced, and she and her mom moved to California. That was where she'd found her calling. Civil disobedience. Professional protest. It started with the Pentagon Papers. Cambodia. A secret bombing campaign ordered by the same presidency which was now in a state of collapse. An air war which had killed thousands of innocent people. She was twelve years old that day on the playground when she was targeted by a couple of boys playing G.I. Joe. A victim of an air attack from the top of the slide. She wasn't in the game, she explained, she was therefore alive; but the boys were adamant about her status as a civilian casualty. Rather than prove her case by walking away, she chose to lie prostrate at the foot of the slide. "You'd better move," the bomber pilot said, poised above her against a deep blue sky; and Lindsey answered that she couldn't, because she was dead. A moment later, his body was whispering smoothly down the metal chute. Her eyes shut reflexively, her body went rigid. Then there was the sound of rubber soles screeching to a halt. The bomber pilot crouched over her, staring with a dim curiosity—and Lindsey remained stationary, slowly apprehending the meaning of what she was doing. Recess ended and she was still there, lying immobile even when her teacher demanded that she come in for math class.

"How long?" I said. "How long did you stay there?"

"About a half hour total."

"Then what?"

"They sent the gym coach out to carry me in. He carried me to the principal's office."

"You got suspended?"

"For a day," she said. "But it was worth it. After that, I wasn't so depressed about my parents anymore. I knew exactly what I wanted to do."

At its north end, the lake fed into a stream, and we crossed on three rocks evenly spaced in the water. Lindsey extended her arms, balancing like someone walking on a tightrope. Up ahead, the field stretched out before us, its tall grass waving and rolling hypnotically, like an ocean. In silence we wandered toward it. The brown stalks grew even with my eyes. Reaching out, I ran my fingers over them, imagining the strings of a harp. Across the lake, my house sat on a spotless stretch of green. I could see my uncle on the beach, the canoe a few feet away, its silver hull reflecting the sun. It was strange to see it all from here, so small and ordered.

"Have you been to the old McCready place?"

Shadows from the surrounding trees played over her face and body. Her thumbs were hooked into the belt loops of her shorts.

"Come on," she said. "We'll go antiquing."

As she stepped forward, the grass embraced her legs and waist. She ran a hand over the golden wheat-like surface. I followed, feeling for a moment the sensation of diving underwater, of being swallowed, unable to see or hear. But trees were visible along the meadow's edge, their branches filled with cicadas, whose chattering poured down like syncopated cloudbursts into the seashell sound of the grass. Over my head, dragonflies zipped back and forth. Farther up, in the blue-and-white sky, a hawk circled, its wings rocking gently in the wind currents. I wanted to go in mind of Lewis and Clark, with an undaunted sense of adventure. But my head was swimming with other things. Lindsey's story had reminded me of a photo I'd found in the library at school, in one of the yearbooks of *Life* magazine. A naked girl, no older than I, running clumsily down a road, her mouth open in a bewildered scream, patches of her skin peeling off, while black smoke obscured the background.

"I don't think he likes me much," she said.

"Huh?"

"Your dad."

We were deep into the field. I could no longer see my house. The air buzzed with the momentary approach and departure of a dragonfly. A cloud passed in front of the sun, and then its shadow broke over the field like a wave, dulling the colors and the heat.

"I saw a picture once," I said. "A little girl, naked, running down a road. There was a lot of smoke behind her."

Lindsey eased her hands into her pockets and glanced down at me.

"Did we do that?" I asked her.

She slowed down. Then, crouching in front of me, she looked seriously into my eyes. "We did not do that. The president did it, Tom. The president and the generals and the soldiers. Not you and me. We didn't fly the planes and we didn't vote for the people who sent them."

Up in the sky, a cloud still obscured the sun, its edge so radiant it seemed to be on fire. The white mass moved slowly. Changed shape, slowly. She was talking about a world so confused and complicated, I couldn't begin to understand its laws. One thing, however, had come painfully clear. The photo of that naked girl had a context, her condition had a cause. I couldn't believe I'd been alive at the moment that bomb had fallen—that I'd breathed easily for the minutes she'd spent running along that road. We'd been fighting a war all my life and I'd never been touched. Now the sun returned to the field, burning with a renewed intensity. Lindsey stood up again and offered me her hand. I held it in my own, without fear or shyness. Ever since I'd met her, she'd been throwing my world off balance. Just then, she felt like the only solid thing in it.

━━

Beyond the meadow, in a small clearing at the edge of the forest, stood a decaying saltbox farmhouse, a barn, and the stone skeleton of an older structure built, Lindsey said, during the eighteenth century. As I'd always suspected, there was something back here. Something archaeological. The ruins of another time.

"Have you ever been here?" she asked.

I shook my head.

"Someone lived here in the fifties. People lived here for two centuries; then they didn't anymore."

I looked into the windows of the house. It was mostly empty. A desk in one room, an icebox in another. Beside the back door, an old-fashioned thermometer recorded the temperature, and a few bricks from the crumbling central chimney lay on the ground below. Nearby, the barn had surrendered to the advance of thick, ropy vines. Its white paint was peeling, flaking off, hanging as if wilted. Most of the windows on the main doors were broken, the frames holding jagged pieces of pane, like broken teeth; one remained intact, except for a small hole in its center, a dark circle in the cloudy surface of the glass. I pulled open the side door and day crept in, half lighting the darkness. At the far end of the room, above the loft, those vines had smashed through the upper window and groped, more slowly than the eye could see, into the musty air of the barn. A ladder led up there, half of its steps rotting and broken.

Walking along the line of horse stalls, I found a rusty plow and, in an open space near the far corner, a pile of books and magazines which someone had tried to burn. Novels, copies of *National Geographic,* volumes of a children's encyclopedia called *The Standard Treasury of Learning.* Most lay scarred with a shiny blackness, missing corners or middles. Some had burned completely to ash, but a few were undamaged, just covered with dirt, webs, or fungi. One of the survivors was Volume One of the encyclopedia. It covered the letter A, and contained special sections on "Animals of the Jungle" and "Atomic Energy." The cover featured a menagerie of dissonant illustrations. On the front: the continent of Africa, an acorn, a mushroom cloud. On the back: John Quincy Adams, an antelope, the atomic symbol.

"Hey, Tom."

Lindsey's voice, tender and distant, reached me through the broken windows. I carried the book outside and walked toward the third building, a single room surrounded by three stone walls and covered by a roof. The fourth wall was inexplicably missing and gave the structure the look of a stage set. With the morning sun behind it, most of the interior lay in dim shadow. But in the center of the dark back wall, a door stood open to the sun-drenched trees and undergrowth beyond, a brilliant rectangle of light and color; and just inside the doorway, a patch of sun warmed the wooden floor. Beside this light, Lindsey was kneeling. As I drew closer, I could see movement on the stone and the floor—the bodies of spiders crawling on thread-thin legs.

"They're Daddy Long Legs," I said.

"Right. But some must be Mommy Long Legs."

A few of them scattered and entered the field of sun before the door. Their dark, round middles bloomed a vivid mahogany, and their shadows followed after them, each leg meeting its twin in perfect time on the dusty wood. I sat facing her, crossing my legs, as she placed a hand against the wall and waited for a spider to draw near, to probe at her skin with pliant forelegs.

Then, very carefully, she inched her fingers under its body, until it was moving over the peaks of her knuckles. Lifting it away from the wall, she held it between us, as if it were something she'd created herself, something impossibly rare, which belonged to me now.

"When I was little, before I moved to California, I used to come here. I made my wishes in this place." She looked at me. "Do you believe in that sort of thing?"

"I don't know," I said.

"I don't know either. I guess it can't hurt, though."

While the first spider walked up her forearm, she reached out once more to the wall, this time with both of her hands, like a blind person feeling and reading. Several spiders detoured around her, but two others, more curious or trusting, climbed onto her fingers and walked in spirals along her arms.

"If there are enough," she whispered, "they can make your whole body tingle. That's when your wish is being granted."

My eyes had adjusted to the shadow. I could see the colors of the stones now. Shades of tan and gray suspended in concrete. I reached out, as amicably as possible, to the cool surface of the wall.

"Touch me here," she said, "on the underside of my arms."

With palms upturned, I placed my fingertips against the tender skin of her wrists; and touching the same place on me, the muted blue veins which led into my hands, she told me to concentrate, to close my eyes and wish for something. In the darkness, I felt the spiders, as weightless and unreal as spirits, walking back and forth across the bridge which joined our bodies, exploring the smooth, hairless surface of my arms. I thought of my mother, and a shudder ran through my body.

"Do you feel it?" she asked.

I opened my eyes to look at her. Lips still parted from speaking, the residue of a dreamy smile lingered on her face. Though we were connected by only the most tentative of touches, I felt unable to move without her prompting. I felt bound to her, the way oceans and seas were bound to the moon—by a cosmological force they obeyed but didn't understand. Her body was still, her breathing inaudible. But she was alive under my fingers. Her pulse, I knew, beat there, though impalpably. A beacon signaling the distant action of her heart.

6 / In the days following the dinner party, I found myself daydreaming, considering how I'd finally met Lindsey's ex-lover, Nile Treadway—and, after a brief discussion of phallic erections, kissed her a single time on the lips. I remembered standing on the porch with her, the novelty of kissing another woman after eight months of unrequited monogamy. After the party, standing somehow together on the dark sidewalk, the door to Lindsey's house shut firmly behind us, I offered her a ride home. Which led to a nightcap in North Beach, and a further trek into the unmapped terrain of flirtation. Much later, I walked her home, and at the gate of her apartment building I kissed her again. More than once. Several times in a row. Individual kisses began to blend one into the other, and pretty soon the activity was indistinguishable from making out.

"Whoa," I said.

"All right," she said.

She wrote her phone number on a scrap of paper with an eye pencil, told me to call the next day. I sat in my car and studied her crooked handwriting. I turned the paper over. It was an ATM receipt, which revealed that at 2:36 P.M. on May 30, she had been at the Wells Fargo on the corner of Broadway and Columbus. A week later, I hadn't called. Nor had I discarded the receipt. I kept it in my wallet, removed it occasionally to study her crooked handwriting; and I remembered that night with Lindsey on Ocean Beach, the helpless emptiness of fucking in a sand dune, of steeling myself through toasts and cacophonies of clinking glass. All eyes on the couple of the hour. Voices fading, leaving only the sound of the waves and the fire. Someone stepping forward and offering the following toast: *"Don't worry about the future, the present is all thou hast. The future will soon be the present, and the present the past."* Glasses met and sang their saturnalian song. Philip buried his hand in Lindsey's hair and kissed her, her body rippling in the heat of the fire, like a mirage . . . I thought of the dinner party, how she'd spoken to me in the dim light of the hallway as if she owned me. Telling me to remember my place, and assuming I'd always stay in it. This piece of paper—this document of another woman's late monetary transaction—seemed to disprove those assumptions, nullify them altogether. A numerical code scribbled in eye pencil. The taste of wine on new lips. The darkness of her skin and the darkness of the night. I'd stood on the sidewalk, watched her unlock the gate to her building. For a moment, it had stood open. She'd held it open, long enough for me to cross to the other side. I didn't. And now I wasn't sure why. I wasn't sure why my first impulse had been to burn Nile's phone number.

                                               ⌐⌐

"Who?" she said.

"Tom. Tom Markham."

A gray dusty pause, during which I considered trying to pass myself off as a telemarketer. A few questions about local politics. A plea for her long-distance loyalties.

"We met at Lindsey's party."

"Oh, yeah," she said. "You write for the *Chronicle*."

"No. I'm a filmmaker."

"Oh," she said. "Oh, yeah. I remember now. The guy with the erection."

"I suppose there are worse things to be remembered for."

"You know it's been a week. I had to stop sitting by the phone. I was getting bed sores."

"How am I going to make up for this?"

"I'm glad you asked. I've just been brewing my morning coffee watching the Weather Channel. They're tracking a doozy of a tropical storm about two hundred miles east-southeast of Bermuda. The whole Caribbean's going under. So whisking me off to Club Med is out of the picture. However, tomorrow is going to be clear, sunny, and eighty-five degrees in Marin County, California."

"Tomorrow's Thursday," I said.

"Shit. I forgot you have a job."

"And you're what, independently wealthy?"

"Teacher's paid vacation, remember?"

"I thought you quit teaching."

"I did. Last month. So what about Saturday?"

"Saturday's good. In the evening."

"The sun," she informed me, "is gone in the evening. It goes to the other side of the world, to warm the people of faraway lands."

"Right. The thing is, I use the weekends to work on my film."

I heard her cover the receiver and fake a yawn.

"Don't go to sleep," I told her. "Seriously, Nile, I really want to see you."

"Then you'll just have to give the puppets the day off. Anyway, you sound like you're coming down with something."

"How about a late dinner?" I suggested.

"I want to go to Cha Cha Cha."

"You name it."

"Have you got wheels?"

"I've got four wheels."

"Okay," she said. "Four-thirteen Filbert. Corner of Kearny. Third floor. Noon sharp."

"Did I say lunch?"

"You handle dinner," she said. "I'll take care of lunch."

To the novelty of a kiss, add a drive through the headlands, a climb to higher altitudes. Brown hills, isolated patches of trees like birthmarks on the body of California. Tattered fog caressing the car. Then finally the ocean, a blue haze in the distance. A slow descent back to sea level. Add to that kiss white suntan oil absorbed by brown skin, my hand pressing into the ridge between her shoulder blades. Stories of a Brooklyn girlhood. Kites snapping in the offshore breeze. Frigid water reaching for the sky, then collapsing into itself. The inevitable topic of Lindsey.

I discovered they'd met at a party in Bernal Heights, held on the birthday of the great nineteenth-century medium, Madame Blavatsky.

"Have you heard of her?" Nile asked.

"No. But I'm a bit ignorant when it comes to Satanism."

I regarded her from behind the safety of my sunglasses. We shared a plaid blanket, just big enough for two. Nile wore an orange bikini, composed of 15% Elastine, which had the wrinkled porous quality of an oceanic sponge; tightly hugging her breasts, it was about as effective as tissue paper in obscuring the twin circles of her nipples. Originally, she had demanded we patronize a nude beach farther up the coast, and though I'd suspected she was bluffing, I nonetheless flatly refused, invoking an obscure papal encyclical about public nudity on a first date. When we got to Stinson and settled down on the fevered sand, she revealed her swimwear with a deft removal of T-shirt and shorts, then lifted from the picnic basket a small ring box, as if to ask my hand in marriage. Sliding the ring—a silver band set with garnets—over her left index finger, she explained that she tends to have trouble with the boys at this time of year. Something about male hormones and the summer solstice.

It was the summer of 1987—

(said Nile, stretching out on her back, and disengaging the orange straps of her bikini)

—when I got the invite for this party, which my friend, Wallace, had actually been planning since he was ten years old.

Wallace had always been very interested in the supernatural. As a boy, he'd lived in an old, old house, and he was certain his room was haunted. He wanted to have a seance, and find out who the spirit was, but of course no one in his family believed him. Years later, after his father died, they sold the house, and Wallace moved here because he didn't fit in very well in Macon, Georgia, anymore. He'd grown up to be a flamer with a head for entrepreneurism, so he put his inheritance into a coffee shop in the Castro, and made quite a nice living and a kick-ass latte to boot. Now, in his spare time, Wallace volunteered in a homeless shelter, and that's where he met this guy who went by the name of Gypsy Ivanovich, an old clairvoyant whose entire family had been killed by the Nazis. He'd come to the U.S. in the fifties and did the Gypsy-tearoom circuit, hung around with Madame X and Sybil Leek, and finally landed a gig as a palmist-in-residence at some café in North Beach, where he had all these famous clients. He told fortunes for the beat poets, and then one night he saw a hyena in Bukowski's tea leaves; a few months later, Bukowski completely lost it.

Twenty years later, I walk fashionably late into Wallace's place and here's this guy wearing an embroidered waistcoat, kerchief around his head, these moleskin pants—and five other guests, of whom Lindsey is one. I meet her, and in all of about ten minutes, my heart is at full gallop. I should digress here, just to say that I was very different then. Just a year out of college and I'd recently completed my latest experiment in heterosexuality (which was a failure of epic proportions) and I was going through this major feminist phase. Sort of hiding my body—I had this boycott going, which I was very proud of, of all books by white males. To give you some idea of how far I'd gone, okay, I'd just read *The Golden Notebook* from beginning to end, and I had this pro-choice T-shirt that had a drawing of a huge vagina on the front and said, "Read My Lips," or something like that. I mean, I didn't wear this thing in public, but I owned it. The upshot of all this is: this woman who's been all over

South America, in the middle of guerrilla wars and the poorest people on Earth, is the closest thing to a goddess I've ever met in my fucking life. She's so mature—she's thirty, I'm like twenty-two—and she's making me pine for the dignity of my own middle age. On top of that, she's this vision of beauty, her hair's starting to go prematurely gray, she's wearing this vintage flapper dress. Pretty soon, fortunes are being told, Gypsy Ivanovich is throwing the Tarot, reading our palms. We're all tipsy on some very expensive French wine. Every time I turn around, Wallace is refilling my glass, and next thing I know, I'm showing Lindsey my palm, my very large and fleshy Mount of Venus.

"This part right here?" she says, and she runs her finger over it; my whole body shivers and I don't even try to conceal my reaction.

"It's the sign," I tell her, "of a highly sensual nature."

She smiles, takes a sip of wine, and her lips look so lush and nourished afterward. I watch the wine slide down the inside of the glass, and I have this flash of her dress sliding down her body with the same slow grace, as Wallace steps up and informs us it's time for the seance.

We walk into another room. There's a table with a single candle in its center. A lamp in the corner with a red bulb. We all sit down, Lindsey on my left, and we place our fingers on the table while Gypsy Ivanovich puts himself under, tries to reestablish contact with his old control, Kapi Re'is—an ancient astrologer who went down with the lost continent of Atlantis. The room's dead quiet. We're all breathing in unison. My head's swimming with wine. Time's passing, I don't know how long, it could have been an hour. The red light's getting thicker, like it's dripping over us. Everything has been brought to a standstill, and I'm wondering if the wine was spiked or if we're all being hypnotized. Then I realize my hand is moving. Drifting to the left, like a planchette, like something's tugging it.

"Water," Gypsy Ivanovich is murmuring. "The Fertile Crescent . . . Drowning of a world . . ."

And my hand keeps moving, and though I know I'm moving it, still, it doesn't feel like I'm in control. It's as if the table's tilting and my hand is just sliding helplessly, obeying gravity.

"Divine justice," he whispers. "The ocean's fatal embrace . . . a fatal embrace."

Then my fingers touch hers, and Lindsey grips them right away, gently but firmly.

"Kapi Re'is," Gypsy Ivanovich says at this exact moment— and his voice actually cracks with emotion. "It's been so long," he says. "So very long."

———

When Nile had finished this story, she rolled carefully onto her stomach. Found me lying on my back, hands clasped behind my head. I felt moved and more than a little charmed, though clearly this tale had been restored and polished by a tragic, retrospective sight.

"When are you going to take that shirt off?" Nile finally asked.

"Oh, soon," I said. Raising a hand to my forehead, I gazed into the sky like an explorer taking stock of proximal terrain. "I'm waiting for the sun to go down a little."

She slid her sunglasses halfway down the slope of her nose, and for a split second I had a glimpse of her distant grandmotherly future. It seemed to me she would age with ravishing grace. By an enchanted wave of the hand, she commanded the shirt to part from my body.

"Off," she said. "Or I'm going to start screaming."

I bared my unremarkable torso. Not unattractive, mind you, but admittedly average in terms of build and muscle tone, its Elizabethan whiteness somewhat eclipsed by a curly pelt of chest hair. This last detail appeared to raise questions in Nile's eyes, as strange anomalies of nature raise questions in the minds of the young. Lying back down, I stared self-consciously at the sky for a few seconds, the blinding light of the sun filtered, brought under control by tinted lenses. Then felt something—her hand, I assumed—trailing speculatively over my chest. My eyes shut and green suns skated across the surface of my corneas. Then the touch was gone; and without hard evidence to corroborate this event, I explained it away, like an incident from the files of Project Bluebook, as the tread of a mountaineering sand spider or a freak gust of wind.

"That was quite a romantic story," I said. "Somehow, though, I still can't see it. The two of you."

"What do you mean? Why not?"

"You're just not her type."

"Really," Nile said with a strained cordiality. "What *is* her type exactly?"

"I don't know, it's just that you have this baroque quality. Mainly, you're an optimist—and Lindsey's so sad."

"Is she?"

"I mean, in the abstract."

She raised an eyebrow, as if to at once concede the point and declare it irrelevant. "Good lovers are never carbon copies of each other. A lot of people thought we were great together. Perfect, in fact."

After a moment, a hand drifted to her face; a finger gently stroked the fullness of her lips. I imagined those lips on Lindsey's body, in all the places mine had more recently been, and found a sensuous curiosity in the rightful place of jealousy.

"Was it serious?" I asked. "Were you in love with her?"

She pushed some sand around, like she was giving the question a proper burial.

"I'm sorry," I said. "Don't answer that."

"Why not?"

"If it's too personal."

"It's not too personal. I adored her, to be honest about it. I mean, I'd been in a few relationships. I thought I'd been in love, but . . . with her it was different. It was like stepping through the looking glass."

"You guys have tea parties?"

She nodded. "I brought storybooks home from work. Read them to her before bed."

"That's ridiculously cute," I said; there it was, finally, that tug of covetous nausea. "What was her favorite?"

"The Adventures of Dinosaur Bob and the Family Lizardo."

She plunged a finger into the sand and drew aimless, looping shapes.

"I don't understand what happened with Phil," she said. "How it could have happened so fast. Like she was running away from something. I just don't see how that something could have been me."

Nile's eyes swung up to mine, naturally and inevitably, and I saw clearly where we were heading. Half believed it was love hollowing out my chest, acting with mythical speed and power. I knew better—I knew it was Lindsey. The thought of her, the absence of her. Nile, I realized, harbored the same feelings and knew the same truth. Lindsey surrounded us both like the stars. Invisible during the day, but always burning and waiting to emerge with the onset of darkness. Looking at Nile, I felt a rush of passion, a strange longing. To touch her, to dive into her. The irresistible urge of Narcissus.

⎣___⎦

It had been quite some time since I'd slept with another woman. Two years, to be exact. Before Lindsey, there'd been Carolyn, my Chicago girlfriend, with whom I'd experienced a week of introductory impotence. By now, that episode had come to possess the quality of a piece of kitsch, a vase or clock so outdated and aesthetically erroneous that the whole notion of the past becomes manageable somehow, providing for one's mistakes and failures a larger, inevitable context of misadventure. After all, hadn't I been engaged for the past eight months in an affair with an older woman? A married woman, whose husband I not only knew socially, but actually had an amicable respect for? Hadn't I been nothing short of satisfying from the very beginning, venturing recently, after close readings of several ancient handbooks, into the realm of the virtuosic? I had never been one to take the sexual act lightly. And perhaps out of fear of the present becoming as misadventurous as the past, I was not a conductor of one-night stands. I explain all this, I suppose, to put that day with Nile in proper context, as by the time we left the beach, our movement toward a common bed appeared to be as unstoppable as the imminent merging of the sun with the western sea. Driving back from Marin, my body tinted by the sun, I found myself examining Nile, trying to gauge her capacity for empathy and patience. Considered the possibility that—despite the breathtaking fact of her nakedness and the evidence of passion flowing from between her legs—I would feel my penis go limp inside its latex wrap, as if collapsing from slow suffocation. And in the turbulent panic of this moment, one thing would remain steady and clear. A lighthouse burning on an opposite shore.

Lindsey.

She had been in the distance all day, tending the beacon of betrayal and guilt. I went through the obvious rationalizations. That she was married and never talked about leaving her husband. That I was young and unmarried. That as the century closed down, as the whole thing got slowly packed up and readied for storage in memory and books, every last soul seemed to have scrambled for the first acceptable body they could get their hands on, without any intention of ever releasing it. And this action, like the rush for a dance partner or a run on a bank, had happened when I wasn't looking, with a simultaneous swiftness that implied universal complicity. Why had I been left out of it all? Why hadn't I seen it coming? Why had I ever left Carolyn— to come here? Could it be, I wondered, as we recrossed the span of the Golden Gate Bridge, that the woman in the passenger seat might hold the answer to this question? And didn't I owe it to myself to find out?

In the end, it happened.

At my place. On a mess of sheets overrun with the smiling faces of the "Peanuts" gang. A light marijuana haze. Shadows thrown by candlelight. To the verge of orgasm, then a caesural break in thrusting. My penis fixed firmly inside her, my fingers continuing to work her clitoris as she took in husky gasps of air. "What's that noise?" she said, her voice hoarse and scratchy. Through the closed door, I could hear Mingus in the other room, tearing around in a frenzy, ripping my couch to shreds.

"That's my cat," I said. "Remember?"

"Is he okay? Maybe you should let him in."

"Let him in here?"

She nodded. "I bet he feels excluded."

I stopped massaging her clit. "You're joking, right?"

"No." She pouted and kissed my nose. "He's in a fit of loneliness. He just wants to be included."

"In human sexual intercourse?"

"He wants to watch," she said, smiling.

"Look," I said, "I hardly know this cat."

We started up again, but after a minute she grasped me firmly by the shoulders. "I don't think I can come," she said, "with him out there, in a fit of loneliness."

She gave me a girlish, pleading look, which compelled me to ease myself out of her and walk across the room, my penis bobbing ridiculously inside its lubricated condom. I opened the door and, a moment later, Mingus entered like a guest on a late-night talk show, giving my bare feet a wide berth . . .

Yes, it happened.

And afterward, lying in Nile's arms, I felt purged of something, and wildly content. I'd sleep with someone tonight. I'd keep her body warm—and wake up with her in the morning.

⌐

In the morning, I was showered and half dressed when she asked me to come over and give her a kiss, just one kiss . . . A good hour later, in an aphrodisiacal daze, I walked late into a pre-production meeting which I'd completely forgotten about. I found the entire staff (all five of them) waiting for me, drinking coffee and eating crullers at the old wooden table. In front of them, the scripts for the new episode, in which Goliath falls in love with a seeing-eye poodle, and Davey overcomes the demon of jealousy to show a blind girl that the wonders of God are not glimpsed by the retina, but by the heart. Final scene, beneath a flagpole. Sound effect: flapping of the Stars and Stripes.

I'd read it, but left my copy at home. Lane suggested I share with Frank the cameraman, who was wearing yet another Deadhead T-shirt which spat in the face of copyright laws: Bart and Lisa Simpson lounging around, smoking doobie. Once I was settled, we all picked up our copies, flipped through, or folded back the cover page. The usual deep inhalations, as if we were the members of a Lamaze class. These scripts arrived weekly in the mail, compliments of writers we'd never met. There were those among us who believed the stories were penned in secret White House strategy sessions with top-ranking members of the Moral Majority and the 700 Club.

"What is this?" Frank asked. "This flag thing is really the limit. What is this shit?"

We turned to Lane, our director. The man behind the magic. The one who dealt with the producers in L.A., the clients. Communicated our passionate commitment to bring Davey alive for the children of America.

"Ask not what this shit is," he told us. "But what you can do with this shit."

We flew through a discussion of the standard opening shots. Tabitha, our storyboard artist, shared her preliminary ideas, jotted notes. Lane slowed us down at the first pivotal moment on page two. Location, a crosswalk. On one corner, Davey and Goliath. On the other, the blind girl and the seeing-eye poodle. Action: Goliath gets woody for poodle, much to Davey's chagrin.

"He's basically a naïve kid, an insecure kid," Lane said, pacing back and forth in a moth-eaten cardigan. "He believes in God. He trusts in God. So how is it, he asks himself, how is it there can be such pain in the world? Such betrayal? That's what this scene is all about. I want to capture Davey's pain, but with subtlety. In the eyes. In the lips. We need to see fear there. A fear of solitude. Tom, you're especially good at this stuff, so you've got the sequence."

"Gee," I said. "Thanks."

Frank the cameraman pointed at his copy of the script, that expression on his face which meant he was thinking in subversive, subtextual terms. "We can set up the shot so the respective couples mirror each other all the way through. Davey looking at the girl—in other words, into his own blind soul. Goliath facing the poodle, or the ambiguity of his own sexuality."

Lane shook a finger with passionate interest. "Tabitha?" he said.

She leaned exaggeratedly over her notebook. "Mirror . . . of . . . ambiguity. Got it."

Frowning at her, Lane began to spin one of his fantasies about turning up the homoerotic volume between our heroes. A boy and his dog via *Midnight Cowboy*. These ideas of ours— never officially communicated to our clients, and largely invisible to the casual viewer—were a weak thread of hope that one day some obscure film scholar might find our work to contain a shred of artistic value. Our two disillusioned prodigies, recent grads from Cal Arts, looked like a couple of mourners at a funeral.

"What's wrong with you two?" the boss asked.

"Nothing," Jamie said.

Cory-Ellen twirled some amber locks around her finger. "I should've been a stenographer."

"What's that supposed to mean?"

"It means we're all going nowhere fast."

"That's not true," Tabitha said. "Look at Tom. We're doing the final sound mix on his film. It's amazing. It's important."

Jamie nodded, his mouth full of cruller. "I saw it. The crash sequence. The blimp exploding into fucking flames, the kid at the wheel going down with the ship. Phenomenal shot."

"When are we going to see the final cut?" Frank asked.

"People, people," Lane said. "When Markham wins his Academy Award, you can tar and feather me. At the moment, we've got a job to do." He gave me a look. "Next major sequence."

"Page three," Tabitha said. "Malt shop. Asshole soda jerk gives blind girl pistachio instead of chocolate."

"Now this is a tough one," Lane said. "She's blind, so we've got to pull her reaction off exclusively in the facial muscles. We need to see a lifetime of suffering."

———

I found I couldn't stop thinking of Nile. We saw each other every night for a week. Discovered we shared a long list of interests, which included surrealism, dim sum, and the mysteries of ancient astronauts. We began talking about sex openly; we planned a road trip to the Joshua Trees, to do some desert camping. Kissing her one night on Market Street, I pulled back to meet her eyes, to brush a hand over her cheek, and felt a fluttering in my chest. The beating of innocent wings. And for a moment, under the purple glow of the streetlights, it seemed the city was revealing a purpose to me, sharing the unexpected secret that I had a destiny all my own. Everything occurred with a startling alacrity, evocative of time-lapse photography, and on a plane of fantastic denial where Lindsey didn't exist. I hadn't spoken to her since the dinner party. Then, one day, she called me at work. Asked if I could meet her at noon on Saturday. In Golden Gate Park.

"Why?" I said.

"Because I want to see you," she said softly.

There was a long, painful pause. The sound of her voice undermined everything, gave everything an overwhelming complexity, as if I'd just graduated from a one- to a three-dimensional world.

"It's supposed to rain," I told her.

"It won't."

Another silence.

"Please, Tom. I miss you. I can't sleep."

That night, after several hours at a dance club south of Market and a few too many drinks, Nile told me the story of how Lindsey had left her for Philip. It had ended with a letter. With the nauseating admission, two weeks delayed, that she'd been with someone else. A man. It meant nothing in and of itself, she had written, but was symptomatic of something else. A deeper imbalance. An undissectible problem whose roots were long and tangled. And suddenly, it seemed to Nile that Lindsey had always worn the glazed look of an amnesiac. She'd often lain limp and distant in her arms at night, crying sometimes after making love and never explaining why. Finally, she'd written some words, closed them in a naked envelope, and slipped them under the door of Nile's apartment.

"Are you over her?" I asked.

She nodded, wiped her eyes. "Yes, I am. I swear." She reached up, touched my lips. "It's just . . . it still hurts, you know. That kind of betrayal. By someone you love and trust, someone you think is your own. It never stops hurting. The feelings sleep very lightly. Do you know what I mean?"

She continued touching my face, and I couldn't help closing my eyes.

"Yeah," I said. "I know."

—

Saturday. As Lindsey had predicted, sunny and fogless. I arrived early at the arboretum, and was drawn to a formation of tables just inside the gates. Apparently, the horticultural society was cleaning out its basement. The tables were covered with aged tracts and treatises on lawn care, shrubbery, and ground cover, all of them priced to sell. For under a dollar, I walked away with two booklets titled "Harvesting and Marketing Your Avocados" and "An Introduction to the Art of Dwarfing Trees," along with a 1947 issue of *Hilgardia* devoted exclusively to sod webworms and other California lawn pests. I thanked the old woman who smelled of gardenias, and started for the spice-and-herb garden. On my way I considered this outdated literature, illustrations of the common pill bug and its barely distinguishable cousin, the dooryard sow bug. I stumbled upon a sentence which read, "We learn the general rules; after that it's a matter of observational experience, learning-by-doing, since the rules do not cover the exceptions, which are many and varied." The grass was a vivid green, dotted here and there with yellow dandelions. At the end of the first slope of land, a small pond held the handsome white bodies of swans, and sunlight sparkled on the water like electricity. Keeping Nile at the forefront of my mind, I seemed to move with the grace of those birds, and to feel all around me the same charged power.

Then I reached the garden.

Lindsey was already there. In a long, white, sleeveless dress. Bent over, nose to a flowering plant. Eyes diverted to the sky, as if embarrassed to be nuzzling an herb she hardly knew. As she drew some hair away from her face, I felt a slow burn in my chest. She saw me and straightened up. Bare arms clasped behind her back. The curves of her body unexploited by her clothing, but viscerally apparent. Her lips widened in a tentative smile. I felt I hadn't seen her in years—that, long ago, our love had almost been lost, foolishly and tragically, but was returning now with an undaunted beauty, as if from the brink of extinction.

"It's not raining," she said.

She leaned back against the low concrete wall, and I noticed she had her sandals in her hand. Her feet were bare. I recognized the earrings I'd bought her in Savannah, Georgia. This minute detail completed the hollowing-out of my chest.

"What are those?" she asked.

"These? Just a few things I picked up. They're having a sale."

Lindsey examined the covers seriously, as if considering bankrolling my future in the avocado business. "I thought you'd steal up on me from behind."

"What?"

"While I was smelling the plants. I thought I could see the future. Like the time you brought me that blue iris. That was strange, wasn't it?"

We stood in silence for a few seconds. Then, with a kind of teenage awkwardness, she reached for my hand. This surprised me, because there was a rule about public displays of affection.

"I'm sorry," Lindsey said. "About the other night."

I just looked at her.

"The party. What I said was out of line."

"That was two weeks ago," I said.

"I know."

"You mean, what you said about me keeping my place?"

"Yes," she said quietly. "That's what I mean."

A gentle breeze touched her dress, pulled the material tight against her hip and leg.

"I'm sorry about that night, Tom. The whole thing. Philip invited her without telling me. We had a huge fight afterward. A row, actually. I left the house and drove around for a while. I came by your place. Just to talk. You weren't there."

A long, weighted pause.

"Where'd you go?" she asked.

"I went to the beach."

Lindsey nodded. She let go of my hand, and I wandered a step or two down the path. The herbs and spices stirred in the wind, and a couple of children entered the garden, followed by their father. All around us, eucalyptus trees arched into a deep blue sky. The grass looked combed, the trees flawlessly pruned, though I'd never seen a gardener here. There were days when it seemed this place required no earthly care. As if it had been grown from a single flawless seed, a cutting from paradise. There were times when its gates were locked.

"You two appeared to be getting along pretty well," she said, giving a kind of laugh.

"Who?"

"You and Nile."

I stared at her blankly.

"What did you talk about?"

"Just . . . small talk," I said.

Lindsey's fingers caressed the leaves of a plant, its cluster of magenta flowers. "Did she talk about me?"

"A little."

"What did she say?"

"She said you looked amazing. She said certain feelings sleep lightly."

"Oh? What kinds of feelings?"

"Why are we here?" I finally said. "Why did you call me?"

"I want to apologize. And I told you, I miss you."

"You said you didn't want to see me."

"I was angry that night," she said. "I didn't mean it."

"You're angry most of the time, Lindsey."

I felt a rush of corrosive emotion. I thought of the past few days with Nile, so textured and genuine. Now they seemed like a failed experiment, like something which had been staged. I regretted them, and I didn't want to. From across the garden, we heard the sounds of a scuffle. The children who had just entered. A girl, five or six years old, stood with her fists clenched melodramatically. A boy, whom I assumed to be her brother, had been pushed to the stone path. For a heavy moment, neither of them moved. Then the boy looked at his knee. It was cut and bleeding. As the father approached and knelt down, his son reached a thin, bony arm around his neck; and his daughter, several feet away, unclenched her fists and began to cry soundlessly. A few moments later, they were all huddled together, the man kissing foreheads and drying wet eyes with the promise of swans possessing feathers both light and dark. Glancing up, he caught me watching, and smiled with a self-assured embarrassment. He looked about forty, with black hair and sideburns that hinted at a stubborn defiance of the passage of time. I placed a hand on Lindey's neck. She didn't stop me. Her flesh was warm with the sun's heat. She too was crying. Staring at me with an unfamiliar intensity, her eyes sharp with some kind of fear.

"Lindsey, what's going on?"

"Please forgive me," she said, her eyes closing gently.

"What's wrong?"

"I don't know. I'm scared, Tom."

Moving even closer, she asked me to hold her.

"You don't want to do this here," I said.

"Yes, I do."

I folded my arms around her, pulled her gently to my body. We stood silent. I rested my face against her hair, felt her hands tracing shapes over my back. Slowly, she moved her head, as if turning in her sleep.

"I'm in love with you," she said. "I can't be, but I am. Maybe you can see why that's frightening. Why I've done some of the things I've done."

I closed my eyes, and a long time passed without speech or movement. How long had I waited to hear these words? Why, having finally heard them, did I only feel dazed and weak and afraid? It was true. I was scared to look at her.

"Do you love me?" she asked.

I didn't answer. I tried to pull away, but she wouldn't let me. She held my face in her hands. "I love you," I said, and then felt the force of her lips. Fluttering wings beat wildly against my rib cage. With a panicked intensity . . . We left the park together. Mounting the stairs to my apartment, I felt claustrophobic, as if invisible walls were closing in on me, the air growing dense with compacted molecules. I fumbled for my house keys and unlocked the door. Surely there was some evidence of Nile lying in the open. Lindsey would recognize the smell of her in the air, on the bedsheets. Suddenly, I realized that I wanted her to know. I wanted something to intervene. To bring this to a stop. The door closed behind us. There, in the hallway, she removed my clothes, and then her own. She took my hand, as one takes the hand of a child, and led me to the bedroom.

———

All that day, wrapped up inside my answering machine, impressed on its magnetic tape, was the voice of Jane. My stepmother. Whom I'd once told, in a tantrum of adolescent hate, to never bother me unless it was a matter of life and death. I returned from work, and found the red light blinking. I set the mechanism in motion. *"It's your brother,"* she said. *"We didn't want to disturb you . . . until it was absolutely necessary."*

"Is my father there?" I asked, shifting the phone to my other ear.

"Yes. He's just beside himself. He cares so much, Tom. He only suppresses his love as a defensive gesture in the context of the father-son power struggle. But when something like this happens—whatever the explanation—as a parent, you can't help but blame yourself. God knows, I feel responsible. Every bit as much." Jane's voice trembled like dishware during a minor earthquake. "We've been through his belongings," she said. "It looks like he left of his own volition. That's some comfort, I suppose. Some of his clothes are missing. Some of my jewelry too . . . and all your dad's tie clips."

"Tie clips?"

"I don't know," Jane said. "Just don't bring it up. He's livid about that part."

"Why now?" I asked. "What happened?"

"Who knows." Her voice was cracked by a deeper, more serious tremor. "It's one thing after another these days. You know how smart he is, but he's failing half of his classes. He won't do his homework. He just reads books his teachers say are completely over his head. They say he can't possibly be digesting the stuff."

"What books?" I said, as if his taste in literature would put us on his trail.

"I don't know. I can't remember the exact names. French writers, I think."

"Maybe he went to France."

"My God, I hadn't thought of that. And French was his highest grade last quarter. C plus. Hold on."

I heard her muffle the receiver and call my father. Halfway through her presentation of the theory, he took the phone from her.

"Why are you putting stupid ideas in her head?" He sounded tired, apathetic, like a general who had chosen surrender over a last stand. "Can't you tell she's hysterical?"

"She sounds fairly rational to me."

"She'd believe anything at this point. She's been crying for two days." My father breathed deeply. "I'm about at the end of my rope here, Tom."

"I wouldn't worry too much. He's probably hiding in some friend's basement."

"We've pretty much eliminated that possibility."

"Does he have a girlfriend?"

"Not that we've ever seen."

"A best friend?"

No answer. I filled in the blind spot of a brief pause: a glass rising to his lips, a swallow, an amber flow of Scotch whiskey winding down his throat, warm and numbing.

"I miss you, Tom."

"I miss you too," I said, forcing the words out.

"I sure wish that you could get back here for a while. Just a few days. Until all this blows over. Jane's trying real hard, but there are certain things I just can't talk to her about. I could really use a sympathetic ear."

I wasn't sure of his precise implication. Perhaps that I'm the only one who shares his inmost need, secret and obvious. To thaw the frozen history of our family's final winter. Go back. Make repairs. Preserve our future at any cost—and never know the truth of the present.

"I can't leave town," I told him. "I've got some problems of my own."

"Oh?" he said. "If it's money, I'll fly you back, all expenses paid. Just like on the game shows."

"It's not money," I said.

"Oh." He took another drink.

"How about you tell me what happened."

"Well," he said, "your brother disappeared, having relieved his parents of approximately six hundred dollars in cash and jewels."

"Quite a heist," I said.

"He took my tie clips."

"I know."

"To spite me, the little shit." I listened to my father take slow, measured breaths. "I wonder why that hurts more than anything else. A stupid little thing like that."

I closed my eyes and felt the urge to comfort him. He was right: the details hurt the most. They sharpen the dull common edges of betrayal, buff its surface until it shines, like a mirror, with your own reflection. The urge to comfort him, flaring brightly one moment and smoldering the next. I'd spent too much time wanting him to suffer. I didn't take pleasure in it anymore—only marveled at its excess and turned away. But I'd long forgotten how to love him.

"I wouldn't worry," I advised. "Too much."

"No, you're right," he said with unexpected vigor. "It's easy to get wrapped up in things. Hell, you've got your problems too. Here I am, thinking I'm the headquarters for the collapse of the entire civilized world. It's just the same old story, really. I don't know why I'm burdening you with this."

I closed my eyes, searched the black field of my mind for something to say. "It's not a burden," I told him.

"Thanks, Tom. That means a lot to me."

I heard him drink. Then the sound of his glass hitting a table top. A sharp, conclusive report.

"How's the optometry business?" I asked him.

"Solid as a rock," he said. "Natural resources may be dwindling, the ozone layer may be disappearing, but there's still one constant in this world. There's no shortage of defective sight."

7 / In the vestibule, I lower my fingertips into the font of holy water. I bless myself. Marco flicks his wet fingers in my face and his mother gives him a backhanded slap. Aunt Carmela has outdone herself this morning. She looks like a movie star from some foreign Hollywood; and though my uncle is tall, broad, and well tanned, he seems somehow secondary, a corollary of her beauty. In the main hall, the organ moans low and even. The stained-glass windows on the east wall glow with the light of the sun, the shadows of tree branches dancing over the fiery colors. A boy wearing white robes lights candles with a long pole-like instrument. He is no older than I, and he steps with confidence from the altar to the tabernacle, genuflecting before the central statue of Christ. As he disappears into the sacristy, I feel a tug of envy and sadness inside. I kneel with my eyes closed. I imagine my mother in a habit, her shape buried in its dark warmth; but images of Lindsey, memories of the day before, steal the oxygen from holier thoughts. The spiders, the way we had touched, how my body had trembled. I want to be back out there, sitting in the ruins, making wishes. Today, life feels mundane and useless. A repetition of the same old rituals. I crave the strangeness of yesterday with a feeling like hunger, a physical ache. Why does it seem wrong to think of her here? Why do I feel compelled to hide her? I turn to Marco, his head framed by one of the stained-glass windows, its illustrations appearing to rise out of his mind. I see then how much he looks like his mother. Like her, he is different and seductive.

We had come in two cars. After the service, Mom and I drove the Plymouth into town to buy some rolls at the Little Cake Box. I couldn't help staring at her new haircut. Close-cropped, combed forward with long crescent-shaped curls alongside each ear. Several people had commented at church, and they were right. There was a modern vitality about her, an unpredictability. She looked young and unassailably healthy. Yet I knew that within the bones of her rib cage, there lay arcane imperfections.

"What are you gawking at?"

"Your hair."

"Do you like it?" she asked, for the third or fourth time.

"I'm not sure yet."

My mother doubtfully stroked the back of her head. "It was an impulse," she said. "Sometimes you just have to obey your impulses."

At the bakery, I stayed in the car while she waited in the Sunday-morning line. She had left the keys in the ignition, and I searched the radio for the music my cousin had been listening to a few days before. I couldn't find it, but settled on a song I recognized. The tune was lyrical, the singer's voice full of some kind of longing. I leaned back and propped my feet on the dashboard. Closed my eyes. Remembered, suddenly, a dream I'd had the night before.

Walking in the field with Lindsey.

Holding hands. In the field, yet somewhere else at the same time. Another country and continent. Planes flew overhead, and I feared their hulls would open up to excrete relentless lines of black cylinders. I turned to Lindsey and found instead that Vietnamese girl from the photograph, unharmed and unafraid. Naked, she gazed calmly into the sky, one hand in mine, the other shading her eyes—and I surveyed her body. Thin like my own. Skin stretched tight over muscles and bone. Between her legs, however, the flesh was smooth, simply notched, as in the photo. I felt embarrassed by her nakedness, but then this feeling was dispersed, blown away by a warm breeze of relief. She was safe, her body unmarred, as if that bomb had never fallen. Somehow, with me beside her, she seemed confident it never would. For a few moments, I lost all knowledge, all experience of ugliness. I felt free of fear and shame. The planes dragged leisurely wakes across the blue, just strolling through the atmosphere. "My dad was in the Air Force," I told her. The girl looked at me and smiled. She placed her hands on my face and kissed me.

———

One o'clock. The sun hanging liquid in an azure sky. I moved through its heat, alone on the lake path. In my hands, an old toy. A rifle made of plastic. Imitation wood grain; a small circular front sight at the end of an olive-green barrel. When the trigger was pulled, the counterfeit sound of a gunshot popped from a thatched hole on one side of the butt, just above the upraised words MADE IN KOREA. At the stream, dappled sunlight spotted the smooth sand, exposing a school of minnows. I passed my hand above the surface, and the fish darted away from the looming shadow. Today, I walked through the stream at its deepest point. The water was cool, reaching almost to my knees, and the current tugged. Just out of my reach, two dragonflies drifted above the water, their bodies delicately joined, one hanging upside down by the abdomen of the other. Damselflies, I corrected myself. A damsel train.

At the edge of the field, I noticed the ground was dry from lack of rain. As I parted the stalks with the barrel of the gun, a dusty grasshopper flitted away. Then I stepped forward, and the grass closed in around me. Except for Lindsey's absence, everything was the same as yesterday. The grass exerting a gentle oceanic undertow. The unwavering voices of the cicadas. Even the hawk continued his circling overhead. I watched him as I walked, stepping forward blindly, the butt of the rifle nestled under one arm, the barrel resting in my other hand. I imagined myself from his perspective. A solitary figure patrolling an un-tamed golden place. Childish desires sparked inside me. I blew on them gently, felt them catch. I raised the gun to the sky, sighted the hawk. Squeezed the trigger. The report, hollow and impotent, was drowned out by the din of nature. Running for-ward, I dove at the ground, rolled onto my back, and fired four times at the sky. The bird went on tracing graceful spirals. I lay listening to the sound of my own breathing, the heat pressing down on me. Already the feeling was fading. The gun felt foreign and ridiculous in my hands. A toy I'd outgrown long ago, but felt unable to discard.

I remained there, motionless, for a long time.

While dragonflies grazed the wheat-like tips of the grass, and a jet—as in my dream of the night before—cut a white wound on the cloudless blue sky, inside me an established emptiness claimed a little more space. My relatives would be leaving that night, and though part of me wanted Marco to go, a greater part of me wanted him to stay. To sleep always in the bottom bunk. To speak to me of things I couldn't quite understand, to inspire endless jealousies, the truth of which would always remain just out of reach. Once he was gone—my connection to Lindsey inevitably severed—I'd be left with nothing but summer's mo-notonous heat. It was mid-July, and I knew that certain changes would soon make themselves felt. Restlessness would creep through me. Freedom would lose its lustrous meaning, and be-come nothing but a lack of structure, an absence of direction. I would wait for storm clouds to blacken the sky and cool the air. Sitting before my window, watching the water of the lake begin to stir, smelling the fertile smell of rain. As the clouds collided overhead, I would feel a particular unease. As the rain fell into the lake, countless pinpoints of water meeting water, I'd glimpse the ends of things, and see inside myself the tender roots of a dark, inconstant nature. Why was it that Lindsey inspired in me these same feelings? The same soundless syllables forming in my heart and lungs?

I stood up, fought off a wave of dizziness. Parallel lines swirling across my vision. A dull pulse inside my skull. I thought about going home. But my parents were on a scenic drive with my aunt and uncle; and Marco had disappeared some time ago, bound for a rendezvous which, judging by his demeanor at brunch, inspired in him a fearful expectation. I had nowhere to go, except for the place I'd already started toward. The ruins of that old home, the remains of someone else's past. As I walked forward, I thought of my dream. Lindsey's effortless transformation into that little girl. The kiss she'd placed on my mouth. On the surface, it was simple enough—a jumbled reconstruction of yesterday. My walk with Lindsey and the photograph I'd asked her about. But why had she kissed me? Why had the dream ended there, with our lips pressed together?

I reached the clearing and the old McCready place—three buildings huddled beneath the afternoon sun, hot and bright at its daily apex. I walked to the back porch of the house, and checked the temperature on the old-fashioned thermometer. Eighty-six degrees. Yesterday, it had read eighty-three. Incredible that after all this time it still functioned, its blood rising and falling day after day. I trailed my fingers over the tube of glass, my eyes following a hornet, his blue-black wings flickering in the sunlight. He ascended, angelic, to the top of the house. There, nestled under the cornice, was a mud-gray hive, hornets sparkling all around it like indigo stars. I peered through the cloudy glass of the back door. I tried the knob and the door opened effortlessly, onto a hallway which led directly to the front door. Inside, on the walls, framed photographs were still hanging. Ancient documents in sepia tones. Matronly women, men with exaggerated mustaches. Farther on, one lay broken on the wooden floor. I bent down. This picture was more recent—a portrait of a teenage girl, colored by hand. Her hair a jaundiced yellow, her cheeks rosy, her lips as red as a piece of cherry candy.

The cracked glass of the frame fractured her face, split one sky-blue eye down the middle, giving her a look of violent blindness.

Rooms branched off the hallway. A kitchen with a caved-in ceiling and an old gas stove. A bathroom, on the floor of which a blue jay lay dead and half decomposed, a few ants pillaging the corpse; the window above the scene was cracked but not shattered, and I imagined the bird had flown into it repeatedly, in a desperate and failed attempt to regain his freedom. At the front of the house, on my left, a staircase led to the second floor. On the right, there was a larger room with a mattress in one corner, a chessboard covered with wooden pieces, several candles of varying lengths and colors. On the mattress lay a flannel shirt and two paperback books. Poetry. One of them had Lindsey's full name written on the inside of the cover, in a child's cursive, meticulous and legible. Flipping through this book, I found that the poems were about love, beautiful hair, touching, thousands of pumpkins floating to shore on an ocean tide, hamburgers made of flowers, bees traveling in covered wagons. This man, I thought, had set down in words the things that filled his head at night; and I remembered the kindred images I'd seen in the nocturnal privacy of my own mind. A praying mantis dressed in the garb of an archbishop. The land of giant pachysandra, swirling with a cinematic fog. The nakedness of a girl, a girl from another land whose body I'd miraculously healed.

"It's not noisy," I heard. "It's orchestral."

Lindsey's voice reached me through the open window which faced the barn and the spider house. She and Marco were entering the clearing, moving without direction; joined at the hands, at the fingertips, by a delicate touch—one I could easily break by calling through the cobwebbed screen.

"It's louder than the West Side Highway," Marco said. "What are those things?"

"They're cicadas."

"What's a cicada?"

"It's a kind of locust. If we look on the ground, we might find one of their exoskeletons."

"I'm not interested in exoskeletons."

Something stabbed me inside as his lips brushed against the back of her neck.

"Stop it," she said playfully. "I'm serious. They're really fascinating."

She released his hand and walked a bit ahead, studying the weedy grass. Marco followed her with a deliberate movement, treading lightly, as if concerned he might scare her away. She wore a melon-orange halter top, tied in a knot at her sternum, and white shorts which didn't cover much of her thighs.

"Are you looking?" she asked.

"Yeah," he lied. "I'm looking."

Lindsey bent down, tucking some hair behind her ear. She plucked a white dandelion from the ground, raised it to her lips. She seemed to kiss it, and the downy seeds swirled around her face.

"I came here with your cousin yesterday," she said.

"That little shit. He told me he walked you straight home."

"Oh, don't tell him I told you. Please."

"I won't tell. I'll just give him an unexplained punch in the arm."

"You be nice to him," Lindsey said seriously. "He's very vulnerable right now."

"I'm just kidding."

"Do you know . . . is his mom going to be all right?"

"I guess so. She just can't exert herself too much. Can't have any more children."

There was a pause during which I considered this summary of the situation. I felt a mildness, a calm settle over me.

"I like him," Lindsey said suddenly.

"Who?"

"Thomas."

"What do you mean, like him?"

"I don't know. I can't explain it. It's just a feeling I get from him."

In my chest, a bubble of heat expanded and gently burst. I watched her stand up. Facing away from Marco, she tightened the knot of her halter.

"He has the most beautiful eyelashes I think I've ever seen."

My cousin took a couple of rapid steps toward her, slipped his hands over her eyes. "What about my eyelashes?" he said. Again he brought his lips to the curve of her neck. Giving a soft giggle, Lindsey angled her head. Kissed him on the mouth. They kissed repeatedly, Marco's hands roaming gracelessly over her body; and wherever his hands went, her skin, her muscle, appeared to grow warm and malleable, like modeling clay worked between fingers and palms. Only yards away from the spider house, the place where we'd touched, he whispered in her ear, pressed his mouth to her ear. I touched my cheek. My fingertip found a trickle of wetness there, and I sensed a strange acceleration within me. A veil lifting from behind the eye, and the sharp edges of things coming clear. With a playful shout, Lindsey broke away from him and ran toward the spider house. The interior was dark and colorless, shaded by the roof, but the doorway on the back wall shone with sun and foliage, a portal to another place. Lindsey ran through it, jumped down to the ground below, my cousin right behind her. For a few seconds, I couldn't see them. There was a panicked squeal. A burst of laughter. Then Lindsey reentered the clearing, running full speed for the house. Her halter was gone. My body igniting, I grabbed the rifle. Ran down the hallway. Past the photographs and out the open back door. A grasshopper somersaulted out of my way as I slid down beside the porch. Crouched down. The front door crashed open. A flurry of fearful laughter. Frantic movement. Then a sudden hush. One hot moment—the heated wood of the house burning through my shirt—then my cousin arrived, taking deep, measured breaths.

"Free Spirit," he said in a singsong. "Free Spirit, where are you?"

Footsteps. I ran along the house, almost tripping over the rusty remains of an old-fashioned lawn mower. As I ducked around the corner, Marco stepped onto the porch.

A long pause.

The lonely *tick-tick* of a cricket.

"Free Spirit . . ."

His call was soft. From the woods came an answer. Rising out of a tender feathered throat. Two notes, plaintive and clear. Then something in my peripheral vision, at the front corner of the house. She stopped in her tracks as soon as she saw me, and we stared at each other, silently. She didn't cover her breasts, which were milky white in the sun. Through the window above me I could hear my cousin moving. Something fell to the floor. Something gave a slow, rusty whine.

"Free Spirit . . ."

Lindsey beckoned to me and then ran across the clearing. I didn't move. But when she reached the spider house, she gestured again, and I found myself sprinting over the weedy grass. She led me behind the structure. The land sloped down. There was shade, wildflowers, and a small white butterfly dancing in the air.

"What are you doing here?" she whispered.

"I don't know."

"Hunting?"

She indicated the rifle, which was still in my hands.

"You can look at me," she said. "It's no big deal."

My body grew strangely warm. The feeling was unreadable, a desire that made no sense, and it occurred to me that perhaps I was asleep. Any time now, Lindsey would turn into that girl, lean close. I wanted to feel her lips and then wake up. A breeze cooled the sweat on my body, and blew some hair into her face. My eyes tracked down her neck, the skin dusted with russet freckles. Her breasts curved to elegant points. Her nipples were brownish-pink circles the size of quarters, growing goose-fleshed and erect before my eyes. She pushed the hair out of her face, and seemed honestly unconcerned by her nakedness, oblivious to her own beauty.

"Let's scare him," she said. "You stay here. I'll get him to chase me to this corner. When he comes around, you shout at him as loud as you can."

Her lips parted in an expectant smile, the grin of a little girl. Without waiting for my opinion, she crept back up the incline. A few feet away, looming above my head, was the doorway of the spider house. Once, there must have been stairs leading from the floor to the ground below, but no trace of them remained; so I had to stand to peer over the threshold, to see her heading toward the house, her back completely bare. A few inches from my face, a spider crossed the wooden floor. I placed my hand in his path, and he paused, one leg tapping silently. The tap-tap of a blind person's stick. Then he circumvented my fingers. It wouldn't work without her. The whirr of the cicadas poured down like rain. Under my eye I could feel the dried residue of the tear I'd shed earlier, the sediment of a strange emotion. What did I want from her? What was it that I coveted so fiercely?

Inside the front room of the house, something was overturned. Objects skating over the floor. The chessboard and its wooden pawns and knights and bishops. Lindsey ran onto the porch, managed to grab the knob of the door. It slammed shut as she bolted into the clearing; then it opened right back up, hit the inside wall with such force that a pane of its glass broke, falling in musical pieces to the floor. Marco leaped from the top step, and I scurried into position at the corner. My chest was heaving, my throat felt closed off. Lindsey slid down the hill, raced past me. But Marco wasn't behind her. I heard his feet hit the wooden floor above. As I turned, his body was already blurring through the doorway. Completing a perfectly timed arc. At the foot of the slope, he hit her with all his weight—and her body, with a violent balletic grace, spun in a new direction. She fell hard onto her back. Then started struggling for breath. I'd heard this before. I'd felt it. Lungs robbed of air. A taste of suffocation.

I wanted to help her—but something fixed me in place. My cousin was kneeling by her now. Staring down at her. His back to me, he hadn't seen me, he hadn't turned around. He was just staring, with what struck me as a dim animal curiosity. Slowly, he reached a trembling hand to her face; and as he trailed it down her neck, over one of her breasts, down the gentle grade of her stomach, I could sense a change in him, a tenuous balance being upset. His fingers rested for a moment at her waist. Then, using two hands, he unsnapped the button of her shorts. His fingers crept under the white cuff, closed around the material, and pulled. Her body impulsively jolted. Her hand flew up blindly, hit him on the side of the neck. She rolled onto her stomach. Marco wrestled the shorts down her legs, revealing her underwear, tiny flowers growing in a field of pink. As he touched the elastic band, Lindsey swung again, caught him full in the cheek and nose. Then, as he'd done so long ago, to a different girl in the broad daylight of the Bronx Zoo, he hit her back, an open-palmed slap that electrified my spine.

All of nature went quiet and still.

The cicadas lost their voices. The leaves on the trees petrified. Bees hovered motionless at the tips of stamens. I felt blind and deaf. Still, I could see her underwear tangled around her ankles; a patch of dark hair between her legs; Marco spitting into his hand. I could hear the distant mechanical vibrations of a small airplane; her breath returning in syncopated gasps; and my cousin whispering with a dissonant tenderness. He forced her legs open with his knees, lowered his body to hers, fumbled between his legs. The muscles of his thighs and buttocks tensed. As he pushed down and forward, a word caught violently in Lindsey's throat. Another push, more powerful and confident, locked them together. Her body convulsed—and with the fullness of her voice, with the clarity of panic, she cried out. From the treetops, the cicadas wailed again, their metallic voices rising in pitch. The leaves whispered, urging her to be silent. I found myself moving away. The rifle fallen from my hands. The seeds of a maple, propeller-like blades, descending and spinning. Halfway up the incline, hidden from sight, I leaned back against the stone wall. I pressed my eyes shut. But the rhythm—a quickening antiphonal tempo—was inside me now. A pulsing heat. A fledgling muscle tearing. No more resistance. Just a miserable dry heave every time my cousin groaned. "I love you," Marco said, and it was only then that I started feeling a sharpened pressure in my eyes. Only then did I realize I was doing nothing. My saliva grew warm and thick. Jealousy turned rancid in my stomach. Up above, that mechanical hum grew louder. The plane appeared over the treetops. Maroon red. Flying low. Its shadow raced through the woods and broke over me like a wave, the roar of the engine drowning out all other sound . . .

It seemed much later that I stirred, as if from a fairy-tale sleep. The sun was burning into the back of my neck with an omniscient heat. Glowing against my closed eyelids. In a crimson blindness, I breathed in the smell of grass and dirt. My face was pressed to the ground. Eyes flickering open. On a clover a few inches from my face: a gigantic worker bee and the flower's white hairs bending tenderly under his feet. Everything was strangely dilated. Atoms and molecules swelled to visible specks, spinning dreamily in the air. Time not so much passing as expanding. I slipped into the space between seconds. It was there that her sobbing could be heard. As subdued and reminiscent as trees dripping water after a rainstorm.

"Oh, Jesus . . . Oh, my God."

"It's normal." My cousin's voice, shaking with some kind of fear. "It's normal the first time."

I didn't move. I stared into the grass and waited. In my peripheral vision I could see the corner of the spider house, the land dropping down. I listened to him trying to dress her; she wouldn't let him. Finally, he said he was going to get the halter. I heard him climbing the slope. A ghostly blur, he turned the corner and froze. He stood motionless, watching me, his fear quietly gathering mass; and in those moments, we became connected by more than kinship. We were bound now. By implicit promises of silence and denial. By the thing between our legs. I wanted only to lie in the grass and sleep. But after he'd retreated, with a soundless circumspect tread, I forced myself to my knees. Dizziness. The countryside, like a music box, in the process of winding down and falling silent. I walked up the incline. The clearing stretched out in front of me. My cousin nowhere in sight. A sharp triangle of sun was cutting across the wooden floor of the spider house. Through the doorway I saw her lying in the grass below. Naked. Trying to get her feet through the holes in her underwear. After she'd pulled it on, a dark spot slowly appeared in the crotch; and I noticed, brushed along one inner thigh, a vivid stroke of blood. Lying on her side, she pressed her face into the ground, and her body silently shuddered. A moment later, I was running away, my heart burning in my chest. At the edge of the field, I knelt. Leaned over to vomit, but nothing came. Nearby, two bumblebees were gathering pollen from the scarlet blossoms of wildflowers. The sound of their wings ominous and religious. Their wings chanting like the throats of monks. A gentle breeze now. The grass of the field whispering secret counsel and the flowers releasing their essence. The smell of a kiss. The smell of a dreamed girl's breath.

8 / Castro Street on a cool summer night. When I arrived at the theater, Nile was standing under the marquee, which advertised a new print of *Dr. Strangelove, or How I Learned to Stop Worrying and Love the Bomb*. She wrapped her arms around my waist, made a show of kissing me in full view of the general populace. Two men passed by, hand in hand, and one said, "Go, honey." Encouraged by this, she backed me up against the front of the building and began making out with me in earnest. Kissing her, feeling her hands slide under my jacket, I felt all the energy of the neighborhood, its hum of pride and the damp chill of tragedy, coursing through our bodies. By the time I heard someone excuse himself—a familiar voice which set off a vague kind of alarm within me—our tongues were engaged in an indecorous sort of jousting match.

Nile and I parted to find Phil, wearing a punchy look of amusement. And Lindsey a step behind him. Her face washed out with a stunned blankness. I watched her eyes veer away from us, take shelter in some image across the street, and immediately something tore inside me.

"I'm Phil. This is Lindsey. We'll be your chaperones this evening."

Nile's throaty, coquettish giggle communicated a thrilled embarrassment at having been discovered. Letting go of my arm, she gave Phil an ephemeral kiss on the lips; then Lindsey a longer one just above the corner of her mouth, which necessitated a slight, but markedly sensual, tilt of the head.

"What are you guys doing here?" I asked.

Phil chose to interpret this as a joke. "We were just passing by. Got swept up in a crowd of pinko intellectuals."

By now, a steady stream of patrons was filing into the theater, past a poster featuring Peter Sellers' emigré Nazi scientist struggling to restrain an arm still instinctually saluting the Führer. Phil herded us toward the box office, where he pulled out a couple of twenties and, waving off my money, dispensed tickets like a father at a carnival. Lindsey studied hers as if it were imprinted with some kind of message, some confusing prophecy.

"Really," I pursued, "this is quite a coincidence."

"What do you mean?" Phil said.

"Running into you guys."

"If you hadn't phoned, it would have been a coincidence."

"I don't get it," I said.

"I called them," Nile explained. "This afternoon."

I looked at her and felt a flash of suspicion, dispelled as her eyes confidently met mine and her lips parted in a gorgeous socialite's smile.

"Hey, honey," Phil said. "This-a-way."

Lindsey took the hand he offered. We all passed into the lobby. Soft yellow light. Red-and-gold carpet, lush and deep. Twin staircases winding up to the balcony.

"Maybe I shouldn't ask what you two have been doing for the past couple of weeks," Phil said.

"Mmm . . ." This from Nile as she removed her jacket and flung it over her shoulder with an almost hyperactive abandon.

"How about you?" I said.

"We went up to Calistoga last weekend. You met my friend Jordan once at the house. He owns that spa up there."

"Right. Mud baths."

"Why don't you boys get some seats?" Nile said. "Right in the middle, right under the chandelier, and we'll pick up a few things."

"No butter," Phil said. Nile winked and tugged Lindsey gently by her coat sleeve. As soon as they had drifted out of sight and we had stepped into the crimson dimness of the auditorium, Phil eased an arm around my shoulders while, front and center, at the foot of the colossal curtain, the organist played "Sentimental Journey" on the mighty Wurlitzer. In this fashion, without speech, we proceeded down the grade of the aisle. Reached the designated area, eased into some seats below the chandelier, which hovered like a giant diamond ring above our heads.

"What?" I demanded.

"Nothing, nothing. I'm just happy for you. My imagination's running wild."

"Don't get carried away." I glanced over my shoulder at the auditorium doors.

"What's wrong?"

"Wrong? Nothing's wrong. Just don't make a big deal out of this—it's only been a couple of weeks."

"Judging from the scene out front, an eventful couple of weeks. Have you been to bed with her?"

I considered responding in the negative. "Deny everything" was the phrase that came to mind. However, for all I knew, Nile would soon invalidate that policy. I looked at Phil. One eyebrow cocked, tongue poised between his teeth, like a runner at the starting block. I gave a weak nod. The whole thing was reminiscent of the distant ordeal of the confessional.

"Had you ever been," he asked, "with that type of woman?"

"You mean black?"

"Black. Jesus, I hadn't even thought of that. She is black, isn't she? Or does she prefer 'African-American'?"

"It hasn't come up."

He nodded philosophically. "Do you see her that way? I mean, do you think of her as black?"

"I don't know. I wouldn't say I *think* of her that way. But it's hard not to notice."

"I'd like to return to this point later," he said, "when time permits. I think there's something of sociological significance going on there. What I originally meant, though, was, had you ever been with a bisexual woman? Before Nile."

"I don't believe so. But who knows? I don't ask for a résumé."

"Well, you're old-fashioned in that way."

Together, as if by common instinct, we glanced back at the doors. Sighted Nile approaching with a tub of popcorn. Waved discreetly. At the end of the row, she eased past the knees of an elderly couple, spilling a few fluffy kernels into their laps. An apology led to a friendly conversation and a sharing of food. They all chewed as the organist segued into something peppy and patriotic.

"In bed," Phil whispered, "do you find she has an attention to detail, a decisiveness that's just lacking in more . . . traditional women?"

"You sound like a car commercial."

Finally, she reached us, handed me the bucket. She remained standing, her head framed by the engraved canopy of the ceiling.

"Where's Lindsey?" Phil asked.

With a nod, Nile indicated the lobby. "Is she okay? I mean, is everything all right with her?"

"Why?"

"Because she just bummed a cigarette off someone. She's out front, smoking a cigarette."

"She doesn't smoke," Phil said.

"I know."

As invisibly as possible, I ate popcorn.

"Have you ever seen her smoke? Tom?"

"Well," I said, my mouth unbelievably dry, "she has one once in a great while. I think she started in Peru."

"Did she seem upset?" he asked Nile.

"Well, you know her. All her actions have this strange pre-scripted quality. It's like she'd been planning to bum this ciga-rette, at that particular moment, since noon yesterday. So she asks some guy, who exhibits no clear symptoms of nicotine addiction, for a cigarette—and of course he's got some. American Spirit, to boot."

Phil stood up, rubbing his hands together as if before a campfire.

"We had a few words earlier. I'll be right back."

Nile eased down into the seat he'd vacated. Sat on its edge, held her chin in her hands. Meanwhile, the organist moved steadily in the direction of a rousing climax, pounding out the chords which made that little voice inside me shout, "Hollywood!"

"Maybe this wasn't such a good idea," she said. "I think she's really freaked out, seeing me with someone else. With you."

This addendum seemed to be laden with some pointed double entendre; I attempted my most generic look. "Well, it's too late now, but you should have asked me. I mean, why are you inviting them out with us anyway?"

"The idea just came to me this afternoon. I thought it'd be fun. Will you stop eating that popcorn?" She confiscated the bucket, placed it on the seat beside her. "So you think that's it?" she said. "You would have known, had I asked you, that this wasn't a good idea?"

"I'm just saying we could have discussed it."

I removed my glasses, cleaned them on my shirttail. The theater an abstract blur of color. The idea of sitting in that seat for the next two hours close to unbearable.

"Has she said anything to you?" Nile asked. "To give you that impression?"

"What impression?"

"That this sort of thing wouldn't be a good idea. I mean, has she ever said anything about me that would give you that impression?"

Replacing my glasses, I studied her face intently, and decided the look of naïveté, of a woman innocently searching for answers, was a brilliant—but nonetheless exposable—forgery. I didn't know what she was up to, but I didn't like it. In the background, I saw Phil ushering Lindsey into our row. Then Lindsey sitting down beside Nile, who, apparently, had cleared Phil's original seat and claimed it herself in anticipation of this final geographical arrangement.

"Sorry," Lindsey said, speaking in our general direction. "I just had to indulge a self-destructive urge."

Her eyes contacted me fleetingly, and the feeling in my chest grew more extreme. A tightness, a thickening heat. I felt like I was choking on remorse and self-loathing.

"I had a sudden craving for a cigarette," she explained.

"I'm all for that kind of indulgence," Nile said. "I've developed a rather homeopathic world view, in the original sense of the word. I mean, I think we have to feed that part of ourselves—you know, the part that wants to destroy the self—in small ways, or else we really are doomed. I mean, I think total abstinence is the quickest road to ruin."

"Spoken like a true educator of our nation's youth," Phil kicked in, from what seemed like miles away.

"Choose your poison," Lindsey said.

"But use it sparingly," Nile concluded.

As if on cue, the organist began his trademark finale, and as he reached down, pulling a lever to initiate the slow descent of his podium, we all applauded. Following the last resounding chord, he stood up, bowed, exited stage left. Then the house lights slowly dimmed. The curtain parted. And as we were bathed in a soft cinematic glow, I peered past Nile at Lindsey. Found her already staring back at me, easing a piece of popcorn into her mouth. Nile's hand landed on my leg, crossed the border of my inner thigh. Then the film presented its silent disclaimer. That the events we were about to witness could never actually happen. We had the assurance of the United States Air Force.

⸺

For what felt like an eternity, we watched the crew of that gas-leaking B-52—their radio silent, their secret code machine out of order—unwittingly do anything they could to carry out their mission, which, if successful, would detonate the Russian dooms-day machine. Beside me, Nile sat with her feet up on the chair, chin resting on her knees. Transfixed. Regularly letting go a breath full of reverence for some bit of dialogue or twist of plot. From time to time she'd lean in Lindsey's direction to share a brief insight or some aesthetic rush. Once, as she bent down to relive an itch on her calf, I was provided a view of Lindsey's face. She looked overwhelmed somehow, as if the ironies parad-ing over the screen were more than she could bear. Beyond her, Philip massaged his chiseled jaw. He gave a wildly amused grin as American leaders discussed sexuality in the postwar world.

Since that day in the park, my body had been throbbing with guilt and fear. But what did I have to feel guilty about? I simply had someone else, just as she did. What did I have to fear? When I was with Nile, the depressed longing which had become as normal to me as hunger or fatigue disappeared, re-placed by a feeling of power and freedom. She leaned back in her seat now, eclipsing Lindsey's face. I lowered a hand into her lap, and she gripped it absently, but firmly. A moment later, she turned to me with a smile that was like the key to some fantasti-cal city. I felt a sudden surge of passionate relief. Yes, in the moon-like glow of the American cinema, I believed myself to be arriving at epiphanic understandings.

"Mein Führer! I can walk!"

Dr. Strangelove struggled out of his wheelchair, took a few miraculous steps through the shadows of the War Room. Then the sound track swelled with a sentimental tune as the world, in a mesmerizing orgy of soundless mushroom clouds, proceeded to come to an end.

Outside the theater, Phil proposed a round of post-apocalyp-tic drinks—and Nile led us to Vesuvio, which I inferred from a nostalgically plaintive tone in her voice had hosted unknowable intimacies in the days when Lindsey had been hers. On Colum-bus, the women walked a ways ahead. Lindsey had her hands thrust in the pockets of her coat. Nile's were gesticulating. The air was brisk and at some point, a gust of cold wind compelled her arm to slip through Lindsey's. They walked like this for a good half block, during which time Phil continued talking about some pointless cosmic discovery he'd recently read about in *Sky and Telescope*.

"That doesn't bother you?" I asked him, pointing ahead.

"What, that?" He shook his head in the negative. "You?"

"Why should it bother me?"

We walked a few steps in silence.

"They're girls," he finally said. "They do that sort of thing without thinking."

At the bar, we climbed to the second floor, a narrow balcony lined with windows overlooking the heart of North Beach. Across the street, the red-light district: the giant neon sign for The Garden of Eden, a snake curling up around a yellowish Eve, its reptilian curves obscuring her private parts. Just below our feet, on the outside wall of City Lights Bookstore, Baudelaire's head presided over Jack Kerouac Alley. We landed a corner table, flickering with candlelight—and after a round of drinks (Nile and Lindsey ordered margueritas on the rocks; Phil demanded I join him in chasing Jack Daniel's with pints of Anchor Steam), the vague unease I'd felt on the street began to lift. As it was I, not Lindsey, whom Nile sat beside, my neck which received the caress of her fingertips. She touched me incessantly, possessively. While, across the table, Phil and Lindsey sat on what seemed to be different planes.

"It doesn't matter how many times I see that movie," Nile said. "I'm floored. I'm fucking floored as we speak." She tilted back her second drink, and a bit of salt clung to her lip. "We're not at the mercy," she babbled, "of technology or government or patriotism. We're at the mercy of irony. Each of us carries it, like a virus. We play by its rules, we communicate it to everything we create. It's the basic building block of matter."

"That's very interesting," Phil said. "But a bit too optimistic for me. Too romantic, in an academic sense."

"How do you mean?"

"Well, I think the whole thing comes down to sex. You've got a nuclear war motivated by a madman's misconceptions of human sexuality. You've got the plane, the bearer of destruction, filled with symbols of sexuality—*Playboy* magazine, the rubbers in the crew's survival kits. You've got Slim Pickens with a giant nuclear hard-on, riding this missile to the ground, delivering the final copulatory thrust . . ."

He continued listing examples with an evangelical fervor. Meanwhile, Lindsey leaned forward into the candlelight, her face and neck darting into relief, the lacy pattern of her bra bleeding through her blouse like invisible ink.

"I think it's a lack of communication," she said slowly, distantly. "The whole scenario is dependent on that. They can't talk to each other, or hear each other." She stared down at the table. "All of them act in isolation, based on false sets of assumptions. They try to talk, but they can't. Even if they could, it wouldn't matter. Language wouldn't prevent the outcome. Nothing can."

This reading had an inexplicable drunken gravity, and we all floundered for a moment in personal silences. I looked out the window; a couple of people had entered the alley, and I thought I saw Baudelaire's eyes follow them in the tradition of haunted portraits.

"At the risk of grinding the gears," Phil finally said, "two weeks from Saturday is Zach's eighth birthday."

Nile sighed, and I imagined her in her classroom, leading two dozen five-year-olds in a discussion about playground morality. After three years as a teacher's aide, she felt it was time to move on. But she was still subject to attacks of melancholy at the mention of her kids; and last week, she had teared up when she showed me her first class photo, in which Zach stood on a riser just above her left shoulder, caught in the act of stealing an adoring glance.

"Eight," she said. "Jesus, I remember when he couldn't get his pencil grip right. I never told you, but we had a big conference about keeping him in kindergarten for another year. We didn't want him to leave, and the pencil grip was the only excuse we could think of."

"I appreciate your leniency. At eight thousand dollars a year, I can only afford kindergarten once."

"Eight thousand dollars," I said. "For a year of kindergarten."

"It's the tempera paint." Nile leaned into me. "The Arabs have the market cornered."

"Eight thousand dollars," I repeated.

"I guess it all worked out," Nile said. "His pencil grip."

Phil nodded. "I bought him a scanner for his Macintosh. He just transfers his work sheets to disk and types in the answers."

I stole a look at Lindsey and saw her eyes dart away from me. I watched her hand slide across the table, into Phil's. He gave her a warm, surprised glance. The waitress swung by and Phil ordered another pair of bourbons.

"Anyway," he went on, "we're having a party, the invitations are out. But I thought I'd make a personal entreaty. We all really want the two of you to be there."

"Your place or Claire's?" Nile asked.

"Ours," Lindsey said; the first person plural stung me, then slipped away unseen, like a jellyfish.

"Hey, look," Nile said. "It's Wallace."

She waved to someone in the alcoholic distance, down on the ground floor. A guy with wavy blond hair, whose health-club torso filled out a black T-shirt, beckoned her to descend. Nile took Lindsey's hand and guided her to her feet.

"You two talk about boy things for a while."

Phil winked in a fatherly fashion. We watched them disappear down the stairs, then emerge by the bar. Wallace, whom I remembered to be the host of the fabled seance, kissed each of them in turn and, holding Lindsey's hand, rotated her 360 degrees. She spun into Nile's arm with a flawless balletic grace, and allowed this arm to linger about her shoulders.

"I'd like to propose a toast," Phil said as our new drinks arrived. "To the erotic enigma of bisexuality."

Without asking for clarification, I clinked my heavy shot glass against his. Held it before my lips for a moment. Heat seemed to rise from the liquid, warming my face. Down at the bar, Nile's arm was still draped over Lindsey's shoulders, as if it belonged there.

"You're feeling it, aren't you?" he said. "The erotic enigma."

I leaned toward him. "I don't want to tip your canoe or anything, but . . . they were lovers, Phil. They shared each other's beds, they enjoyed each other's bodies."

"Yeah . . ."

"Well, you might consider being less cavalier about it."

"Who's cavalier? I accept their relationship as historical fact."

"What's that supposed to mean?"

He shrugged. "It means it happened and it's over. It also means that what they shared has been so distorted—by time and retrospection and subconscious mythmaking—not even they can know its organic truth anymore. Those are two women over there, Tom. You tell me they were lovers and I nod my head. I can buy it. But viscerally, it means very little to me. It's just an idea. You and I can't understand it, because we're not gay."

"You and I fall in love," I said. "I mean, not with each other, but we have sexual desires, we fall in love with other human beings. I think there's enough common ground to understand it. To be afraid of it."

"You're telling me I have something to be afraid of?"

"Not afraid." I paused to ask myself why I was pursuing this so vigorously, and was unable to find a suitable answer. "It's just . . . you're possessed of a minor misconception. Their affair wasn't lukewarm. Nile was in love with her."

Phil turned his attention to the bar, where something akin to flirtation continued to thrive.

"Can you sit there," I said, "and tell me you're not jealous?"

He massaged his jaw like a guy in an electric-razor commercial. Drank pensively. "I'll admit there's an element of jealousy. Look, Tom, I don't deny the validity of the whole thing. But I look at the two of them, and I'm incapable of feeling threatened. I'm too preoccupied with the sexual excitement of imagining them naked together."

I waved him off.

"I realize you can't relate to this specific example. Since for you getting in bed with Lindsey would probably be like getting in bed with your older sister, but let's be honest here. At some point, everyone thinks about fucking their sister—"

"Jesus, Phil."

"Can you sit there and tell me the sight of the two of them doesn't inspire your imagination?"

"I don't know."

"Why don't you be honest for once in your life?"

"What?"

"Just admit it, kid."

I looked away; I hated it when he called me that.

"Admit it," he repeated.

"All right," I said. "I think about it."

Somehow this answer took him by surprise. Fixing me with an odd stare, he nodded uncertainly. "What do you mean, you *think* about it?"

"Huh?"

"I didn't ask you if you *think* about it. You sit around *thinking* about it?"

"No," I said. "Not on any regular basis. I've just thought about it. The thought has crossed my mind."

He eyed me for a bit longer. Then rose suddenly to his feet.

Strode off to relieve himself. In his absence, I removed my glasses and North Beach dissolved into visual confusion. Eve and the snake merged into a single hybrid entity. Headlights wound up the streets like strings of luminous pearls, and Baudelaire looked suddenly like Edgar Allan Poe. I shut my eyes, rubbed my temples. Some Cuban dance music kicked in on the jukebox. My head swayed gently in tempo.

"What are you doing?"

I opened my eyes and found Lindsey standing within arm's reach, standing over me. The past pulling like an undertow. This love I felt for her. I didn't want it. I wanted only to be rid of it.

"What do you think you're doing?"

"I'm having an affair," I said. "Just like you."

There was a long pause. I reached for my drink, which blazed a trail of fire down my throat. Nile was still at the bar, chatting amiably with Wallace; and as if she knew, by some magical romantic instinct, that my eyes were on her, she glanced up and sheepishly bit her lower lip. This wasn't a one-night stand, or a two-week fling. I didn't have to let her go—and furthermore, I didn't want to. When I turned back to Lindsey, she was staring at me. Uncomprehending. As though I'd stabbed her, held a knife even now in the soft flesh of her stomach.

"You're sleeping with her?"

"Lindsey, you don't have any right—"

"Are you?"

I allowed silence to answer the question.

"What about the other day?" she said.

"I shouldn't have met you. I wish I hadn't."

"Do you remember what I said?"

Again I didn't answer. She seemed to be staring through me now, as if at something on another dimensional plane, something which was growing clearer and more terrifying with every passing moment. I felt a panicked burst of compunction. I stamped it out, I smothered it. Lindsey walked swiftly in the direction of the stairs. Halfway there, she ran into Philip. He started to say something and she pressed her hand against his chest. When he grasped her gently by the shoulders, she pulled away and disappeared around the corner. Back at the table, he eased into his seat as if into a hot bath. Seconds later, Nile's hand landed on my shoulder, and my body bolted to nervous attention.

"What gives?" she said. "Where's Lindsey?"

Phil looked at her empty seat, shook his head with hopeless irritation. "She must be getting her period."

———

Shortly thereafter, I watched Nile slide into the back of Philip's Saab. She'd said she was tired and had a hike the next day, and when I offered to drive her home (my car was in the Mission at the time, about thirty blocks away), she raised a carefree eyebrow and said, "That's okay, I'll get a ride with them." She kissed me long and hard, then added, "I'll owe you . . . with interest." She jogged across the street, where Lindsey was climbing into the front without so much as a farewell glance; and as the car started and left me behind, I felt profoundly lost. Somehow, Phil's soft tap on the horn, the sight of his vanity license plate, BK2NTR (translation: Back to Nature), made everything infinitely worse. In the Mission, I lay for a while in Dolores Park. Staring up at the dull gray canopy of fog, I felt the globe's drunken spin, and thought of something Phil had said earlier. How they had a saying in Africa. *Ot Nilis, ot nihil*—"either the Nile, or nothing." They said this because the river, Nile Treadway's aqueous namesake, was the lifeblood of their land. Should its waters fail to swell once a year, fail to bathe the desert in great brown floods, then Egypt, the Sudan, Abyssinia would die in an equatorial furnace. Philip had shot an epic documentary there, tracing the path of explorers who'd sought the source of the river in vain for two thousand years. And like Philip—like Ptolemy before him, like Stanley or Livingstone—I imagined riding the river's crocodiled currents and seeking out its truth.

What had she been doing tonight?

I thought about what Phil had said. That they were girls. Flirtatious, physical by nature. Certain actions were performed without thinking. This failed to ease my mind, as it seemed clear that none of us were thinking. In my apartment, my cat, Mingus—whom I'd recently saved from a sleepy death in some feline concentration camp—sat on his hind legs, staring at the scratch post as if receiving extraterrestrial transmissions. There's something wrong, I thought. There's something wrong with my cat. Meanwhile, on a table across the room, the heart of my answering machine was beating wildly. My finger hovered over the Play button. The words coiled up in there were doubtless better left unheard. No sooner had I decided to deal with it in the morning, to turn the entire communicational system off for the night, than the phone rang.

"You get my messages?" my father asked.

"I just walked in the door."

"We found something," he said. "A note."

"What kind of a note?"

"Written on the back of a postcard. Jane found it. In the bathroom. In a box of feminine napkins."

"What does it say?"

"I'm getting to that. The front is one of those 3-D pictures, okay? The Virgin Mary appearing to a little girl at Lourdes. You know that story?"

"I know it," I said. "What did he write?"

"This is a direct quote," my father said. "Are you ready?"

I pressed some fingers to my forehead.

" 'I beseech you not to send the police after me for I am carrying a gun, and the first bullet will be for the policeman, the second for myself.' "

There was a lengthy silence.

"You getting an idea of what I'm dealing with here? He finds this all highly comical. Meanwhile, Jane thinks the kid is wandering the country with a gun in his pants. Would you just say a few words to her?"

"Say what?"

"Just tell her. That he doesn't have a gun."

My fingers pushed harder at my temple. "How would I know, Dad? How would I know if he did or not?"

———

I woke to a dark room and a ringing telephone. No one sleeping beside me. I picked up the handset, dropped it, dragged it by its cord up to the bed. "Hello?" A strange delay. No response. For an unreal moment, I expected my mother to speak. But it was a boy's voice. Unfamiliar and undeniable.

"Guess who?" he said.

"Matthew, where are you?"

"Staking my claim, man. There's salt in them thar hills. I'm gonna make a killing out here. But seriously, guess where I am. There's enough salt to melt a glacier, but it ain't Margaritaville." He made a clacking noise with his tongue, the sound of a clock running down. I heard a giggle and my brother telling a third party to cut the shit.

"Are you with someone?" I asked him.

He returned with an uncanny parody of Don Pardo. *"Tom from San Francisco, California, is a cartoonist. He's created many of our best-loved characters of the silver screen. He comes from a pathetic little family in a crappy little town in Connecticut. His father's a professional asshole and his stepmother is a stupid bitch who thinks Dostoyevsky is a kind of vodka. He has one brother, who is currently touring the country with MTV VJ Mighty Missy."*

"Hi," I heard—a raspy voice speaking through a mouthful of chewing gum.

"Matthew. Where are you?"

"Chill, man. Jesus. So you can't solve the riddle? Enough

salt to melt a glacier, sure as hell ain't Margaritaville." Again the
tongue clacking. "Solve the riddle and I'll let the girl go."

A high-pitched shriek.

"Utah," I said.

"Bingo! Don, tell him what he's won. *Well, Tom, you and
a guest are the proud owners of a one-way ticket to Chernobyl,
U.S.S.R. Don't forget your chemotherapist, 'cause this place is hot.
Back to you, Chuck.*"

"Are you all right?" I asked.

"Okay, okay, if you don't want to go for the big money,
fine. But listen to this, Tom." I heard him flipping pages. "Have
you read Bataille? Georges Bataille?"

"No, I haven't."

"Well, you're gonna love this, 'cause you're, like, an artist.
This is my new favorite line in the history of literature. 'Chapter
Two—The Antique Wardrobe.' Are you ready?"

"Matt—"

" 'That was the period when Simone developed a mania for
breaking eggs with her ass.' "

Finally, a three-second pause: a moment of silence for
French pornography.

"Matthew," I said, repeating his name as if to convince myself it was really my brother. "Have you called Dad and Jane?
They're freaking out. It's been six days."

"I'm not talking to them anymore. They're part of a life I've
left behind. You know what Jack Kerouac said, Tom? He's no
poet, he's no surrealist. But his words strike a chord. 'Go west,
young man . . . and get as much pussy in the process as is
humanly possible.' "

I heard the girl accuse him, without amusement, of sleaziness.

"Hey!" he said. "Come back here! Don't walk over there!
There's Mormons in that tabernacle!"

A scratching sound. Once more I spoke his name. He'd left
the phone dangling, and all I could hear was the dull moan of
traffic. I imagined him not returning, lost again and disappearing

forever this time, following his strange trajectory into nothingness. Why did I feel accountable for all this? Why did it seem
the blame was mine?

"Hold on!" I heard him yell in the distance. "Operator,
don't touch that dial!" Then the phone was in his hands again.
"Listen," he said.

"No, you listen, goddammit. I want to know where the fuck
you are and what the hell you think you're doing. I want to
know now, or I'm going to hang up the goddamn phone."

A slow whistle. "We've got a live one, Chuck. Okay, I'm
in Salt Lake City."

"How'd you get there?"

"Greyhound luxury liner."

"Who are you with?"

"Dolphin."

"Dolphin?"

"You asked her name."

"Who is she? How old is she?"

"She's a young lady who's open-minded to the idea of
breaking eggs with her butt cheeks while doing a headstand on
an armchair while I jerk off and come in her face. It's all in the
book. She's fifteen."

"Matt, please. Tell me what's going on."

"Nothing," he said in a tone of casual honesty. "It's summer
vacation. I'm just doing some traveling."

I took a deep breath and lay back on my bed. Outside the
window, the Twin Peaks radio tower was thrusting its spiky arms
into the night sky, flashing its silent beacon.

"Vacation," I said calmly. "What's your final destination?"

"I'm glad you asked. Like I quoted, I'm going West. I get
in Thursday night."

"Get in? Where?"

"San Francisco, Californ-eye-ay. Land of fruits, nuts, and
vegetables. I've always wanted to see homosexuals walking down
a public street hand in hand. You've got that, right?"

"What time on Thursday?"

"What time. I've got this all written down in my mind. I've got a real busy schedule. We're trying to see the sights. We've got the Navajo sweat lodge tomorrow, Reno the next day. It's an existential gamble. It could be Friday. I'd better call you back on this."

I gave him my number at the studio, asked him to call me once a day. I told him not to stop again, to just stay on the bus. On Thursday, I'd pick him up at the terminal. He said nothing while I made these suggestions and requests. When I was finished, there was a silence connecting us—an uneasy and somehow intimate silence.

"You mean," he finally said, "you want me to come?"

I felt the gears of my mind shifting. This question. His voice, stripped of all veneer. I listened to him breathing, the phone pressed against my ear. Like listening to sounds trapped in a seashell. Whispered secrets. I was involved now. Implicated.

"Just answer me two questions," he said.

"All right."

"Have you ever been to Utah?"

"I have, yes. Once."

"Do you believe the story about the Utah state bird?"

I didn't know it. He gave me a brief synopsis. Brigham Young. A religious pilgrimage. Crops threatened by a plague of locusts. The specter of cold starvation. Then, from over the hills in miraculous waves . . . seagulls . . . hungry and angelic.

"Do you believe it?" Matthew asked.

"No," I said. "No, I don't think so."

"Of course not. I knew you wouldn't, 'cause it's a load of crap. I was at a Dead concert the other day, and it was the same thing. Everybody standing around yelling, 'I need a miracle! I need a miracle every day!' What the fuck is that? You're scared? You feel threatened by things you have no control over? Who the fuck isn't? But there aren't going to be any seagulls. There isn't going to be any cavalry riding over the plains. There isn't going to be any Lazarus rising from the dead. 'Cause when you're dead, it's over, Tom. When you're dead, it's for life."

I thought he choked off a sob, but I couldn't be sure.

"Am I right about that?" he asked.

There was a lengthy pause. In the background, the girl was lobbying for a chili burger.

"Will you shut up!" he shouted. "Just shut the fuck *up!*"

"Fuck you," I heard.

When my brother spoke again, it was into the phone; his voice was soft, personal. "Am I right about that?"

"I don't know."

"Think about it," he said. "That's all I ask. Just think about it."

9 / The sun has set behind the hills. I am sitting on my bed while my father talks about the State of the Union. How the slogan on that pin serves no useful purpose. What our country needs to do is come together and rebuild. Stop taking sides, stop denying responsibility. The truth is, we are all to blame. Confusion. Fear. Troubled years. A torn fabric which must be mended . . . While he talks, as if just to fill the silence, the sky loses detail and hue. A few crickets and frogs begin to chatter and croak, a nocturnal orchestra tuning up. Scattered above and behind him, the model kits we have assembled together—the triceratops, the Klingon War Ship, King Kong with the glow-in-the-dark Fay Wray—hover in the grayness of dusk. They seem far away or aged. Just memories I will always associate with him. He leans back, switches on my desk lamp to repel the heavy advance of night. I think of how dark the spider house must be. Now, beneath a blackening sky, urged on by the lifeless sheen of the moon, the old McCready place gives more of itself to decay. Those vines reach out, strangling a rotted rain gutter. Another chimney brick loses its footing and drops to the ground. Fungus propogates over dank and rotting walls.

I had left her there.

And a few hours later, I'd watched my uncle's station wagon disappear down the lake road, my cousin a dark shadow in the backseat. He hadn't said goodbye. Somehow, we'd managed to avoid each other all afternoon. Strangely, as he moved farther away, I felt no relief. Only an intensification of fear. As if my guide through some foreign landscape—an endless desert or some range of snowy mountains—had suddenly vanished, leaving me to navigate on my own.

"How'd it wind up in your shorts?" my father asks.

"What?"

"The pin."

"Marco," I say. "He gave it to me."

"Where'd *he* get it?"

I shrug to disavow any knowledge of its origin, and for some reason this feels like one of the more significant lies I've ever told.

"I guess it's his idea of a joke," Dad says.

I hear my mother walk down the hall. She does not peek her head in. She does not join us. My father waits for their bedroom door to close, and then he proposes something. He offers me a job. Fifty cents an hour. Helping him out at the office for the rest of the summer. This doesn't sound like such a bad idea. Working for him, I can save for a plane ticket to some exotic locale. Maybe that place where the monarch butterflies congregate, covering the ground and trees like orange snow. Anywhere beautiful. Outside the window, above the hills, I can see one bright star burning. My father sits motionless and silent beneath it, as if he has no other place to go. At such moments, moments when he looks alone or lost, he often tells me he loves me. Then I feel close to him. I begin to understand that somehow he helped to create me. But tonight he only kisses my forehead, and advises me not to sleep in my clothes. Watching him move away, I feel desperate. As he pulls the door shut, I call to him, but the word sticks in my throat and he doesn't hear it. A few minutes later, music from the stereo joins the sounds of night. An accordian. A chorus of women oohing in a melancholy fashion. A cool breeze reaches me through the window as I turn off the light and settle into darkness. Wide awake, I imagine the spiders cowering like me. Hiding in the holes and cracks of that ancestral foundation. Waiting for morning.

10 / I barely slept that night. In the morning, there was a pressure behind my eyes, and as the blood-orange sun spilled in from the east, I felt desperate and childishly afraid. That day, I moved Davey—little Christian of clay and rubber, passive soul that he was—through the darkness of his tiny bedroom, brought his hands together in the antiquated attitude of prayer. With a pin tool, I removed his open eyes and substituted closed ones. Shot two frames. Two snaps of the camera shutter which echoed through the cool expanse of the stages. I checked the log sheet, rewound the audio. Davey, in a pre-pubescent falsetto, spoke through the headphones. *"God . . ."* I opened his mouth, shot two frames, rewound. *"God, I know . . . God, I know I'm not worthy . . . I know I'm not worthy, but show me . . . I'm not worthy, but show me the way."* I repositioned the camera and the lights for a low-angle close-up. Took a meter reading, checked focus. His head filled the frame now, and as I stared into the viewfinder, I had a strange sensation. It seemed I was looking into a magic mirror; it seemed I was seeing my own lost face.

Someone called my name. Frank (whose T-shirt today featured Snoopy on top of his doghouse, taking hits from a water pipe) was holding up the phone in the outer hallway.

"I want you now," Nile said.

"What?"

"I want you to come over here now."

"What's wrong?"

She reminded me that I'd loaned her *The Tao of Love and Sex*. She said something about a thousand loving thrusts. There were several feats, set forth by the ancient Chinese masters, which she wanted to accomplish before sunset.

"I'm at work," I said.

"It's almost lunchtime."

"I'm sorry, Nile."

"Tom . . ."

"What?"

"The Libation of the Three Peaks," she said. "The Tide of Yin is rising. The Palace of Yin, Tom."

I put her off. I locked myself in the bathroom, sat on the closed lid of the toilet seat, and cried. What the hell was wrong with me? I tried to convince myself I didn't know. But I did. Had that really been my brother on the phone last night? The Matthew I knew didn't speak that many words in a month, much less in a single conversation. Had we *had* a conversation? The Great Salt Lake Desert. A Greyhound bus. The space between us shrinking. Memory set the scene. Utah. Giant rocks sculpted by wind and water: spires, arches, miniature cities on the horizon. Barren expanses. Images wavering in a salty heat. Imagined things. Illusions.

———

The amusement park in Santa Cruz. A boardwalk lined with shops. Cavernous video arcade, blaring with the sounds of space-ships, machine guns, and kung fu. Cooling sand beach and a half-moon over the bay. A massive pendulum built in the image of a pirate ship; hollowed-out logs drifting peacefully through the channels of an airborne river; the roller coaster rattling in the distance, screams of terror drifting in and out of hearing. As Nile and I gained altitude, the Ferris wheel lifting us in a slow backward curve, I gazed up into the sky, dotted with stars. Felt Nile gently rocking our seat, and had the sense of floating with her in a life raft. Visions of deserted islands, Adam and Eve, messages setting sail in ancient wine bottles. I thought of the

Bugs Bunny short with the fat and the skinny castaway, hungry and in hot pursuit of rabbit meat. Hoodwinked into seeing Bugs off on a passing ocean liner—*Goodbye,* they call to him, *arrivederci, don't forget to write*—they are left regarding each other with the ravenous hallucinatory look of the starving. One dissolves into a hamburger, the other a hot dog.

"Have you seen that one?" I asked her.

"That one scared me," she said, her face drifting through yellow light. "I must have died of hunger in a past life, because that one, and the one with Chilly Willy, when he's at the arctic ice station—he's got these black circles under his eyes, you can see his rib cage and his little face is all hollowed out—you know that one?"

"Uh-huh."

"God, he's there with that dog and they've got one bean. One fucking bean. Animators are masochists, aren't they?"

"I suppose they are. Most of the ones I know had disturbed childhoods. They watched *The Gong Show* and experimented on their sea monkeys."

A cool breeze came in off the water, but the air was warm. Nile wore a tank top and shorts, and had her hair pulled back with a batik scarf, which (she'd mentioned in passing) had been a gift from Lindsey.

"What about you?" she said. "What about your childhood?"

I stared out at the bay, a dark blanket pulled up to the chin of the beach. "What about it?"

"What did you want to be?"

"A priest."

"That's all?"

"Well, then a cartoonist."

"I had a rather long series of dreams," she said. "First, I wanted to be the person who polished the ice at Rockefeller Center. I wanted to design new musical instruments. For a while, I wanted to have the world's longest fingernails. I wanted to be in one movie, playing Grace Kelly's daughter, win an Academy

Award, and then never act again. It changed like every month because my family was so steady and normal. *Both* of my older sisters wanted to be lawyers. We'd spend summer afternoons playing moot court."

"They put you on trial?"

"You wouldn't believe what I've been convicted of," she said coquettishly. "How about you? Do you have any brothers or sisters?"

I told her I didn't.

"An only child?"

I drew her toward me and the seat rocked. My hand rested on her bare shoulder; I breathed in the fruity smell of her hair.

"The other night was strange, wasn't it? With Phil and Lindsey."

I nodded ambiguously.

"Have you talked to her?" Nile asked.

"No."

"I thought you were pretty close."

"We are," I said. "In a sense."

"But you haven't called, to see if she's okay?"

"Okay?"

"She seemed pretty upset. If memory serves."

"I didn't think it was that big of a deal."

She watched the pirate ship arc into the night sky; as it swung back in our direction, the lights of other rides bled over its hull, then pulled away again as if on a tide.

"You weren't with us later," she said. "In the car."

"The car?"

She raised an eyebrow, bit the inside of her lip. "When they dropped me off, she was crying."

Her tone had started out utterly casual; now there was a heaviness in her voice. I remembered meeting her earlier this evening. We'd made love before driving down here—and when I came inside her, when I heard my name spoken by her, filtered through urgent gasps, the suspicions of that night had almost been washed away. I didn't want to talk about it, I didn't want to talk about anything but us.

"She was crying," Nile repeated.

"Well, what do you mean? Openly? Hysterically?"

"No, quietly. I couldn't even hear her."

"But you could see her?"

"Not really, no. I was in the backseat."

"Then how do you know?"

"When we got to my house," she said, "I leaned forward to kiss them good night. I could taste the tears on her cheek."

With a visceral rush, we crested the top again. In the distance, a log boat headed unstoppably for the falls, and I felt a weird omniscience, as if only I had knowledge of its passengers' imminent fate. I looked at Nile, at the world orbiting her profile—and noted the arrival of a familiar sensation. The feeling of standing in the rain, shivering, throwing pebbles at a window.

"I was going to call her," Nile said. "But it's been so long . . . since we've really talked."

"Listen," I said softly. "Do you think we could talk about something other than Lindsey?"

"Like what?"

"Anything," I said. "We're always talking about her."

There were a few moments of silence. Far below, the operator disengaged the motor, and we eased to a stop, one position shy of the top.

"You jealous?" Nile said. "Because she was crying over me?"

I felt a poke in the ribs.

"You jealous? Of my ex?"

She got me in a ticklish spot and I jumped. The car rocked violently and Nile fell into my arms with a melodrama straight out of the silent cinema. Her eyes were enormous and dark, her lips slightly parted. We were advanced to the zenith of the park, and hung there utterly alone, as if free of all earthly constraints. But no sooner had we started kissing than our seat began a slow, methodical descent. Before we knew it, we were back on solid ground. Gravity seemed oppressive and the stars impossibly distant. We blended into the crowd. To our left, taking a great hydraulic breath, the pirate ship paused briefly at its apogee, and a momentary hush fell over the park so Nile could whisper something into my ear. "You're very handsome," she said. "Buy me a hot dog."

———

The next evening, Phil came over to my place under the pretense of borrowing a book for his trip to New Zealand. Stepping tentatively inside, he wandered around the living room, loitering in front of my framed lobby poster of *The Beast from 20,000 Fathoms*. On the poster, buildings crumble, well-dressed civilians scatter as the drooling dinosaur smashes his way down a city street. In ragged capitals: THE KING OF PREHISTORIC SEA GIANTS RAGING UP FROM AGES PAST TO TEAR A CITY APART! Splayed on a mess of pillows below, Mingus regarded him with a lazy distaste.

"This is your cat?" Phil asked.

"That's my cat. Yes."

I offered him a beer, and he asked if I had anything else.

"Kahlúa," I said.

He gave me a look which accused me of something or other, a fatal deficit of masculinity.

"It was a gift," I explained. "I haven't even opened it."

"No man should be without a good bourbon."

I nodded, then disappeared into the kitchen, returned with a couple of dark foreign ales. Phil and I had never been alone in my apartment together. Before his arrival, I'd conducted a paranoid search for any personal articles belonging to his wife.

"What's his problem?" Phil went on, still contemplating the cat.

"Don't mind him. He's always like that. It's been a month and he's yet to rub up against my leg."

"You think it's indifference, or active dislike?"

"I think it's death-row syndrome."

Phil sat on the couch, and I settled down on the arm of an easy chair, wary of getting too comfortable.

"At the pound," I said, "there seemed to be two camps among the condemned. Some of the animals went crazy when I walked in, like they were begging me to have mercy. Others, I could sense an apathy, a resignation growing on them. I think I chose Mingus because it seemed that, among all his peers, he cared the least. It's like he was already dead."

"Your instincts are in fine working order," Phil said. "This cat provides all the aesthetic advantages of taxidermy without the loss of the animal's original organs."

"I'm trying to think of him as a pet in progress."

"I think that's good. I think you've got realistic expectations, which is good. But hell, what do I know about cats? We always had German shepherds growing up." There was a hopeless frustration in his tone, as if the subject of domesticated animals stirred up memories and passions which were better left alone.

"I got the invite," I blurted out.

"Huh?"

"To Zach's party."

"Mmm," he said.

"I don't think I can make it. I'm going out of town."

Phil shook his head, informed me I had to be there. "I'm serious, this is mandatory. If he finds out you're not coming, he'll reschedule the whole goddamn thing."

"I've got these plans," I said.

"Tom, listen. The kid adores you. He's always talking about that trip to Chinatown, the pot stickers. Once a child vomits in your presence, he never forgets you."

"I'm flattered—"

"He wants to be an artist, he wants to make animated movies just like you."

I took a deep, tortured breath, wondered why I'd brought it up in the first place. "I'll see what I can do," I said.

"Do that. Or I may be forced to give him your phone number. You want eight-year-olds calling you up with guilt trips?"

I shook my head and we tipped back our beers. I found him the book he wanted to borrow. A critical look at the films of Stanley Kubrick. Still sitting, he turned it over in his hands, flipped through, and looked at some of the pictures. When he spoke again, his voice had slowed down, his tone had bottomed out.

"What's going on with Lindsey?"

I just looked at him.

"I realize the other night you were trying to tell me something. You were hedging."

"I'm not sure what you mean."

He leaned forward suddenly, his eyes intense, his face unshaven—and I felt like a trapped animal. A cinematographic subject.

"Let's cut the crap, Tom. Something's going on. It has been for weeks."

The ambiguity of these sentences touched down on me like a funnel cloud, sent the contents of my mind into a whirling chaos. Was he talking about his marriage or my affair?

"I haven't seen her for a while," I said.

"We were out together two days ago."

"I mean, in private. You know, we haven't talked in a while. Between work and Nile—"

"Well, trust me, she's gone plum loco. And it's not her period, because there aren't any tampon wrappers in the bathroom trash."

I recalled him telling me one time, over several rounds of beer, that she was a very light bleeder. But heavy on the premenstrual syndrome, heavy on the swelling of breasts. He thought I'd be interested in these facts about an old childhood friend.

"I've been thinking about what you were saying the other night. About Nile." He transferred his beer to his other hand, held the bottle by the neck, raised an eyebrow at me. "Will you relax?" he said.

I realized I was still sitting on the arm of the chair, and eased myself down into a cushiony embrace.

"For about two weeks now, Lindsey's been like a different person. Distant, cold, preoccupied with something, though she swears she isn't. Completely disinterested in sex. It started right around the time of that dinner party. That night, after everyone left, we had a fucking row about my inviting Nile."

He looked around the room, as if to be sure no one was sneaking up on us.

"A row," he repeated.

At this point, Mingus bolted across the room and skidded to a dead stop in front of the scratch post. He stared at it intently.

"What in the hell is he doing?"

"Phil, before you go any farther, I think you're misinterpreting what I said."

He stroked his chin, and I could hear the sound of fingers on stubble, like the nocturnal scraping of a tree branch over a windowpane. "The other night," he went on, "after Vesuvio, in the car, she was crying. We get home—now keep in mind, we haven't slept together in weeks—we get home and she attacks me. Tom, she fucked me until I saw stars."

This statement struck me physically, a blow to the head. Sound and sight violently obliterated. When I came to, Philip was placing his beer with a careful resoluteness on the coffee table.

"Now, what do you make of that?"

"I really don't know," I said.

We sat for a few moments in a graceless silence. My thoughts digressed. I remembered how Philip had opened his arms to me at the wedding, helped me land my job in San Francisco. Welcomed me into his home time and again, handed me drinks. For the first time, I considered confession. I almost told him it was me. The harmless childhood friend. I almost told him about everything he'd already lost.

"I realize you've got a conflict here," he finally said. "If she's confided something in you, I wouldn't expect you to tell me."

"Phil—"

He held up his hand. "Just do me one small favor. I'm leaving for New Zealand tomorrow. Could you try to fit her into your busy schedule? Make sure she's okay?"

I shrugged vaguely.

"I'm serious. I'm worried."

His voice was laced with tenderness; it was like poison to me. "Sure," I said. "No problem."

Turning away, I caught Mingus staring at me with an especially virulent disdain. I looked back at Phil, and his eyes, too, gleamed with a strange calculation. Blinked. And I thought I could hear the sound of the lids closing, opening. Like a couple of spy satellites, they seemed to be gathering clues. Taking pictures of enemy terrain.

———

The next evening, I was in the Persian Zam Zam Room. This was an establishment with certain rules. You ordered only martinis. You didn't sit at the tables after five o'clock. If the old bartender didn't like your look or demeanor, if he left you unattended, you got up politely and exited. These rules weren't posted anywhere. You learned them from experience or word of mouth. The ignorant were expelled. The chosen sat at the semicircular bar, washed in a crimson glow, drinking a cocktail which the proprietor had perfected over the course of three decades. It was about eight o'clock, the tables were empty, and the bar sparkled with graceful triangles of glass. A cold mist seemed to rise from the surface of each drink, as from a lake at dawn. Cozy and dark, with a couple of ogee arches and a wall painting of a guy strumming an oud, the place had been around since the 1940s. It was a gorgeous anachronism, belonging to a lost time, before the hippies and the homosexuals, before the old acerbic bartender's city fell to ruin. Here it was believed that men should order the drinks, and that women ceased to be women, in some fundamental way, with the extinction of evening gloves.

I was waiting for Lindsey.

She had called me that afternoon at work. She said she had something to tell me, though she didn't specify what it was. I had a few points of my own to make. Mainly, that our relationship had grown completely untenable. That Philip had the look of a detective in his eyes. And Nile—well, I had to admit there was something suspicious, something Machiavellian, in her dark pupils, but I'd seen something else too, however young and imperfect. I knew I had. And I'd felt it inside myself. The other night, after returning from Santa Cruz, we'd made love in her bedroom, and orgasm had been reached during the finale of Verdi's *Macbeth,* the sounds of consummated love synchronous with the climactic lamentations of Maria Callas and company. In the dreamy, hilarious moments after this event, I'd divined the strange fact that Nile and I could belong to each other. I'd felt I was seeing the blueprints for a new and providential future.

The bartender's stomach strained the buttons of a red vest. He placed my glass on the bar, lowered in a toothpicked olive, then poured out the contents of a silver tumbler. We'd never been formally introduced, but I thanked him by name. Bruno. Minutes passed. I kept an eye on the entrance. Haight Street, overrun by three generations of counterculture, was visible through red-tinted windows on the swinging doors, mystical portholes revealing a glimpse of a strange and dissolute future. I was into my second drink when she arrived. The murmur of the street rushed in, then withdrew. At the coat tree, Lindsey shed her suede jacket. She wore a gray turtleneck, tight and ribbed with vertical lines; dark slacks; shoes with heels high enough to make me feel short.

"Hi," she said casually, almost buoyantly. She kissed me on the cheek, eased onto the neighboring stool. "How are you?"

"Well . . ."

"Did you get a haircut?"

I nodded.

"It looks different. Turn your head."

Her fingers trailed over the back of my neck, and a cool thrill plunged the length of my spinal column.

"Do you have a new barber?"

"Yeah."

"Is it a woman?"

"Yeah."

"Is she a lesbian?"

"I suppose so."

"She uses a straight-edge razor?"

I couldn't see how this line of questioning was at all relevant, but I had the distinct impression of being maneuvered into something. Bruno slipped a napkin in front of her in the furtive style of a bribe. I was too preoccupied to remember my responsibilities.

"I'd like a martini," Lindsey finally said.

He remained standing before us, fixing me with a look of fatal reproof, then moved off.

"That was bad," she said. "You're on the blacklist."

She crossed her legs, lit a cigarette. It seemed to me her fingers were trembling.

"So," she said. "How's Nile?"

"That wasn't my idea. The other night."

"Oh, I know. That's got Nile written all over it. She's a bit theatrical, in case you haven't noticed. She used to play opera on the stereo when we made love. She liked to come in the final act."

I felt a subtle sting, the precise nature of which I couldn't identify. These words had to be sardonic, but there was no trace of anger in her face or voice. Her tone was more than congenial; it suggested an intimacy that was entirely uncomplicated.

"Does she still do that?" Lindsey asked.

"Do what?"

"Come during the final act."

"Do we have to talk about this?" I said.

"I don't see why we shouldn't."

"Well, do we have to have this kind of conversation?"

"What kind?"

"Passive-aggressive. Highly subtextual."

"You mean, postmodern."

"Whatever."

"I'm not being passive," Lindsey said, "or aggressive. I'm honestly curious. I feel a new bond with you now. We've both been with the same woman. I want to compare notes."

I nodded while I ate my olive.

"I mean, I have good taste, don't I?"

"I like her," I said. "We have a lot in common."

Lindsey laughed in a way that reminded me of her husband's nasal snort. "Okay . . . but . . . are you having good sex?"

"It's great," I said flatly.

"I believe it. You two are the best lovers I've ever had. Different, of course, but each superlative in your own way. She's a virtuoso when it comes to mouth and tongue, and you have an extremely profound phallic technique. For Nile, sex is high art. For you, it's religion. She's black and you're Catholic. It's an extremely erotic combination."

Bruno placed a glass in front of her, poured out her drink. It rested like a sculpture on the edge of her napkin. I handed him a five-dollar bill, and he displayed little desire to handle my money.

"A toast," Lindsey said, "to a perfect match, as they say in *Fiddler on the Roof*."

I didn't pick up my glass, but she clinked it anyway. She sipped, then bit off half of her olive.

"You two looked . . . just absolutely enamored of each other. I mean, really, like a couple of Parisians. Phil couldn't get over it. He's so proud of himself." She touched my leg momentarily, and I felt a reflexive surge in my groin. "You looked happy."

She waited, patiently, for confirmation of this conclusion.

"I like her," I repeated.

"That's all? You just like her?"

"I don't know."

"Phil was prepared to lay ten-to-one odds that you're in love."

I studied the bar, a jewel set against the mirrored wall. Someone approached the jukebox and triggered the groggy trumpet of Louis Armstrong. Behind the bar, Bruno mixed endless martinis, and beside the cash register, a younger version of him smiled from inside a silver frame. Dark-haired, dressed in a Navy uniform. On a shelf above the bar, a plastic model of a snarling fighter plane rested in the shadow of a bottle of Sheep Dip. I heard the first raspy line of the song: Mr. Armstrong wanted a kiss to build a dream on.

"Are you?" Lindsey said.

"Am I what?"

"Falling in love?"

"I don't know, Lindsey."

She gave a kind of smile. "Well, there's no rush. For the time being, you're getting laid in grand style."

"I know you're mad," I said. "I suppose you have a right to be—"

"I'm not mad, Tom. Honestly, I'm not. This is the best thing that could have happened. Really. I mean, I'm not going to deny that it shocked me at first. It was sort of like a cold shower. It's torture for a few minutes, but then it gets to be exhilarating."

She inhaled, relieved the cigarette of its ash, sipped her drink.

"I don't know what you expect from me, Lindsey."

"I don't expect anything."

"There isn't any point in suppressing your anger."

"I'm not angry," she said. "I'm grateful. I've been feeling really crazy lately. Uncertain about some things, and this really helped put it all in perspective."

"Uncertain . . . about what?"

She extinguished the cigarette. "It's not important anymore. What's important is, there's going to be change. You and I, we're going to leave the last eight months behind us. I'm going to work on my marriage, and you're going to fall in love. Phil and I are going to move, and you and I are going to forget about each other."

"What do you mean, 'move'?"

"We're moving to New York."

"What?"

"We're moving to New York."

"You hate New York."

"He's agreed to stop working abroad for a while."

"Lindsey, he was at my apartment last night. He didn't say anything about this."

"We decided this morning," she said, "at three A.M. We made love and I realized I do feel a lot for him. I just can't access the feelings because of you. And I want to give them a chance to flourish." She fingered the fragile stem of her glass. "He wants to have a baby. We're going to try and get his surgery reversed."

I looked at her for a while. Then I reached for my drink, which had lost its icy edge; it went down like medicine. There was a definite panic massing inside me. I remembered how, late one night, after one of the dinner parties on Russian Hill—the guests gone, Lindsey upstairs shedding her evening clothes— Philip had talked to me about his first marriage. After Zach had been born, he'd done something stupid. He'd allowed a urologic microsurgeon to excise his vasa deferentia. As he described, in gory detail, the post-operative bleeding and swelling of his testi-

cles, I'd felt nausea creeping through my insides; then a deep
sympathy as we discussed the foolhardiness of sacrifice; and finally
a ridiculous optimism and pride, as if his infertility, his symbolic
castration, was somehow a substantiation of my own sexual validity. I'd felt like I'd won some kind of election.

Now I watched his wife extract another cigarette from the
pack.

"Do you have to do that?" I said.

"What?"

"Smoke."

"I've told you," she said. "They're organic."

"Hemlock is organic, Lindsey."

"True enough." She placed her thumb on the striker wheel
of a silver butane lighter. Without a doubt, her hands were
shaking.

"I don't believe any of this," I said.

"Well, you've always had problems with faith."

"No one decides to move to New York at three in the
morning. You're just angry about Nile, and the truth is, you
have no right to be."

"Don't tell me what rights I have and don't have."

She turned away, and I could see that she was tired. Very
tired, maybe sick. We surrendered to silence. Lindsey smoked.
My eyes settled on her napkin. Given only to female patrons,
each bore the seal of Persian Aub Zam Zam: a drawing of two
Middle Eastern lovers sitting under a tree, the man holding out
his arms in a gesture of supplication; the woman, topless but for
an open vest, turned away from him. The words beneath them
read, COME FILL THE CUP, AND IN THE FIRES OF SPRING, THE
WINTER GARMENTS OF REPENTANCE FLING.

"You're lying," I said softly. "You're saying these things to
hurt me."

Her eyes closed, and an expression formed on her face which
suggested that this conversation wasn't going as planned. "I don't

want to hurt you. I never wanted to. I know I keep doing it and that's one reason why I'm leaving."

"Running away," I corrected.

"Call it whatever you want."

"That's what it is. You've done it before and it doesn't work, because it's an action rooted in denial and fear."

"It's going to work this time," she said. "Because we're both going to agree it's over. Completely. We don't talk anymore. We don't write letters or call on the phone."

"What?"

"We have to agree on that."

"Well, I don't agree. I don't know what the hell you're talking about. You don't ever want to talk to me or hear from me? What does that mean?"

She didn't answer.

"What are you going to tell Phil? What's the explanation for a falling-out that's that severe?"

"When we get resettled," she said, "I'm going to tell him what happened."

I shut my eyes. The ground beneath my feet was eroding, washing away. I could feel myself losing balance, trying in vain to defy gravity. The song on the jukebox grew increasingly sad. It was a live recording, and as the trumpet solo ended, an audience which had parted long ago applauded again together. But it was only a record, a document. Like the model of the fighter plane, the photo of Bruno beside the cash register. Artifacts of a time which cried to move again and never would.

"The last eight months have been a mistake," she said. "A bad one."

"Don't say that."

There was a long silence. The cigarette burned unchecked in her hand, ashes scattering on the surface of the bar. I removed it from her fingers and pushed it into the ashtray. Then I reached up to touch her face. Lindsey's eyelids fluttered closed, and a tear escaped from inside. Leaning forward, I cradled my hand around the back of her neck. I kissed her gently, and when I felt her lips respond, it seemed I could feel the truth changing and maturing. I saw everything now with a sharpened sight. Nile was nothing but a place to hide; she was no more real than Philip. This was our reality. Irreplaceable, unspeakably beautiful. I remembered what I'd never forgotten. I loved her. Flooding with fear, I told her so.

"Did you hear me?" I asked.

A form entered our peripheral vision. It was Bruno. With an expression that was final and unyielding, he confiscated our glasses.

"I need these seats," he said.

"I apologize," I said.

"There's no lovemaking in here. This isn't a parlor house."

Lindsey had already dismounted from the stool and was heading for the coat tree. By the time I reached her, she was halfway into her jacket.

"Don't call me," she said. "I can't see you anymore. I've made up my mind. When I'm with you, I lose perspective."

"You've got it backwards, Lindsey. This is what's real."

She had her face angled to the floor. I brushed her hair back, and her cheeks were wet, shining in the reddish glow.

"I love you," I said.

"You're wrong about that. It's not love."

"It is, Lindsey."

"It's not, okay? For either of us. It's something else. Something very old and tangled. We're wrapped up together, but we're not in love. Not in any pure sense."

A cool tremor ran through me; when I spoke again, my voice was shaking. "You said it the other day. You meant it, I know you did."

"You can only make believe for so long, Tom. You can deceive yourself the longest, but eventually something happens. Something that forces you to see things as they are."

The look on her face was strangely new. Composed of feel-

ings I couldn't name and which terrified me for their sheer in-
scrutability. Suddenly, all around me, I could feel a strange
imminence. Like the thickening of clouds, the light of the sun
dimming, a cool climatic change. Something spotting my mind,
like the first heavy raindrops of a summer storm.

"What are you talking about?"

"Nothing," she said.

She tried to move, but I held her by the arm.

"What are you talking about?"

"Let me go."

These words were loud enough to be overheard. The song,
I realized, was over, though I couldn't remember it ending; and
there was a new silence in the room, heavy and voyeuristic. I
let go of Lindsey's arm, and she leaned back against the wall as
if she were winded or dizzy, the jacket hanging from one side
of her body. We stood there for a good thirty seconds. The same
song started up again. Finally, she looked at me with a kind of
exhausted surrender. She pulled the hair back from her face, and
by this action appeared to be stripping herself naked, in order to
show me everything. Every wound that had ever healed and
scarred, every one that was fresh and bleeding. I felt I'd been
involved in all of them, that I'd inflicted or cleansed every single
one. My heart was racing now, my eyes were stinging. For some
reason I thought of my brother, speeding west, across a desert
swimming with false images.

"You look sick," I said.

"I am." Her voice was a whisper, like leaves stirred by the
wind, like blades of grass touching. "I've been throwing up. In
the mornings."

As she spoke these words, all sound collapsed into a uniform
murmur. In the distance I heard the trumpet of Louis Armstrong,
ancient and plaintive. Leaning her head back against the wall,
Lindsey closed her eyes and began to cry. Silently. All at once,
everything made an impossible miraculous sense. What a strange
sensation I felt then. A weird vertigo. The borders of the past

and the present growing indistinct. Merging. Like some single-celled organism rejoining its divided self. It seemed I'd already known. It seemed I'd always known. She had missed her period—and the thing eclipsing it was ours.

PART TWO

11 / Brother.

From the very beginning, the word rang hollow and mean-ingless in my head. But he was—fruit of my mother's womb. Her last creation and sacrifice. A boy whose birthday would always fall, in relentless synchronization, on the anniversary of her death . . . My father had remarried quickly and without fanfare. An "actress" named Jane, who starred in shows at the Candlewood Playhouse. Years earlier, she'd had a chorus role on Broadway, in the short-lived production of *The Girl Who Came to Dinner,* starring Jose Ferrer and Florence Henderson. I despised her; and upon seeing her in the local production of *Show Boat,* developed a violent distaste for the musical, for the idea of shout-ing one's innermost secrets to anyone within earshot. Even at twelve, I could sense her fear of me, the certainty of her own inadequacy. In a world which had proved me utterly powerless, she was the one thing at my mercy. She treated me like her own son—and waited patiently for reciprocity which never came. Even on nights when I was starved for an embrace and found myself in hers, I never returned her desperate love. Never closed my arms around her. Only lived a few moments in un-faithful warmth, and surrendered to illusion.

No, she would never be my mother.

But Matthew . . . still a baby . . . too young to question . . . to remember.

One night, my father and his new wife sat me down in the living room, and while my brother lay upstairs, in the crib which had been mine—forgotten for years in the attic, like Rapunzel's inescapable spinning wheel—they spoke to me of the power of the truth, the dangers it could pose. In her melodic voice, my stepmother told me I'd suffered a terrible loss. But I'd had a foundation with my mother. A life with her. It had been cut short, but it was a life, and I had memories of her love for me. What did Matthew have? Not a single memory. If we were to tell him what had happened, no matter what we said, he'd always feel responsible. And for a young boy, a little boy, that feeling could be devastating. It would be a long time before he could understand. Until then, it was up to us to give him as real a family as he could possibly have.

"I want to be his mother," she said. "His real, true mother."

My father's eyes rose slowly from the floor, eyes that had once been an incomparable blue. Clear and stunning as the tropical water in glossy pictures from *National Geographic*. Tiny light-and-dark specks in the rings of the pupils, like splashes from a diver's impact. That diver, I imagined, had been my mother; and now the blueness was growing dull, hardening into a cold gray, and it seemed he was locking her away there. That she was something freezing in the ice of his mind.

"Sometimes," he said, "sometimes hiding the truth is the only thing to do."

———

At six, he is morose and silent. Dark-haired and dark-eyed. Obsessed with the catacombs in Rome. Drawing at school pictures of our mummified ancestors transplanted into the walls of our basement. Seeking out small dark places himself (coffin-like, womb-like) to hide in.

December.

The lake behind our house icing over. Flurries swirling out of a blank sky, while downstairs, my father shouts at Jane. The Johnny Walker Red is missing. The entire bottle. A thing not easily misplaced. From my bed, I see Matthew heading for the attic staircase. The definitive creak of the third step. Climbing. Disappearing. A minute later, my father's head pokes into my room, asking politely for information. The whereabouts of the liquor, the whereabouts of my brother. I consider covering for him, then locating him upstairs, exhuming him from an empty cedar box. I, a teenage diplomat, with the power to broker peace. Instead, lethargically, I point to the ceiling . . . My father's weight hitting that third stair. Matthew squealing, setting my flesh crawling. Carried down two flights of stairs to the liquor cabinet. The scene of the crime. I walk out to the landing, my book in hand. Listen to my father's interrogation through the hail of my brother's screams. Jane's voice, like the cry of a bird lost in a storm. I descend, and turn the corner into the living room. My stepmother crying and my father telling her not to touch him. Not to touch the boy on the floor, their son, whose nose is streaming blood, until he provides an answer. Asks again: *Do you have an answer?* And I watch my brother, quiet now, clamber to his feet. Tearless. Blood pooling in his hand, he walks toward the sofa, as if to the bottle's hiding place. Reaches out— and paints a red streak across the white wall.

12 / I called in sick, and spent a day just walking. I walked through Golden Gate Park. Past the museums and the stables; through a garden blooming with roses; beside the lake where people were sailing miniature boats. At Ocean Beach, the fog had yet to lift. Everything was shades of gray. I watched pelicans feeding, pirouetting above the water, and performing uncanny vertical dives. The ocean seemed to be pulling them down, swallowing their bodies with a kind of lustful hunger. Farther north, it smashed against the offshore rocks, as if in the hope of breaking them to pieces. There was nothing romantic about the ocean today. It was showing its power and its age. I sat on the sand, against the concrete wall which ran the length of the beach, at times without another human soul in sight.

The night before, we had stood on Haight Street, emotion urging us into the back of a cab, where I took her hand and met the cold obstacle of her wedding ring. Her house was dark and empty. Upstairs, Philip's heirloom grandfather clock announced the half hour. Lindsey snapped on a light, and the shadow of the stuffed albatross leaped to life against the wall and ceiling, giving the momentary illusion of startled flight. Philip was well on his way to New Zealand by now, and I remembered his words of the previous evening. *Fit her into your busy schedule. Make sure she's okay.* I watched Lindsey pull the curtains closed, her eyes meeting mine and moving away. I followed her upstairs. Wordlessly, I removed my clothing; and then hers. The bed was unmade and I knew the sheets hadn't been changed. I thought I could smell Philip's musky odor on the pillows . . . In the morning, she rose suddenly, crossed to the bathroom, closed the door. A few seconds later, I heard her dry-heaving. Standing naked at the door, I listened to her throw up miserably, cough, and spit.

"Are you all right?"

"I'm fine," she said, her voice artificially steady.

"Do you . . . need anything? I mean, can I do anything?"

Another pause.

"Make some coffee."

I dressed in last night's clothes, which smelled faintly of cigarette smoke. In the kitchen, I poured some beans into the grinder; the sound of its motor, of the blade chopping and tearing, was loud and barbaric. I measured the coffee into the French press, filled the teakettle with water, set it on the stove. It was a little after seven. No sun, a chill in the house. I sat at the table while the coffee steeped. I poured myself some, and held the warm mug in two hands. When Lindsey came downstairs, she was fully dressed. Jeans and a sweater. Hair wet. She sat down across from me, and we waited for something to happen.

"I've been for the test and the counseling," she said at last, her voice slow and husky. "The appointment's on Saturday. In the morning. I need you to be there."

For a moment, I looked at her with a total lack of comprehension. She'd made an appointment, reached a decision, before she'd even told me. I thought about standing up and leaving without a word. Leaving her alone. Instead, I glanced at my wrist, which was lacking its watch. I told her I'd left it upstairs. In her room, I felt like an intruder. I checked the bedside table, the floor, the tangled covers of the bed; and as the scope of the search grew wider—to include the top of her dressing table, littered with jewelry, and the bathroom where beads of water still clung to the shower door and ran down its glass pane like tears—I felt a childish fear swelling. Something irreplaceable lost. A mistake which could not be rectified, no matter what I did.

"You find it?" she asked, still in the same place at the table, a cup of coffee in her hands.

"I just remembered . . . I didn't wear it."

I sat back down. The radio was humming, almost inaudibly, with the mellow voice of some public broadcaster. Lindsey held her mug near her mouth; fine wisps of steam snaked up from inside.

"So you'll be moving to New York?" I said.

She nodded.

"You don't have to. I mean, I'm sure I'll leave in any event."

"What about your job?"

"I hate my job. I mean, what am I doing on that show? Fucking Christian propaganda. If this country ever swings to the left, I could be jailed for working on that shit."

We sat in silence. On the radio, they were talking to the ten-year-old winner of the National Spelling Bee—a girl from Georgia with an accent, tender and soothing, like the smell of some beautiful flower.

"Where will you go?" Lindsey asked.

"I don't know. Portland, maybe. I have a friend who works for Will Vinton. You know, I never liked San Francisco that much. It's too gray."

"It's always gray in Portland," she said. "It rains there."

I looked again at my naked wrist. "Should I call in sick?"

"No." A fleeting, appreciative smile. "Saffron's coming over. She's going to take me out to Marin."

"Lindsey, we need to talk."

"No," she said. "There's nothing to talk about."

"I don't love her."

"It's okay if you do."

"I don't *love* her."

"She's not the problem, Tom. We are."

On the radio, they dared the girl to spell "pulchritudinous," and as she broke the word down into its component parts, I latched my fingers together, closed my eyes, and saw clearly.

Emptiness massing like fog. Obscuring the light of the future. The emptiness of a bed, of nights spent in someone else's arms. The emptiness of her insides, unburdened of me. The vague image of my brother rose out of this void. Unreal and tenuous. Waiting for shape. I walked out of the kitchen, through the dining room and the living room. I was halfway down the stairs, my throat and eyes aching, when I heard her call me. She stood at the top of the dark staircase. On the wall behind her, the albatross hovered, loyal and portentous.

"Will you be with me?" she said. "On Saturday?"

I gripped the banister and asked what time. Ten, she said. Ten-fifteen. Her body just a silhouette. No definition. No substance . . .

On the beach, the wind had picked up. A salty mist blew in with the waves and clung delicately to the lenses of my eyeglasses. The damp cold forced me inland, back into the park, and I wound up in the aquarium. In the dim halls, traversed by young families and an occasional couple, I felt cloaked. A shadowy figure traveling through oceanic realms. Peering into tiny segregated worlds, glowing with coral and the whirling bodies of psychedelic angel fish; darters with fins like plumage; camouflage artists blending into stone and sand. I watched the eerie rantings of the queen triggerfish, her lips uttering furious inaudible sentences; the slow motion of anemones, anchored to rocks, their arms waving gently in the water; a herd of sea horses, graceful amputees managing a pitiable beauty; a moon jelly, its transparent body rippling and undulating.

The aquarium was teeming with children.

They darted through the corridors, bold and brightly dressed. They clung to their parents, seemingly afraid of a darkness pulsing with strangers, or stared mesmerized through the tiny windows. A little girl kissed at a school of frail pink minnows, and they shied away in unison. An infant, held against a father's shoulder, slept oblivious, dreaming amorphous dreams. And farther on, there was a boy. Seven or eight years old, untethered to adults, he stood motionless in front of one tank. Seconds went by. A half a minute. He didn't move. I started toward him, approaching from behind. I stopped a foot away and peered over his shoulder. The fish under scrutiny was a specimen of concrete ugliness, floating immobile, thick and gray. A watery gargoyle with a jagged upper lip, two fangs which rose from its lower row of teeth like sharp stalagmites. It hovered at one end of the tank, above a chunk of dull coral, and stared back at us with commanding hatred. I read the backlit information panel. *Native to South American waters . . . has been known to attack swimmers . . . too belligerent to share a tank with a member of its own species.*

The boy pulled away from the glass, his breath leaving a tender oval of condensation. He turned to me, unsurprised to find me at his shoulder. His eyes narrowed with a vague recognition. But I didn't know him.

"I feel bad for this one," he said.

Looking back to the tank, he tapped curiously on the glass. I almost reached out and pulled his fingers away, expecting the fish to dart at them with demonic vigor, with enough force to crack the barrier.

"They can't even give him a friend," he said. "But it's not his fault."

He appeared sure of this, though he spoke with the measured restraint of someone coming to new and unsettling conclusions.

"It's not his fault," he repeated.

"Why not?"

"I don't know," he said. "It just isn't. They should have left him where he was."

I looked at the tank, and then at the boy. He had strange upswept eyebrows, and a pink smoothness on his forearm, which appeared to be the result of a serious burn. Suddenly, as if snapping out of hypnosis, he scanned the immediate area, looking for someone.

"Where's my mom?" he asked, expecting an answer from me.

But already he had caught sight of her. At the end of the corridor, near a wall of glass, she was pointing to a somersaulting dolphin for the benefit of a younger child concealed in a stroller. Before he ran to her, caught by a wave of greenish-blue light, he looked once more with confusion into my eyes. As if he knew me. As if he couldn't quite figure out who I was.

———

Days passed with a strange languor. The feeling that I'd lain down in a field of poppies. My eyes, from time to time, opening. Slowly, mindlessly. Somewhere in the blind alleys of my brain, I understood what was happening, but the knowledge remained trapped and inaccessible. In the evening, the sun would disappear into the Pacific, and I carried with me the image of a black silhouette standing before the water, growing increasingly indistinct as night closed over the day. Like a long-lashed eyelid, the sky blinked—once, then again—before admitting darkness, deep and aphrodisiacal. In Nile's bedroom, it seemed the stereo was always playing opera. The bed always unmade. A stuffed white whale, wearing a sailor's cap and missing one beady eye, lay beached on silken shores. Candles burned on the windowsill; and the light, wrapping around the wrought-iron bars of the headboard, sent a warped shadow of parallel lines over the wall and ceiling. In this place, I tried to lose myself in illusion. But the more fiercely I gave to her and took from her, the more times I spoke her name, the more palpable an abstract presence became. Something that hovered, something that swallowed thought and emotion, and nullified them.

"Hey," Nile said. "Hey. Markham."

The smell of come and sweat slowly lifting. Warm breath on my face. My arm, stretched across her body, a marbleized streak.

"This is going to sound bad," she said. "Freudian."

I didn't look at her.

"I was thinking of my father. I mean, not the whole time,

but for a second. Because on Saturday mornings, I'd climb in bed, you know, with my parents and he'd hold me on his chest and roll back and forth. Crash me into the pillows and sheets and make these sounds, like thunder."

"Uh-huh."

"It was a dramatization . . . of life on the high seas."

Silence was filled by an orchestral crescendo. We were knee deep in another musical drama. Gaul, 50 B.C. Love triangles, jealous rage, moral myopia, funeral pyres. The same old story.

"Anyway," Nile went on, "the way we just made love reminded me of that."

"You're right. That is sick."

"I didn't say 'sick.' " She slid away. After a few seconds, she got up, padded naked over to the window. A candle burned on the sill. Her shadow loomed, pulsed on the ceiling.

"Aren't you cold?" I asked after a while.

"I like it."

"I didn't mean 'sick.' Come back here."

She shook her head.

"What are you being so oversensitive for?"

"What are you being so distant for?" She walked across the room, pulled on the shirt I'd recently removed. She half sat against her desk, waiting patiently for an answer.

"What?" I said.

"What. First of all, I spent half the afternoon cooking that soup. I bought the lobsters fresh. I killed them myself. That was the best damn lobster bisque I've ever made."

"It was incredible, Nile."

"You ate half a bowl."

"I just wasn't hungry."

"Then we have a nice deep fuck and you're all churlish afterward. 'Yeah, you're right, you're sick.' What the hell is that?"

"I'm sorry. I'll be nice."

"It's too late now. You've shattered my post–orgasmic calm."

She reached down into a ceramic ashtray, lifted out a half-smoked joint. Considered it for a moment, then put it back down. Crossed her arms.

"Are you angry with me?" she asked.

"Angry? What are you talking about?"

"You seem angry."

"I'm not."

"It's been different," she said. "Since that night."

"What night?"

"With Phil and Lindsey."

The sound of her name caused a sudden shift in my perception. For a moment, I could see invisible rays of light, the fullness of the spectrum.

"I have no problems with that night."

Nile stared at me.

"I'm not jealous," I said. "And I'm not angry."

We regarded each other for several seconds with a charged uncertainty. Then a reluctant smile fluttered across her lips. She pointed at the stereo.

"Lohengrin," I said.

"Does this sound like German?"

I listened more carefully. *"Dido and Aeneas."*

"Christ," she said.

"H.M.S. Pinafore."

"I'm not coming back over there until you make an intelligent guess."

"Aida. Leontyne Price."

"Oooh. Not bad."

"That's it?" I said, amazed.

"No, it's *Norma.* Maria Callas." She drifted back to the bed, straddled my waist. "There's a way you can make up for your bad attitude," she said. "My parents are going to be in town next week. I want you to come to dinner."

"Nile—"

"You owe me. Jerk. Anyway, it won't be that bad."

"I'll do something else," I said. "I'll do your laundry."

She gave a bestial sort of laugh, her one blatantly uncultured attribute. "You don't know the difference between bleach and fabric softener. You're coming."

I rolled over, and she dropped down in front of me, as if to block my escape.

"Promise," she said.

"All right, for God's sake."

She kissed me, rolled over onto her back. A few seconds elapsed. She looked like she was already having second thoughts.

"Now what?" I said.

"Well, there's just one thing. My dad, he's sort of pedantic."

"What does he teach again?"

"Intellectual history. It's sort of . . . religion, philosophy." Her fingers interlocked and made a wavy motion. "He's going to want to know where you stand on the question of original sin."

"Original what?"

"But you're a Catholic," Nile said, "so I'm sure you have some very developed ideas on the subject."

"Actually, I never resolved my thoughts on that issue."

"It's really very basic. Do you believe every person inherits the sin of Adam and we're all utterly helpless, or are people responsible for their own sins and able to emancipate themselves from God?"

"I don't even know if I believe in God," I said.

She nodded at me as if waiting for further elaboration. "It's not a big deal," she finally said. "Some dads want to know what you think about the designated-hitter debate; mine wants to know about original sin."

"There is no designated-hitter debate."

"Whatever," she said.

┗━━┛

That night, with Nile sleeping soundly against my back, I thought of Zach. I remembered a trip Lindsey and I had taken to Big Sur. We camped in an open field and, after sunset, lay in our sleeping bags outside the tent. Our voices, washed in the distant murmur of the ocean, rose skyward, lighting the signal fires of the constellations. It was the only time we'd spoken of a child. Elliptically, tenuously. What had she said? That Zach made her cry inside. That he made her think of me. Of everything I'd offered her in Chicago. Everything she'd run away from. My heart had pounded against the bars of my chest. Silence. Had either of us ever seen so many stars? The sky bent along its crystalline perimeter with the weight of them; and later, our eyes unerringly open, a giant rock entered the atmosphere, its minerals igniting as it sailed slowly and silently under the Milky Way. "Tom," she said in a whisper, and I didn't answer. I couldn't . . .

I slipped out of the bed. Nile murmured in her sleep. In the living room, I stood by the windows. Down below, North Beach was nearly deserted, its lights blown out like candle flames extinguished by the wind. I realized then the specificity of my hopes for the future. A little girl, named for some genius poet; a small low-key wedding; one of those houses up on Twin Peaks, built high above the city like the nest of an endangered bird; our very own bed, layered with flannel sheets, new and unadulterated. I felt a sudden, violent rush of nausea. The ignition of tears. That shooting star—our star, that meteor which even now was racing in an unknowable orbit—tracked over the black shade of memory. It was nothing. Nothing but a scratch on the emulsion of the night sky. On Saturday, we would drive across town, consoled by the humanity, the propriety of our legal rights. Some gleaming machine, in a matter of seconds, would safely empty her uterus of all fetal tissue. Then we would separate; and I knew we'd never come together again. The end—quantifiable and irreversible—was only days away. Time was passing, and I was doing

nothing. Nothing but waiting. Idly, vainly. Sitting in place. Staying in my place.

Why?

When, inside Lindsey, permanence was taking shape. A
wordless explanation. A justification made of flesh and blood.
Part of her wanted it. I was certain of this desire, and also terrified of it. *I love you,* she had said. And only now was I seeing
past the concrete meaning of those words. Like a planet, they
were surrounded by an atmosphere, a gravitational field. They
possessed an axis of rotation. They orbited an invisible star. How
I wanted to hold Lindsey's daughter in my arms. To witness the
mistakes of a child, and apply the salve of forgiveness.

━

Thursday night. In the underground dock of the Greyhound
terminal, I watched the bus empty itself of travelers. A copper-
skinned Native American: eyes clouded over, face tracked with
deep furrows, a wasted piece of land. Young mothers followed,
collections of children in tow. Then old women, struggling with
stubborn luggage. A Norman Bates type, wearing the haggard
look of the newly unemployed. Finally, a woman of higher so-
cioeconomic status, who wanted to know where she could file
her complaints. The bus driver, a tall black man with a walrus-
tusk mustache, stared at her dispassionately while the illustrated
dog on the side of the coach attacked from the rear, leaping
vigorously at her jugular vein.

"Now you've let everyone off this bus," the woman was
saying, "without conducting a search, and I want to see your
superior officer."

"This ain't the armed forces, lady."

"I'm telling you," she said, "I had sixty dollars in Oakland.
Two twenties, a ten, and two fives."

"You got serial numbers?"

She eyed him suspiciously, as if this could be a step in the right direction. "How do you mean?"

"The serial numbers . . . of the allegedly stolen bills."

The entire bus visibly rocked as a giant of Southern stock, with a frizzy red beard and (I couldn't believe this) a Confederate baseball cap, thundered down the steps. The woman eyed him as he squeezed past, his mass seeming to bend the very fabric of adjoining space. A couple of kids, unloading the baggage, cracked a joke about Rosa Parks. Chalk one up for their history teacher.

"Now what were you saying?" the woman went on. "About serial numbers?"

"For the love of St. Peter," the driver said.

I scanned the windows, the bus apparently empty. Then movement toward the rear. A head rising into sight like a periscope—a girl surveying the interior—then dropping down again. Another bus, at the far end of the subterranean cavity, gave its horn a warning blast and started backing up. I leaned against a pole and waited. Meanwhile, the plaintiff—fiftyish, possibly a suburban divorcée on a belated voyage of self-discovery—was advised to search the coach before the custodial crew arrived. Stubbornly, she reboarded and worked her way toward the back. Body popping up in successive windows, like a target in a shooting gallery, she finally reached the spot where the girl's head had surfaced. Looked down and visibly blanched. A momentary paralysis. Then she turned away and once again disembarked. Holding a compact before her face, she checked her makeup in the post-apocalyptic light.

"I've been driving these buses for twenty years," someone shouted. "Don't tell me I stop in Elkhorn. I've never even heard of Elkhorn."

Back in the window, the girl stood up, wiped her mouth. Then my brother, holding a hand to his forehead as if testing for fever. He kissed her passionately and strode up the aisle; she followed, opening a stick of gum. As they came down the steps, I was shocked by how old he looked. His hair, cut severely short, was bleached blond. He wore a weathered, calculating look, and a T-shirt with the "Phillies Cigar" logo peeling away like a decal on an aging plastic model. The girl was a definite finalist in the Humbert Humbert Love Object Competition. Hair pulled back with candy-colored barrettes; a skin-tight top ending just below the rib cage, hugging formative breasts and laying bare a pierced navel.

They stepped over to the baggage and the girl rooted around for something; Matthew had only the backpack slung over his shoulder. The woman, who had relocated the driver, led him back to the scene of the crime. She crossed her arms as he cleared his throat.

"You kids know anything about sixty dollars?"

My brother shook his head.

"You want to waive your right to unconstitutional search and seizure?"

"Fuck, no," my brother said.

The driver shrugged and walked away. Sighting me, Matthew gave a military salute and started over, leaving the girl to manage the transport of a huge cylindrical bag. The woman, victim of the ways of the bus, was muttering to her imaginary lawyer.

"That bitch," Matthew said to me, "hasn't shut up since Cheyenne, Wyoming." He batted his eyelashes, slipped into an irrelevant Southern belle accent. "Ah grew up on a smaaall cotton *plan*tation in Macon, Ala*b*ama. Of course, by *they*-en, slavery had been *long* abolished. But mah *gran*daddy was a real forward thinkah. He bought *stock,* you know, in the undah-ground *rail*road. That was his *claim* to *fame.* He called me Peach Pie and I was *they*-ah at his death bed. Along with all those who had stayed—" he clasped a hand to his chest—"in voluntary servitooood."

The girl struggled up to us, and let the bag drop to the ground with a thud. "Fucking hair curlers," she said.

We all stood surveying each other; a bus, bound for the

nation's capital, swung by, its headlights flashing like an aurora behind my brother's head.

I extended a hand to his companion. "I'm Tom. Matt's brother."

"Dolphin," she said, shaking firmly. "Matt's chiropractor."

———

In the car, they both sat in the back. I could see Matthew in the rearview mirror, and I was shocked again by the fact of his maturity. Deeply unnerved by something around the eyes which was undeniably my mother's, which seemed to have appeared only since the last time I'd seen him, a year and a half earlier. This change was subtle, but the myriad others were not. He'd always been distant and solitary, so incommunicative Jane had once taken him to New York City to have tests conducted on his ears and vocal cords. Now, with his arm around a girl he'd picked up two thousand miles from home, he talked ceaselessly about his journey. An epic travelogue peppered with random quotations and puns, delivered at breakneck speed with an occasionally spooky lyricism. He talked about America's highway system. Circulatory. Great asphalt veins. Carrying life. Never resting. Cars like cells, both healthy and diseased. Rushing to heal the nation's wounds or slowly eating away at it. Killing it. How beautiful the gracious die in amber waves of pain . . .

"The bus is real," he said, breaking out a cigarette. "It's like a moving biosphere. You know, that scientific place where you go in and you never come out? I mean, they let you off the bus, but only to eat at predetermined locations, only to walk around bus *terminals*. Are you getting what I'm saying? It's not an actual kind of freedom, it's not a Jeffersonian freedom, because you're always *linked* to the bus. You have no life out*side* of the bus. Have you seen *Ben Hur?*"

"Ben who?" Dolphin said.

"Not you. Tom, have you seen it?"

I glanced in the mirror, met his eyes for a moment. "I have, yeah."

"You know that scene where the slaves are rowing the boat? The bus is like that. Except there are no oars."

Dolphin leaned forward between the bucket seats, chewing tropical bubble gum. I cracked my window. "Hang a right on Van Ness," she said.

I looked at her.

"I mean, if you don't mind," she said. "Dropping me off at my house."

"Your house."

"Yeah, you know, home sweet home?"

In the back, my brother was drawing seriously, obliviously, on the cigarette. I turned up Van Ness, and Dolphin lingered at my shoulder. She latched her fingers together over the gearshift and explained, while methodically cracking her knuckles, that she was a California native. She'd been in Utah visiting her aunt—walking around one day, trying to score some weed, which in Salt Lake City was like trying to find a Komodo dragon in Siberia—when she saw Matt sitting on the ground, against a wall engraved with wisdom from the Book of Mormon. She asked him what he was reading about and he showed her the cover of his paperback: a disembodied eyeball floating in a smoky mist. *The Story of the Eye,* by Georges Bataille. The death of God, he said, the dark side of the erotic. He got her stoned and they took it from there.

"Yeah, the bus," Dolphin said. "I had a plane ticket back here, but it's like why fly when you can experience life from a new perspective. I mean, when you can discover things about people. Like I talked to this woman who accidentally killed her baby. They had no heat in their apartment, so she turned the stove on. A gas stove. Fell asleep, left it on all night. The next morning, bam, the baby was dead in its crib."

"Crib death," my brother offered, surprisingly concise.

I glanced in the rearview mirror. He was staring out the window, the streetlights dousing him with violet fluorescence.

"There's tragedy on the bus," Dolphin said.

I heard the slow inflation of a bubble, then its miniature explosion. A warm breeze of masticated fruit.

———

Several minutes later, we came to rest in front of a Victorian palace in Presidio Heights. Three stories. Central porch, balcony, and pediment. Arched windows, balustrades. Two cypress trees standing like sentries in the garden.

"Your dad's, like, the gardener for this place?" my brother said.

"Fuck you."

"Just kidding, just kidding." He exited the car, ran around to her side, opened the door valet-style.

"Thanks for the lift," she said to me. "Can I ask you, though, were you really in Vietnam?"

"In what?"

"Come on," Matthew said, pulling her by her shirt; she waved as she wheeled away. "You want him to have a flashback?" my brother said.

I switched on the radio, considered this girl's subtraction from the population of the car. Like a departing lover, she would take with her the items she rightly owned—in this case, conversation and the pretense of normalcy. After the phone call, I'd figured she would be a vagabond, at the mercy of my hospitality; in a way, I'd been counting on it. Now she fumbled with the keys to her parents' mansion, while my brother's hands explored her from the rear. She finally got the door open, dragged her bag over the threshold into warm yellow light. Kissed him. Then Matthew started back. Jogging. Doing one graceful turn to marvel at the grandeur of the house, the syncopated rhythm of his footsteps audible in the neighborhood's lavish silence. At any moment, I expected him to break into a musical number.

"Gag me with a silver spoon," he said, diving into the passenger seat. "Her dad's a real estate magnet."

"Mag*nate*," I said. I eased us downhill, making for more picayune districts.

"Do I know how to snag 'em? Smart, rich, fashionable, healthy, wealthy, wise, *moneyed*." He counted these points off, using two hands. "And the clincher is, she loves, and I mean *loves,* to perform fellatio. She loves to swallow, she loves the taste of it."

"First of all, will you slow down?" I told him. "For starters, just slow down."

"Why does everyone keep telling me to slow down? But maybe you're right. I should linger on the details."

"Second of all, I don't want to hear any more about this girl's sexuality."

"Why not?"

"Because she's fifteen."

"Sixteen," he said. "Sixteen. But numbers don't mean anything. The calendar's arbitrary. Have you ever asked yourself why we still mark the passage of time with the names of Roman emperors? Julius, Augustus, Septimus, Octavius, Novembrius. Right now, we're under Roman rule and we don't even know it. Now, that's the mark of an empire. Anyway, my willie is like in a coma right now—"

"Let's talk about something else."

"Why?"

"I told you why."

"You know what your problem is?" he said. "You're repressed. You know what the first sentence of *Story of the Eye* is?" He took a breath. " 'I grew up very much alone, and as far back as I recall, I was frightened of anything sexual.' Alone and frightened. Well, that's not going to be me anymore. I'm out of that fucking house and I'm never going back. I mean, look at me. I'm gone for a week and I've seen the world. I've stood in the sun and seen a thunderstorm, an entire storm, on the horizon. I ate a hamburger made of buffalo meat, and you should have seen the shit I took the next day. I got my first blow job, man, on the shores of the Great Salt Lake. Every time I see salt for the rest of my life, I'll remember that. And salt is everywhere, every time you turn around, there's a salt shaker. Now I find out her dad is Donald Trump. It's like my life is charmed. Like I'm leading a charmed life all of a sudden."

He reached into the backseat, pulled a tattered notebook and a pen from his backpack. Scribbled something down in the inconstant glow of the streetlights.

"I'm writing a novel," he said. "It's going to be a classic of pornographic literature. Opening lines are important, so I'm keeping a list of opening lines. What do you think of this? 'There was a moment when I realized my life was charmed, having understood, only after the fact, that I'd come in the mouth of the aristocracy.'"

I glanced over at him, simultaneously stepping on the gas pedal to push us up a forty-five-degree hill. The car labored as if trying to break free of Earth's gravitational pull; Matthew waited earnestly for my review, eyes blinking out some frenzied code.

"I like it," I managed. "I like the rhythm."

We crested the hill and he shifted onto his knees, to see out the back window. A sprawling view of the bay and the bridge.

"God, that's beautiful," he said. "This is the most beautiful place I've ever seen."

⎣⎯⎯⎦

It was nearly midnight when we got home. I set him up in the extra room, sparsely furnished with a futon, a pole lamp, a desk, and a bookcase. A tapestry hung on one wall, an old sunburst clock on the other, non-functional. My brother surveyed the place while I lingered in the doorway, considered broaching serious topics. I watched him kneel down at the bookcase, filled mostly with histories of animation, books on technique and film theory. The bottom shelf, however, was a solid line of monographs: Bosch, Dali, Miro. He trailed his fingers lovingly over the spines, removed the one on Magritte.

"Are these your favorite artists?" he asked.

"Yeah; I suppose so."

He opened the cover, flipped through until he found the painting of the woman's face which doubles as a naked body, breasts for eyes, vagina for mouth. My brother stared at this for a long time.

"Do you draw like them? In your cartoons?"

"I don't make cartoons," I told him. "I use puppets. It's three-dimensional."

"Like *Gumby?* Like the California Raisins?"

"Sort of. More detailed than that. Speaking of work, I have to go there tomorrow."

He forced his gaze up from the image. A terrifying thing. A mouth incapable of speech, nakedness which cannot be covered. In his eyes, a sudden lucidity.

"Have you called Dad?" he asked.

I nodded. "I told him you'd called me but I didn't know where you were."

There was a long pause.

"I appreciate that, you know. I mean, I don't want you to think for a minute I plan to take advantage of your hospitality. This is a purely temporary situation. And you don't have to worry about me. I'm a hundred percent self-sufficient. I'll just be writing, hanging with Dolphin, looking for a job."

I nodded slowly. "We'll try this for a few days. Until you get your thoughts together."

"I won't forget this," he said. "I'm serious. My memory's photographic."

I fell into bed without washing up or removing my clothes. After midnight. I'd been sleeping poorly for days, taking prescription sedatives I'd borrowed from Tabitha at work. I swallowed one now with a sip of stale water, drifted into a dream which was an almost perfect clone of reality. Everything exactly as it should be, except for my estranged brother entering my room, sitting on the bed beside me, and informing me calmly that everything was all right, he'd called our father, who had agreed he could stay here indefinitely; Dad was putting the official documents in the mail. I snapped into consciousness, turned to where I thought I'd been looking, and Matthew was no longer there. The door was shut. It was one-thirty, and he was pacing on the other side of the wall. Frenetic movement punctuated by sudden outbursts of hushed speech.

What was wrong with him? What was he doing here?

I asked the same questions of myself and could find no suitable answers. Why wasn't I with her? It seemed that if I called her now, spoke to her in the midst of this darkness, I could convince her of many things. Surely she was awake—and like me, no matter how tightly she pulled her blankets up around her neck, unable to relieve herself of a mortal cold. Surely she was waiting. I picked up the phone, held the receiver in my hand until it started to beep. Dialed the first three digits of her phone number. Then felt the arrival of doubt. Gray and slow-moving, it threw my world back into shadow. My brother, by now, had left his room. I could hear him in the bathroom. Masturbating. Grunting roughly and then crying out, as if he were losing his balance on a steep and treacherous path. A flurry of panicked breath as he climaxed. I felt the steady throb of fear. Fear of Saturday and everything that would follow it, everything that wouldn't. Eventually, the television came on in the distance, a soft tinny murmur that lulled me to sleep.

13 / In the morning, I feel the urge to clean myself. Not in bath water, which will turn tepid and cloudy, but under the shower. Under a hot stream that will wash steadily over my body, wash away the invisible corrosion which has formed overnight. In the bathroom, I remove my underwear and regard myself in the mirror. Different somehow. Changed in some unquantifiable way. Or is it just fatigue? I step under the water and, feeling light-headed in the heat, kneel down on the floor of the tub. Wet warmth pours over me. I press my cheek against the cool ceramic tiles. Where is Lindsey now? Has that wound between her legs begun to heal? Is it possible that she hasn't moved? That she lies even now among the ruins of that farm, half naked, eyes at rest, but the history of her tears etched into her face? I imagine the grass around her dripping with morning dew; a spider climbing her leg, discovering that stroke of blood, turned now to a rusty red. I imagine myself in the place of my cousin. A safe dive from the top of a waterfall. Deep underwater breaths. Shame rises up from my stomach, hot and vulgar. Never. I will never take that dive.

⊔

I sat on the deck, in the shade of the wind-out umbrella. Watching the Paris house. Above me, a bumblebee floated under the umbrella, buzzing loudly. Lured by the painted flowers, he repeatedly attempted to draw pollen from the fraudulent stamens. His wings, from time to time, would give a sharp sound, like an electric shock, and I'd feel myself snap out of a reverie which had no color or substance. As if from a great distance, I heard our telephone. Then my mother calling my name. I understood all this, but I didn't get up. I wiped my forehead with the cold sweating glass which held my orange juice. I was about to drink when I noticed a gnat had drowned inside. The door behind me squeaked open.

"It's for you," my mother said. "The phone."

Inside, I picked up the receiver and heard someone chanting in a robotic falsetto: *"Please return the egg."*

"Hello?"

"Please return the egg," the voice repeated; and as if I were awakening from a long amnesia, primordial images and memories filtered back into my consciousness. A giant egg washed up on the coast of Japan . . . the miniature girls, intercessors from Monster Island . . . Godzilla breaking the misty surface of Tokyo Bay . . . a siren in the night, terrible footsteps, like the heart of the Earth pounding.

"Roland," I said.

His voice fading, my best friend started babbling in faux Japanese. In the background I could hear his mother's electric coffee grinder, so I knew he was home. Another epic family vacation had come to a close. I'd almost forgotten about him, and his voice seemed irrelevant somehow, part of some other invalidated life.

"The world must not know of this," he said. *"Promise to keep my secret."*

"Will you shut up for a minute?"

He said he had to see me. He had to sleep over, immediately. I could tell from his tone that he had something in his possession, something which his devotion to melodrama would allow him to discuss in only the most furtive of terms. With dead-calm gravity, he asked me if we had any soda bottles in the house.

"We've got soda," I said.

"Soda *bottles.*"

I said I couldn't be certain of this, and Roland informed me that I had to be. If I couldn't find any, I was to walk into town and buy one. A glass soda bottle with a long neck. We made plans, passing messages back and forth between our mothers, like a couple of translators. He reminded me once more about the soda bottle.

"Is that clear?" he asked.

"I've got it."

"Tom, I'm serious about this. The future of civilization—"

"Will you shut the hell up?" I said.

I hung up the phone and found my mother watching me from the counter. She didn't chastise me for using the word, only gave me a long, weighted stare, then lowered the top of the waffle iron.

"Would you like to warm up the syrup?" she asked.

I squeezed some Aunt Jemima into a silver pot, turned the burner on low. The radio played softly. A fan whirred in the corner. My mother was saying something about vegetables. Starting a vegetable garden. I poured the syrup into a small pitcher, positioned it next to my plate; my mother, according to diet, would eat hers plain, with just a few pieces of fruit on top. We sat down. Butter melted in the square wells of my waffle. I cut into it, and watched syrup flood the plate with a surreal lethargy.

"What's wrong?" Mom asked with a seriousness, a gentleness, that pierced me.

I looked up at her, at the strange angularity, the uncharted beauty, created by her new haircut. I tried to work up the strength to tell her. I knew what I'd seen—and yet I didn't. So how could I describe it? And if I did, what consequences would follow? Had I really done nothing but hide and listen? Had I really run away—and left her there?

"I'm sorry," I said, almost inaudibly.

"What, honey?"

"I said I'm sorry . . . that you can't have butter and syrup."

Her hand brushed over my forehead, through the hair above

my ear. Behind her, past the windows and beyond the lake, the tall grass swayed with a sad, daunted grace. It looked sentient somehow. As if it knew what I was hiding. As if it knew.

That morning, I began work at my father's office. Dusting the frames, cleaning the non-prescription glasses, washing the front window, which said "Colonial Opticians, Benjamin Markham, Optometrist." My father had painted the words himself, the Old English letters, black and gold, arching across the glass. Just inside the window, on a bed of velvet, rested his collection of antiques: from the nineteenth century, a folding lorgnette, its tortoise-shell handle long and intricately carved; from the twentieth, Grecian-spring Oxfords which folded together to look like a single lens, and several eccentric women's frames, dressed with tiny rhinestones and strokes of gold. In the mornings, the sun lit the window, and the shadows of the letters lay over the vintage fashions like a thin ghostly shawl.

The outside of the pane was filthy. I used a squeegee to soap the glass and wipe it dry. I stood on a stool to reach the top corners, sweating into my short-sleeved shirt. From his desk, my father looked up and gave me an okay sign. He wore his white coat and a gold name pin. An optometrist now, but once a member of the armed forces. I knew little of his service days. I knew that, in his off hours, he'd chased jackrabbits over the dusty infinity of the Lone Star State, pushing eighty in a buddy's old Jeep and still unable to keep pace. I knew that, every winter since those days, a recurrent frostbite reminded him of nights spent beneath the frigid hulls of our country's air power. A gun in his hands and orders to kill anything that didn't identify itself. There was only one photograph from this era, a black-and-white shot enclosed in one of our family albums above a clipped *Beetle Bailey* comic strip. My uniformed, sunglassed father standing in front of a sign for the Airmen's Club. Something about the picture had always haunted me. His youthful sternness, the way his blue eyes were darkened behind black lenses. Or perhaps it wasn't the photo at all, but the unseen things that lay outside it.

Back in the office, my sweat dried cold in the air conditioning. I sat on the bench beneath the mock eye chart that read, in ever-shrinking block letters, YOU ARE ATTRACTIVE, GENEROUS, WORLDLY, CREATIVE, AND, IF YOU BELIEVE ALL THIS, EXTREMELY EGOTISTICAL. At the desk, my father was leafing through a glossy catalog. He held it up and showed me a photo of a giant contact lens. Thin, weightless, and soft.

"This is the future," he said. "This is a revolution."

The phone rang, and his voice grew pliant with sympathy as he listened to a tale of ocular woe. The caller's voice buzzed like a fly in the receiver, elderly and womanly. From a small table crowded with magazines, President Nixon stared up at me, typewritten words tattooed on his red-shadowed face. *I want you to stonewall it plead Fifth Amendment cover-up or anything else.*

"Yes," Dad said, "that's a shame, but nothing we can't correct."

I stayed at the office until noon, glad to have something to do, something else to think about. When my father ran out of jobs, I sat by the window and read *The Lion, the Witch and the Wardrobe*. The whole time I kept an eye on the street, waiting for her to walk by. I imagined her looking in the window, sighting me, and waving casually. In her eyes I'd see that yesterday had been some kind of illusion. She'd be restored like the girl in my dream. The hands of the clock inched forward. Gradually, the angle of the sun betrayed the spotty job I'd done on the window. The shadow of my father's name and title evaporated. I moved into the back room and sat in the examination chair, surrounded by its spidery appendages. From there I could see Dad in the workshop, sorting through a box marked FRAGILE. I stepped up to the threshold of the workshop, where carpeting gave way to a painted cement floor.

"When's my next exam?" I asked him.

"Oh, in a year or so," he said absently. "Your vision's perfect. Twenty-twenty."

"I don't know," I said. "Things have been kind of blurry lately."

"What kinds of things? Things that are distant or things that are close?"

"I don't know. Everything, I guess."

He continued unpacking the box and sorting through its contents: his latest order of blanks, the lenses he received from some company in Hartford. Using the saw, he would now cut them to fit the patterns of his customers' frames. Like making keys, he said, to unlock the doors of distinction and clarity.

"Maybe you could give me an exam," I said.

"I can't right now. But soon."

Finally, he turned to me. His tie fixed to his shirt with a slender gold clip. His face freshly shaved and a tiny blood mark on the underside of his jaw.

"In the meantime," he said, "try not to walk into any telephone poles."

I returned to the examination chair, pressed my face into the olive-green upholstery. If only he would examine me, I wouldn't have to say anything at all. The room dark. My chin resting in a smooth plastic cup. The tiny beacon of his ophthalmoscope. Coming nearer, overtaking my vision. A brilliant serene blindness. My father's warm breath on my cheek. Surely as he gazed into the blackness of my pupil, he'd find it there. Burned into my cornea—a latent image on the emulsion of my eye. The truth of yesterday, revealed without a word.

⌞　　⌟

Walking home, I passed St. Edward's and saw children playing kickball and eating on the lawn in back. Lunchtime at Vacation

Bible School. In years past, this had been one of the most tedious experiences of my life; but what I would give now to lie back on the carpet and hear Sister Margaret strum a pleasant chord on her guitar. Since my First Communion, I'd lost all fervent interest in things religious, while Catherine Paris had gone on to join the Passion Players (landing the role of the Virgin Mary in the Nativity pageant) and the Children's Choir (singing a solo rendition of "Day by Day" which was deemed so stirring it became a regular feature of the 10:30 Folk Mass). Strange to think that, before Roland—when I was a greener boy and less political in my affections—Catherine had been my best friend. I'd feel ludicrous approaching her now. Nonetheless, I found myself following the path which ran along the side of the church, waving to Sister Margaret and marching right up to Catherine, who sat in the shade of a maple with the freckled redhead who'd backed up her story about the rapture. They looked up at me in perfect synchronization, right hands holding Thermos cups from identical Snow White lunch boxes.

"Can I talk to you for a minute?" I asked.

She took a dainty bite from an egg salad sandwich. "Go ahead."

"In private," I said softly.

The redhead's pink Thermos cup froze at the edge of her lips, her open mouth displaying a mash of Velveeta and Wonder Bread. I held my polite expression steady. Catherine chewed her food thoroughly, swallowed, and rose to her feet.

"If you touch me," she said, "I'll scream."

We walked in silence along the perimeter of the kickball diamond, and it became clear to me that, one way or another, I was destined to make a fool of myself. No doubt Catherine had agreed to talk to me for the express purpose of witnessing this event. Her blond hair was tied in pigtails and her stick-thin arms kept bouncing back and forth—touching in front of her, then behind her, then in front of her again—as if she were a device built on the principle of perpetual motion.

"I've decided to become a priest," she said suddenly.

"You can't be. You can't even be an altar boy."

"My mom said maybe by the time we're grown up, the Pope will let women be priests."

"I doubt it," I said.

"You doubt too much. Doubting Thomas."

I felt a surge of hostile energy, reminded myself I wasn't here to fight. There were more important things to talk about; the question was, how to bring them up. Catherine bent down, picked a white dandelion from the lawn, twirled it in her fingers as we walked.

"Do *you?*" she asked.

"Do I what?"

"Still want to be a priest?"

"No."

"Why not?"

"I don't know. I just don't."

"That's called a fall from grace," she said.

This had all the earmarks of being instigatory, yet her expression had softened. The sneer was gone.

"Is that why you're not here this summer? 'Cause you had a fall from grace?"

I shrugged. "I don't know. It's boring. I wanted more time to read."

"You're right," she said, a kind of pathos underscoring the words. "It is kind of boring."

Expelling a current of breath, she dispersed the fluffy head of the dandelion, and it was then—as the seeds scattered over the green lawn—that I found the resemblance. Not in the hair or the bee-stung lips or the front tooth pleasantly skewed, but in her eyes. Like Lindsey's, they curved up at the edges, a barely noticeable feline sweep.

"We saw the aspergillum the other day," she said.

"What?"

"It's the little baton the holy water gets sprinkled from. Father Coine showed us. There's a sponge inside the end, a sacred sponge. He let us shake it two times each. Don't you love it at Easter when the priest walks down the aisle shaking it over everyone? Don't you love that feeling when the water lands on your face?"

She'd closed her eyes, and when they opened again, there was something warm and hazy about them, something vaguely unnerving. I remembered that kiss in the coat closet of Miss Aloia's preschool; and it occurred to me that that incident still connected us, invisibly but indelibly, as certain animals of disparate species are connected by a common, long-forgotten ancestor.

"Guess what?" she said.

"What?"

"I'm going to your school this year."

"Mount Carmel?"

"No, dummy, Harvard. Of course Mount Carmel. I guess we'll be in the same class."

She went on to inform me that she actually read on a sixth-grade level. Her gaze drifted toward the sky, she quoted from *Charlotte's Web.* "It's my favorite book. E. B. White. He's my favorite author. What did you say you were reading?" I handed her *The Lion, the Witch and the Wardrobe.* Opening to my bookmark, she read the title of Chapter Thirteen. " 'Deep Magic from the Dawn of Time,' " she said, a dormant fondness stirring in her eyes.

"Is this your favorite book?" she asked.

"One of them."

"Guess what?"

"What?"

"Our favorite authors both have two initials in their names."

I raised an eyebrow.

"E. B. White. C. S. Lewis."

"Oh . . ."

"Remember when we were in preschool," she asked, "with Miss Aloia? It seems so long ago."

"How's your sister?" I finally said.

"My what?"

"Your sister."

"Oh, her. Bratty, as usual. She's been locked in her room since yesterday. Won't eat at the table. Keeps playing the same record over and over again. My mom says she won't put up with it much longer." She took a couple of sudden balletic steps forward. "I just can't wait till September," she said.

"September?"

"For school," Catherine said. "I can't wait to have a nun for a teacher. My mom says we'll probably carpool."

I just looked at her, and she smiled that old sweet smile, that wet mouth of hers reminding me of a bygone morning when our lips had met among the raincoats and rubbers of our peers. There was no chance of that mistake being repeated.

"You think it's possible," she said, "that the Pope will change his mind?"

"I've got to go," I told her. I started in the direction of her picnic spot, my only exit route. The redhead quickly averted her gaze.

"Pray for me," Catherine said.

I had no idea what that was supposed to mean.

━━━

A few hours later, I felt a surge of normalcy at the sight of the Mercedes. The car pulled up beside me, classical music bleeding through the sealed windows and an eruption of flowers in the middle of the front seat, obscuring Roland's face.

"How do you do?" Mrs. Harris said in her lilting aristocratic accent.

With two hands, she managed the flowers, arranged in a white vase. A bumblebee appeared, skipping over the petals, droning around her straight black hair, her high cheekbones. My father said there was Cherokee Indian in her, whether or not she wanted to admit it. Roland walked over to me, his Battleship game in hand.

"I'm glad your mom's feeling better," he said stiffly.

Shocked by his politeness, I was speechless for a moment. Mrs. Harris gave me a sympathetic nod and blinked her dark eyes, blowing at the bee, which had taken a liking to a tender yellow trumpet. Inside, she presented the flowers to my mother with the ceremonious formality of a visiting diplomat; and as soon as she'd left, her son became his old self again: bossy and verbose. We descended downstairs on the customary landslide of stories and descriptions ("The Taj Mahal," he kept saying, sounding freshly awestruck, as if he'd brought the place home and was gazing at it). Then he handed me a long narrow box, unwrapped and tied with a silky ribbon. This was my souvenir from Indonesia. Vigorously, Roland scratched his unruly head of hair, which, for an as-yet-undiagnosed reason, always smelled faintly of tobacco.

"God, it's fuckin' hot," he said. "Go ahead, open it."

I slid the ribbon off, removed the cover. Inside lay a long wooden stick, intricately carved. Upon closer inspection, I saw that it was made in the image of a dragon or snake, with fangs and a round hole at the mouth.

"What is it?" I asked, peering into its maw.

Roland took it in his hands. From a hidden storage space in the wood, he removed a pointy piece of metal, weighted at one end. Sliding this, end first, down the creature's throat, he lifted its rear end to his mouth and, taking a deep breath, sent the dart whistling into the wall of our den.

"Holy shit," I said.

"Yep, holy shit. It's an Indonesian blow gun. Hand-carved."

He pulled the dart from the wall, cleaned the tip. "These little jewels can puncture an artery, so don't shoot 'em at anyone you don't want to hurt."

"That's cool," I said. "Thanks."

It took me a few tries to get the dart to stick firm. Once I'd mastered it, I didn't want to stop, but when I turned to Roland, I found something impish still squirming behind his eyes. Wordlessly, he locked the door to the stairs. On the couch lay his Battleship game. He knelt before it, and the expression on his face—a flash of spirituality, as if he were kneeling before a tabernacle or at the foot of some shrine—suggested the imminence of miracles. I dropped down beside him. His hands rested devoutly on the lid, which featured a photograph of two smiling children, gleefully waging war.

"I've been in Canada," he said, "for the last two weeks, visiting my cousins. Every day I had to wake up and say the name of the day in French. *Lundi, mardi, mercredi,* fuck-a-flea. Instead of 'please,' I had to say *s'il vous plait.* A royal pain in the ass. A bunch of *merde,* as they say up there. You don't know what I went through. But, Tom, I'd do it all again for what's in this box."

A momentary pause.

"Do you know," he asked, "what's legal in Canada?"

I gave this some thought. "Killing a praying mantis?"

He shook his head. Then—very carefully and dramatically— he removed the lid and revealed a cache of fireworks: countless bottle rockets, long and lithe; jumping jacks and cherry bombs; strings of miniature dynamite wrapped in waxy paper. He picked up a small cylinder, the color of cardboard, about the size of a C battery.

"This little sucker is called an M-80," he explained. "It can blow off a human hand."

I stared in disbelief at this glorious stockpile of contraband— a treasure seemingly looted from the sunken destroyers and submarines of this naval board game. Unexpectedly, Roland's arm closed over my shoulders, and this gave me a rush of emotion. The horrible tightness in me slackened.

"How'd you get them?" I asked.

"My cousin's private stock."

"He gave them to you for free?"

"I won them on a dare," he said.

"What do you mean? What did you have to do?"

Roland removed his arm from my shoulder, ran a hand through his hair, and I got a whiff of that aroma, the smell of unsmoked cigarettes. "You know my cousin Simone?"

I nodded.

"I had to lick her snatch."

"Her what?"

"Her pussy," Roland said. "Her vagina."

I stared down at the fireworks, each of which carried a DAN-GER warning in red print. "How old is she?"

"Nine."

We stashed the box under my bed and, without another word about dares or genitalia, changed into swimming trunks. In the lake, as we swam and dove off each other's submerged shoulders, and the afternoon began to close down, I kept thinking of what he'd done in Canada.

"What was it like?" I asked him.

"What?"

"You know."

There was a long silence. Water dripped off our hair and trickled down our chests.

"Have you ever eaten an oyster on the half shell?"

I shook my head.

"You're lucky," he said. "Consider yourself lucky."

━┛

The promise of the fireworks buoyed me throughout the rest of the day. Thoughts of Lindsey receded, until she was something blurry and distant on the horizon, like the skyline of a city seen from afar. Our idea was to head for the open country of the field, the cover of the grass, after my parents had fallen asleep. Around ten-thirty, as the sound of my father's snoring became audible, we collected our gear: two flashlights, several books of matches, an empty Nehi bottle, and a backpack filled with a selection of fireworks. Outside, the air was cool, the sky clear and sparkling with stars. We walked along the lake path, our beams bobbing over matted crabgrass, over the scalloped imprints of sneakers left in the dirt—my footprints and Lindsey's, from yesterday and the day before. Along the lake, frogs were making gutteral conversation. A sliver of moon reclined above the Paris house, giving no light. The path ended, and the field waited just ahead. Dark and undivinable. Fireflies whirled through it, straining to light it from within, rising and swirling, coasting over the wheat-like tips of the grass. Inches away from my face, abdomens flickered into phosphorescent existence, then were lost again. A cool breeze blew toward us from distant territories, bearing the earthy, dewy smells of night. I glanced back at my house, a hulking shadow not far off. The Paris house, at the other end of this shore, kept roughly the same distance. We shone our beams into the grass, laying jagged tracks of light. The field seemed as dense as a jungle.

"You could get lost in there," I said.

Roland looked at me, not unconcerned; then he raised his eyes to the stars.

"Orient yourself," he said (last year, he'd had a brief flirtation with the Cub Scouts). "The Big Dipper. See it? The handle points to your house."

We parted the grass, stepped into it, and the stalks shuffled closed, surrounded us. We walked side by side, our flashlight beams blending together. Gradually, the sound of the frogs receded; the darkness grew blacker, and we soon realized that this was because the battery in Roland's flashlight was dying. We made a small clearing by stamping down the grass, then settled down in a tiny arena of yellowish light. I dug a hole in the ground, secured the Nehi bottle inside. Searching the sky for the Dipper, I found its invisible outline. I knew there were other images up there, hidden in the maze of the stars. A winged horse, a bull, a hunter. One of those bright specks was the North Star. One of them might be Venus, its hot, gaseous surface shimmering in the light of the sun.

"Okay," Roland said. "T minus thirty seconds."

He had a rocket positioned in the bottle. I moved closer to him, held the light while he fished for the matches. The grass whispered, swaying in a gentle wind. The fireflies flashed their silent beacons. Unwillingly, I thought of the spider house, the old McCready place, and shivered. The percussive rhythm of the crickets was all around us, relentless and repetitive. Like the panting breath of my cousin. The crickets sounded like that. Though I knew it was impossible, I thought I could hear Lindsey crying. I looked in the direction of the Paris house. At the edge of the field, their outdoor lantern gave off a diffused auroral glow.

My breath came heavier.

Time was passing, but yesterday refused to fade. Inside me, rage was cramping—the realization that I'd merely banished my feelings to some dark corner of myself. It seemed certain they would always be there, sleeping lightly, lying dormant. A fall from grace, Catherine had said. Was I falling? I turned again to the sky. Peaceful and unchanged for millennia. But weren't suns, even now, expiring? Going dim and gray, or exploding in volcanic colors? Weren't planets dying in the cold or burning in impossible heat? I watched Roland turn back the matchbook cover, then pause. Suddenly, he handed me the pack, and took the flashlight.

"You do the first one," he said.

The features of his face were barely visible. I couldn't tell if this was generosity or cowardice. I studied the matches, lined up in rows like a tiered choir, their red heads harmless now, but containing somehow the formula for heat and flame. I'd performed this action before, to light the Advent candles at Christ-mastime. Now, with the crickets growing louder, as if gathering around us in great curious numbers, I tore off a match. My heart raced as it had yesterday. The same pulsings of fear and anger and excitement. Yes, I'd felt that yesterday. I'd listened and stared, sickened and confused—but also fascinated.

"Let her rip," Roland said.

I saw him with clarity then. His face thin, his jaw angled and defined, his eyebrows dark. The flashlight's dim bulb aging him before my eyes, removing through some weird luminescent surgery the excess of childhood. I knew the same thing was happening to me. I didn't have to see it, I could feel it—a sensation which was epiphanic and frightening. I dragged the match through the friction strip. Sizzling, it flared up bright or-ange. To the end of the fuse, which ignited with a spitting sound; to the threshold of my lips, where the tiny flame warmed my face for a half moment before my breath extinguished it. We scurried back as the rocket lifted off with a whining hiss, arcing back toward the hills, over the heart of the field. It exploded distantly in the black sky, a brief flash of yellow white. Then its spine fell lazily back to Earth, tracing a fading orange line. Ro-land laughed and slapped me on the back, and I felt my fist close hard, as if I wanted to hit him. The smell of the match, of gunpowder, lingered in my nostrils. Above us, for a dizzy second, the stars swam around as if in a whirlpool, then shot back to their rightful places. They were like pins, I realized, holding the veil of this universe in place—and beyond them, out of sight, was a lighted place, which I could never return to.

⎣　　⎦

We got home just after midnight. The house dead quiet. My father still snoring. Everything the same as we had left it. Roland, who claimed to be suffering from jet lag, climbed into the top bunk. I settled in below him and, almost immediately, felt myself drifting away. On a peg which extended from the headboard, my rosary beads—milky white and phosphorescent—glowed weakly in the dark. I tried to reach up, to touch them. But my arm felt leaden. They were too far away. Too far . . . I dreamed of a woman, an opera singer holding a tragic and magnificent note. The sound echoing over itself and reproducing in great concentric movements. Suddenly, the glass of sleep was shattered. My eyes snapped open. Still night. But the sky stained an impossible crimson. The music louder than before. Had I left one dream only to fall immediately into another? Then I noticed, in the air, a smell reminiscent of dying matches; and I saw through the wailing voice's disguise. It wasn't human at all. It was mechanical. The firehouse siren. My body went cold and motionless with a fear I understood but couldn't name. The siren sang more softly, then built again to crescendo. Above me, the top bunk creaked.

"I can't do it," Roland murmured. "I can't say it in French."

"Roland . . ."

Another creak. A long dark pause. Then my best friend, awake now, swore under his breath. A single awestruck vulgarity. He slid down, hit the floor. In nothing but his white briefs, with the slow, awkward tread of an astronaut walking on the moon, he crossed the carpet; and as he approached the windows, his skin changed color to match the sky.

"Tom . . ."

"What?"

"Get over here."

"What do you mean?"

"Get over here. Now."

The light clicked on in the hallway, a thin line of white appearing at the base of my doorway. Feet hit the stairs and descended. My father. In a moment, my mother would open my door. I knew this as surely as I knew I was not dreaming.

For some reason, I didn't want her to find me in bed. For some reason, I wanted to be nearer to Roland. I swung my legs around, stood up. My eyes cleared the windowsill. I saw, but refused to believe. Hadn't we been out there minutes ago? Hadn't my eyes closed, my body surrendered to sleep only moments ago? Across the lake, the tall grass was drowning in light. A full half of it was on fire, and in the far northern corner, the general vicinity of the old McCready place, trees were burning like torches.

The bedroom door opened.

"Let's shut the windows," my mother said. "Move, Roland."

Turning to the clock on my desk, I hoped to find some kind of contradiction, some proof of unreality. I stared at the fluorescent hands, laboring to decode their phantom chronometry. Roland and I had returned at midnight. It was some other hour now. My mother closed both windows, and through the glass the flames were like a cinematic special effect. The burning bush, the pillar of fire in *The Ten Commandments*. Moving slowly in the direction of the Paris house. What did I want from her in those moments? A touch on the forehead. A kiss. Something to reassure me that our bond was unbreakable, no matter what happened. No matter what I did in life. But I received neither of these gestures. She was in some other mode now, distracted and efficient. She left the room to close the rest of the west-facing windows; and Roland and I, avoiding each other's eyes, considered the explanations. A spark which had lived long enough. A spent rocket left smoldering. The one we hadn't seen explode, the one we'd thought was a dud. "We didn't do this," he said, but there was no confidence in his voice; he spoke the words as if reading aloud from a textbook. Our town's only fire truck, blasting its horn, went racing up the lake road. As it pulled into the Paris driveway, its headlights spotted someone carrying an armful of belongings out the front door. Someone else was spraying the side of the house with a garden hose. The truck rolled over the lawn and into the tall grass. Red lights swirling. I closed my eyes and remembered the black, endless expanse of the field. The sulfurous ignition of a match. The Big Dipper pointing toward home.

14 / Day's end at the studio. About to head home when Lane summoned me into our little screening room, known lovingly as The Gas Chamber. "I want to show you something," he said, guiding me into the third row. He signaled into the projection room to our summer intern, Jonathan, and the screen flickered to life with the rough cut of the latest episode. The sound came up to speed. Davey and his dog, Goliath, trudging through the woods, decked out in hiking gear. Lost. Goliath sneezes, his olfactory sense of direction dulled by a head cold. Davey consults the compass. In close-up, the needle spins drunkenly, then the whole thing breaks open like a defective stopwatch. Davey's trademark biting of the lip. Goliath's eyes glancing from side to side. Cut to an omniscient aerial shot. Distant coyote howl. Then Goliath's oafish voice-over: *"We're in trouble now, Davey."*

In the back, the phone rang. Jonathan announced that it was Lane's wife, requesting that he pick up their daughter from her after-school art class. After some back-and-forth, Lane reached for the phone on the rear wall. Meanwhile, on the screen, dark clouds gathered. A fat raindrop splashing on the tip of Davey's nose. Low growl of thunder. This was my sequence.

"Why can't Adele get her?" Lane was saying. "What do we pay the girl for?"

I slumped in my seat, recalled a barbecue at his house last year. His daughter opening fire on the entire staff with a water Uzi. He told her he was glad she was challenging traditional gender roles, but there were certain tenets of nonviolence which had to be observed at public functions; she had responded to a nickname born in some private, unknowable context. I thought of Matthew. I'd called several times today and no one had answered. This morning, I'd found his door open, the lights on, the bed made as if it hadn't been slept in. The extra key I'd left on the dresser, gone. A note sitting on the blanket which read, in almost illegible uppercase letters, "GONE FISHIN."

"Raining?" Lane said. "No, it's only an animated storm."

A deafening clap of thunder. Then the skies open up. Our heroes start running. Low-angle tracking shot. Davey stumbles. Falls into close-up. Flash of lightning illuminates his terrified face.

"Go on without me, Goliath."

"Never, Davey. I'll never leave you."

Lane hung up, leaned forward in his seat.

"Look, Davey. A cave."

"A cave!" Davey cried in a pre-pubescent falsetto. *"God must have led us here!"*

The room lit up with a flash of lightning. The puppets ran for shelter, lashed by the relentless downpour. A few moments later, they were huddling, shivering in a rocky womb. *"It's all right, Goliath. God will protect us."*

Davey's eyes rise ambiguously skyward. Rumble of thunder. Fade to black.

The film stopped rolling. The low lights brightened. Lane, wearing a moth-eaten cardigan, turned to me, glowing with fatherly pride. I couldn't believe it, but his eyes were moist.

"That's gorgeous," he said. "Goddamn gorgeous."

"Thanks."

He nodded a few times, clasped his hands together. "That's what makes this show worth doing. The vision, the desire to elevate the material to a higher plane. The ability to turn shit into art."

"I think 'art' is putting it a little strongly."

"I'll stand by that classification," he said. "In any event, I don't want to see an erosion in the quality of your work, or in your commitment. So why don't you tell me what's going on."

"On?" I said.

"You show up to meetings without scripts. You're a day behind on your latest log sheet. You look like hell. And I believe you told Frank this afternoon to go take a light reading of his asshole."

I leaned back in my chair, paid some attention to the ceiling, like a kid in the principal's office. Lane waited patiently, and I remembered a drunken conversation at the AFI Animation Conference a few months earlier. After a talk by Chuck Jones and three highballs at a place called the Tuxedo Junction, I'd told him about Lindsey. That night Lane had seemed to me, for a few abstruse moments, my ideal father. Again now, he wore on his face an expression which was open, sincere, paternal.

"Do you remember that woman I told you about . . . at the AFI Conference?"

"The writer. Who was in El Salvador."

"She's pregnant," I said. "By me."

Lane nodded, as if considering a deep intellectual paradox. "I thought she was married."

I just looked at him.

"It's yours. You know that for a fact?"

I explained Philip's situation, and my employer performed a wormlike movement in his seat. In the back, the projector emitted a soft mechanical whine as the reels spun in reverse.

"What are you going to do?" he asked gently.

"She wants an abortion," I said. "What I mean is, she's going to have one. Tomorrow. And I'm going with her."

We sat in silence for a good half minute.

"You want the kid," he finally said.

"The point's moot."

"But you want it."

"Actually, no. Well, there are moments . . . the truth is, it's just not tenable."

He nodded slowly.

"I'm going to be fine in a few days," I said. "Deep down, I think it's all for the best."

Lane edged closer, touched my knee. "Listen," he said, "if you want someone to talk to, I have a friend—"

"It's all right," I said.

"Just listen to me. You may not be carrying the child, but the loss, the impact of the loss is every bit as real."

"I appreciate your concern, but I want to forget about this, not talk about it. I want to forget about her."

"That's natural, Tom, but don't deny your feelings. Your anger and your grief are real, and valid."

"Look," I said, "I'll get back on schedule if you just give me a few days."

"This isn't about work," he said.

"If you have to let me go, that's fine."

"Let you go? Don't be ridiculous."

I took a deep breath, and when I released it my body shuddered. I looked briefly into his face. He reached out and placed a heavy hand on my shoulder.

"I have to go home," I said.

I saw Tabitha on the way out; she was carrying a miniature church. "Hey, have a great weekend," she said. "Don't do anything I wouldn't do."

⌐

I returned home to the smell of marijuana and paint fumes. The stereo blasting the word of one of Seattle's lesser musical prophets. Passing the bathroom, I could hear the shower running, a girl's voice singing along. The door to the extra room stood open. Inside, all furniture had been herded into one corner, and my brother, wearing plastic goggles, was on one knee aiming a paint gun. He squeezed the trigger and a ball of red exploded across the opposing wall.

"What the hell are you doing?"

My words were sucked without a trace into the void of music. Striding into my bedroom, I crouched down at the stereo, where a pile of new CDs stood a foot tall. There was a strange power and clarity to the sound, and I realized my boxy speakers had been replaced with sleek black monoliths, each topped with a green Christmas bow. I stopped the CD player. Down the hall, from behind the bathroom door, a girl continued the verse in a lyrical rasp, unconcerned by the sudden disappearance of guitars and percussion.

"Sotto voce!" my brother shouted; then the dull click of the trigger, the sound of packed liquid splattering. I returned to his doorway, watched him lie on his belly. Take aim. When I spoke his name, he turned sharply, raised the goggles.

"Holy mackerel, where'd you come from?"

His eyes blinked wildly; the gun barrel drifted to the side of his head, and I felt my insides seize up. He relieved an itch above his ear.

"Would you watch where you're pointing that?"

"It's just paint," he said; a faint smile, inspired by my presumable concern for his safety.

"What are you doing?" I asked.

"Interior decoration." He rose to his knees, pointed to the wall at my left. I peered around the doorjamb to find a giant forgery of that Magritte painting—the naked face—presiding over the room like a graven image.

"I spent a long time on the pussy hair," he said. "That was the toughest part. What I'm doing now, I call this Rorschach Painting. I just got started, but I figure about fifty shots and there ought to be something up there that could really be analyzed, you know? Something that, like, rose from my subconscious and found expression through these bullets. I'm trying not to think too much while I fire."

Dolphin sidled up next to me, wrapped in a towel, combing out her wet hair. "Can I borrow some boxers?"

My brother didn't answer.

"Tom? Can I?"

I regarded her with disbelief: a long curl of wet hair had actually been placed into the corner of her mouth.

"Hey, where are you going?" Matthew asked.

I slammed the door of the bathroom behind me and pissed. When I opened it, he was standing right outside, paint gun in hand.

"I got you a present," he said. "Did you see them?"

I sat against the sink, nodded. "Not to be rude, but how'd you pay for them?"

"On the way out here, I worked for a while as an Okie. Met this guy named Joad who was in the uranium business."

Dolphin appeared in the doorway, still combing, still in the towel. "I like your apartment," she said. "I love your bedsheets. Snoopy and Charlie Brown. That's 'cause you're, like, a cartoonist, right?"

"Shut up," Matthew said. "I'm in the middle of a story."

"Why don't *you* shut up? You and your goddamn stories. They're all bullshit."

I watched my brother's eyes narrow to slits. His hand met the nape of Dolphin's neck and rested there lightly as she worked on a knot. "You think you know what's real?" he said. "What's real and what isn't?"

"Yeah, I know what's real. You're 'real' full of shit, that's what's fucking real."

She continued brushing, wincing and swearing under her breath. Suddenly, her face registered a deeper pain. A second later, the towel had fallen away, and my brother had her naked front pressed against the wall, the paint gun at the back of her head.

"That's it," I said. "Give me that thing."

"I'm just trying to prove a point."

"Give it to me."

"She thinks she knows what's real. Living in a fucking palace, a new car for Christmas."

"I'm getting a Jag," she mumbled into the plaster. "From Santa."

"Matthew, give it to me now."

"It's just—" he said. "It's just, I didn't know I was fucking such a realist—"

He glanced back at me, and I thought I could see true irrationality in his eyes, a total lack of control. I imagined his finger squeezing the trigger, the paint ball bursting against the back of Dolphin's head. An evening spent in the emergency room. Some real-estate-baron father to answer to. Probable suspicion of statutory rape.

"Matthew," I said. "This isn't funny."

"It's not supposed to be funny. Just real. And real isn't funny."

"You are so full of shit!" Dolphin shouted, her voice rising in pitch. "You don't know about anything. You don't even know who you are!"

On his face, that fleeting lucidity, as ephemeral as a sun shower. The animal look disappeared. The gun dropped away from her head. I stepped slowly between the two of them. Closed my hand around my brother's arm. Held it. When was the last time I'd touched him? I took the gun away, the butt still warm with the heat of his palm, and he wandered down the hall. Into the living room. He stood by the window, gazed out at Dolores Park. Mingus hopped up on the sill beside him, and my brother's hand reached down to stroke his orange head. I could hear Dolphin behind me, adjusting the towel.

"Are you all right?" I asked.

"Yeah. I've been in tighter spots." She stepped slowly into the bathroom, closed the door.

In the living room, I eased myself onto the couch. Eventually, Matthew moved away from the window, settled in on the far cushion. As he pulled his legs up, his knees pushed through the ragged holes in his jeans. I gave him a serious look, considered a lecture about trashing my apartment, taking hostages in the hallway. This, however, would lead to deeper, more complicated issues. What he was doing here. What was wrong with him. I couldn't deal with it. Not tonight. I tilted my head back until it rested against the wall, closed my eyes. For some reason I felt dizzy, and the resulting effect on my equilibrium put me in mind of a wrecked ship, listing starboard and sinking.

"You gonna tell Dad?" he said.

I gave him a blank stare.

" 'Cause there's no point in bringing him into this. I mean, for all intensive purposes, those two are dead, so you can't really reach them by phone in any event. I'd fake my *own* death, but then I'd have to fake a resurrection and I just don't have the funds to mount that kind of a production at this point in time. You know what I mean?"

"Sure."

"Tomorrow I'm gonna start pounding the pavement. Job search. This is just temporary."

I nodded dismissively. "In the meantime, if you're going to stay here, we have to get a few things straight. First of all, I can't have fifteen-year-old girls showering in my apartment, walking around in towels."

"You mean sixteen-year-old nymphomaniacs."

"Listen to me. If her parents ever found out she'd been here—"

"She is, you know." He began to whisper. "She sees a therapist and everything. Her mother buys her birth control pills. It's a disease, actually."

"Are we clear on this?"

"Absolutely. Now what do you say to a little cannabis major?" He lifted an imaginary joint to his lips, his eyebrows leaping up and down Groucho Marx-style, and I saw an opportunity to do some investigating.

"Do you have anything else?" I asked.

"What do you mean?"

"Mind-altering substances."

He nodded ambiguously. "I might," he said.

The bathroom door opened and my brother went through a wild routine: shushing me, swinging his feet onto the floor, picking up a nearby magazine, then paging through it languidly. Dolphin appeared in a V-necked Adidas shirt and a pair of loose maroon jeans with scissored cuffs. My brother jumped to his feet.

"My stars, you look absolutely ravenous. Now when did such an *int*eresting monster get such an *int*eresting hairdo?"

She clasped his hand, did a turn like a music-box ballerina, modeling an utterly shapeless outfit ending in a pair of world-weary sneakers. I was forced to respond to a wordless request for my opinion.

"Ravenous," I said.

"All right," Matt said, clapping his hands and rubbing them together. "I'm gonna go drain the lizard, then it's on to greener pastures."

His feet squeaked over the hardwood floor; Dolphin plopped herself down on the couch.

"Where are you guys going?" I asked.

"Movies. Want to come?"

I shook my head, thanked her for the invitation.

"Did you see my boobs before?" she asked suddenly.

"No," I said. "I swear to God."

Her face clouded over with a vague disappointment. "They're small."

In the ensuing silence, I noted that Matthew had failed to close the bathroom door. We could hear a liquid gurgle in the distance, like the action of some polluted spring.

"So," I said. "Is Dolphin your real name?"

She smiled, shook her head.

"Where'd you get it?"

"From Matt."

I leaned toward her slightly. "I can't see any resemblance to a sea mammal."

"One day, he just said, 'Beware the nets of the tuna fisherman,' and I said, 'What the fuck is that supposed to mean?' and he said I was beautiful, like a dolphin."

The toilet flushed, and I gave thanks for small sanitary gestures.

"No one had ever named me before," Dolphin said, as if this were the reigning heartbreak of her life. "Well, except for my mom."

                        ▃▃

After they left, I peered into his room. The smell of paint hung thick in the air. Matthew's engorged backpack lay on the floor, surrounded by dirty clothes. In the main compartment, I found a sandwich bag filled with marijuana, rolling papers, a Walkman, and a few cassette tapes. A small box cluttered with earrings, brooches, necklaces—Jane's jewelry; and, scattered among these suburban baubles, my father's collection of tie clips. I unzipped the outer pocket and countless photographs spilled onto the floor. Square and white-bordered. My mother and I at a motel swimming pool. I at my homemade altar, feeding her Communion; her tongue waiting, eyes closed, while I lifted a wafer of compressed Wonder Bread from my plastic chalice. I looked at five, six, seven more. They all featured her. Before our Christmas tree; at a picnic; in the canoe. Finally: along the Bethlehem parade route, craning her neck, surrounded by flag-wavers. The fire engines rolling up Main Street and I, a boy of ten, standing at her side, looking distrustfully into the camera. Her belly swelled, she is visibly pregnant . . . I sat stunned on the floor for some time. Mingus wandered in, stretched out beneath the Rorschach wall, and pawed at the air. It was still wet, this representation of my brother's subconscious. Splotches of color . . . neurons firing . . . exploding stars.

He knew.

That he was not the person he'd believed himself to be. The person he'd been told he was.

Again I looked at the photo and felt a coldness seeping into me. Molecules slowing, changing their state. It was almost Saturday. Somewhere, there was an empty obstetrical chair, a laundered gown, a machine lying in wait. A building whose architecture would betray no secrets. I remembered driving one afternoon on Van Ness. Stopped at a light, my window rolled down; and on the sidewalk a few yards away, a handful of people. Rosary beads fell from their hands in graceful arcs. Their mouths moved in unison. A piece of a familiar sentence reached me through the din of the city: *"Mother of God, pray for us sinners . . ."* One of them, noticing that I was staring, walked over and handed a leaflet through the window. I didn't look at it. I didn't hear what the man said. As I drove away, for some reason I thought of the wasps which had lived under the eaves of my boyhood home. Hovering outside the windows. Crawling along the screens. Testing for weaknesses, and inevitably finding their way inside.

My mother.

She was not one of them. I didn't really know her, but I know she was not one of them. A zealot, a crusader. She simply obeyed the rules of her faith, and in the hours before delivery, she must have asked herself the same questions I was asking myself now. What am I doing? What am I complying with? When she went into labor, felt her sickened heart seize up and die, I wonder if she was thinking of me.

⌐⌐

I woke up to a mad chirping. Hit my alarm clock to no effect. Then detected the smell of breakfast gone awry. Locating my glasses, I stepped into the hall. At the far end, my brother had a chair in his hands and was in the process of swinging at the smoke alarm. The plastic cover flew off but the sound continued unabated. He wound up for another attempt.

"Hey!" I said. "Hey!"

"You gotta teach these things who's boss!" he shouted.

I held out a hand, as if trying to calm someone with a dangerous weapon. It took him several seconds to apprehend what it was I wanted. The chair. Which he finally handed over. Standing on its seat, I thrust my head into deafening altitudes and disengaged the nine-volt battery. In the sudden silence, everything seemed to vibrate visually. I closed my eyes. After a moment, I could hear something sizzling in the kitchen. The smell of charred bacon hung thick in the air. The toaster gave a distant, lazy report.

"Matt," I said.

"Yeah, Sarge?" He stood there looking up at me, ran a hand through his mangy hair.

"Something's burning."

He snapped his fingers, strode off singing under his breath. *"Something's burning, I dunno . . . what it is . . . but it is . . . gonna be great . . ."*

I followed him into the kitchen, where eggs were coagulating over a blue flame. There was a smoky haze in the room; I went to crack the window and saw that it was pitch black outside. The clock on the wall read two-fifteen.

"The worrrrld is turnin' . . . the Oscar Mey—er's burnin'. Why am I singing this shit? I travel millions of miles, and let me tell you, the phrase 'light year' is a serious misnomer." He snapped his fingers repeatedly, paced on the linoleum, the pan of eggs banking and weaving in his hand. "Story idea, story idea. Father Time's Corporate Headquarters. Long table. The big man's sitting at the end with his hammer and sickle; everybody else, everybody else, hourglasses for heads." He covered his mouth, dropped his voice into a gravelly baritone. *"Boys, we've gotta come up with a year that's every bit as tasty, satisfying, and long-lasting, but*

won't cause cancer, heart disease, flab at the midriff, et cetera in lettera.
The sand slowly sifts through through the heads of the company's
top spin doctors, every last one of them a licensed physician *and*
accomplished disc jockey." He came to a sudden halt; confusion
flickered across his face like lightning. "Shit, that's not going to
work." He dished the eggs out. "That's not going to win the
fucking Hugo Award, or the fucking Nebula. I've gotta stop
thinking like Douglas Adams and start thinking like Harlan El-
lison." He pulled a shallow pan from the oven which held the
gruesome remains of the bacon. "Oh, Jesus," he said, prying off
what he could with a fork. "Jesus Jesus Jesus, it's enough to
make you convert to Judaism. Sit down, sit down, the baby
chicken embryos are getting cold. That's fresh-squeezed tangelo
juice, so drink up. Now I know there's some manna somewhere
in this desert." He rotated 360 degrees, then darted over to the
toaster, returned with two slices of bread, sat down, bent his
head. "Our Father a fart unleavened hollow be thy game." His
hands clapped together, a sharp whip-snap. "You hungry?" he
asked.

I stared at him blankly.

"I'm so hungry," he said, "I could eat a witch's tit."

He shoveled some eggs into his mouth, and I could hear
shells crunching between his teeth.

"Do you know what time it is?" I finally said.

"Time for a complete breakfast."

I watched him pick up a piece of bacon, insert it in his
mouth; moments later, he was bending over the trash, spitting.

"Is this a joke? Or are you trying to piss me off?"

He looked at me, confused. "It's breakfast."

"It's two in the goddamn morning."

"Time doesn't mean anything," he told me, sitting back
down. "We think it passes, but it really doesn't. The past, the
present, the future are actually all occurring simultaneously. What
I'm saying in my novel, which is actually sci-*fi* pornography, is

that sex works the same way . . ." He babbled on, gesticulating with his glass of tangelo juice, quoting Georges Bataille.

"Shut up," I said.

"Okay, but listen—"

"I said, shut up."

"Hey! Don't tell me to shut up. Who are you anyway? You're just some fucking cartoonist. I don't even know you, man, so just watch your goddamn language."

My hand shot out and slapped the glass out of his fingers. It struck the wall with a resounding smash, and droplets of liquid tangelo, shards of tinted glass, rained down on the table. Finally, the house was silent. Matthew, with one eye closed, used his pinkie finger to clean from his cheek what could have been mistaken for a tear. In the subsequent moments of dead quiet, I felt the Earth spinning toward dawn. Inside her, something coming closer to being real. To being unreal. Where had it all started? When did my boyish adoration turn into need, a panicked need to have her always? The answer was sitting right across from me. It was locked within the square borders of those photographs he'd discovered and stolen. I grew dizzy with rage. I couldn't stay here. If I did, I'd hit him—and I refused to do that. I refused to repeat the actions of my father.

I walked into my bedroom, picked up the phone. Matthew appeared in the doorway.

"Who are you calling?"

"Get out."

I dialed. Three rings.

"I'm sorry," he said. "I won't cook anymore."

"Hi. You've reached the International Headquarters of the Audrey Hepburn Fan Club—" The message clicked off; several seconds of confusion ensued. Then a groggy "Hello."

"Nile?"

"Tom?"

"Can I come over?" I asked, and felt a criminal pang in my chest.

A few minutes later, I was outside. At the end of Dolores, I could see the lights of Market Street, a flow of nocturnal traffic. On the opposite sidewalk, a shopping cart. A homeless man who spent summers in my neighborhood, just discernible at the grassy foot of the park. I unlocked my car and suddenly remembered the story about the Mormons and the Utah state bird. What had my brother said that night on the telephone? That there would be no seagulls. No cavalry riding over the plains. No Lazarus rising. He was right. There was no magic in the world. No miracles.

———

Candles burning. Quivering shadows. In a white silk chemise, Nile lowered me onto the bed, informed me that there was nothing she liked more than being roused in the middle of the night; she'd spent the past twenty minutes waking up, leafing through her highlighted copy of *Little Birds,* by Anaïs Nin. She began removing articles of my clothing. I felt myself changing, growing warm and hard as the music suffered a plaintive diminuendo, violins and cellos crying alone as Nile lifted the chemise over her head. Candlelight skated along her body. Her black nipples stood erect in the cold air. Without warning, she took my hand, pressed it into the moist flesh between her legs—and my mind seized up with the image of Lindsey in a few hours' time: legs comparably parted, but bound in stirrups. The passivity of it, the trusting passivity, turned my stomach. My penis ached. Something clawed at my stomach. Some kind of hunger. Whatever I did here, nothing satisfied it. I felt wet warmth cover me over, her hand and mouth enclosing me. The advance and withdrawl of orgasm. She told me to beg her and squeezed until the pressure hurt. Then released and squeezed again to draw drops of clear come, like blood beading on a fingertip. I felt crippled and helpless, impotent despite the hardness of myself.

"Not like that," I said.

I lifted myself off my back, rose to my knees. Brought Nile's face to my own. Kissed her. And as I slid my hand down her belly, she snapped it up and twisted me around, slammed me onto the mattress, proving the serviceability of the self-defense program at the YWCA.

"Ouch," I said, my face pushed into the pillow.

"Now you just do what I tell you," she said, "and everything'll be all right."

Her tongue trailed over my cheek and I felt—what? Not passion, but ambiguity and anger. A desire for some kind of redress. As she eased off, loosed her grip on my arm, I grabbed her, wrestled her onto her back, and got on top. Pinned her arms with my hands, her legs with my legs. I kissed her mouth, shoved my tongue past her teeth. My cock pressed hard between her legs; her wrists, writhing under my hands, felt small and powerless. On the floor, I spotted her bathrobe.

"Don't move," I told her.

Reaching down, I removed the terrycloth belt from the robe. I knelt over her, and she stared up at me with a paralyzed innocence. Then slowly, with the grace of a diver preparing to yield to gravity, she lifted her hands until they met the bars behind her head. I fastened her wrists together, forced her legs open, and pushed my tongue through the dewy curls of her pubic hair. I made her come—and while she was still moaning, eyes shut hard, I buried myself inside her. Watched her give a sharp cry. Watched her body, slackened by orgasm, tighten again. Muscles and tendons taut, like overtuned strings. Her breath heavy and fast. Despite halting declarations that she couldn't anymore, I kept on. Until she finally let go a single prolonged sound which seemed to be composed of nothing. Nothing but pain and sadness.

I removed the condom, and the feel of my trapped semen, the slimy warmth of it, disgusted me. I felt exhausted, lonelier than I could ever remember. The sound of Nile's breathing filled the room. Deep, shivering gasps which seemed to threaten the life of the candle flames.

"You going to let me go?" she asked.

I untied the knot and she massaged her wrists. Her eyes met mine briefly, then darted away as I reached out to caress her cheek. Eyelids fluttering, then closing. I considered kissing her, then thought better of it.

"Well," she finally said. "No one's ever done that to me before."

I cleared my throat, almost inaudibly; my heart was pounding.

"Was it all right?"

She stared at the ceiling. "I think so. I mean, yes. It hurt a little."

"You should have said something."

"I did, sort of. I guess you didn't hear me."

Her chest continued heaving; the lines of her rib cage fading in and out of sight. The air in the room was humid now. Sweet and acrid. Finally, she looked at me. I received that smile which had become familiar over the past week. Hesitant and vague. She lifted a wrist to my lips, and I understood that I was supposed to kiss and make better the part of her that hurt.

"It felt great," she said, a note of apology in her voice. "I mean, more than great. Three orgasms, you know, who can complain?"

She kissed me, then slid out of bed, relieved the ashtray of its customary joint. Lit it on a candle flame. Sat beside me and took a drag. We smoked in silence for some time, and under the drug's influence, tarnished memories regained their luster. My mother had never seemed so real, or so irreversibly lost.

"Do you do that to other people?" she asked.

"Do what?"

"Tie them up."

"I don't sleep with many people," I said. "I told you that."

"But do you? I mean, have you ever?"

I shook my head.

"You never have?"

"I never have."

"Why tonight, then?"

"You twisted my arm."

Nile stretched out on her side, gathered some covers up around her chest. Head resting on a pillow, she stared down into the folds of the top sheet.

"Why are you angry with me?"

"Oh, Nile . . ."

"Did you do it because you're angry?"

"Of course not."

"You seemed angry."

"I wasn't."

"You seem angry now."

"I'm not," I said, and this at least was the truth.

She reached out languidly, and I handed her the joint; it burned like a fuse in her hand.

"I had lunch with her yesterday," she said.

"Uh-huh . . ."

"I just want to be open about it. I mean, these things have a way of outing themselves at strange times, in weird contexts—"

"It's fine," I said. "Why shouldn't you have lunch with her?"

Nile nodded slowly. "She's so unhappy, Tom."

A wave of cold heat broke over me; my face, I imagined, was visibly flushing. I lay back out of the light. Marijuana's vague paranoia was spreading through me, and I imagined I'd feel a lot better if she'd put out the cigarette.

"It was spooky," she said. "Just like when we were together. She told me there was nothing wrong, but I knew she was lying.

She looked so tired, so worn. She kept staring at this other table. She couldn't stop listening to their conversation."

"What were they saying?"

"It was a mother and her daughter. They were having this afternoon together. The girl was maybe nine and she kept calling it a safari. They were going to the De Young after lunch to see some exhibit. She turned to me all of a sudden . . . and asked me to forgive her."

Nile's eyes shone in the candlelight; then a luminous tear tracked down her face. She wiped it away, and I felt pressure behind my own eyes. I placed my hands slowly over my face. A mother and daughter on safari. How many times had I seen children in the past few days, and felt melancholy start falling, like a long and steady rain? A stretch of time elapsed without words, without movement. Nile sniffled, composed herself. I'd found this show of emotion frightening at first—tears which hinted at a pure and selfless love. Now I realized she was just like me; that she'd been to a place where dreams were half real, where hope masqueraded as fact. And suddenly, my heart grew big enough to admit empathy.

"I'm sorry," I said.

"For what?"

"I know . . . that you're still in love with her."

For a long moment, she didn't move, just lay on her pillow, eyes closed as if in sleep. Then she slid into my arms and held me as if I were someone long lost. I stroked her head, felt her tears dripping onto my neck. Her body was warm and strong, but with every passing moment she seemed to grow more ephemeral. Like a cloud changing shape, losing its resemblance to something real, and dispersing. On the stereo, the three princi-pals of the opera wrapped up Act One; and after a brief pause, the orchestra began an ominous introduction.

"This is the saddest part," Nile said.

"What's she saying?"

"She's saying . . . 'They're asleep, they won't see . . .'"

"Who won't?"

"Her children," Nile said. "She's thinking about killing them."

She fell asleep on my chest while Maria Callas debated infanticide in the bel canto style. Outside, the sky was lightening. A dull gray light which promised nothing.

15 / I have always tried to be elsewhere. Always. As if running from him. As if that little boy were something to run from. While he was growing up, learning to walk on the same carpet, the same hardwood my mother had walked on, I was living in a dormitory at the foot of New Hampshire's White Mountains. Translating the *Aeneid* from the original Latin. Learning how to smoke pot from a water pipe, how to conceal the smell of alcohol on my breath. Living with the truth, concealed from me for three years, and recently discovered in a class on current issues.

Abortion.

It was autumn, and I remember walking through a squall of fiery leaves. Running her pregnancy backward in my mind, returning my brother to her insides. I saw the slow deflation of her stomach. Matthew's reversion to a primal, meaningless stage of existence. Even if it was a sin, she could have done it then. Before he was really alive . . . That day, I felt half-healed wounds tearing open. The flimsy refuge I'd built of isolation and denial collapsing, swept away by a blast of October wind. This was no tragic accident. She'd had another option. Legal, but unchosen.

━━━

In the spring, she visited me, in the brown Duster inherited from her father, the same car I'd spent so much time in the summer my mother had died. It was a Saturday afternoon, and while I waited for her on the rock wall outside North Dorm, I could hear distant cracks and cheering from the varsity diamond, hidden on the far side of Macedonia Road. In my hand I held a rose. Deep burgundy red, just beginning to unfurl. I shielded the quivering petals from the sun and the breeze, and stared at the bridge which spanned the muddy waters of the Connecticut River. I was thirteen. Lindsey was twenty-one, in her last year at Cornell. Those nights in her teenage bed belonged to a different, finished time. We never spoke of them. But every few weeks, we talked on the phone about other things. Occasionally exchanged letters. In her last one, she'd told me that in May, after her graduation, she would be leaving the East Coast. Moving back to California. She'd gotten a fellowship to study at Berkeley. Journalism and Latin America. We would keep writing, she said. Someday I'd come and visit her. But these promises meant nothing. I'd been walking around St. Paul's for weeks with a burning hollowness inside me. She couldn't be leaving me. I wouldn't let her . . . When a brown car emerged from the trees on the far side of the river, my body tensed. I fumbled with the rose and brushed my hair back. The car eased to a stop in the lot below. The passenger window open. Lindsey leaning across the seat, looking up at me, her black hair long and wind-blown. As I climbed in, she immediately noticed the bruise under my eye, the half-healed cut that scarred my face.

"What happened?"

Carefully, she kissed me on the cheek. Then saw the rose. Velvety, dark as wine. I pushed it in her direction.

"Thanks for coming," I said.

Her face went through a rare transformation. She looked young and unprepared. I waited for her to ask again about my face. Instead, she kissed me once more, this time closer to the corner of my mouth. A moist pressure which made my nerve endings tremble. A kiss which seemed to last a split second longer than the first, and have behind it a different intention. Or was I imagining things? I wasn't sure—and as we drove north, at times when the car fell silent, I couldn't think of anything else.

We spent the day at a state park in the White Mountains. Lindsey had brought a blanket and food in a picnic basket. A waterfall sparkled in the sun. We hiked to the top, and waded in a pool which afforded a view of the surrounding meadows. All afternoon, cumulus clouds migrated across the expanse of blue. I hadn't seen her in months; and only now, in her presence, did I realize how empty I'd felt since Christmas. In January, in Connecticut, we'd made snow angels, ice-skated on the lake; walking back to her house, I'd tackled her, and felt the wonderful sensation of her weight pressing down on me, pinning me against the cold ground. Since then, the emotions inside me had evolved at an alarming rate. They pounded now in my head, in my chest, between my legs. Feelings that outshone everything else. Algebra, Shakespeare, Ancient Greece. Burning away like tinder in a brilliant, disorienting heat.

"You promised to decline nouns for me," she said.

"I was kidding."

"Well, I wasn't." She raised an arm and draped it, melodramatically, across her forehead. "Tom," she said, "speak Latin to me."

Her tank top and shorts had parted, and I could see a line of stomach flesh, her belly button. I could see, under the pink and blue stripes, the outline of her breasts, and the tiny peaks of her nipples. *Pulchra puella,* I thought. *Beautiful girl.*

"I'm waiting," she said.

"*Arma virumque cano.*"

"What does that mean?"

"I sing of arms and of the man."

She pursed her lips dubiously. "Say something feminine."

"*Pulchra puella.*"

"Ooh, that's much nicer. Now translate."

I looked into the lenses of her sunglasses, each filled with a reflection of the sky. "Are you still friends with that girl?" I asked.

"What girl?"

She knew what girl. Her name was Rebecca. I'd gone with them the year before, to demonstrate against a nuclear reactor in Seabrook, New Hampshire. On that day, they'd touched in a suspicious fashion. This girl was a double major—Film and Astronomy. They got high together and talked about the universe. I'd been wondering about them since examining a lesbian spread in *Penthouse*. Oral sex. The vagina, the vulva, the clitoris. I'd read extensively about these subjects.

"You know," I said. "The astronaut."

"You mean Rebecca?"

I nodded.

"Sure, we're still friends."

"So you go to movies together? That kind of thing?"

"Movies, dinner, the library."

I rubbed a thumb over the palm of my hand. Over the intersecting lines and curves, the angles and arcs of my future. "Are you in love with her?" I asked.

Lindsey propped herself up on her elbow, eyed me over the top of her sunglasses. I couldn't tell if she was annoyed or amused by the question. Either way, she wasn't going to answer it.

"What about you, Valentino?"

I shrugged.

"It's Saturday night. Are you going to meet some little girl on the soccer fields?"

"No."

"Some little Helen of Troy. Some little Helen of Southampton."

"Shut up," I said, a pressure building in my throat. There had been someone, the previous semester. Blond hair, perpetually flushed cheeks. We went to movies and dances. We messed around in the music practice rooms. All of my friends wanted her, so why didn't I? It all seemed so childish and regressive:

her passivity, nights that went no further than kissing, tortured discussions about the removal of brassieres. Even after she'd agreed to let me touch her, the shuddering of her body confused and frightened her more than anything else; and afterward, no matter what had happened or not happened, I always felt guilty. And I always had to sleep alone—lying awake, certain that Lindsey was sharing with someone else all the things I wanted so desperately. All the things I'd had with her once before.

"Who is she?" Lindsey asked, her tone different now. She wasn't teasing. She wasn't looking at me.

It was getting late, the sun falling toward the hilltops; and I could see a swarm of insects in its slanting light. I thought about the drive back. There was nothing to delay us. Nothing but antiques stores, all of which would be closed by now, and an occasional inn, glowing with soft expensive light. Soon I would be alone again. The river flowing south. On the walkway in front of the dorms, boys massing with their girlfriends. Girls who would never understand, who could never give me what I needed.

"I think I forgot something," I said, standing up. "At the waterfall."

When I got there, I cupped water in my hands, wet my face, and fought the feeling behind my eyes. I thought about her departure, only a month away, and I understood that today might be our last time together. Might it be the last time I'd ever see her? The rush of the waterfall filled my ears and I saw, suspended inches above the water, attached to a series of rocks, a majestic spider web. It had three levels, like the floors of a house, and the angle of the sun made the strands of web luminous against the dark water. Soon a hand landed on my shoulder with a warm pressure. A shiver ran through me. Her fingers moved along the skin of my neck as she knelt down beside me.

"What is it?" she asked. "What's wrong?"

"Are you really going?"

"What?"

"Are you really going to California?"

"I have to," she said.

"I don't see what the big deal is . . . about Latin America."

"Well," she said, "the Sandinistas. Remember, I told you about them. They're about to seize power from Somoza. When that happens, the future of Central America is going to change."

I nodded dismissively. She reached out and touched my cheekbone, the faded bruise. Asked again, more seriously this time, how it had happened. Was someone hurting me? I stared at the web, at its thin, intersecting veins.

"You can tell me anything," she said. "You know that."

"Can I ask you . . . anything?"

"Of course."

"Do you think it's murder," I asked, after a long silence, "to have an abortion?"

She eased away from me, and I noticed our shadows, stretching over the grass and meeting at a far-off point. When I looked at her again, her countenance had washed out, her skin had paled.

"Do you?" I repeated.

"No, I don't. I think it's a woman's right. To end a pregnancy if she needs to, or wants to."

"Would you do it?"

"Why are you asking me this?"

"I just want to know what you believe," I said.

"I already told you."

"I want to know what you'd do."

"I'm not sure if that's any of your business, Tom." She turned away, her voice going cold and distant. "But nobody makes that decision lightly. Without pain. Nobody."

The waterfall pounded out its steady rhythm. Lindsey was here and elsewhere at the same time. Beautiful and frozen. She took slow, measured breaths; and I struggled to control myself, to keep my voice steady and unbroken.

"I figured something out," I said. "Something everyone

knows and no one ever told me. Not even you. My father acts like it was all some tragic accident. But she didn't have to, Lindsey. Even if it is murder, she could have done it when she first got pregnant. Before he was really alive. My father acts like it was all an accident. But you don't just wake up pregnant one day, unless you're the Virgin Mary. Somebody has to fuck you first."

Lindsey shut her eyes. "Tom, don't talk that way."

"All right, I'll hide the truth, like everyone else does. Because it's ugly. Because we should all just forget it."

"That's not what I mean. You know that's not what I mean."

She touched my hand and held it firmly, tenderly. Did she suspect, could she possibly know how much of my sperm had died on this same hand? Expired while my heart and mind reeled with lambent fatigue, and woke up from the illusion of her—to embarrassment, futility, loneliness.

"How could she?" I asked, half expecting an answer. "When she knew? When she knew what could happen?"

———

A few minutes later, I'd told her everything. How on selected Saturday nights, after lights-out, I was guided into a makeshift boxing ring. Pennies taped to my knuckles, hands wrapped in thick turbans of gauze. I'd been taught by my Senior Fellow— a boy with a subtle Texas accent, the heir to an oil fortune— how to jab, how to guard myself, and to throw an uppercut. I told her about a boy from Chicago who'd quit, and subsequently had been branded a homosexual. After dinner one night, I'd watched the head waiters hold his face in a puddle of spilled milk, prodding his ass with a broomstick until he admitted to assorted sodomies. I repeated that it happened on Saturdays, after the school had gone to sleep; and when she asked if it would happen that night, I lied and said yes.

"Have you told your father about this?" she asked.

I shook my head.

"When's the last time you saw him?"

"Christmas."

In the car, I stared out the open window, at the side of the road. Asphalt and foliage raced and blurred. Wind rushed over my face and stole my breath away. As she drove, she ran her hand through my hair, and tried to get me to talk. But my throat seemed closed off, my vocal cords petrified, as they had been countless other times since my mother had died . . . The road was completely in shadow now. Only the tops of the trees, the summits of the eastern hills, were still touched by sun. The countryside was losing its definition and color. Lindsey seemed tied to this change. Fading away. Growing indistinct against a larger background of darkness. I thought about the nights I'd spent boxing. How much I dreaded them, and how much I needed them. When I fought, I felt my rage and confusion given form. While it was happening, those few minutes of violence, that feeling of mindless lucidity, compensated for the bruises and cuts—for the horrifying realization I'd have later, in private, that I'd drawn the blood of a boy I had no quarrel with . . . I brought a hand to my face, and tried to erase the evidence of a tear. She must have noticed, because her fingers ceased their hypnotizing rhythm. Her hand paused, lingered on my neck with a kind of nervous pressure. The motor of the car humming. The radio saying unintelligible things. Then she told me she wasn't taking me back tonight. We would stay somewhere. We'd get a room and go back in the morning.

⌐⌐

Before we found an inn, we found a carnival, rising into the darkened sky like a distant city. We parked in a dirt lot and stepped into the violet light, the smell of popcorn and hot dogs. With a curl of tickets, we headed for the Tornado. Lights bloom-

ing like neon flowers along its spine. Spidery metal arms. Cars
racing in dizzy figure-eights. We stood in line near a string of
game booths, their shelves lined with cheap stuffed animals that
seemed unbearably lonely despite their numbers. A speaker
churned out the steam-whistle sound of recorded calliope music.

"Do you know where the calliope got its name?" I asked
her.

"The what?"

I pointed to the speaker. The whistles of the instrument,
squeaking and wheezing air, pushed out endless runs of defi-
cient notes.

"Calliope," I said, "was the Muse of eloquence and epic
poetry."

"What did it mean," Lindsey asked, "what you said this
afternoon? The Latin words."

"I can't tell you."

"Say them again."

"Pulchra puella."

"What do they mean?"

I shook my head.

"Tell me," she said.

The Tornado slowed and came to rest. Its passengers disembarked, struggling to regain their equilibrium. The gate was
opened and I ran for an empty car. It was painted turquoise blue,
glimmering with specks of gold and sporting pointy fins and
conical red taillights. Lindsey hopped onto the seat after me,
pulled the safety bar shut. When the operator locked us in, he
moved me to the outside, even though I was smaller, so my body
would bear the weight of Lindsey's once we started spinning.

"Man on the outside," he said.

Lindsey and I sat shoulder to shoulder, the closest we'd been
all day. In a moment, we were under way, the car coasting
toward the iron railing, then back to the flashing bulbs at the
ride's center. As we picked up speed, her body eased uncontrollably into mine. I drank up her weight, and looked up into the

gyrating night sky. The Big Dipper hung above the treetops, larger than I'd ever seen it before, tilting precariously over New Hampshire, as if about to spill the ingredients of the galaxy on top of us. We laughed while the girls in other cars screamed in panic. I met Lindsey's eyes and felt the night, everything it could inspire and hide, falling over my imagination. Her hair fluttering against my cheek. Her body pressing into mine, drawn to me and held against me by the magic of centrifugal force.

———

At the Fox & Fox Inn, we posed as brother and sister. An older man with a full beard, a pipe, and a heavy Boston accent (Mr. Fox, I presumed) showed us a room with two beds and an antique butter churn in the corner. I walked inside and leaned against the mattress. The beds were identical, divided by a small table and lamp. Mr. Fox handed Lindsey the keys, said we could pay his wife in the morning. In his pipe smoke, I saw the fleeting image of a flower budding, blooming; then the petals fell away. I felt a pang of nervousness as Lindsey pushed the door shut, and the latch bolt clicked fluently into place. The stairs creaked through the wall as our host descended. Then it was absolutely quiet. We sat on one of the beds, playing gin rummy with a pack of borrowed cards. Gradually, the sounds of other guests shuffling through the hallway, using the bathroom, faded away. Before we knew it, it was midnight, the crickets trilling in the silence.

"Which bed do you want?" she asked, in a stage whisper.

"I'll take this one, I guess."

She nodded, but didn't move. I gathered the cards and placed them on the night table. Still she sat there. On my bed. Breathing. Staring down at the quilt.

"Tomorrow, I'm going to find the dean and I'm not leaving without some guarantees. If anything else happens, I want you to promise you'll call me. Promise me."

"I promise."

"I know I'm leaving soon," she said. "But just because I'll be far away for a while doesn't mean that's how it'll always be. People drift apart and come back together. That's the way it is in life."

Her face was shadowed and golden in the low light, her eyes serious, the green of the irises almost opaque. Anything could happen here. In this silence, this stillness.

"I'll miss you," she said. "I love you . . . and I care about you. No matter what."

My heart seized up at these words. I had to shut my eyes and shake off the memory of my mother. Toward the end, her belly swelled, an oxygen tank at her side, she'd spoken similarly, while my brother eavesdropped from the shelter of her womb. What did Lindsey mean, love? What did she want me to do?

"You'll visit me, in California?"

"Yes," I said.

She bent forward to hug me, and suddenly her hair was touching my face, the metal of an earring lying against my nose. Her neck smelled faintly of soap. Then, with a paradoxical inelegance, she was gone. Pulling back the quilt of the other bed.

"I have a great picture of us," I said, still sitting. "You haven't seen it. I have it at school."

"Really . . ."

I thought I heard a quiver in her voice. "From last summer. That picnic. Remember, we were eating corn on the cob?"

"Yeah, I remember." She climbed into the bed with her clothes on, reached for the light switch. "I'd love to see it. Tomorrow, okay?"

The room lapsed into darkness and I turned away from her. Soon, consciousness would evaporate, as time had relentlessly evaporated. Lindsey lay only an arm's length away, but it felt like miles. As many miles as she would put between us tomorrow, at the wheel of her car; and a month later, in the seat of a jet. Moving. While I sat still. I could leave, I thought, once she'd fallen asleep. Take her money and anything I could find down-stairs, and run away in the Duster. Drive to California. Perhaps the wind rushing through the windows would blast the empty wounded feeling from my chest. Maybe the wind of the Pacific would send it away forever. I was crying again, positive that I was in love with her, and filled with terror at the absurdity of it . . . Lindsey spoke my name, a soft and broken whisper. Then she was beside me on the bed. Holding my head in her lap, saying calming, meaningless things. My arm, I realized, was wrapped around her waist, my fingers touching the skin at the base of her spine, caressing it in slow circles. When she tried to move away. I reached out with a thoughtless strength and grabbed her by the wrist. Began to tug gently. To pull her down.

"No," she said

I held her more tightly, pulled harder, and she violently withdrew her hand.

"Stop it."

"Why?" I said. "Why not? Like those other times."

Sitting back against her own bed, she wrapped her arms around herself, as if she were cold. Remained there, motionless, staring at the floor. In the silence, I remembered the carnival. The way the rides had changed at closing time. As their lights shut off, they seemed to be cooling, rusting to immobility. When Lindsey and I backed out of the parking lot, that miniature city looked sadly dead, its inhabitants already extinct, just the museum skeletons of what they had been a short time before. The end of a prehistoric period. Now I listened as she slid under her quilt, as she breathed deeply and evenly, and I thought I heard a single sob absorbed by her pillow. Or was it an owl, a rusty weather vane obeying the touch of the wind?

Then I heard it again.

A few moments later, I was no longer on my bed, but stand-ing beside hers. Reaching down, lowering a hand to her hair. She didn't protest. She didn't stop me from lying down beside her. The sun had been gone for hours, but now darkness truly fell over us. That night, I felt blind. Lindsey guiding my hands to things I would never see. Only feel and imagine. I remember the softness of her skin against my face. The flesh between her legs, like living sea glass, like living velvet. I remember an extravagant climb in altitude, then the effortless embrace of a place just beyond gravity's reach . . . Afterward, in the still warmth of each other, we seemed to harden, as clay hardens in the heat of a kiln. Lindsey lay on her side. I rested my lips against the downy nape of her neck. Silence grew thick. Consciousness began to give. "I love you," I whispered, certain that she was asleep, and imagined I was changing the course of her dreams.

16 / I found myself leaning over a sink, confronting a reflected image. Someone kindred—but not me. This person was older, his face worn with mistakes I didn't understand. He had to be somewhere soon. He had an appointment. Footsteps padded into hearing; the bathroom door gave a mournful sigh as it was pushed open several inches. Nile's eyes were leaden with fatigue; she crossed her arms over her chest, each hand weakly gripping the opposite shoulder. She seemed embarrassed, and I remembered how she'd cried herself to sleep. How she'd failed to deny the obvious: that she was still in love.

"What are you doing?" she said.

In explanation, I lifted a plastic cup from the sink, filled it with water. Her head rested against the doorjamb.

"Will you come back to bed now?"

"Actually," I said, "I have to go."

"Go? Where? It's Saturday morning."

"I have something to do."

"What?" she said softly, her eyes on the floor. "What could you possibly have to do?"

"Something," I explained.

I considered the exterior of the drinking cup: the citizens of Pooh Corner wandering in pastoral bliss. Nile turned away without speaking, and returned to the bedroom.

My body reeked of sex. I had to shower, and though I didn't want to do it here, I couldn't go home either. I couldn't bear to face my brother and the wreckage of last night. So I stepped under Nile's shower and washed myself with her soap. I hadn't slept. My body felt drained and feeble. In the mirror, I'd looked startlingly pale, like someone in need of medication. Now, as hot water poured over me, a strange pattern invaded my vision. The room leaned over. I lowered myself to my knees, felt my stomach crawling with nausea. I stared at the drain, at the water's steady flow. Afterward, the cold air felt good. I searched the medicine cabinet for a new toothbrush, and couldn't find one. Stared at Nile's for some time. Then finally picked it up, and tried to wash the taste of her from my mouth.

In the bedroom, she appeared to be sleeping, covers pulled up to her face. The clock read 8:53. A space heater whirred in the corner. My clothes were strewn over the floor, a sock missing. I snapped on a small lamp.

"What are you doing?"

"Looking for a sock."

"Could you talk to me for a minute? I mean, have you got a minute?"

I approached the bed, sat on the edge of the mattress. Quite some time passed with Nile lying silent on her side, staring out the window.

"I know you're upset," she said.

"Nile, please."

"Don't give up on me, okay?"

"I'm not upset."

"Well, it's just . . . you know, you wake me up in the middle of the night, fuck me like there's no tomorrow, then we have a slightly scary conversation and a couple of hours later, you up and leave. I mean . . . you know?"

"I want to stay." I touched her through the bedsheets. "I have a commitment."

"You have to believe . . . she's something separate. Don't you have someone whose memory runs through you? Do you have someone like that?"

I didn't answer.

"Those people," she said distantly. "Once you lose them, you're never supposed to have them again."

"What do you mean?"

"Just that I think it's necessary, or maybe inevitable, to spend your whole life wondering . . . about what might have been. Just wondering. Not trying to find out."

She sat up, drew closer. Holding my chin with her fingers, she kissed me tenderly; and I felt an aftershock of that emotion I'd known at the start. Something so pure and innocent. It seemed to me that real forgiveness lived in her. The potential to bury the past together and begin again, on ground leveled by honesty. But it was too late for that. The situation had grown far too complicated, and I'd done things I'd never believed myself capable of.

"Promise me you won't give up," she said.

Nile's hand brushed over my cheek, and the touch sent shivers through me.

"I want to forget her," she said. "I want you to help me."

———

A few minutes later, I was on Fillmore Street. Stepping into an overpriced vintage shop where I'd once bought Lindsey a perfume bottle of enameled Venetian glass. The place had a large sidewalk window, but the inside was always dim, lit indirectly by floor lamps, Tiffany Wisterias with stained-glass shades. I breathed in its pleasantly stale air, heard music leaking out from a rear room, some ancient jazz which crackled and strained. I walked past flapper dresses and a rack of narrow ties to the jewelry case, where the proprietress, an older woman in an evening gown, smoked a cigarette from a long holder. Lace mitts, dark and delicate, lay over her arms like Spanish moss. Her gray-white hair was long and pinned back. High cheekbones sloped to meticulously painted lips. As I approached, her lips widened dreamily, her eyes narrowed in the fashion of a sun-drenched cat.

"How are you?" I asked.

"I," she said, "am copesetic. You?"

I nodded, indicated the jewelry which stood between us. "I'd like to buy a ring. For a woman."

The cigarette, I noticed, was unlit. I tried not to look at the bare expanse of her neck and shoulders, the pendant necklace which touched, at its nadir, the dark, slightly weathered ravine between her breasts.

"Amicable or intimate?" she said.

"I'm sorry?"

"The nature of the gift."

"Intimate. An engagement ring, if you have anything along those lines."

Pensively, she gazed down into a vast collection of antique jewelry, all of it lying together with a natural randomness, as if it had been washed up by a tide.

"What's her ring size?"

"Ring size . . ."

"That's important," the woman said gently.

"Is it absolutely necessary?"

"Few things in life are absolutely necessary. Let's put it this way. One is more likely to purchase a ring which will fit if one knows the ring size of the person who will wear it."

I allowed this theorem to sink in. Then I glanced nervously at my watch. "I don't know it."

"That's not surprising. Now, one of the challenges a man in your position faces is finding out ring size without betraying his intentions. Going through a female friend is a time-honored option, but you've got to choose the agent carefully. I don't care what anyone says, the female urge to gossip is primal, in certain members of the species irresistible."

"I don't mean to be uncouth," I said. "But I need it now."

She raised an eyebrow, smiled that feline smile. "Of course, in the case of fiery errands such as yours—can we characterize your errand as fiery?"

"Whatever it takes."

"—there are ways to make an educated guess." She opened the glass door of the case. "What's her shoe size?"

"Shoe size?" I sorted through the chaos of my mind for some relevant memory.

"How about bone structure?" the woman said.

"She's thin, but she has hips."

"Height?"

"Mine. An inch shorter, maybe."

"So . . . five foot ten, or eleven?"

I nodded. "Ten."

The woman produced a large metal cone, engraved with lines and numbers. As she slid rings over the narrow end to measure their circumference, I caught my reflection in an epic standing mirror; and though I seemed small and young, the size of the glossy image, the richness of the surroundings, and the mirror's slight upward tilt conferred a sense of majesty on me and my marital campaign. I tried to work up some corresponding confidence to still the nervous throbbing in my chest.

"I prefer 'betrothal' to 'engagement,' " the woman was saying, her voice velvety, though the sheen had dulled over time. "Engagement . . . too many unsavory associations. Debt security, business employment, military combat. Betrothal, on the other hand, has a single meaning, and its etymological root is the Anglo-Saxon word for truth. Sadly, in most English dictionaries, it follows directly after 'betrayal.' "

Here, she fixed me with an odd stare. Sad and sympathetic. As if she'd managed to divine the specifics of my personal affairs.

"Here's a possibility," she said, handing me a ring. "Those are emeralds and pearls in a filigree mount. Late nineteenth century."

She tried a few more, the rings whispering musically as they slid down the cone.

"Here's another. That's a diamond, claw-set. Same period, roughly. More Art Nouveau than Victorian."

"What size are these?" I asked.

"They're sevens. I think that's the best guess."

I bent down in front of the glass. My eyes picked over earrings, brooches, necklaces, pendants trailing long threadlike chains. Beside a pin which featured two golden dragonflies joined at their abdomens, I saw a ring with a long, narrow setting. It resembled an eye standing on end; its gems sparkled white and green.

"How about that one?" I said. "Next to the dragonflies."

The woman's delicate fingers trailed across the wings of the insects, and I half expected them to come to life and dart out into the dim light of the shop. When she dropped the ring over the cone, it halted just shy of seven.

"That's an Art Deco. Emeralds and diamonds, maybe 1920."

She held it out to me, and I turned it over in my palm. There seemed to be an energy emanating from it. It was nothing like Lindsey's current edition, a basic contemporary thing from Tiffany's. This had character, history. Gems cut in the spirit of Cubism. It spoke of Picasso and Gertrude Stein. A rejection of realism.

"This is perfect," I said, producing my wallet. "Don't tell me how much it is."

She held my credit card at the magnetic trench of a small keypad.

"You're sure you don't want to know the price."

I smiled, shook my head. She ran the card through, and while we waited for confirmation from some invisible authority, she lectured about Art Deco, and I soaked in the details of her maturity. The sculpted lines of her face, her whitened hair, the slightly flaccid skin around her collarbone, the wrinkles between her breasts. Lindsey was a quarter century shy of sixty, but with an effort of imagination, these same signatures of age could be seen on her body, as images are visible in the stars if one knows how to connect them.

"Do you have any children?" I asked.

"Three," she said.

"You're very beautiful."

Averting my eyes from the monetary total, I signed; and when I met the woman's eyes again, I found her affectations had fallen away. She looked older, less perfect, and somehow more desirable. "Be sure to leave the ball by midnight," she said, then handed me the ring, closed now in a tiny velvet-covered box.

17 / Morning.

A fire engine. A police car. Shiny and displaced, like forgotten toys. The grass gone and the field as barren as a moonscape. Stripped of mystery and beauty. Just a stretch of scarred land, threading smoke signals into the air. But the Paris house is safe. Untouched. Only stained with dark soot. On the end of the dock, with my mother's binoculars, Roland and I can see closeups of the investigators. Digging, taking pictures, searching for clues. For some time I watch a technician carrying a silver box, pointing a kind of microphone to the ground. According to my best friend, this is a Geiger counter, and the destruction we see before us has been caused not by a smoldering bottle rocket, but by an ancient god, a giant reptilian monster who will soon surface in more populated and cosmopolitan regions.

"We have to stop him, before it's too late."

"This isn't a joke," I tell him.

"Return the egg," he says in his Japanese falsetto. "Return the egg."

I hear the deck door open. I see my mother in the doorway, the phone, which rang several minutes ago, pressed to her ear. She motions to me, so I hand Roland the binoculars and walk along the creaking swaying dock. In the kitchen, I find my father standing solemnly by the telephone, my mother sitting at the table, her hands clasped together.

"It's Father Coine," she says.

Though I am already perspiring from the heat, a cold chill ripples through me. His home, I suddenly remember. The parish rectory. Hidden by the slope of the land, at the far end of the field. My father's next words reach me through a shady film of disbelief. Life ended. A soul parted from its body. I shut my eyes and images flash uncontrollably over the surface of my mind. Father Coine's luminous robes. A girl running down a road in some faraway land, patches of her skin burned away. A boy kneeling among stalks of grass, holding fire in his hands. These ideas are like pieces of a puzzle, and I can almost see it whole when my father says something else. That the fire was not an accident. That traces of gasoline have been found in the ruins of the old farm. The McCready place. Someone deliberately burned it down. Inside me now, a shifting, a swelling wave of relief. I am innocent. I share no connection to this crime. Then I remember Lindsey—a girl abandoned under a summer sun, her inner thigh streaked with blood—and I hear an impossible secret whispered to me, too softly to be fully understood.

18 / With an antique engagement ring in my jacket pocket, I climbed Russian Hill. The fog was burning off above this favored neighborhood, the bay warming to a lapis blue, but farther west the sky was still congested. Just after ten as I pulled into her driveway. Through the second-floor windows I could see a stretch of mahogany wall, Philip's epic bookshelves lined with the history of nature photography, a wing of the stuffed albatross. I rang the bell. Turned the ring box over in my pocket. Probably she was still dressing. Perhaps erasing the evidence of tears. I rang again. Was it possible that she'd left without me? I caressed the velvet pelt of the box, wandered toward the car. A hollow, desperate love ate away at the hull of my stomach. Suddenly, the front door opened. Lindsey gave me a blank look as she stepped onto the welcome mat, a leather bag slung over one shoulder, a book in her hand. She dropped her keys, bent down. An artful descent to one knee, a genuflection. I gripped the box as she walked toward me. Suede jacket over the brown print dress she'd once worn on a drive to Bodega Bay; the eyeglasses, sleek and curvilinear, which she generally used only for reading; her expression ambiguously weighted as she halted an arm's length away. "Morning," she said, and my chest flooded with a sudden premature heat. The kind that tempts flowers to bloom before their time.

"Did you sleep?" I asked.

She shook her head and glanced at her watch. "We should go," she said, and made her way to the passenger side. The doors of the car closed with cold metallic thuds; the keys, which I'd left in the ignition, jangled and swayed. Lindsey didn't look at me, only drew some hair back to afford a view of her profile. Her left index finger was bare; she'd removed her wedding ring.

"Where are we going?" I asked.

"The Sunset. Judah and Twelfth."

We drove all the way to Van Ness in silence. Traffic moved slowly. Buses hulked at our side. Lindsey stared out the window, at their long rectangular advertisements for radio stations, soft drinks, and Hollywood films.

"I had a strange conversation this morning," she finally said. "With your brother. He said you'd gone out. He said if I saw you, to tell you he was sorry . . . about the bacon."

"You called me?" I said.

"How long has he been here?"

"Thursday. Thursday night."

"What's he doing here?"

"I'm not sure."

"He's writing a novel," Lindsey said. "Do you know that?"

"He's mentioned that, yes."

"Do you know what it's about?"

I shook my head, slowed for a stop light.

"It's about a teenager who's visited by the Virgin Mary when he masturbates. Pretty soon, they're having an affair together. You can imagine the rest."

The traffic light changed to green. I turned onto Fell Street, ducking under one of the abandoned freeway overpasses. Broken by recent shifts in subterranean plates, it ended in midair, an exit to no place at all. We crested a hill, hit a ghostly wave of fog. Down below, I could see Golden Gate Park, the road forking, the left lanes leading to the Sunset District. In my pocket, the ring seemed to be giving off an urgent heat.

"Are you scared?" I said.

Lindsey didn't answer, just kept staring out at other people's porches and front doors and windows.

"Because I am. I'm scared that we're letting fear dictate the terms here. I mean, do you feel in control? Because I don't. I mean, I'm driving, but I don't feel in control."

She nodded distantly.

"Do you?" I asked softly.

"No," she said. "But that's nothing new, Tom."

The park was just ahead of us now, the meadow where thousands had once gathered in the name of love. All of it veiled by a white mist. I was preparing to bear to the left, but then the arrow for a right turn flashed to life. My hands tightened around the wheel. I checked the mirrors. I checked Lindsey, who was removing her eyeglasses, tucking them into a small padded case. A moment later, we were coasting smoothly in a new direction. The Sunset District veering off without us. It took her a surprisingly long time to notice that we were on the wrong side of the park.

"You know," she finally said, "it's in the Sunset. On Judah."

I hung another right on Park Presidio, artery to the Golden Gate Bridge and points north; and I could feel her stare, like a change in the weather, as we achieved the brisk speed of fifty miles an hour.

"What are you doing?" she asked.

"I'm taking control."

I slid into the left lane and overtook a station wagon with a curriculum vitae plastered onto its rear window: UCLA, STANFORD, VULCAN SCIENCE ACADEMY. Then, without another word, I pulled out the ring box and placed it in her palm. Silence filled by the steady hum of the engine. The car speeding northward and a phantom presence traveling inside her.

"Are you going to open it?" I asked.

She didn't answer.

"It's an antique. It's Cubist."

She held the box in two hands while cross streets—avenues back to the heart of the city, back to her appointment—approached, then slipped behind us. I reached out and brushed her freckled cheek, her black-and-gray hair, gently with my fingertips.

"I want you," I said. "A life with you. A home."

"Tom—"

"I'm not asking for an answer right away. But open it now. Just look at it. We'll get out of the city. Later, let me put it on your finger. We'll go up the coast. Somewhere we can think and talk. That place with the garden, above the ocean."

"I can't do that."

"Yes, you can, Lindsey. We can do anything. You just can't see that right now."

I wove my fingers more deeply into her hair. Her eyes closing. Her fingers closing around the box as we dove into the darkness of MacArthur's tunnel. Concrete bending over us. The echoing roar of cars. On the other side, the fog was gauzy and torn and shining. I merged with traffic; and sunlight bloomed over our bodies as the bridge swung into view. I thought about crossing it. I thought about driving north, farther than we'd ever gone before. Driving until we reached a place that was all our own. Though a handful of cars were slowing for the final city exit, most of the traffic was rolling swiftly onto the span. There was no toll in this direction. No one to halt our motion, nothing to block our escape. Without a question, without so much as a glance in her direction, I drove on. The ocean stretching out at our left. The city falling behind us. In those selfish moments, it seemed we were being carried on the crest of some impossible wave. It seemed I could feel reality bending, conforming to my own will. How long did it take for me to think of her, to look at her? She had her forehead angled against the cold surface of the window. Her breath was steaming the glass and her shoulders were trembling.

"Lindsey?"

"Do you know what you're doing to me?" she said. "Can you imagine what you're doing?"

I felt a warm chill, the confusion of someone who wakes up

remembering nothing. For a long moment, there were no names, there was no past. We were simply moving without a purpose or a destination. I knew only that I was doing something horribly wrong, that I loved the woman sitting next to me. I loved her so much, I couldn't see past the fact of my own need. As we neared the northern end of the bridge, I found myself easing into the right lane. Taking the Vista Point exit. Circling into the parking lot. I'd hardly stopped before her door was swinging open and she was walking away. I sat in a motionless silence, watched her step down to a stone observation deck lined with scenic binoculars. What was I feeling in those moments? Not remorse or contrition, but a sorrow that grew out of some long and obfuscating history, a recognition of everything that was blocking her sight. All around me, people were talking and taking photographs, posing in front of the bridge and the bay and the city in the distance, which looked as perfect and inauthentic as a scale model. I parked. I passed through the sounds of foreign languages and through the paths of video recordings. Behind her, at the low stone wall, I placed a hand on her shoulder.

"I want the keys," she said.

"Listen to me."

"The keys."

"I'm not giving them to you."

She backed away, and regarded me with an expression I'd never seen on her face. It seemed to heat the air around us. It seemed capable of burning away all the love she'd ever felt for me.

"You're not going there," I said. "Not until you talk to me."

"There's nothing to discuss."

"You owe me that."

"I don't owe you anything. I didn't ask you to fuck up my life. I didn't ask for any of this."

"But it happened," I said. "It's happening to both of us."

"No, it's not, Tom. This isn't happening to you. It's happening to me."

Impulsively, my eyes sought out the center of her body. She turned away, and I grabbed her by the arm. "Don't touch me," she said, violently shaking me off. "Don't touch me like you have some right to tell me what to do."

"I just want to talk."

"Well, I don't. I just want this to be over. I want to start again."

"With Philip," I said calmly.

"He's my husband."

"You don't love him."

"That's really not your concern."

"You don't love him, Lindsey. You never did. This is what you want."

"Don't tell me what I want."

"Your desire is as deep as mine. I can feel it."

"It doesn't matter," she said. She stared out at the bay, at the tiny silhouettes of gulls against the sky and white sails floating peacefully over the water. "Sometimes, Tom, it's not enough to want something. Everyone has dreams and fantasies, and everyone has an obstacle standing in their way."

"There's nothing in our way."

"That's a lie. It's what we both wish was true. But it's just a wish."

"I don't know what you're talking about."

"Stop pretending," she said. "As if denying it can erase it. We've been silent so long. But you think about it all the time, just like I do. It's with you all the time."

There was a long, cold pause.

Then, with her arms folding over each other, hugging her own body, Lindsey moved away. I became aware again of the people around us. Voices. Cameras. Children peering into the sights of the giant binoculars. There were things I wanted to say, things which had been trapped in my mind for as long as I could remember. I was beside her now. Close enough to see the tender lines at the edges of her eyes and on the surface of her lips.

"I'm sorry," she said. "I can't tell you how sorry I am, and how I wish things were different. I'll never forgive myself for what I did to you, but I can't change it, and I realize now I won't ever make it right. No matter how hard I try or believe, it'll never be right. And I'm promising you that, after today, I'll never try again. I'll never hurt you again."

"Look at me," I said.

"I can't."

"You're wrong, Lindsey. It's not what you did to me. It's what *we* did."

Her eyes joined mine now, and I thought I saw them flicker and brighten with understanding. I noticed, cupped in her hand, enclosed in her fingers, the ring box. She'd carried it out of the car. She hadn't let go of it. Hope flashed through me, electric and impetuous. But then she hid the ring inside the pocket of her jacket, and the brightness in her eyes was already gone.

"You're confused," she said. "You always have been."

"I was there."

"You don't remember."

"I remember. I remember leaving my house and walking to yours. I came to you, every time."

I watched her eyes close, the lids sealing shut as if she were trying to black out some image imprinted inside. The wind lifted her hair, pulled the skirt of her dress tight against her legs. All around us, the fog was burning away into nothingness, the blue sky widening.

"You don't remember," she said. "You don't remember everything."

These words were just a broken whisper. No force behind them. But like some necromantic spell, they transformed everything around me. People lost their voices and froze in place; sound dropped off into a cavernous silence; and I had the dreamlike sensation of standing at the threshold of a familiar room, its door always unlocked but never opened. I knew what was inside and at the same time I didn't. Maps of ended time and lost places; magic lanterns, the toys of childhood, whose pictures lay still and dormant; the tender light from some mysterious and undying source, creating shadows in the shape of desire. There was a choking feeling in my throat as I placed my two hands firmly on her face and tried to make her look at me.

"Stop it, Tom."

"I love you," I said.

"You're hurting me."

But I didn't release her. My fingers fought the rigid muscles of her neck until she broke free. Then, drawing the windblown hair out of her face, she did look. She stared at me. And I could see, reflected in her fractured, uncomprehending eyes, the extent of my trespasses. I could sense, beyond her irises and pupils, the final assembly of conclusions which weren't valid, which were based on fatal misinterpretations. A moment later, she was walking away, up the stone steps to the parking lot; and as I followed her, I felt a strange weightless rush, a tightness in my chest, as if my body, like the body of a diver, were rising too quickly to a foreign and native surface.

"Don't touch me again," she said.

"Lindsey, please—"

"I was happy before. I had Philip and my writing. Since you've been here, I've felt like a ghost. You've done something to me. You've stripped me down to that girl I used to be. The closer I get to you, the more real she seems. And I hate her. I hate the things she did and the mistakes she made."

"Stop," I said. "You're not thinking clearly."

"Yes, I am. For the first time in a long time. I've made my decision, and you have no right to try and change it. You can revise history all you want. But you were just a boy, and you didn't come to me for what I gave you, what I took from you. I know what I did, and I'm not going to be anybody's mother. Not anyone's. Not ever."

Tears were streaming down her face now; and in her eyes there was a fear I didn't know how to contain—a fear which, I now realized, I didn't even understand. It was stronger than everything: love, regret, her desire for all the things which stood to be lost. If she didn't keep her appointment today, she'd schedule a new one tomorrow, or the day after that, and there was nothing I could do to stop her. In this place where choices were made, where things were conceived or headed off or brought to a halt, I had no power. Suddenly, it seemed my entire life could be distilled down to that single fact. I didn't know what I was doing anymore. Only that I'd rather be with her, hurting her, than alone.

"If you do this," I said, "I'll tell him. I'll tell him everything."

"I don't care anymore. I don't care about anything."

I grabbed her arm, more roughly than necessary. I spun her around to face me. What was left to say, to do? "What about tomorrow?" I said. "You'll feel guilty and dirty, and you won't be able to go back." As I finished this sentence, there was a blur in my peripheral vision. Things fell dark as her hand struck my face. The landscape, the image of her, went wildly crooked, and I realized she'd thrown my eyeglasses out of whack. A split second later, it happened again. Pain branched out from the center of my face, my hand rose automatically at the taste of blood, the metallic flavor of old coins. "Give me the keys," she said, her voice barely audible, "and get in the fucking car." I reached into my pocket for the key ring. In exchange, she handed me my glasses; though the joint on one side had snapped, the lenses were intact. A group of tourists came into focus, then shied away in unison like a school of startled fish. In the car, I tilted my head back, applied pressure to the bridge of my nose. As Lindsey fell into the driver's seat, she threw something against the windshield. It bounced around and fell to the floor. The ring. Its velvet-skinned container. Sounds broke violently from her throat as she tried, repeatedly, to fit the wrong key into the ignition. I'd seen her like this only once before; and as I had that summer day, so long ago on another coast, I felt atrophied by fear. Blood rushed down my throat, thick and nauseating. Above, patches of fog floated through a cold blue sky; and the bridge loomed over us, its towers and cables massive and skeletal, like the reconstructed evidence of something long extinct.

19 / A strange detachment numbing my mind as my mother drives us around the lake. The sky arcs overhead, a cloudless slate of blue. Where are the stars? Not gone, only hidden, covered over with the paint of day. For the first time in a long time, our car eases up this driveway, gravel crackling under the tires. Mrs. Paris is standing in the yard with another woman from town, and when she sees us she walks over. She wears a long silky toga dress. She kisses my mother on the cheek, and tells me to let myself into the house. Catherine is expecting me. Here, only yards away from the field, the smell of wet ash is more potent; the damage of last night, concrete and undeniable. I push the front door open. How long has it been? Three years? There is the spinet piano still in the same place, that weird geometric painting, a fluffy cat whose name I remember to be Lucy. There is the staircase with its regal red carpeting; and there at the top, in overalls, her strawberry-blond hair tied in pigtails, is Catherine.

"The Sacrament of Extreme Unction," she says.
"What?"
"The final sacrament. He died without it."
I climb the stairs and she leads me down the hall. Past a door which is shut and muffling the sound of soft music. This, I know, is Lindsey's room. We pass it without comment, and enter a place it seems I once visited in a dream. The furniture an unforgettable banana yellow. The wallpaper, a squall of daisies against a blue background. On the white bedspread, a couple of Holly Hobbie dolls lean into each other, gossiping about my

return; and above the desk, a Maryknoll calendar hangs from a tack, featuring a picture of a Catholic missionary surrounded by dark-skinned children.

"It's okay," she says. "You can sit on the spread."

I lower myself to the edge of the bed as Catherine hands me her boxed set of E. B. White books. Using colored pencils, she has enlivened the opening illustrations of *Charlotte's Web*. Fern struggling with her ax-bearing father; her brother holding an air rifle; Fern feeding her pig from a baby bottle, like an aspiring mother. The music across the hall is faint and melancholy. I slip the book back into the box, then hand it to Catherine. She rearranges the titles, sets the whole thing down on her desk. We sink into silence.

"Do you want a Shirley Temple?" she says all of a sudden.

I look at her ambivalently.

"We've got real maraschino cherries."

She exits the room. I listen to her footsteps. Slow and steady down the hall; then, once she thinks she is out of hearing, a spastic flurry. I walk over to the window. Men treading on the field's barren surface. Police cars. A yellow fire engine gleaming in the sun. From here, with the grass gone, I can see what remains of Father Coine's house. One half of it burned away and collapsed . . . How mercurial my impulses are. The need to know. The urge to hide. That music is clearer now. A woman, accompanied only by a guitar, singing about California. And before I turn around, I already know that she will be standing in the doorway. My vision swims at the sight of her. Her beauty, her poise, surrendered to some desperate shadow. My body goes hot and cold at once, as my suspicions grow sharp and clear. Last night, while I was lighting matches, watching bottle rockets shooting skyward and crying out against gravity, she too was in the tall grass. Fireflies sparking all around her. A can of gasoline in her hand. She heard the final whispers of the field. Maybe she asked the spiders for forgiveness. Then she lit a match of her own. To destroy the place where it happened.

"Tom," she says.

A single syllable breaking under the weight of fear and desperation. I know exactly what she is going to say now, exactly what she needs me to do. To not do. As I stand facing her, I feel, for the first time in my life, intimately connected to the mechanism of the cosmos. Isn't our planet, at this very moment, rotating? Flying through space in a giddy solar orbit, a lone moon tracing circles around us like some giant restless insect? As she approaches me, the borders of reality seem to contract, until I can see that planets and stars are just ideas that exist in books, and the universe is a microscopic thing composed only of the two of us. As she joins me at the window and touches my cheek, I feel a wave of dizziness wash over me. A claustrophobia which feels just like growing up.

20 / The fog. A low white ceiling pressing down and blowing in waves up Judah Street. She parked the car, cut the engine. While we waited to cross the street, I felt my nose, my upper lip, checking for traces of fresh blood. I'd cleaned myself up as best I could in the vanity mirror, but my shirt was spotted with rusty drops; a dull pain rippled over my face. Lindsey hadn't spoken a word to me since leaving the bridge. Hadn't looked at me or touched me. She just drove, like someone obeying a commandment, like someone trying to break free of the gravity of her own desires. But now she gripped my hand, held it tightly as we were given the right-of-way. In front of the building, there were people waiting. Rosary beads hanging from their hands in graceful arcs. As we neared that place, it seemed I couldn't see color anymore; I could no longer judge distance; and light began to fade, as if a cloud, some dark cataract of truth, were moving over my retinas.

"Don't go in there," I heard. "Please."

One of the women was walking alongside us. Beneath an overcoat, she wore a pink sweater, a silky scarf at the neck. She smelled of perfume. Her fingernails were painted red.

"Don't choose this," she said. "Don't choose death over life."

"Leave us alone," I said.

"You're not murderers. I know you aren't."

I met her eyes then, eyes filled with all the unconditional sympathy I'd ever wanted. She reached out and her shiny red fingernails scraped over my skin. A few feet away, the others were speaking in a gentle monotone. Praying for the soul of our unborn child. A moment later, we were inside. Lindsey letting go my hand. The heavy door closing behind us.

21 / That morning, all of Bethlehem crowds into St. Edward's. The day is hot and the doors stand open. On the east wall, the stained-glass windows, overwhelmed by mid-morning sun, glow like overexposed photographs. Colors melt together, threatening to run in brilliant volcanic rivulets over the walls and floor. There is a heat inside me too. As if, two nights ago, a tiny ember of Lindsey's fire had traveled over the lake to settle secretly in me. Hidden and glowing, fanned by the promise I have made her. By a pact which feels crucial and unbreakable and horribly wrong. On the altar, beside the tabernacle, the perpetual flame keeps watch over the consecrated hosts. I stare now at the crimson light, mesmerized by its steady flickering; until my eyes are drawn away, coming to rest, like the magnetic needle of a compass, on her. She is wearing a summer dress. Dark brown and girlish. She angles her face to the floor as she follows her family up the center aisle, and disappears from my sight. Then, in her wake—at this point in time which I believe to be the end, but is only the first of many endings—the beginning returns to me with a shimmering clarity. This same building, dark and silent. A girl dressed in the garb of some other reality, walking barefoot over the velvety altar. Talking to me. Changing me somehow, in a way I will not understand for a long, long time. The first hymn begins. Father Coine's coffin is carried up the center aisle. A strange priest, a bishop in liturgical headdress, waves a silver baton, and a rain of holy water falls upon the dark polished wood.

22 / As we sat in that waiting room, in its jaundiced light and its void-like silence, a familiar coldness reached into me. The slow advance of an enormous nonentity. There were three other people with us. A young woman, alone; and a couple not dissimilar to us, though closer to each other in age. The women documented their medical histories, pen tips whispering against paper. The men attempted, unsuccessfully, to blend into the surroundings, to hide like creatures gifted in the art of camouflage. We sat motionless. We breathed. We waited for our lovers' names to be called.

"Are you all right?" she said.

"What?"

"Your face."

I nodded.

"I can't believe I did that."

She brought a hand to her forehead, her left hand, and I focused on her naked ring finger. I thought of the object I'd purchased barely an hour ago, lying somewhere on the floor of my car. I thought of her wedding day, the peacock which had been painted on her arm and long since washed away. Was it possible that if I'd never come to California, by now she might have been happy?

"Ms. Paris," someone said.

A nurse stood at the threshold of the waiting room. Lindsey rose to her feet and I rose with her, my heart beating furiously.

"You can't," she said in a barely audible whisper.

"What do you mean?"

"You're not allowed."

I just looked at her, breathing air that was growing thinner every moment. All around us, emotion seemed to be breaking down, molecules of sadness and longing dividing into their constituent elements. Her lips moved as if to form words, but there was nothing to say anymore; and with her first step in that other direction, I felt pathways being sealed off, bonds breaking, lines of sight being altered. When she disappeared down that dimly lit corridor, we became unreal, the two of us. Bodies made of memory.

———

I asked the nurse how long it would take, and then I left that place. Hurrying past those people on the sidewalk, I headed for the park. The day was still cold, but up above, the sun wore holes in the thick skin of fog; and the tourists and the citizens were biking and walking and parking their cars outside the arboretum. All around me, the world seemed to be changing in accordance with loss. Laughing people, families, children—they all existed on some other plane. I couldn't touch them anymore. If I tried to, my hand would pass through them unfelt. For the rest of my life I would try to explain, and they wouldn't even hear me. After today, we would separate, and I knew we'd never come together again. After this, we'd never dare kiss again. Never dare touch each other again, for fear that our bodies would crumble into dust. I tried to imagine the outlines, blurry and shifting, of some other reality. A city I'd never been to. A woman I'd yet to meet. Some distant point in the future when this day, all of its pain and power, would stop burning in my mind. Like a sun losing its light and heat, collapsing inward, and swallowing emotion, images, sounds. Drawing all evidence into some dark unreachable place.

Hadn't my mother disappeared in that very way?

I walked aimlessly. Past beds of flowers. Down to the pond

where the swans glided on their own reflections, where an old man was ripping up bread crusts and throwing them into the colorless water. Yes, I thought. She is where my mother might have been. Change that one decision, thaw the frozen history of our family's final winter, and all of life would be different. No grief to blind me. No nights spent in a teenager's arms. Was Lindsey right? That I hadn't seen the truth of what had happened. That I still couldn't, and I never would. I lowered myself onto a bench, a knife-like pressure behind my eyes. Was my memory accurate and complete? Had my mind censored, erased, rewritten the truth? I thought of light shining beyond the visible spectrum, of chords ringing silent, vibrating at frequencies too low to be heard by the conscious ear. It didn't make a difference. It didn't matter what she had done, or what she was doing now. I'd never stop loving her.

⌐⌐

It was less than an hour, but it seemed I was wandering for days. As if following some natural instinct, I retraced my steps. I exited the arboretum, walked past the baseball fields dotted with uniformed players. Up ahead, the carousel—hidden in its circular, dim-windowed shell—spun beside the playground's swingsets and slides and jungle gyms. I stood at a distance, at the top of a gentle slope, and felt like a dead spirit eavesdropping on the tender sensations of the living. Cool air against skin. The steady throb of a heart. I closed my eyes and listened. The voices reached me like the distant cries of ocean gulls. The music of the carousel bled into the air, rising and falling. The bodies of horses. The silhouettes of children.

⌐⌐

When I returned to Judah Street, that same woman floated across the sidewalk. Perfume, pink cardigan. I thought of firearms. I imagined a pistol, loaded with sacred purpose, concealed inside that sweater. But there was nothing of the lunatic about her. She was just a woman. Perhaps a mother. Perhaps a mother who might have been.

"She heard us," she said.

I didn't stop walking, but glanced at her. Her eyes igniting with optimism and hope. She repeated her words, and I felt my body slowing, halting.

"It's true," she said to me.

"What do you mean?"

"Your friend. She's not in there anymore. She spared her child."

A moment later, I was running up the block, running for the car. I found Lindsey sitting on the hood, feet propped on the fender, her hands buried in the pockets of her suede jacket.

"Where were you?" she said.

"I was just taking a walk."

I approached to within a few feet of her and stopped. Afraid to get too close. Afraid to speak. As if any further movement, any question, would cause the scene to lose shape and dissolve. I'd open my eyes and find myself lying on the grass in the park. A streetcar approached from the west, its body glistening with oceanic mist; and under cover of its passage, wheels rolling over scar-like metal tracks, Lindsey dismounted from the car. She came to me. She walked into my arms, pressed her face into my neck; and I held her there for some time, feeling her eyes opening and closing against my skin, the caress of her lashes.

"What happened?" I finally asked.

"I'm not sure," she said, hugging me more tightly, bathing my heart in a misty heat. "I need a little more time."

PART THREE

23 / She needed to be alone. She was going to walk through the park; if the fog burned off, she'd go all the way to the ocean. Then she would start thinking. I watched her disappear into the trees, the tactile memory of a single impassioned kiss on my lips; and as I started the car and pulled away, as the morning and that half-lit waiting room fell behind me, I felt like a teenager taking a driving test. Conscientious and manic. High on the fumes of freedom, the promise of uncharted roads. At a stop light, I reset the mileage counter, squirted some washer fluid onto the windshield, adjusted the temperature control. My hand searched for another task, hovered near the center of the wheel, on the verge of testing the horn. The light turned green and there was something miraculous about this, about the color green and the word "go" and the simplicity of the invention we call the traffic light. At my apartment, with the help of a Valium, I curled up on the couch and became weightless. As I slept, I heard no sounds, dreamed no dreams; and when I woke up, I felt at peace. Outside, the sky was dimming. Night closing over California. I stepped into the hallway, into a hallucinatory glow. In the center of his room, dyed by the light of a red bulb, my brother was kneeling at the feet of a statue. The Virgin Mary. She was clothed in flowing garments and a veil, hands clasped under her chin. He had a small paintbrush and a container in his hand, and was applying to the lower part of the statue some kind of clear liquid. Pornographic magazines were scattered all over the floor, pages ripped.

"Where'd you get that?" I said.

"It's a beautiful piece, isn't it? This church was having a major going-out-of-business sale. I mean, a real everything-must-go kind of deal. Serious bargains on religious dress, if you're into that sort of thing."

He shuffled through one of the magazines, found a photo, and ripped off a section of it. Pasted it onto the spot he'd just painted. I now noticed that the statue's feet and the hem of her garment were covered with a mosaic of unappareled women.

"I'm sorry about last night," I said.

It took him a while to turn and regard me with a confused expression.

"For getting angry," I explained. "For walking out."

He resumed his work, and I continued standing in the doorway until the phone rang. As I approached it, a nervous euphoria raced drug-like through my veins. In the dusky living room, Mingus sat on the window sill, watching the advance of the evening fog. The television was on, murmuring to itself, bleeding light.

"Hello?"

"Are you coming?" I heard, and felt an odd mental tug, as if I were staring at a trick image from perceptual psychology—the vase which becomes two opposing profiles. "You said you'd come."

"Come where?"

"To dinner . . . with my parents."

"Nile, I can't."

"Then why did you say you would?" Her voice was flat, without definition.

"I thought I could—"

"I know where you went," she said.

In the distance, I could hear my brother tearing glossy paper, dissecting.

"I figured it out a while ago. After that night at the movies. You guys are bad actors."

"What are you talking about?" I managed.

"The amazing thing is, I don't think Phil can see it. I guess he spends too much time with animals. He's lost touch with human nature."

There was a long pause, during which I felt the old panic, the familiar disbelief, moving through me. Did I really think that, faced with the corporeal fact of her husband, Lindsey would confess what we'd done? Map out the merciless topography of our adultery? Choose me?

"You know," Nile said, "you're ruining her life."

"I have to go. I can't see you anymore."

She gave a humorless laugh. "Can't you see, Tom? She doesn't love you . . . or me. She doesn't love anyone."

I didn't respond. Then a click—and the hum of the dial tone.

"Who was that?" Matthew asked. He was standing in the doorway, the hall behind him glowing with the light from his room.

"No one," I said. "A friend."

He nodded, raised a hand as if he were about to launch some orchestra on a symphonic voyage. "There was a man," he said, "drinking coffee with Reality in a cheap café, when some soap bubbles floated through the intersection outside the window. The orange sign was flashing DON'T WALK, but the bubbles ignored it and just floated right on through. They were pioneers and were soon followed by other bubbles. They floated over the tops of cars, above the heads of pedestrians. Pretty soon, they were arriving in great numbers and a wide variety of sizes. Traffic stopped, people stared in wonder. The bubbles were like a river. Flowing down the street, dividing, multiplying. And when the man drinking coffee looked closely, he could see the whole world in each and every bubble. So he stood up and left his coffee, and he left Reality sitting there and he walked out into the street. And he let a bubble close over him and pick him up. And then he was on his way . . ."

"To where?" I asked.

"It depends. Look into your heart. Your heart is the great kaleidoscope. Do you know why?"

"No."

"Because it's full of crushed glass and mirrors."

I wandered toward the window. The sky had lost its grip on daylight. Nile was wrong. It was different now. I had proof.

"Tom," my brother said distantly.

"Yeah."

"Are you in love?"

On the curved windowpane, I could see the tinted reflection of the hallway: Matthew standing, warped and blurry, like an image inside a crystal ball. I nodded.

"Me too," he said. "It's all happening just like she told me it would."

"Just like who told you?"

When I turned to face him, Matthew's eyes were shut in the fashion of someone making a wish. "It's going to be okay, Tom. We're going to be whole again."

⌐⌐

In the bathroom, I thought about what had happened that morning, and what I had done. I felt criminal and yet closer to her than ever before. Closer to the life I longed for. Suddenly, it seemed that this life was possible. Not only possible—but waiting, gestating. A future as certain and intractable as our past. In the shower, hot water running over me, I rested my body against the cool ceramic tiles. My chest felt overfilled with air, oxygen that choked me with its purity . . . Something around the eyes inherited from her. Something about the mouth which was undeniably mine. Like Matthew had said (was my brother some kind of clairvoyant?), we would soon be whole again. All of us . . .

There was a rap on the bathroom door, then it opened. "Someone here to see you," Matthew said.

"What?"

"Someone's here."

"Who is it?"

"I don't know. She's sort of old, but beautiful."

Lindsey poked her head into the doorway. "Can I come in?"

"Please. Absolutely."

With an exaggerated wink, my brother withdrew. Lindsey closed the door behind her, waving at the swirling motes of water as if they were insects, and wearing a vaguely bewildered smile on her lips.

"That's him?"

"The one and only."

"So . . . what happened?"

"He took some money from Jane's pocketbook and stole my dad's tie clips."

"I mean before that. Why did he leave?"

"I don't know yet," I lied, as those photos of my mother flashed over my mind. I'd opened the curtain a bit, and for some reason I felt self-conscious, ashamed of my nakedness. Lindsey approached the edge of the bathtub, the mist parting and wrapping around her again like a veil. Fine drops of deflected water budded like dew on her face.

"He's handsome," she said. "He looks like you . . ."

"He does not."

"Yes, he does. You both have this thing around your eyes."

"He looks like a Holocaust survivor," I said.

Lindsey raised an eyebrow in concession of the point. "He does look a bit undernourished."

"It's the Greyhound diet."

"He came on the bus?"

I nodded. Already we were running out of small talk. The morning, and all its unresolved contradictions, drew near, like a flock of birds moving in unison.

"How are you?" I asked.

"I'm good . . . You?"

"Good. I slept. Most of the afternoon."

"I slept some. In the arboretum."

"On the grass?" I said.

She nodded. "It got warm. I just curled up in the daisies. Took a nap."

"Would you . . . have you eaten anything? We could go get some dinner."

She appeared to be considering this idea. Then, averting her eyes, she reached out and touched my chest, pushed her fingers into the hair. Rested them there. As if divining things from the beating of my heart.

"I'm embarrassed," she finally said.

"Don't be."

"You must think I'm a fucking loon."

"Come on, Lindsey."

"This past week, this morning . . ." She shut her eyes. "It felt dangerous, Tom. Like I could hardly control myself."

"I know. I know what you mean."

"All I could think to do was run. It seems to be what I do best."

I placed my hands on her face and slowly guided her mouth toward mine. "Lindsey," I whispered, kissing a tear from the slope of her cheek.

"I can't help it."

I started to turn off the water, but she intercepted my hand, held it and brought it to her lips.

"I was changed," she said. "I was in the gown."

She didn't speak again and I didn't press her. The longer the silence went on, the less capable I felt of speech, as if my vocal cords were slowly petrifying. As if language were falling away, a shed exoskeleton. Slowly, she lifted her shirt over her head. I watched her unbuckle her jeans, unclasp her bra. Desire squeezed my heart and set it pounding, but the feeling was different somehow. Devoid of guilt and rivalry. As if we belonged to each other now. Wordlessly, she stepped into the bathtub. The water tracked down her body in rivulets. I held her for a long time—motionless—until, like people awaking from a deep sleep, we began to move again. Her hands streamed over me. Her breath came from deep in her lungs. I ran my fingers down her neck, touched her breasts, and she winced, though I'd applied little pressure. She asked me to be gentle. They'd been growing tender for days.

When we emerged from the shower, we could hear a guttural hum emanating from the stereo, pulsing through the walls. The apartment was completely dark now except for Matthew's red light. Wrapped in towels, Lindsey and I proceeded down the hallway hand in hand, as if we were approaching the heart of some Gothic mystery. Matthew was kneeling at the foot of the Virgin, wearing nothing but a pair of boxer shorts. He was still working, ripping up magazines. The statue was papered halfway up the legs. He saw us, waved blankly, and continued humming along to what had revealed itself to be human chanting.

In my bedroom, I flipped on the light, and something moved on my bed. Lindsey gasped, reflexively grabbed my arm. I snapped the light back off.

"What the hell was that?" she said.

"That's Dolphin," I whispered.

"What?"

"My brother's girlfriend."

A petulant esophageal response was grunted into my pillow.

"You let them sleep in your bed?"

"I'm having some discipline problems."

We dressed in my walk-in closet. I gave Lindsey a shirt and sweater. I gave her kisses before her body was covered. One on each nipple; one in the humid hair between her legs; one on her belly, where it seemed I could already feel a voluptuous distension. Then we returned to Matthew's inner sanctum—into the dreamy light and the voices which were echoing through the catacombs of the bass register.

"Matt . . ."

"That seals it," he said.

"Seals what?"

"My decision. Monosyllabicism does not behoove the serious artist. Nor does duosyllabicism. I am therefore changing my name to Matthias." He shuffled through an edition of *Penthouse Letters,* found a photo, and ripped off a piece of it. Pasted it onto the spot he'd just painted.

"I want you to meet someone," I said.

"I'm a little busy," he said. "Could you get back to me sometime around the vernal equinox?"

Lindsey wandered into the room, hands behind her back; Matthew's eyes followed her surreptitiously. She said hello, told him her name, and his face flickered with an uncertain recognition.

"We've met somewhere before," he said.

"You remember? You were really young."

"It's coming back," he said, snapping his fingers. "The Russian Front, '63. You gave me a Zagnut bar. You saved my fucking life, soldier."

I walked in, leaned back against the Rorschach wall. Lindsey stepped toward the statue, toward my brother—and the chanting seemed to grow more urgent. In the red light, all movement occurred with a weird lethargy, as if we were trying to function in an atmosphere composed of translucent liquid.

"What are you doing?" she asked.

"It's a companion piece to my novel."

"You're a writer?"

"I don't want to define my artistic identity too narrowly, but that's part of it. Words are important, opening lines are crucial."

"I agree," Lindsey said. "I used to be a journalist."

My brother crossed his legs on the floor. This posture, combined with his near nakedness, endowed him with an overwhelming innocence.

"What are you now?" he asked.

"I don't know." Somewhat timidly, Lindsey reached out and touched the cheek of the Virgin. "Where'd you get this?"

"Garage sale."

"Must have been a strange garage."

"You could say that. Most definitely."

She turned to the giant Magritte face, studied it in the stance of a museum patron. "You a fan of surrealism?"

"More than a fan," he said. "I'm the American New Wave."

I heard the door to my room open. A moment later, Dolphin appeared and was washed, with the rest of us, in crimson. She looked newly awakened and was wearing one of my T-shirts, which barely dropped below the latitudes of her privates. I introduced her to Lindsey and she waved lazily, stood behind my brother, whose head slowly tilted back to gain a view of her crotch.

"Matthew," I said, a tired parental rebuke.

"Would you agree or disagree," he asked us, "that 'cunt' is by far the loveliest of names for the vagina."

"Whose opinion is that?" Lindsey asked.

"Mine. But I have been influenced by certain French writers of dubious repair."

"What's that fucking noise?" Dolphin said, her voice creaking like a rusty hinge.

"The Gyoto Monks," my brother informed us.

"I've been dreaming of frogs," she said, raking her hands through her hair. "Giant motherfucking frogs."

Matthew stood up suddenly, and Lindsey's eyes veered immediately away. An erection was straining against the white cotton of his underwear.

"Why don't you put some pants on?" I suggested.

He glanced down and seemed genuinely stunned by the status of his penis. "Jesus," he said. "I gotta talk to somebody about this."

___

The four of us drove out to Baker Beach, at the edge of the Golden Gate. It was a clear night, there were stars visible over the ocean. The bridge, lit up and shining with headlights, seemed close enough to touch. Matthew grabbed Dolphin's hand and whisked her off in that direction, yelling, "Epic! Epicurean!" As their voices drifted just out of earshot, I felt Lindsey's arms wrap around me from behind. "Epicenter!" Matthew shouted, and Lindsey laughed into the back of my neck.

"It's funny, but it's not," I said.

"Don't be such an old fogy."

"I have to be. If I don't keep an eye on him, no one will."

Her lips brushed against my earlobe. "That was cute," she said. "That was downright fraternal."

I wormed away from her, began removing my shoes and socks.

"You just can't admit that you like him."

"I'm sure his performance is endearing in a small dosage. But he's been going like this for three days straight. Did you see the walls in my apartment? He did that with a paint gun."

"He's just trying to get your attention."

I shook my head. "I thought at first he was on speed or coke. I think it's something else. You can't have a conversation with him. He's completely scattered, he's hyperactive or something. He doesn't seem to sleep, he keeps quoting Georges Bataille. It's spooky because he used to be so quiet and inward."

"People change," she said. "He's not a little boy anymore."

"There's something wrong with him, Lindsey."

"Yeah, I'd say there's something wrong. There's something wrong with your father and his goddamn emotional vendetta."

She marked me with her eyes. Implicated me. I couldn't

hide my flaws from her, and I did feel flawed. Ashamed of how long I'd harbored the same resentment and nurtured the same grief. Feigning anger, I started toward the water, the vague comfort of the waves. A moment later, Lindsey was at my side, gripping my arm, taking my hand.

"I'm sorry," she said.

"You just don't know what it's like—"

"Yes, I do."

I tried to withdraw my hand, but she wouldn't let me. How long had I waited for this simple sensation? To move away and find myself gently moored, gently held in place. She ran her fingers over my palm, over the intersecting tracks which hide the truth about life and love.

"Do you feel healed," she asked, "after all these years of hating him and hurting him? Has the pain gone away, or has it just been sustained?"

My eyes shut with a childish force. "I'm just not ready . . ."

"The thing is, Tom . . . he's here now. He came to you. He wants your help."

Again I could hear his voice—a buoy rising above and sinking under the sound of the Pacific.

"There are people," Lindsey said, "who can turn pain into love. Like alchemy."

"I'm not one of them."

"Yes, you are," she said, the tone of her voice synonymous with the touch of her fingers. "You are."

I eased my free hand into the pocket of my jacket and fingered the ring box, which I'd brought along in case of a sudden downpour of romance. I wanted to drop to my knees in the presence of the ocean and the stars and that giant suspension bridge and ask her to never leave me. But Matthew was jogging into view, singing "The Battle Hymn of the Republic."

"What do you think?" Lindsey asked him.

"I think I'm in paradise. I can't believe people actually live here."

"There's an application process," she said. "You have to prove that you're either a humanist or a romantic."

"I'm both," Matthew said. "I'm human and I'm romantic. Right, lovergirl?" He draped an arm over Dolphin's shoulder.

"Give me a break," she said. Then, turning to Lindsey: "Do me a favor and don't start in with any hippie shit."

"Hey, mellow out." Matthew stroked her hair. "My brother would never date a hippie. Would you?"

"She used to be one."

"No, I wasn't," Lindsey said defensively. "I just liked the scene."

"See," Matthew said, "she was just in it for the drugs. Dolphin's got this thing about the sixties."

"It's not a *thing,* okay?"

"Oh, right, I forgot. You're a sociologist."

"And you're a writer. Like you could write your way out of a thimbleful of piss."

"Yow. I don't know what that *means* exactly, but I'm hurting. Prep me! *Prep me!*"

"Shut *up,* for the love of fuck."

"It's not a thing," my brother clarified. "It's a theory."

"What is it?" I asked.

"Forget it," Dolphin said.

"No, really, I'm interested. And I was just kidding. Lindsey wasn't a hippie. She just looked like one."

Matthew, who had beaten a retreat of several inches, sidled back up to Dolphin and laid an encouraging hand on her shoulder. She pouted, shoved her hands in her pockets, and strode off in a westerly direction.

"What did I say?"

"Nothing, nothing," Matthew replied. "She's just a little moody. To be completely candid, the theory has a lot of holes in it. Essentially, it looks at idealism as a limited natural resource, like oil or trees. You guys used it all up, leaving us with an eosophobic void." He adopted an expression of sympathetic skepticism. "Too much MTV and too little Marx."

"What's eosophobia?" I asked.

"Fear of the new day."

"I'll go talk to her," Lindsey said.

"That's a good idea." My brother touched her arm. "Get her talking about lip color, it'll loosen her up."

We watched Lindsey move off. After a few steps, she looked back and gave us a reassuring smile. Then jogged to catch up with Dolphin, her feet kicking up sand.

"Your wife's beautiful," Matthew said to me.

"She's not my wife," I laughed. I walked toward the bridge, and he fell in beside me. Seeing that my feet were bare, he stopped to remove his sneakers and socks, left them lying by a piece of driftwood.

"What do you think of Dorothy?" he asked.

"That's her real name?"

He nodded. "Is that amazing? I mean, everyone spends half their life watching *The Wizard of Oz,* the same time every year on CBS, but how many people actually *meet* someone named Dorothy?"

"That's a good point."

"So what do you think?"

"She's cute," I admitted. "Very cute. But that's strictly off the record."

A smile broke over his face, full of satisfaction and a giddy passion. "We did it," he half shouted. "We made love today."

"Really . . ."

"My first time," he said. "God, she was sweet and tender. She showed me her clitoris. Have you heard of that thing?"

"I have, yeah."

The sand was cool under my bare feet, the breeze cooler.

"I know what you're thinking," Matthew said. "That I'm too young to be having sex. I've heard it all at school, and I admit there's some validity to that position. But in the end, you've got to look at the big picture. I mean, I could be sitting in Burger King tomorrow, just about to take a nice bite out of a flame-broiled Whopper when some sexually repressed fuck walks in with some ammo to unload. I mean, when that's reality, it's time to start rethinking sex education."

"Well . . ." I said.

"Don't worry, I was very responsible. I changed your sheets."

We walked along the shore. My brother was strangely silent, staring up into the sky. I tried to figure out a segue into a serious discussion.

"You know what Georges Bataille wrote?" he said. "He wrote that the universe seems decent to some people because decent people have gelded eyes. He said they can't be frightened when strolling under a starry heaven."

"Are you?" I asked. "Frightened?"

"Sure. I mean, look up there. It's like the reflection of the world. Dark, with little lights that are too far away to touch. Everybody wants to know what's up there and there's no way to find out." He wandered into the surf for a moment, then drifted back to me. "But what does that mean, 'gelded'?"

"It means castrated. Like when they cut the balls off a horse."

His eyes shut in sympathy or fear, and stayed shut as he walked a blind straight line.

"Are you afraid of anything else?" I asked.

He nodded slowly. "Roosters . . . The crowing of roosters, because that means it's dawn. I always think of St. Peter when the cock crows, and how shitty he must have felt, knowing that Jesus was right the whole time. Then I get to worrying, you know, maybe it's like that for everyone."

"Like what?"

"Jesus tells him, 'You'll deny me three times,' and Peter says, 'I'll never deny you,' and then he does it three times in one night. So I worry, you know, that maybe everyone hears the cock crow. One morning you wake up and you hear it, and you realize you fucked up. Eventually you wind up crucified upside-down. Just an upside-down version of Jesus. And maybe if He hadn't put the idea in your head in the first place, everything would have worked out all right. You ever think about that?"

"All the time."

"Really?"

"Well, not in those exact terms. But I think a lot about—well, about the idea that whatever you do, whatever your intentions, you'll end up in the same place. And when you get there, you'll see this terrifying logic. It'll all be set in stone, and you'll see that you never really had any freedom of choice. You can't change it, and you never could have."

"You mean," Matthew said, "because God planned it all."

"Not God, exactly. But sort of."

"You're frightened too," he said softly.

"I suppose so."

"Of what?"

"The past," I said. "The future, maybe."

"That leaves the present. Are you frightened right now?"

I shook my head. Matthew stopped walking and sat down at the edge of the wet sand, stared out at the ocean. I crouched down next to him, watched the end of a wave approach his feet, wash over them, burying the tips of his toes.

"Last night," I said, "I didn't mean to get upset. It's just, Lindsey and I . . . we've been having some problems . . ."

The next wave climbed up the beach and his feet were another inch deeper in sand. Very slowly, he reached into his back pocket. Pulled out a small square of paper. It took my eyes a moment to adjust in the darkness, but I soon recognized it as one of the photographs. The July Fourth parade. Slowly, the image of our pregnant mother racked into a ghostly focus.

"Did you know," he said, "that we're both in this picture? That's you right there . . . and this is me." His finger rested on her swollen stomach, caressed it in tiny circles. "What's her name?"

"Monica . . ." I said.

He stared at the photo, mouthed the name without sound. Then he said, "She's my mother."

I eased down onto my knees.

"That makes you my brother," Matthew said. "Not a half brother. A whole. A hundred percent."

"I'm sorry."

"That's okay. Because I'm here now." He looked at me directly. "You can take me to her."

"What?"

"The place she went to after I was born."

A pause. A chill tracing an icy line through me.

"I've seen the house," he went on. "The Virgin showed it to me, in the form of a hologram. It's by the ocean. It's on the rocks high above the ocean. I know you go there, and I want you to take me."

"Oh, Christ, Matt."

"I know you've been waiting for me. Both of you."

I scanned the beach for Lindsey. She was nowhere in sight. Suddenly, I felt terrified of what was happening inside him—and all I wanted to do was run. As I always had. Run away, deny him, betray him.

"She's dead," I whispered. "You know that."

"That's the old story."

"It's the truth."

"No, that's the old story," he said with irritation. "That's history. But haven't you heard? History's bullshit. The people who write it are liars. Just like you and Dad and that bitch who *says* she's my mother—"

"We did lie to you . . . for too long."

"You're all a bunch of fucking historians."

"Let me tell you what happened," I said. "She had a weak

heart. She got pregnant . . . with you. Her doctors wanted her to have an abortion—"

"Can we cut the bullshit and get on with my destiny?"

"Do you know what an abortion is?"

He glared at me. "It's when a mother kills her baby."

"Some women have them to save their own lives. Mom didn't want that. She wanted to give birth to you, and the strain of giving birth killed her. She died in the delivery room . . . and you lived."

"You're making this difficult," he said, his voice quivering. "You're saying one thing and Mary's saying another. Now who do you think I'm going to trust?"

"I'm telling you the truth."

"Then where's her gravestone, Tom? Why isn't she buried in the churchyard?"

"What churchyard?"

"In Connecticut."

"She grew up in New York," I said as gently as possible. "She's buried in the Bronx."

The water rushed up the shore, gripped our feet. I felt the sand eroding beneath me, the seductive tug of the ocean. My brother stared into the darkness for a full minute. I wanted to reach out to him, I started to, and couldn't complete the action.

"Let's go home," I said. "You need some sleep."

"I'm not going home." His voice was shaking violently now. "And fuck sleep. You close your eyes and that's when it starts happening. They geld you when you're not looking."

"Hey," we heard. Lindsey and Dolphin were coming toward us, their bodies luminous against the water.

"Tell them to stay away," Matthew said. "Tell them."

As soon as I was out of reach, he bolted away, slipping in the wet sand, then finding his balance. The breeze whistled past my ears as I followed him. Breakers hit the beach in a dreamy syncopation. He was fast and I felt drunk with grief. He was not running away, but after something. A tiny light. A star long dead.

Dimming with each step he took in its direction. I didn't catch up until he'd fallen to the sand. His breath was heavy and he was on the verge of tears.

"I don't want my eyes gelded," he said. "But I want the universe to be decent. You can't have it both ways."

"It's all right," I said. I placed a hand on his heaving chest.

"It's not all right. Can't you see? There's a difference between people who are frightened under a starry heaven and people who aren't. Just like there's a difference between Jesus and Peter. One gets crucified right side up, the other gets crucified upside down. Are you starting to understand?"

My voice was gone.

"Are you?" he said. "Starting to understand?"

September 1975.

The days growing short again. The stars igniting earlier every night. A strange August has come to an end. Nights spent in the bed of a teenage girl who lived across the lake. Lindsey Elizabeth. I find myself writing this name on sheets of blue-lined paper, like an exercise in penmanship, as if to master the curves and loops of the letters is to understand. I am nearly eleven. Beginning the sixth grade. This year, my report card will devolve. I will stop praying in chapel. I will play Puck in an abridged version of *A Midsummer Night's Dream,* and forget my lines. I will look at girls, seventh- and eighth-graders, and I will see the naked planes and slopes of their bodies. I know the secret of each and every one of them . . . She is gone now—three hours away, starting college in Ithaca, New York—and in the daytime, I feel a friction inside myself. Heartsickness and relief. But in the dark, in the regressive solitude of my own room, emotion is unambiguous and terrifying in its purity. I am suffocating. I am freezing to death. I can't exist outside the warmth of her body . . . My brother will wake up crying in the middle of the night. Sometimes my father will let him wail for hours. Until the baby's voice is hoarse, until he has exhausted himself back to sleep. Sometimes I will leave my room and stand outside my father's closed door, and hear that he too is crying, irregular sobs dampened by mattress or pillow. I will touch the wood of the door, the cold metal knob. Then walk downstairs. Prepare the formula, as he has taught me. The air in the kitchen is cold, and I hold my hands close to the reddening coils of the stove top.

This year, there will be no Indian summer. Even in August, nocturnal drafts swept down from Canada, uncharacteristic and luxurious. Lindsey left her window open and we used blankets. Her body an abstract force in the darkness, like gravity, like a magnetic storm; and when I woke in the morning, it felt as if I'd washed up on some foreign shore. The rising sun, filtered by the leaves of a willow tree, playing silently over the floor and the bed, or rain slanting down from a gray sky, and the sound of it on the lake like the wingbeat of birds. She was solid then, bound together by skin and bone. Her black hair long and tangled. Eyes flickering behind closed lids. Lips slightly parted and the whiteness of teeth visible beyond. One morning, very early, staring at her from across the pillow, I performed the action myself. My heart racing, but in a new variation of its newfound rhythm. Something pushing me from behind, while I crossed meridians of fear and desire, and finally felt my lips touch down on hers. A moment later, she stirred. Drew me toward her. Into a nakedness so warm it seemed to singe the downy hair on my forearms, the tips of my eyelashes . . . Upstairs, my brother continues to mourn and make demands. I pour the formula into a plastic bottle capped with an artificial nipple. As I climb the stairs, I see the light in the nursery is on. My father is reaching into the crib, raising him up. A cool relief washes over me, because I don't have to touch that body, feel my brother's life in my arms. In this moment, as I meet my father's graying eyes, full of sympathy for me, full of love—which invokes no reciprocal feeling, none at all!—I see a world devoid of color and meaning. I see the void created by the absence of women . . . Later. Hours of night stretching out before me. Hours of vulnerability to the weird agenda of my own mind. What will I dream of before morning? Where will I be? In a canoe with my mother, lost on the ocean, beautifully alone with her and paddling into infinity; or terrified by the sight of her, pallid and glossy, imitating sleep? Tomorrow, my classmates will continue to treat me with the deference, the soft forbearance, which is the due of the bereaved. I know that I am like a lens, a magnifying glass which shows them the minute details of their own good fortune. To-morrow, I will look at older girls and notice the hardness at the tips of their breasts. I will write that name in cursive script on a sheet of blue-lined paper, and remember those nights when I was mercifully lost with her. If I feel the stirring of tears, I raise my hand, and Sister Madeline Mary excuses me without ques-tion. In the bathroom, locked behind a metal door, I wipe my eyes. Then, full of an undefined shame but unable to resist the temptation, I lick my fingers. Salt water. Scentless. Unlike those other tears of hers. Shed in darkness. Filling the lines and whorls of my fingertips, and leaving their strange olfactory evidence. In the mornings, as I walked home, as the dragonflies fed over the lake and the sun dried the dew on the grass, it was still with me. The smell of verdant moss, of a humid day broken by rain. The essence of her.

25 / We dropped Dolphin off at home, and brought Matthew back to Lindsey's. I drew him a warm bath; Lindsey prepared the guest room. She turned down the bedcovers, left a pair of pajamas on the mattress. A little later, bearing a Valium and a glass of water, I knocked on the door and found him already in bed. Reading one of Phil's issues of *Sky and Telescope*.

"This'll help you sleep," I said.

He swallowed the pill without question. "Who's Philip Davenport?" he asked, looking at the mailing label on the cover of the magazine.

"Some friend of Lindsey's," I said.

"He's her husband, isn't he?"

My brother gave me a long, cool stare. I sat down on the edge of the mattress. We didn't move or speak for quite some time, and it seemed I could feel the last of his energy bleeding away, see his muscles slackening, hear his heartbeat slowing.

"The cock is really crowing," he remarked.

"No, it's not."

"She never even saw me. They took me out of her and she was already dead."

"She loved you."

He turned his head into the pillow. "How can you love someone you never met? Never even saw?"

"She held you inside her. You were real to her."

My hand settled on his shoulder, and he considered it with a kind of confusion, as if it were some creature of uncertain temperament.

"We're so alike," I said. "We've both lost the same thing. We both want the same thing."

"What do we want?" he asked.

I didn't answer, and he repeated the question—a whisper, an echo.

"A family," I said.

My brother's eyelids blinked slowly, twice. Then settled closed. I sat there for a while longer. Until sleep staged its gentle ambush. Until his breathing was steady. Then I rose carefully to my feet, switched off the light. For some reason, I picked up the magazine. I left the door wide open.

—

On the way upstairs, I met a cool draft. Lindsey was sitting out on the porch, beneath that sky which remained miraculously clear. In the distance, the bridge arced over the water. The vista point where we had been this morning was, from here, indiscernible; but I could feel it out there, throbbing with the impossible heat of a phantom limb.

"I can't guarantee anything, but I think he's asleep."

She didn't speak, just handed me the photograph which Matthew had had on the beach.

"He found it," I explained, "in Connecticut."

"Is that what this is all about?"

I nodded, joining her at the little wrought-iron table, where a candle flickered inside the glass chimney of a hurricane lamp.

"When I saw that," she said, "my whole body went cold. I have one picture of you, of us. I know where it is, but I never take it out. That's how it's always been . . . I remember, when I was in Central America, I felt so far away from you in so many ways. I started to feel it all slipping away, fading away, and losing its hold over me. I was finally ready to forget and start over."

"Why didn't you?"

"I realized . . . I didn't want to."

"Sometimes," I said, my voice soft but unwavering, "the deeper you hide something, the stronger it gets. You think you've moved past it, but really you've only learned how to look away."

"Is there a difference?"

"I think so. Some things can't be left behind or erased. If you live without them, you're not really living."

Inside the curved glass of the lamp, wax dripped down the body of the candle, cooling and hardening. In the light, Lindsey's skin was a flawless amber, her face ancient and ageless, more beautiful, more valuable than anything else I'd ever known. Was it possible that all the mistakes we'd made, all the pain and hurt, were part of that beauty, one of the reasons for its pricelessness?

"I've been waiting so long," she said.

"For what?"

"To hear you say these things . . . and the things you said this morning . . . some of them."

"This morning—"

"Don't," she said. "I don't want you to apologize. I want you to tell me."

"Tell you what?"

"Everything you can remember. The way it was for you."

I studied the photograph in my hand. I stared into my own lost face and the boy stared back with an unnerving prescience. As if, for the split second that the camera's shutter had been open, he'd seen his own distant future, his own face impossibly aged, lined with unreadable desires.

"I won't deny I was confused, even frightened at first. But I always knew exactly what we were doing."

She held my hand and locked her fingers gently into mine.

"We were righting things," I said. "We were restoring each other."

"Tom, I want to believe that."

"Believe it."

"But even if I do, it doesn't change the fact that what I did was wrong. There have to be limits. Lines you don't step over, no matter what."

"Sometimes people outgrow those limits, Lindsey. Rules and laws. Definitions of right and wrong. Sometimes people rebel against them. Aren't there times, you think about those nights and your mind becomes so lucid. It's more than memory, more than pictures in your head. At those moments, can't you feel again how that girl felt? Desperate. Like she might die without someone to care for. Someone she knew she could trust."

"How do you know that?"

"Because . . . it was the same for me."

She lifted my hand and pressed it to her cheek, and a tear traced a warm line over my finger. I spoke her name then, as if just to hear it, as I had that very first night, standing at the threshold of her bedroom. Now, once again, my brother was sleeping. My mother—still irretrievably lost. Still a child's ideal that never grew up. Had so little changed in all this time? Had I moved forward at all?

"I still dream about lighting that match," she said. "That moment. I despise it. And at the same time, I hold it close. I can't abandon it."

"It was an accident, Lindsey."

"It was a consequence. There's a difference. And there's no excuse, no justification for what I did. I believed there was, but I was wrong. And I'll tell you something, Tom. The thing I'm most afraid of is that I'd do it again. Because when that place caught fire, I felt so strong. Running home through that meadow, I believed the air in my lungs was pure again."

"Why did you ever come back?"

"I think I wanted someone to suspect me, to start asking questions. I wanted something from you, but I didn't know what. When you came to me that night, and you were hurting so much, and so was I, I couldn't send you away. I couldn't see why we should be alone . . . when we could be together."

After a lengthy silence, Lindsey rose to her feet, wandered slowly out of the candle's reach. The darkness slipped over her like a garment. I followed her. Stepping up behind her, I placed my hands on her shoulders. The fog was finally coming in, wrapping its tentacles around the towers and the suspension cables of the bridge. Lindsey's body shivered as she breathed in the darkening air.

"I know what I want," she said. "For the first time in so long, I know. But I'm afraid of how we got here."

"Don't be."

"I don't want to turn away anymore, but the impulse is so strong. Don't you ever feel that way? Don't you ever want to forget?"

I nodded, and it seemed I could sense Matthew turning in his sleep, dreaming of undefinable things. "It doesn't work," I said. "I know that now."

"You're not afraid?"

I shook my head. "I've always known we could be together . . . if we could just find our own place."

"Is that what this is?" she asked, as if indicating something directly before us. Something real but invisible. The border of a foreign country. I grasped her left hand, the ring finger still bare, as though it had always been that way. She leaned into me, and I held her in an embrace which lasted a long time. Traffic murmured in the distance. A horn blast, gentle as a sigh; the dreamy wail of an ambulance. When Lindsey finally raised her face to mine, it underwent a rare transformation, blushed with a new faith, with the slow movement of dreams once again taking up residence inside her. Her eyelids closed, her lips moved. "I'm pregnant," she whispered, and as I held her, listening to her breathing, slow and steady now, I imagined the course of the oxygen. Its dispersal into her bloodstream. Its microscopic arrival deep inside her. Across the bay, the headlands were as dark as sleep; and to the west, the lights of the bridge strained against the fog, tracing an arc of luminous dots over the water. It seemed I could reach out and gather up in my fingers that string of light. Those glowing beads. For weeks now, I'd thought it was fear swelling in me. I was wrong. It was freedom.

———

In the days following, Matthew was like a landscape obeying a change of season, preparing for a long, cold hibernation. Calm, almost listless, he said his novel had proved to be a piece of shit, and he wasn't writing it anymore. Likewise, the Virgin stood unfinished, in a flood of nudity which had ceased just short of her mouth and nose. He started sleeping excessively. In the morning, I left him in his bed, and often returned from work to find him in the same place, or staring at the television, at some grim documentary about the Holocaust or the Model T Ford. He ate little. Food I cooked for him would end up in the toilet bowl, or I'd find it the next day beginning to spoil under the couch. One night, Dolphin called, and after introductory formalities, he told her to fuck herself with a cucumber. I took the phone from him.

"What's his goddamn problem?" she said.

"He's having a bad week."

"Tell her to fuck herself," he mumbled. "With a squash."

"I've still got a pair of your boxers," Dolphin said to me.

I pressed at my temple, fought off a hot flash of paranoia. That real-estate-baron father, twenty years hard labor for not keeping a lock on my underwear drawer. The line went dead, thanks to my brother, who was stretched across the couch, in the posture of Michelangelo's reclining Adam, arm extended to the phone cradle, forefinger severing the connection.

"You're not scoring any points with her," I said.

"She's a cunt."

"I thought you were in love."

"I was mistaken," he said, his face blank and pale. "I've never loved anyone in my whole life . . ."

I tried to talk to him. I offered to tell him more about our mother. But he acted like I was speaking another language, and appeared to have forgotten what had happened on the beach. I couldn't find the photographs. He'd hidden them, or destroyed them. And as if he knew I'd called Connecticut, could feel our father's arrival forming over him with the invisible slowness of an icicle or a stalactite, a film of resentment began to glaze his eyes. My apartment grew unbearable. Gray and hopeless. But outside, San Francisco shone with specificity.

Lindsey and I were planning.

A nocturnal wedding. The authorship of our own vows. A trip to Europe or the South Seas. We made love without contraception, and with each repetition our claim of parenthood felt more valid and unassailable. Still, there was Philip. He was due back from New Zealand in a few days. Saturday, he and Lindsey were scheduled to host Zach's eighth birthday party. We discussed this business over an early breakfast on Haight Street, Lindsey's face gently flushed, still glowing with the morning's pleasure the way the sky still glows after sunset.

"It's a problem," she said. "Because I don't want to ruin his birthday."

I nodded.

"I mean, their relationship is so fragile as it is . . ."

Bebop played from the rear. Something hit the grill and sizzled.

"Stop staring at me," she said, blushing.

I made believe I was snapping out of a trance.

"Look at something else."

"Why would I want to do that?" I asked.

The food arrived. A feta scramble for me. Blueberry pancakes for Lindsey, which she shellacked with orange marmalade. On the far sidewalk, the Haight's resident wizard held a pose of medieval serenity. He wore a black robe and cape, a rubber-ball nose, a pair of Mickey Mouse ears. A handlebar mustache curled up golden around his cheeks. He held a wooden staff topped by a shrunken skull. I watched the approach of a family of tourists. The little girl, noting the ears, pointed excitedly at his back. Then she saw the rest of him, and the muscles in her face seized up. Not with fear precisely, but with a kind of unutterable knowledge.

"We could tell him after the party," I said. "On Sunday."

"What do you mean, 'we'?"

"I mean you and me. Us."

"You want to be there? I don't think that's such a good idea."

"Why not?"

She stared down at her breakfast for a while. "I don't know. I just think he deserves some privacy."

The waiter filled my coffee cup, drifted to the next table with the lethargic grace of a bumblebee.

"What do you think he'll do?" I asked.

"Do?"

"When you tell him."

She fingered one of her earrings. Outside, the morning's curtain of fog slowly parted. The sun shone, with a tentative brilliance, on storefronts painted red, purple, turquoise.

"Maybe you should move out now," I said. "Before he gets back."

"If you're worried about my safety, you can put your mind at ease. He doesn't get angry."

I gave her a skeptical look.

"What I mean is, he's not capable of violence. He'll blame the whole thing on himself."

After a long pause, I said, "Maybe you should write him a letter."

"Oh, Tom."

"No, I'm serious. I mean, that's what I'd want. I wouldn't want to hear the words, out loud."

She closed her eyes. "Can we have a few minutes?" she said. "Before you have to go?"

I checked my watch. I was already late for the dailies. Even now, Davey and Goliath were standing by a bus bound for Boise, Idaho, a little blind girl and her Seeing Eye poodle in the window, waving goodbye. Even now, Goliath's canine heart was pounding. It was breaking.

"I wouldn't tell him everything," I said.

Lindsey placed her fork on her plate.

"I just wouldn't tell him everything."

Our waiter returned with his perfectly sculpted hair and his mythological physique. He indicated the marmalade jar. "Are you in a mood?" he asked her. "Or are you serious about marmalade?"

"Both. When it comes to marmalade, I'm in a serious mood."

The two of them discussed the merits of the house jam, the art of preserving, which Lindsey had once studied under the tutelage of a great-aunt. I imagined her in our own home, presiding over a double boiler, the air thick with the aroma of strawberries, oranges, apricots. Across the street, the Mickey Mouse wizard seemed to be watching us. Expressionless. He twirled a waxed end of his handlebar mustache.

"By the way," the waiter said, "that's a gorgeous ring."

"Thank you." Lindsey shot me a brief, sheepish glance, then turned to the guy as he moved off. "It's Cubist."

——

I returned home that night, and found Matthew on the couch watching TV in the dark. He didn't acknowledge my presence. Neither did Mingus, who lay stretched out at his feet in an imitative posture, like some kind of disciple. The room, warm and stuffy, smelled faintly of his body odor. I opened a window and leaned back against the sill.

"How was your day?"

"What the fuck do you care?"

I sat there for a while, waiting for something to happen. The movie on television was asking us to believe that Yul Brynner and William Shatner were brothers in Czarist Russia, the former a spendthrift womanizing soldier, the latter a saintly monk. At the sound of the word "Karamazov," Matthew let go a fart which, in terms of length and resonance, was the work of a professional.

"That was impressive," I said. "But I'm going to excuse myself, if you don't mind."

I hung up my jacket in the anemic glare of the television and noticed that the hallway floor was spotted with what seemed to be little phosphorescent rocks. I stepped forward and picked one up. Jagged, surprisingly light. I reached for Matthew's dimmer switch, and that crimson glow washed over the room—and over the now decapitated body of the statue. Fragments of the head lay scattered all over the floor. A length of metal piping, the size of a billy club, rested at her feet.

I walked back to the living room, paused in the archway.

The light from the television flickered over his body. His posture hadn't changed. He looked dead, his skin the color of mold.

"We have to talk," I said.

No answer. On the TV, the scene had changed. The Karamazov family, as doomed and dysfunctional as any in twentieth-century America, was debating the existence of God.

"Matthew . . ."

"Why don't you shut up?" he said, his voice thin and pained. "The more you talk, the more my head hurts."

"You still have a headache?" I said.

"It's not a headache."

"What do you mean?"

One of his fingers moved slowly to the base of his skull.

"It's a tumor," he said seriously. "It's lodged in my medulla oblongata. It's choking off vital nerve centers."

I stepped into the room and sat down in the armchair. The remote control was on the coffee table, beside a cashed pipe of marijuana. I muted the sound and silenced that monk, whose boyish eyes were growing damp, full of pity and blind faith.

"Listen to me, Matt. I don't know what to do anymore. I don't know how to help you."

"There's no cure," he murmured. "It's too advanced."

"I tried to make you an appointment today . . . to talk to somebody. I'm having trouble finding an opening."

"You think I'm crazy?"

"No. Just that . . . you need to talk to someone. Someone objective, who can help you see what all this means."

He buried his face in the cushion, as if the idea were fundamentally insulting. Facile and trite. I felt embarrassed for having suggested it.

"Listen," I said. "I want you to take a bath. Then we'll go out and get something to eat."

"I've stopped eating."

"No, you haven't."

"There are kids starving in Africa. I don't want to waste food."

"We'll go have burritos," I said. "Then we'll go to a movie. Your choice. We'll invite Dolphin."

"That'll be difficult."

"Why?"

"Because she's dead."

I took a deep breath and stood up.

"Don't let it upset you," Matthew said. "It happens to everyone. It's natural. Like this movie. It's a historical epic, and someone always dies in historical epics. And you know what kills them?"

I had started across the room, picked up the telephone, and was now placing it on the coffee table.

"Do you know?"

"No, I don't."

"History," he said.

I held the receiver out to him. "Call her."

"You call her," he said. "You take her to the movies and you bring her home and you get to know her in the biblical sense. She'll love it. She thinks about you when she comes, you know. I know that because it's your name she's moaning, not mine."

My stomach knotted up, but I acted like I hadn't heard him. Just continued to placidly offer the phone. The dial tone was a steady sinister hum, like bees in a hive.

"Come on," I said.

Very slowly, he reached out, drew the receiver toward his ear and mouth.

"Hello?" he said. "Mom? I just thought I'd call and say fuck you."

A second later, he was on his feet. The phone sailed across the room, hit the wall with a musical clang. My hands had shot out, too late, to stop him—one was closed around his throwing arm, the other his shirt front.

"Hit me," he said. "You've always wanted to, so just do it."

I let go of him, but didn't move away. We just stood there, Matthew making sounds in his throat, as though he wanted to cry and couldn't. On the floor, the phone beeped; then a robotic voice began to issue instructions. I walked over and hung it up.

"You're sending me back," he said. "Aren't you?"

"Matt . . ."

"Just answer the question."

"I don't know what else to do."

His features were unreadable in the grainy light.

"Tell me," I said, "what to do."

He returned his body to the couch. With a tentative meow, Mingus came out of hiding, leapt elegantly onto the open cushion. On the television, Mr. Brynner had his hands closed around the neck of a man whom I assumed to be his father, while Mr. Shatner said a panicked prayer in the background.

"You can just tell," Matthew said, his left hand absently stroking the cat, "someone's going to die in this movie."

———

The next day, Nile called and said she wanted to arrange a meeting. She'd be grateful (and I quote) if I'd have some coffee with her, as things had ended in a fashion too ragged for her tastes. She believed we'd shared something of significance, and there was no excuse for not honoring that meaning with a corresponding closure. At 8 P.M. on Tuesday at Café Trieste.

"All right," I said.

"Good," she said. "This will be a perfect opportunity to return each other's personal effects. Try to find that earring, will you? And don't forget the garter belt. I'm sure you'd like to frame that piece, but it's the only one I've got."

I arrived late and Nile arrived later. While I waited, I drank a cappuccino, my eyes wandering aimlessly over the newsprint of the *Chronicle*. I looked up from the arts section to see her striding through the door. Clad in those black bell-bottom pants, a tan faux-leather jacket. Carrying a shopping bag from Nordstrom. Her gaze swept over the place searchlight-style. I stood up, obeying some antiquated instinct, and she walked right up to me, kissed me on the cheek. Perfunctorily. Nonetheless, it shocked my nervous system.

"Do you want something?" I asked.

"A double latte."

At the counter, I ordered hers, and another for myself. I needed something to do with my hands, something to keep them steady. I hadn't seen her since that last night we'd spent together, and I was deeply ashamed of what I'd done. Yet it was more than that. More than shameful anxiety spreading through me. Earlier that afternoon, I'd gathered together her things. I'd found the earring under a magazine on the floor, and added it to the small pile on the bed. A pair of Felix the Cat boxer shorts, a Kate Bush CD, the garter belt, and a pair of panties. I lay back on the mattress and held the earring to the light. A tiny female figure. Oval head and conical torso, simple horizontal arms. Based on sculptures by the Akan people of the Ivory Coast. Kept by native women to induce conception and to assure the birth of a beautiful child. *I'm not a native,* she'd said one night, *but I'll remove them anyway, just to be safe.* I lay there for a long time before I picked up the panties and held the crotch to my nose and mouth. Something remained. Growing solid inside me, pressing against an unhealed place.

"Thanks," Nile said, as I returned with the drinks and a piece of chocolate cheesecake. She had shed her jacket and was wearing a crushed-velvet top which I tried, unsuccessfully, not to look at. She smiled, her lips thick and painted, her teeth large and white.

"Hi," she said.

"Hi."

Without delay, she took a bite of the cake.

"Oh," I said. "I'll get another fork."

"You can use this one, silly. I don't have cooties." She handed it to me and I could find no alternative to putting the utensil in my mouth.

"Did you find the earring?"

I nodded as I chewed, and relief washed over Nile's face.

"They were a gift," she said.

"Oh?"

"From this woman I was seeing for a while. It's nice to have mementos, things to remember people by. Don't you think?"

"I do, yeah."

"Because relationships end, you know, but the connection doesn't. I think when people are intimate with each other, sexually, they're giving part of themselves to someone else. And I don't mean giving in the sense of sharing in some temporary way. I mean permanently. You *impart* a fraction of yourself to someone, and he or she carries it with them always, and vice versa." She sipped her latte, daintily cleared some foam from her upper lip, then licked it from her finger. "I think that's what makes adultery and cheating on people so serious. Because the physicality may end, but the transgression never does, because there's always that fractional component of 'the other' active inside you."

"Sounds a bit parasitic," I said.

She shrugged. "I think, at its most extreme, you could characterize it that way. But at the other end of the scale, it's more like a kind of ore, a mineral that lies buried."

I nodded, hands closed around my mug. A lull in the conversation was bridged by the sound of the espresso machine, of milk being transformed into a weightless froth.

"You look great," Nile said. "And I don't just mean physically. You look happy."

"Thanks."

She seemed to be waiting for reciprocation, which I couldn't bring myself to provide.

"How about your cat? How's he? Mingus."

"Oh, not so good. He's really apathetic. I bought him a scratch post, but he just sits there and stares at it, sort of tentatively paws it. Like the apes with the monolith at the beginning of *Space Odyssey*."

"Hmm. He always got pretty animated when we were screwing," she said, her tone utterly blasé. She reached for the fork. "Maybe it was the frequency of my voice. Does he do it when you fuck Lindsey?"

As insouciantly as cheesecake can be chewed, she chewed her cheesecake.

"She used to be very quiet in bed," Nile continued. "Hardly made a peep no matter how good it was, and as you know, I happen to have a bit of a talent for oral sex. She's a lot different now. Much less passive, and a lot louder . . . I left that part out the other day. I guess I felt guilty for some reason, I'm not sure why. In any event, the feeling has passed."

I stared at her, quietly. "What are you talking about?"

"What do you think I'm talking about?"

"You know," I said after quite a long silence, "I didn't come here to fight. And I don't really care what happened last week."

She shook her head. "You care. You just think, on a relative scale, it doesn't matter. But it happened and you can't erase it. While you were at work playing with your dolls, she was mine. She was begging *me* and it was my name she was saying and it was the taste of me in her mouth."

Without another word, I stood up, grabbed my jacket and the bag she'd brought. Outside, the air was warm, and destined to get warmer—I could sense it, the way animals feel the imminence of an earthquake. My pulse throbbed in my temple as I walked downhill, trying to remember where I'd parked.

"Hey! HEY!"

I turned around.

"If you think I'm walking home with a bag from the *Gap*," she shouted, "you're fucking crazy."

Nile charged down the sidewalk, took the Nordstrom bag from my hands, and dumped my stuff onto the concrete. Then she transferred her belongings, her breath coming in rhythmic heaves.

"You fuck," she said. "You son of a bitch. I deserve better than what I've gotten from you, *and* her. What is it with you two anyway? Doesn't intimacy mean anything to you? Doesn't it have any sacred value? You can just walk away after that shit you pulled the other night? Leave me at eight in the morning with no explanation, never call, just blow off a dinner you *said* you'd come to, and I've got to sit there with my parents with a sore vagina? I had a bladder infection, you fucking bastard, and it felt like someone was branding my insides."

"Yeah!" some stranger shouted from across the street. "You fucking bastard!"

Nile started north, the heels of her shoes clacking sharply against the sidewalk. Fading. Slowing. Until she stopped about a half a block away. Dropping the bag, she rested against the front of an apartment building. I crouched down and collected my things. Then slowly walked up to her, leaned against the same brick wall. High above us, on Telegraph Hill, Coit Tower stood like a saint, keeping watch over its adoptive city.

"I'm sorry," I told her. "I know an apology isn't good enough, but I am."

Her fingers, which had been clenched in a fist, unfurled like the petals of a flower. Stepping closer, I slid my hand into hers, and she held it, tightly.

"Please," she said. "I don't want things to end like this. I like you. I really like you."

We stood there holding hands, Nile's face angled skyward, her lips slightly parted. I stared at her profile, remembering the things that had happened and imagining all the things that wouldn't. She turned to me then. Her front teeth bit down on her lower lip. When I tried to look away, her hand stopped me, her fingers cool and firm against my cheek. I closed my eyes and thought of Lindsey, as if to have her in my mind was compensation. I could smell the coffee and chocolate on Nile's breath. I could feel, not a kiss, but the shadow of one. Her lips just shy of mine, conducting a slow magnetic energy. Her arms wrapping around my waist, her body pinning me to the wall.

"God, I'm dripping," she said. "Arguments are the best foreplay."

"I can't do this."

"Yes, you can."

"Please," I said. "Don't touch me again."

"Don't fight me, Tom. You know what's going on here. We both know."

I looked into her eyes and felt terrified by the feeling in my chest. Those wings, beating wildly. Her hands touched my face.

She caressed me as if I were more than a lover. As if I were a promise, a thing to cultivate.

"Take me home," she said. "Make love with me."

I let go of her waist and removed her hands from my cheeks. A car drove by and its headlights flashed over us, revealed our shadows blending on the pavement.

"She's pregnant," I said.

Nile's eyes flinched, then moved away. The sound of the car was swallowed by the larger clamor of Columbus Avenue.

"It's mine," I said. "I mean, I'm the one."

"How do you know?"

"We just know."

"Well," she said, so quietly I could barely hear her. "Should I express . . . my condolences or my congratulations?"

I didn't answer.

"I'd better go," she said.

"Let me walk you home."

"No. No, I think I want to be alone. In fact, I think I need an extended period of solitude. Solitude and celibacy. Perhaps of a religious nature." She forced a smile, her eyes shining like crystal. She was about to cry. In those moments, I wasn't sure what I was accountable for. I couldn't tell the difference between responsibility and wrongdoing.

"I'm really glad we got together like this," Nile said, picking up the bag. "It's just good to have some closure, you know?"

I stepped toward her with the intention of giving a hug. She kissed me on the mouth. A single kiss, rushed and urgent, as if she were late for an appointment. Then she was walking away. I listened to the sound of her heels. When she'd rounded the corner and had passed out of sight, she started running.

⌞ ⌟

At Lindsey's house, the living room windows were open. Light glowed warm and yellow inside. She had Joni Mitchell on the stereo, and the music drifted down to the sidewalk. An album she'd played that summer. Melancholy and spare. I hadn't heard it in years. The chords, the melodies were like the echoes, long delayed, of every night we'd spent together. I rang the bell, and her silhouette appeared in one of the windows.

"It's me," I said.

A few seconds later, the door unlocked itself. Lindsey waited for me at the top of the staircase, in leggings and a long undershirt. Her hair was pulled back in a ponytail and she was wearing her eyeglasses.

"I wasn't expecting you. I thought you were going to stay with Matt."

I nodded. "I just wanted to see you, for a little while."

She led me by the hand into the living room, where the feathers of the albatross trembled in a tepid breeze. "I was working in the back," she explained, walking toward the stereo and lowering the volume. "Maybe I should change this music. It's a little depressing. You've got to be in the mood."

"I love you," I said suddenly.

A smile playing over her lips, as she pronounced the same words. We kissed and I touched her face, her arms. I put my hands under her shirt and felt the warmth of her flesh. I touched her everywhere, to cover over the tactile memory of Nile. To bury it alive. I was aching with desire and contrition.

"Saffron's coming over," she said.

"Soon?"

"Yes."

"Really soon?"

"It's a tragedy . . ." She placed her lips carefully against my ear. " . . . but you can't have me." She bit my earlobe and eased out of my arms, made a show of tending to her disarranged hair. "I'm drinking tea. Would you like some?"

"All right."

"I've got quite a selection. I went tea shopping today. Because I'm going to stop drinking coffee."

I followed her into the kitchen, where she filled a ceramic pot with water. The newspaper, I noticed, was spread out on the table. The apartment listings. She had three ads circled in red ink.

"So . . . I looked at a place today. In Noe Valley. A really gorgeous Victorian. Second floor. I want some altitude, don't you? It was a great space, but I don't know about that neighborhood. It's pretty yuppified . . . Okay. I've got chamomile, raspberry, something with a scary old lady on it, and orange pekoe."

She turned around and caught me wiping a tear from my cheek.

"Hey," she said. "What's going on?"

I shook my head, and as she approached I started crying in earnest. She took me in her arms and I felt so relieved, so happy and full, that it seemed I couldn't take another breath. I thought of what Philip had once told me about diving under the ice canopies of Antarctica. How he'd felt the urge to lose his exit hole, use his twenty minutes of air to swim as far as he could, then surrender, gazing at the glow of pristine ice. Part of me wanted that now. For oxygen to grow scarce, for the world to go dark. As if I needed no more than the promise of us. As if prescience, no matter how accurate, was somehow superior to the future itself. But a moment later, that feeling disappeared. Lindsey's arms were strong and confident. Her body was changing, even now. I didn't have to let go. Not for a long time.

"I love you, Lindsey."

"I know."

"I've never loved anybody but you."

"Don't get me started," she said. "I wept in front of the realtor today." She hugged me more firmly. "I've been crying all afternoon."

━

I'd been right about the weather. I woke up the next morning to find orange light bleeding all over the city. The fog had stalled in the oceanic distance, and heat was rushing in from the north and the east and the south, like something escaped from a cage. The DJ on the college station, talking about eighty-plus degrees, placed a call, live and on the air, to the mayor's office, requesting that all San Francisco's beaches be declared "nude for a day." The secretary refused to patch him through, so he set about advising general anarchy, backed up by the insurgent guitars of The Surf Teens. Matthew's door was closed, all was quiet inside. Late the previous evening, Dolphin had dropped by, and they'd talked for a while without incident. She left around midnight, wearing the exhausted, tireless expression of a wartime nurse. I showed her to the door and she paused on the landing.

"Why won't you let him stay?" she asked.

We regarded each other without speaking. It wasn't judgment or hostility in her eyes. I didn't know what it was. Only that it unnerved me; it kept me awake. Sunday, our father's arrival, seemed a long way off. Yet, when I thought of Philip, minutes and hours elapsed at breakneck speed. Lindsey and I were still undecided about exactly how to tell him, and what to do about Zach's party.

It was Wednesday.

The sun leaning over us. The sky an unblemished canopy of blue. That day, I moved Davey, inch by inch, onto his knees before an altar dimly lit. Sometime after three, I was summoned to the telephone—and the voice on the other end sounded fatherly and priestly, the voice of the one person who could hear me and forgive me.

"Are you in New Zealand?" I said.

"No."

"You're back?"

"We wrapped early. Listen, could you meet me later for a drink?"

I tried to analyze his tone. Definitely urgent, but basically calm. Lethargic, even. Jet lag or despair? I remembered the words he'd spoken before he left. *Try to fit her into your busy schedule. Make sure she's okay.*

"I've fallen a bit behind here," I said. "I was planning to stay late."

Tabitha passed by and directed her uncanny Mae West impression at the receiver. "He's *working* tonight," she said, giving me an aphrodisiacal wink as she headed for the screening room.

"How about eight?" I suggested.

"You talking to me or Zsa Zsa?"

I covered the receiver. "He thought you were doing Zsa Zsa."

Tabitha splayed both hands over her chest and shouted, "I just *adore* a penthouse view!"

"She sounds spirited," Phil said. "Is she hot?"

"She's very hot."

"Is she single?"

"You looking for a date?" I asked.

"I'm thinking of you," he replied flatly. "As always, I'm thinking of you."

———

The second floor of Vesuvio. Windows open and the sound of the street pouring in. On the stereo, some beatnik with a hypnotically deep voice, speaking over a catchy bass rhythm. On the wall across the alley, that giant portrait of Baudelaire looming in the dusk like a voyeuristic god. I found Phil at the most distant table. He looked up, startled, as I claimed the opposing seat.

"Sorry I'm late."

He responded with a total lack of concern, as if time were a concept which had lost all relevance. His first pint of beer was almost gone, and an empty shot glass remained in its vicinity, like an orbiting moon. The waitress appeared without delay and we ordered a round. Anchor Steam and Jack Daniel's.

"This town's hot as hell," he said.

I nodded. "How was New Zealand?"

"Gorgeous. Weird. We met a Japanese research team in the forest, looking for moas."

"I thought the moa was extinct."

"Slaughtered," Phil clarified, "by Spanish cocksuckers in the 1700s."

"So, what, they were looking for bones?"

"No, the real thing. They were hiking around playing synthesized moa calls. Dead serious."

"Looking for giant extinct birds."

"Giant extinct *flightless* birds. Every once in a while, there's a sighting. It's like Bigfoot or the Loch Ness monster."

"Oh . . ."

"Pathetic," he said. "But someone has to carry the torch. Keep on believing there's still mystery on this planet, and things left to discover."

The drinks arrived and Phil told me to put my money away.

"To crackpot idealism," he said.

We clinked shot glasses. The bourbon tore smoothly down my throat, and I immediately wanted another. Lindsey hadn't called me all day. I didn't even know if they'd seen each other. But I'd been rehearsing speeches for hours, envisioning scenes which ranged from the pitiable to the violent. Philip collapsing into tears in public, the two of us drinking to his destroyed marriage until we stumbled out into the street well after midnight, falling down and vomiting—or Philip escorting me out to the alley where, under the painted gaze of Charles Baudelaire, he would beat the shit out of me. I watched him sip his beer, then return it, with a report reminiscent of a courtroom gavel, to the table.

"I had a dream on the plane," he said. "It scared me halfway to hell. Remember when I went to Venezuela for that *Nova* piece? The tarantulas? It started there. I'm at the Piaroa feast eating barbecued arachnids. The Indians are picking their teeth with the fangs. I start getting real dizzy. I look down at the spread, flickering under torchlight, and the spiders begin to move like they're coming back to life. I pass out. Next thing I know, I'm on a boat in the middle of the ocean. With Lindsey. We have to get somewhere, it's urgent. There are crocodiles in the water and baby egrets are falling out of the sky. The crocodiles are eating them and the water's turning red. Suddenly, all of our navigational devices quietly stop functioning. We're in a fog. An iceberg floats by off the starboard bow. Then the fog lifts and the stars are out. Perfectly clear, as if the sky has been polished. And I'm overwhelmed by this gift of nature. Steer by the stars, I think to myself, until I realize I can't, because they mean nothing to me. I can't read them. The ability, I think to myself, has been deselected by evolution. Now I start looking for Lindsey. She's not on deck anymore. I'm scared out of my mind because maybe she's fallen overboard. I walk below, into a subterranean catacomb filled with half-fossilized bones. Up ahead, there's a phosphorescent bead curtain, made of the silk lines of the New Zealand glowworm. I part the curtain and there's a moa. Standing. Alive. I'm half the size of this thing and I notice it's crying. Not making noise, just tears falling discreetly from its big eyes. Then I start crying. Because I realize I'm dead. I got a bad tarantula."

I nodded grimly.

"Do you believe," he asked, "that dreams can be prognostic?"

"Well . . . I don't know."

"Because I walked into the house this afternoon. Unannounced. I just slipped my key into the lock and walked upstairs because, you know, I live there. And I get upstairs and what do you think I find in the living room?"

I swallowed hard. "A moa?"

"Guess," he said pointedly.

My mind was a profound blank.

"How are things with you and Nile?"

"Me and Nile?" I cleared my throat. "Well, we broke up."

"You broke *up?* Is this that serious?"

I just looked at him.

"Is it that serious?" he repeated.

My pulse was racing. A drop of sweat trickled down my rib cage. "It's serious," I said.

He slumped back in his seat, scanned the area for the waitress, who was nowhere in sight. He tipped back his beer. A few bubbles of foam clung to his upper lip. We sat in silence while I tried to remember my rehearsed lines. God, how I respected him in those moments. His fatalistic calm. An almost soldierly composure.

"Is it more than sex?" he finally asked.

I held his stare and truly saw him. Unshaven, tired, soon to be drunk. To his left, outside the window and beyond his field of vision, a mural of degradation: strip clubs, adult bookstores, the neon sign for The Garden of Eden. "Fuck," I said; and gradually, a change came over him. Not something visible, but something I could feel, like a rise or a drop in temperature.

"Are they in love with each other?" he asked.

It took me several seconds to process this sentence. For a moment, I thought I'd simply misheard him. Yet why was there no hostility in his eyes? My brain's neuronic gears shifted. I moved a hand around as a prelude to stammering.

"You got upstairs," I said. "And what happened?"

"Well, they were clothed at least. Nile's on the couch crying, *miserably,* there's a rose, a fucking red rose, lying on the coffee table, and Lindsey comes out of the kitchen with a cup of tea that she promptly drops to the floor at the sight of me. Clichéd enough for you?"

I shut my eyes.

"Tom?"

"Yeah . . ."

"Are you all right?"

I shook my head ambiguously.

"I don't mean to upset you, kid, but I'd like to know what the hell is going on here. They're in fucking *love?* Is this what you're telling me?"

"Did you talk to Lindsey?"

"No. I turned around and left."

"Would you—" I said. "I really have to pee. I'll be right back."

In the basement bathroom, I splashed cold water over my face. I hadn't eaten since lunch and I was already buzzed. It was cooler down here. The music prodded at the ceiling and guilt settled over me like dust. I knew what I had to do. Take a deep breath, march back upstairs—and tell him the truth. I knew I wouldn't. Not tonight. Somehow it seemed safer to maintain his ignorance, as if Lindsey and I would be able to slip away, unde-tected, while his attention was diverted. I bent over the sink. I couldn't bear to look at myself in the mirror. The more I thought about it, the more I felt like some territorial animal, powerless against its own instincts for survival and happiness. And what about Nile? The idea of her showing up with flowers and tears didn't surprise me. In a way, I found the news comforting, a balm for my raw conscience. At least someone was taking care of her. At the first-floor pay phone, I tried Lindsey. Three rings, then the answering machine clicked into action. "Riders on the Storm." Thunder crash. Keyboard solo. I mounted the narrow staircase and returned to the table. A fresh shot of bourbon was waiting for me.

"The thing that kills me," Phil said, "is that on the most pragmatic level I'm responsible. I created the conditions. I invited her to that damn dinner party. Or was—Christ, was it going on before then? And that's why Lindsey was so pissed that I was trying to set you up with Nile, and so violently pissed when she saw the two of you together that night. Excuse me, but I'm developing a revelatory rash here."

I downed the bourbon and the alcohol dealt a soft blow to my equilibrium. The room tilted and swayed, as if the bar had just put out to sea.

"Am I right about this?" he asked.

I didn't answer.

"How long has this been going on?"

"I don't know."

"Kid, you look sick."

"I've felt better."

"Is this coming as a shock? I mean, a month ago, you were warning *me,* remember? It was here in this very building. You told me to take them seriously."

I nodded.

"And Nile sat here that night and had the gall, that fucking . . . *Jezebel* . . . had the nerve to sit here and talk about irony. Remember? 'Irony's the basic building block of matter'?"

"I remember."

"Jesus. I mean, everything's coming clear. I've been feeling this for months and denying it. I knew she was seeing someone. I knew it."

There was a sudden lull in the bar—the music stopped, conversation thinned out—as if the gravity of Philip's words demanded a moment of silence.

"I owe you an apology," he said then.

"What?"

"In my more paranoid moments . . . I thought maybe it was you."

I glanced away and felt a wave of nausea. The room pitched starboard. Baudelaire raised an eyebrow. I removed my eyeglasses, throwing everything into a meaningless blur. I had to leave. I wanted to sleep. I couldn't bear another moment of consciousness.

"It's fucking ridiculous, I know. I mean, you're like her little brother."

"Speaking of siblings," I said, "I really have to go."

"What do you mean?"

"My brother's in town. He ran away from home."

"Are you serious? Isn't he, like, twelve?"

"He's sixteen," I said. "He's having some emotional problems."

Philip nodded slowly. I should have gotten up right away. I didn't.

"I realize now," he said, "my attitude about them, that heterosexism, was just a defense mechanism. Part of a larger network of denial. Something's dying between us, I've sensed it for a long time, but I've been too scared to acknowledge it. Is Nile the cause, or is she just an effect?"

"I don't know, Phil."

He turned to the window. It was dark now, the neon and the streetlights shrouding the neighborhood in unnatural hues. A bus rolled by, plunging into the heart of the Financial District, and the electric wires twanged and pinged like the strings of some ethereal guitar. How could he be made to understand that what was happening here was a phenomenon far more complex than adultery? Was it any kind of solace to learn that a thing being lost was never truly possessed to begin with?

"I love her," he said. "More than I ever loved Claire."

His eyes stared, unblinking, at the street. This went on for an interminable length of time. I just kept sitting there, the room weaving gently on an ocean of lies.

"I'm not going to lose her," he told me. "Not to a twenty-five-year-old girl. Not to anybody."

⎿

I tried Lindsey again from a pay phone on the street. Where the hell was she? I called my apartment, but the phone just rang and rang. Doubtless she'd been trying to reach me there, and for all I knew, my brother had disabled the phone. My mind, alcoholically lucid, seemed certain of this. He'd ripped it out of the wall. I started for my car, which was parked on the edge of Chinatown. It was stupid to drive. I did it anyway, concerned that I'd need the car later. Rolling down the window, I coasted slowly and defensively to the Mission. In my apartment, the shower was running. He was cleaning himself. A good sign. I checked the answering machine. Sure enough, it had been disconnected. I walked into the bathroom without knocking and hit a wall of steam. I went straight to the curtain, pulled it open as I spoke his name. On her hands and knees, Dolphin gasped, but didn't try to cover herself.

"Shit," I said, averting my eyes. "What are you doing here?"

I walked back into the hall, searched the place for Matthew. Somehow I knew he wasn't there. His door was open, the light on. The room stank of semen and sweat, the wreckage of some kind of sex game involving raw eggs and bondage. Shells lay scattered around the room and one of the kitchen chairs trailed pieces of twine from each leg. The seat and the hardwood floor were wet and glistening. Nausea gripped me deep in my gut, and as I neared the bathroom, the feeling was something more like terror.

"Dolphin," I said. "I'm coming in, okay?"

I knelt down by the tub, separated from her by the curtain. Seen through the clear plastic, her body was without detail. She was still on all fours.

"Are you all right?" I asked.

"Your brother," she said, "is a little nuts, I believe."

"Did he hurt you?"

There was a lengthy delay before she responded. "I've been hurt worse."

I parted the curtain and placed a hand on her back. The water ran over my arm, soaking my shirtsleeve. Her wrists and ankles were chafed, dotted here and there with spots of blood.

"Should we go to the hospital?" I said.

She shook her head.

"I think we should."

"He didn't rape me," Dolphin said, somewhat defensively. "I know what rape is, okay?" She looked at me, her eyes bloodshot. From crying, I assumed. Then she started rinsing them.

"What's wrong with your eyes?"

"Nothing."

I repeated the question, as tenderly as possible.

"They're burning," she said. "He came in them, all right? Anything else you want to know?"

I stood up slowly and closed the curtain, told her I'd be in the living room if she needed me. Out there, I sat on the couch and my own eyes began to sting. The only thing restraining the tears was anger. I imagined beating him senseless. He was completely beyond my control now, and I found myself hoping he'd run away again. After a while, Dolphin emerged from the bathroom wearing my robe. She sat down in the armchair and stared into space. Mingus entered the room with the attitude of an accomplice trying to play it cool.

"Why do I get involved with fuck-ups?" Dolphin asked. "Why do I only love guys who are off their hinges? You know? Why do I feel like I'm thirty years old?"

She gave me a long look, as if she really expected me to attempt an explanation. When she left the room to get dressed, I picked up the phone. This time, Lindsey answered.

"Jesus," I said. "Where have you been?"

"I can't talk right now," she said.

"Why not?"

"I'll call you later."

"Who the fuck is that?" I heard in the background. A moment later, the phone was in her husband's hands. "You disappoint me, Nile. You really do. You fuck with my hopes for humanity. I use this word rarely, because I find it almost nauseating in its vulgarity, and almost impossible to find someone who is actually deserving of the annotation. But I've been thinking long and hard about this for the last couple of hours, and I've decided that you are. You're a cunt."

There was a spasmodic clicking. Then the line went dead.

⌐▬▬⌐

By the time Dolphin was dressed, I'd made a cup of coffee and was feeling the tentative touch of sobriety. Still, I didn't want a passenger in the car with me. I offered to call her a cab. She refused, saying she had no reason to go home at the moment. We walked, together, down to the street, where a warm breeze disturbed the leaves of the palm trees. The grass of the park was dotted with people, the tennis courts illuminated, and the soft pops of the balls sounded like the murmurs of distant hearts. "It's too beautiful to go home," Dolphin said. She slung her backpack over her shoulder and extended her right hand. "Well, been nice knowing you," she said, then started walking uphill. She was a half a block away, I was opening my car door, when she shouted my name and spoke her final words: "I'm keeping your underwear."

⌐▬▬⌐

I had to ring the bell three times before someone appeared at the living room windows.

"Who the hell is it?" Philip said.

"It's me. Thomas."

I stood there, staring up at the moon. It was floating high above the peninsula, directly over her house. A quarter of it glowing white, the rest barely visible, gray and larval. Waiting for the shadow of the Earth to recede. Lindsey opened the door. A checkered dress, black-and-white, like her hair, ended just above the knee. I could barely see her eyes in the darkness of the foyer. Behind her, the stairs were lit, curving up and out of sight.

"What are you doing here?"

"I didn't like your tone of voice. I didn't like his either."

She gave me a look which was vaguely chastising. "You going to hold my hand for the rest of our lives, every time we cross the street?"

I stared at her for a few moments, feeling worn and raw inside, abraded by love. Then I reached out and took that hand. "You want me to leave?"

"To tell the truth, no. I'm glad you're here. *I'm* leaving. I'm packing some stuff and I'm going to Saffron's. You can take me. I'm too worked up to drive."

"You told him?"

"No, not even. I can't do it. You were right, I should have written a letter."

I glanced at the stairs, moved closer, and held her. I buried my face in her hair. I kissed her forehead.

"Come upstairs," she said. "Talk to him while I pack."

I followed her to the second floor, where Philip, with a drink in hand, was browsing his record collection. Lindsey continued upstairs. I wandered in the direction of the piano.

"Welcome to Bleak House," Philip said. "Your timing is impeccable. What can I get you?"

"Nothing. Thanks."

He sipped his drink and the ice clinked harmonically against the glass. "What do you think? Billie Holiday, Mozart, Nico, R.E.M.? I've got it all. What's appropriate for this particular set of circumstances?" He looked at me. "What would you play?"

"I don't know."

He kept searching. "How's your brother?"

"My brother . . ."

"The one you were going to check on."

"He wasn't there."

Phil set his drink down and pulled out *Cattle Call* by Eddy Arnold. He displayed the album cover, as a garçon displays the label on a bottle of wine: Mr. Arnold strumming his guitar, his cowboy-booted feet propped up on a saddle, a giant pair of steer's horns mounted above his head.

"Music's vital," he said, sliding the record from the sleeve. "It's more than an accompaniment to experience. It bonds itself to experience, then becomes a kind of cognitive key. A specific piece of music opens a specific chamber of memory." He lifted the turntable cover. "Usually, the bond is created arbitrarily. From time to time, however, one has the opportunity to create it consciously. To fit the music to the experience. Are you with me on this? So the question is: if your thirty-four-year-old wife of two years was leaving you for a twenty-five-year-old girl . . . what would you play?"

He lowered the arm, and the stylus touched down with a gentle hiss. A few moments later, Eddy Arnold was yodeling, Wyoming-style. Philip lowered himself into one of the giant armchairs, shut his eyes reverently; and as the first verse came to an end, he lifted a hand to his face, and placed a finger against each eye to stem the flow of tears. I stood frozen by the windows, waiting through horrible moments for him to speak again. He didn't. And as invisibly as possible, I left the room under cover of the music. I climbed the stairs to the third floor, found Lindsey in the bedroom. She, too, was crying. Something about this, the synchronicity of their emotions, made me want to hide somewhere and cover my face.

"Why are you crying?" I said.

"Oh, I don't know. What's he playing this music for? He knows I hate it."

A traveling bag waited on the chair. The top drawer of her bureau was open, half emptied of lingerie and socks. Several dresses lay on the floor by the closet, having slipped from their hangers. I thought of Philip ascending the stairs later, half dead with liquor, to confront this room, vacant but still full of her.

"Are you taking these?" I asked, indicating the fallen dresses.

She shook her head, and I rehung them. Then I started making the unmade bed.

"What are you doing?"

"I don't know," I said.

"Can you get my computer from the study? Then I'll get my writing and that's it, okay?"

I walked down the hall, and as I passed Philip's heirloom grandfather clock, it announced the hour of ten. Deep, ominous throbs which were swallowed by the sound of the music. In the study, I packed Lindsey's laptop into its case and caught sight of a framed photograph which sat beneath a lamp on a corner table. Their wedding. A close-up portrait. Philip in the turban and those flowing robes; Lindsey in the sari, her hair braided, the peacock, rendered in henna, on the soft underside of her arm. Suddenly, the music fell away to a whisper, and I could hear the sound of conversation downsairs. I stepped out into the hallway, walked to the top of the staircase.

"You've been here before?" Phil was saying.

"Yeah. I slept here. I read one of your magazines."

"Why'd you sleep here?"

I shouted his name, and almost tripped on my way down the stairs. Philip was standing by the stereo, Matthew by the albatross. His backpack slung over his shoulder, he was trailing a finger over the bird's head. He regarded me with a completely blank expression.

"I thought I'd find you here," he said. "I came to say goodbye."

"Come here," I told him.

He turned back to the bird. "Was this alive once?" he asked.

"Where have you been?"

"Nowhere."

From behind me now, I could hear footsteps on the stairs. They paused just shy of the floor.

"Hi, Matt," Lindsey said.

"Hello . . ."

"Where have you been?" I repeated.

"No—fucking—where."

"Actually," Phil said, "he's been here . . . sleeping. I was wondering how that came to be."

"I don't know what he's talking about," I said, starting across the room.

"Don't be like Peter," Matthew said. "Don't deny me in my final moments. Don't deny her."

I walked up to him, and I could smell on him the odor of that room. Raw eggs, sweat, and sperm. "I've been to the apartment," I said. "I saw Dolphin."

"Who?"

"What the hell is wrong with you?"

"I don't know what you're talking about."

My veins ignited like tinder. I grabbed his arm and had the distinct feeling of having grasped more than him. Something other than him. Something dead and yet preserved, as flawlessly as an insect trapped in amber.

"Why did you do that?" I said.

"I didn't."

"Tom," Lindsey said, "what are you talking about?"

"When I got home, I found her in the shower on her hands and knees. She'd been tied up."

"It wasn't me. I didn't do that." He yanked himself free of me and stumbled into the center of the room. "I didn't do it," he said, his voice breaking. Then he turned to Lindsey. "I swear on my mother's grave I didn't do it."

"It's okay," she said. She stepped down to the floor and extended a hand, palm turned upward. "Come here," she said; and slowly, he walked in her direction, into her arms. She held him as his shoulders trembled, as his breath came in gasps.

"I've got this feeling," he said. "This horrible feeling . . . that she'll never talk to me again."

Lindsey stroked his hair.

"Did I hurt her?"

"I don't know," she said.

"I think I did . . . I really think I did." His body shook; his arms tightened around Lindsey's waist. "Some sins can't be forgiven, you know. You could spend your whole life doing penance, and it wouldn't help." He slid to his knees. He pressed his face, his cheek and ear, into her stomach as if listening for something. The telephone rang. Nobody moved. It rang three times; then in the distance the answering machine picked up. I heard Saffron's voice but couldn't make out the words. At some point, the record album had reached its end, or Philip had stopped it. There was silence now, as Lindsey knelt down and cradled Matthew's face in her hands.

"I've prayed for this hour to pass," he said. "For this cup to be taken from me. It's no use."

"What do you mean?"

"I have a tumor. In my brain."

Her eyes contacted me momentarily, then returned to him. "Do you want to go to the hospital?"

"It's too late for that."

"No, it's not."

She smoothed the hair above his ear. A sob escaped from his throat as he lifted a hand and touched her hair. I watched him draw her face to his and kiss her on the mouth. Something cold trickled over my spine. For a long moment, we all lost our voices and our freedom of movement. Then Matthew rose slowly to his feet and backed away. His eyes were wet. A tear rolled along the edge of his nose as he unzipped his backpack and removed the paint gun.

"That's not real," Philip said.

"It's paint," I heard myself say.

"Okay, kid." Phil stepped forward and Matthew fired at

him. His chest seemed to explode from the inside out. Blood which was a thick bright green. His glass shattered against the floor. He doubled over, shouting and swearing. When I moved, my brother shoved the barrel of the gun into his own mouth.

"Christ," I said. "Please. Don't do that."

Staring at me hypnotically, he withdrew it just enough to allow speech. "Why not? The cancer is everywhere. Like weeds. My brain's like a garden no one cares about."

"That's not true," Lindsey said. "We care. Both of us do."

"It doesn't matter. Every father kills his son and every son embraces that death. Embraces it willingly. This is *my* choice. Not his, not hers. Mine."

His shoulders were heaving, the gun knocking against his teeth.

"Are you watching?" he asked me. "Are you looking at me?"

He closed his mouth around the barrel. His finger tensed against the trigger. He pulled it. And nothing happened. An impotent click. His legs folded underneath him, as if the bones had spontaneously snapped. A moment later, I was kneeling on the floor beside him. Carefully, I removed the gun from his hands. Then I touched him. I wiped the wetness from his cheek, and found myself moving closer. Drawing him toward me and holding him while he cried. Embracing him for the very first time.

"Everything makes sense now," he said. "The heavens are so starry, I can see galaxies that have been dead for a hundred million years. I know why Dad hates me. Why you hate me."

"I don't hate you."

"Somehow, I think I've always known. It seems I can re-member you, bending over my crib one night. You must have told me everything, you must have told me the truth, and that you'd always hate me. I seem to remember that. And I just want you to know that it hurt, but I understood. I forgot for a long time, but that night, I really understood. If you'd taken a pillow and held it over my face, I wouldn't have protested."

"Matt . . ."

"It's not like Cain and Abel," he said, his voice dropping almost to a whisper. "You should have killed me then. I would have killed me . . . and I wouldn't have tried to stop myself."

"I love you," I said.

"You're lying. You can't love me. Because it's my fault."

"It's not. It's nobody's fault."

"I killed her," he said. "I broke her heart."

His arms wrapped more tightly around me, and I felt the weight of a lifetime compressed into a few fleeting seconds. The sudden birth of everything we'd never been to each other. And then a strange acceleration. As if, only now, the universe were beginning its process of expansion. I looked at Lindsey—an arm's length away, waiting for me. Collection of cells. Commencement of life. With every passing moment, it came closer to being real. Closer to being a child. Philip was sitting on the arm of the couch, his shirt and hand stained with paint. A stroke of green marked the side of his face with a primal symbolism; and I imagined him at some aboriginal festival, seated by a fire, the creatures of the outback sleeping or hunting by night. Pity was working to close off my throat, but I swallowed hard, and prepared to tell him. That it was me. That I was the one. Not Nile. As the phone rang again in the distance, and again no one answered, Matthew eased out of my arms. His eyes dark and bottomless. There was no hope in them, but somewhere in the lids and lashes, in the bridge of his nose and his eyebrows, there was that vague trace of our mother. In those moments, I thought about how much of life was composed of lies and distortions and hidden things. Is this what I'd been waiting for? Is this what everyone waits for? The time when fictions fall away. The time when truths are brought to light, and you feel your flawed heart catching fire, and you see as if for the first time. The beauty of responsibility. The freedom that breathes inside fear. "Philip," I said, rising to my feet—and slowly, very slowly, a kind of wave seemed to swell all around me, like the sound of an orchestra tuning.

26 / In the days before I met her, Lindsey Paris stood on the summit of Twin Peaks—high above San Francisco, the world revealed in all its massive complexity by a tiny square of paper she'd dissolved on her tongue—and fancied herself a goddess. The one who first beheld the nakedness of the Golden Gate, envisioned a city built on hills, imported fog from the ocean. The same who spun the myth of the Barbary Coast, and lived on the rocks above the Pacific, in the Gothic grandeur of Cliff House. Long ago, she had wept while her city burned, then dried her eyes and set about the task of rebuilding it on the foundation of its own ashes. That epic suspension bridge had appeared to her in a dream. It was she who brought it into being, then coated it with a skin of maroon orange. Those splashes of color dotting the concrete walkway had been licked by the wind from her celestial paintbrush. They were like drops of her own blood . . . That is the girl she was—and this is the woman she became. A writer. A documenter of history. A mother . . . I was there that day. In a room which smelled vaguely of pot-pourri. Hardwood floors, a queen-size bed, floral prints on the walls. I held her hand, I spoke to her while the midwife waited between her legs. Deep breathing. Cries of pain which brought everything into a new and timeless focus. For me, it was like this: like approaching the edge of a flat world, and an unimaginable void beyond, only to discover that the sea unfurls itself endlessly, spontaneously. The plane of the Earth curls around, rolls itself into a perfect sphere.

⌞   ⌟

Whenever I see, on television, some spectacle of the natural world—a wasp and a scorpion battling like ancient gladiators; a baby crocodile struggling out of its egg and searching instinctually for water; an albatross finding its only mate after a year of separate wandering—I think of cinematography. I think of the person behind the camera, and I wonder if we will ever hear from him again. If there are certain crimes which are unpardonable no matter how much time goes by, no matter how much of life covers them over . . . After that last night on Russian Hill, I saw him only once. By then, Lindsey and I had moved into a place in Dolores Heights. She was in her second trimester, and we had an ultrasound image, which looked like a transmission from some deep-space probe, a photo of interstellar dust or some inchoate solar system. It was nearly midnight in the Persian Zam Zam Room, and the sight of him in that crimson light put me in mind of visiting spirits.

"Hey, kid."

I introduced him to Tabitha ("from the studio," I said, "she does storyboards"), and the muscles of his face tightened into a smile. We were celebrating that night, because my film had been selected by several festivals, and had a chance at a couple of minor prizes, a shot at being seen at the country's handful of art houses. Philip offered up a halfhearted toast and we all sipped our martinis.

"So," Tabitha asked in the ensuing silence, "how do you two know each other?"

"A mutual friend," Phil said.

"I'll get us another round," I said.

"Not for me. I'm on my way out."

He shook Tabitha's hand. Then he turned to me and shook mine.

"Zach asks after you," he said. "You should give Claire a call sometime."

"I will," I lied; and in his eyes, I searched for some evidence of forgiveness, some hope that the future could redefine the past. But I found only the ashes of our counterfeit friendship. His eyes looked gray and hard, like the eyes of my father.

⌐————⌐

It was some time earlier that I'd agreed to meet Nile Treadway. On a weekday. In broad daylight. At a busy downtown bistro. We hadn't spoken since that night in North Beach, when I'd told her, on the street, that I'd be having a child with her ex-lover. When I thought about that evening, and the way our affair had died at my hands, I felt the impulse to turn myself in to the authorities. To present myself for arrest, throw myself on the mercy of some court of romantic law. I felt guilty of crimes which no one would hold me accountable for, no one except myself; and it was with a sense of moral mission that I approached that lunch on California Street. I would hold her hand. I would offer a concise but comprehensive apology. I would reassure her of the extent of her mental and physical gifts. There would be discreet tears and julienned vegetables. There would be confession and absolution.

"Markham," I said to the maître d'; and was led not to a table for two, but to a table for three, where Nile was already sitting, drinking white wine with another woman, laughing. They looked up at me simultaneously, their faces full of amusement and contentment.

"Tom, Mika. Mika, Tom."

Her new lover was a performance artist and poet from New York. Filipino. Long black hair. Signature eyeglasses. We discussed the state of the animation industry, Lucille Ball and Karen Finley, bloodshed in the Persian Gulf. We discussed the big news. That, in a few days, Nile would be pulling up stakes and moving to Manhattan. Into Mika's place on the Lower East Side.

"Congratulations," I said.

"And congratulations to you," Mika said. "Nile tells me you're having a baby."

"My wife and I. My fiancée."

"How's Lindsey?" Nile asked. "Is she beautiful pregnant?"

"Yes. Very beautiful."

"I wonder what it's like to make love with a pregnant woman." She turned to her new poetess lover. "Have you ever wondered about that?"

Mika pursed her lips, adopted the aimless contemplative look of some Hellenic philosopher. The plates were cleared. The check was paid. It was time to go. Time to take leave of each other. On the street, Nile hugged me confidently. And while I was in her arms, I waited for her to whisper something concise and comprehensive. I waited to feel the lingering radiation of what we'd almost had. I didn't, and the absence filled me with a wonderful kind of regret. As she disappeared into the noontime crowd of the Financial District, I thought of Lindsey, growing heavy with love and desire. Pathways being cleared, bonds strengthening, lines of sight growing sharper. The sun was warm, the air perfectly cool. It was that time of year when San Francisco feels the breath of paradise. Soon the flowers would be thriving in the park. It was nearly September.

━━

Five years have passed since that summer.

Those days feel to me now like some primitive stage of history, ruled by superstition and savage emotions, replete with omens and signs. We no longer live in San Francisco. But we remember its beaches and landmarks, its hills and the fog pouring over them like a slow-motion avalanche. We remember the city's windows and streetlights shining at night. So beautiful and serene.

And we know, we know that far below, its bones will always be fractured. We know about the cracks in its subterranean foundation. Here, in the Middle West, life is different. Skyscrapers. Subway cars coasting on elevated tracks. Here, the summers are hot. Sometimes the elderly die of suffocation in their airless homes. Sometimes the young die on street corners, the last thing they hear in this world the sound of tires on asphalt. But on an evening like this one, along the shore of Lake Michigan, there are also swimmers, lifeguards in a rowboat, triangular sails in the distance turning salmon pink . . . Will you believe me when I tell you a little girl sleeps down the hall from me? That in the hours after thunderstorms, the night air charged with electricity and coolness finally sweeping down from the north, she sleeps beside me, curled against her mother's body, the two of them breathing in unison?

One night in Northampton, Massachusetts, my brother fell into a deep sleep after swallowing, with a bottle of sarsaparilla, several weeks' worth of tranquilizers. This was his first year of college. He was eighteen, and for some time had been on Lithium, as treatment for bipolar mood disorder, also known as manic depression. His relationship with the medicine, however, had been turbulent, and he'd recently stopped taking it for philosophical reasons. Because it was an anesthetization of the self. A numbing, a smothering of organic identity. Because in addition to protecting him from the darkness, it blocked out the light, the euphoric perfection of mania . . . I walked into his hospital room with my father. Jane and his girlfriend were already there. After a while, he asked them all to leave, and I sat alone with him. There were flowers in a vase. A couple of cards from close family friends. A small pile of books—Foucault, Kierkegaard, Sartre. A big stuffed alligator, toothless and missing its right eye, lay beside him on the bed. A member of his girlfriend's childhood collection. We talked about life at his prestigious Northeastern university; about my wife and child, the little girl I referred to as his niece. Then there was a long silence, filled by the dampened sounds of the psychiatric ward.

"I've been thinking of taking a long sea voyage," he finally said. "Like in the old days."

"What old days?"

"The old, old days, when they put the loonies on ships. What do you think? The salt air might do me good."

I studied the dark circles around his eyes. The lids fell closed, and I wondered how near he had come to locking them shut forever. If he had been serious. If he'd known what he was doing, any more than he'd known that night at Phil and Lindsey's.

"You don't need a cruise," I said. "You need to take your medicine."

He nodded, his hand inching to the edge of the bed. Waiting there, patiently, until I reached out. Then his fingers closed around mine. A tear traced a slow line over his cheekbone. When he spoke again, the words sounded tattered, as if they were catching on sharp spikes in his throat.

"It's hard to say goodbye, Tom."

"What?"

"It's hard," he said, "to live in everyone else's world, once you know what it's like to live in your own."

He opened his eyes and looked at me directly. Pleading for answers; full of a helpless fear of the future. Yet I knew then, with an instinct that felt somehow fraternal, that he would be all right in the end, that the darkest days of his life were coming to a close. And in those quiet moments, while I held his hand and he mourned the loss of who he thought he was, I envied him. He was bruised and afraid and far off course. But he was my mother's stronger son.

I live now on the North Side of Chicago. A block from the lake. I share this third-floor apartment with Lindsey Paris—who, for several months, has been feeling the anxious depression particular to the thirty-nine-year-old—and our daughter, Isabel. Old enough now to climb the ladder of a slide. To put her emotions into words. Soon she will be one of an elite corps of children. Boys in gray shorts and maroon cardigan sweaters. Girls in sky-blue jumpers. A world of weather charts, crayons, show-and-tell, afternoon naps. Band-Aids applied to skinned knees. Storybooks with clear moral messages.

Sometimes, at night, I watch her sleep.

The glow of a cartoon night-light. Her lips slightly parted. Her eyes moving behind closed lids, an indecipherable dream code. Concrete and spectacular. Time flowing through her, the way light flows through a prism; and it seems I can see myself—the boy I was—more clearly than ever before. Young and vulnerable. Sick with grief. Filling with secrets too brilliant to be faced directly. I touch her long dark hair, and feel an ancient constriction in my throat and chest. I feel drugged and brutally lucid. Inside my head, memory thrums as gently, as ominously, as bees in a meadow. I know Lindsey hears it too, this same sound in a different key . . . Back in our bedroom, I wake her with soft kisses. Her hair falling past her shoulders. Skin pale, but light freckles lying like dappled shade over her face and shoulders and chest. The secret eccentricity of a beauty mark, mahogany brown, riding the crest of her pelvis. Her sex, humid and slick, embraces me. Warmly and deeply. So deeply I feel I've lost my way inside her. I find myself crying, I don't know why. She kisses the tears away. She brings us to orgasm, and as we come she says to me, *This is forever, my love. Forever* . . . Fingers woven into mine, she lies still on top of me. Breathing hard against my neck. Her vagina contracting powerfully. Then she settles into my arms, her head in the hollow between my shoulder and chest.

These are the nights.

I hold her. I breathe in the smell of her hair, her hair which always tangles together at night, as if birds are weaving it into a nest while she sleeps. I lie awake, filling with a knowledge that seems somehow forbidden, yet inevitable and necessary. Something around the eyes inherited from her. Something about the mouth which is undeniably mine.

My daughter . . .

Let me tell you the truth. About the boy and girl who met in, of all places, a church. About your mother, and the man who was her husband, but not your father. I will not rip incriminating pages from this text. Hold my hand now. Watch us sin. And believe me when I tell you: you too are beautiful in your illegitimacy. With the strength to close doorways and open new ones. With the sharpened sight of the transgressor. Let me tell you of those days, the most powerful of your existence, when you were a vague, undefinable thing. How you conceived for me my happiness. My future. This is the story of how you came to be. This is the story of why I love you.